Marion Zimmer Bradley's

Sword and Sorceress 34

Edited by

Elisabeth Waters

SWORD AND SORCERESS 34

Edited by Elisabeth Waters

ISBN-13: 978-1-938185-59-5
ISBN-10: 1-938185-59-5

Trade Paperback Edition

October 29, 2019

A Publication of
The Marion Zimmer Bradley Literary Works Trust
PO Box 193473
San Francisco, CA 94119-3473
www.mzbworks.com

ACKNOWLEDGMENTS

CONTENTS

INTRODUCTION

by Elisabeth Waters

This will be the last volume of *Sword and Sorceress*, and the end of an era in my life. I started working on *Sword and Sorceress* with the first volume, back in 1982. At first my job was keeping track of the manuscripts and the SASEs (self-addressed stamped envelopes) that came with them, preparing and sending out contracts, and making sure everyone got paid. Marion loved reading slush; even if a large portion of it was dreadful, she was always thrilled to find a new gem. She was much more interested in nurturing the next generation of writers "so I'll have something good to read in my old age" than in making money, but *Sword and Sorceress* did make money and developed a following, even as I gradually took over more of the editing and picked up the whole job with *Sword and Sorceress 22*.

Fast forward 37 years, to when (a) I hit retirement age, and (b) we noticed just how many writers whose stories we were still paying royalties on had died—several with very messy family situations and without wills. So we began efforts to simplify my job to the point where it can be done by someone else, because I do not expect to live forever.

I have loved editing *Sword and Sorceress*, and I will miss the thrill of getting wonderful stories each year (although not so much the agonizing part at the end of the reading period when I have to send back half the stories I wanted to buy). I have found so many new favorite authors from this series and made so many wonderful friends among both authors and readers. Thank you all.

CHAOS HEART

by Marian Allen

One of the nice things about doing an anthology by invitation is that I can ask for the stories I want. I've always loved Marian's stories about Pimchan and the All-Father, so I asked her for one. I'm glad I did.

Marian Allen writes science fiction, fantasy, mystery, humor, horror, mainstream, and anything else she can wrestle into fixed form. She has had stories in both on-line and print publications, including multiple appearances in Marion Zimmer Bradley's *Sword and Sorceress* anthologies. Her latest book is her science fantasy *The Wolves of Port Novo*. She blogs daily at Marian Allen, Author Lady (MarianAllen.com).

Pimchan's Female shook the workout room's rosewood filigree screen, rattling it against the doorway, and continued rattling it until she was granted permission to enter.

The Warrior Pimchan, drawn from battle meditation, scowled. She knew such impropriety meant a matter of import.

"Enter, if you must." She stood, feet braced apart, fists on hips, short trousers and sleeveless tunic showing her burnished red-gold muscles, the runes tattooed on her shaven scalp gleaming in the sunlight from the open portion of the arena.

She might as well have saved herself the imposing posture. The Female, small at eight, bowed briefly in the doorway and scurried in, jabbering in her thickest Honeycomb accent.

One of the benefits of a wandering Warrior's travels was the ability to understand or decipher the Blessed Land's many dialects. Although Pimchan had been "gifted" with the care of and tribute from the town of Mountain Cloud years ago, she hadn't lost her knack.

Still, just to be certain, Pimchan said, "A Warrior is here?"

The Female calmed, now that Pimchan had taken the message, and said, in clearer speech, "A male Warrior and his female attendant. Somboon and the Guard escorted them from the Eastern gate."

Somboon was the chief of the town guard, a man Pimchan admired very much, in spite of his apparent inability to keep his underlings from deriving amusement from her every visit to the barracks. Their poorly hidden grins were directed toward Somboon and not herself, or she would have demonstrated to him how to keep order in the ranks.

It didn't surprise Pimchan to see, in the corridor beyond her Female, her Male (the Female's twin); old Lek, the clever companion discarded by a foolish Warrior who valued youth over experience; and Nadia, Pimchan's former Female, now freed and named and employed as household Overseer.

Pimchan spoke to Nadia. "I will open the compound to my fellow Warrior, myself. Make food and drink ready, in the event I offer him hospitality. My Male will come with me to receive any orders."

Nadia gave the Male a pointed look, cautioning him to be on his best behavior.

The Male unbarred the heavy screen that guarded the compound and folded it back, its myriad bells jangling.

The visiting Warrior wore a cloak with a hood which shaded his face. His companion's head was nearly engulfed by a conical straw hat. Somboon stood to the Warrior's right, sword drawn, and the Guard surrounded the strangers, far enough back to at least raise an alarm if they were turned on.

"You wanted to see me," said Pimchan. "I am here."

"That's abrupt, Mistress," said a voice she knew. "Although this worthless student deserves no better."

It was Nandan! So his companion was surely—she looked more closely and saw it was—Tyana!

Nandan had been Pimchan's Male when Nadia was her Female. While Nadia had trained for housekeeping under Tyana, Nandan had taken the Warrior path and, not too many years previously, had set out on the life Pimchan still longed for, wandering the Blessed Land, searching out wrongs to right in the All-Father's name. Tyana had chosen to accompany him, leaving

Nadia in charge of Pimchan's household—or, as Nadia often seemed to think, in charge of Pimchan.

Pimchan's first impulse was to grip Nandan's arm in friendship and camaraderie, but the fact that he had come without announcing his identity held her back.

"Enter. Welcome."

Nandan pointed at Somboon and shook his head. Pimchan considered for the space of a heartbeat, then said, "Somboon, take ease in the Chaos Garden. My Male, have refreshment sent there to him. The Guard may go about their business. These people are known to me."

Somboon bowed, dismissed his subordinates, and followed the path to the Chaos Garden.

The boy scurried into the house, staring back over his shoulder at the strangers.

"You have new slaves," Nandan said, sounding almost wistful.

"The ones I had before grew up. They make me proud. But I hear one of them has a problem and needs my advice. Will you come under my roof and enjoy what poor hospitality I can offer you, my comrade?"

When they stepped into the dining area, faces still shrouded, Nadia began to bow, then straightened abruptly.

"Nandan! Tyana!" She gave the woman a quick and hearty hug, knocking her hat off, and slapped the man repeatedly on his biceps, shaking back his hood. Nandan's shaven head bore more tattoos than the one with which he had left. Pimchan cataloged the ones she could see: strength, quickness, health. Simple, easy to apply on a basic level, capable of growing more powerful and complex with experience and mastery, if the bearer was lucky and capable. Good choices.

Pimchan's Male and Female gawped at such liberties taken with a Warrior. Behind them, Lek's wrinkles parted like a curtain, showing a gap-toothed smile, he having known the abused and abuser since their infancy.

Nadia turned to the new slaves with a fierce frown. "This is how you are *not* to treat a Warrior or a Warrior's attendant. I'm allowed to, only in this particular case. This man is my brother, and this woman was to me what I am to you."

The children looked sideways at one another, as if neither could imagine wanting to throw their arms around Nadia, but both were wisely silent.

"Serve us," Nadia ordered the children, apparently assuming she would be at the table.

Pimchan said, "And don't forget refreshments for my Chief of Guards in the Chaos Garden. Nadia, Lek, you may join him there or you may go about your business."

Nadia looked ready to protest, but the seriousness on her brother's face caused her to close her mouth and bow as if there were no question of objection.

Within the hour, Pimchan summoned Nadia, Lek, Somboon, and the children.

Gesturing to the slaves, she asked Nadia, "Can these two puppies be trusted to hold their tongues outside this room, or should I send them away while we talk?"

Nadia replied to Pimchan, but she might as well have been drilling holes through her charges with her eyes. "They know that this household is inviolate. Nothing done or said or supposed here passes beyond the compound walls."

"Very well. Nandan, let me summarize what you and Tyana have told me. Correct me if I miss anything important or have misunderstood."

Nandan nodded.

Pimchan said, "Nandan came across a merchant and his bodyguard being attacked by bandits and helped fight them off. Some of the parcels had come undone. One of the exposed pieces was a blue steel kukri inscribed with runes."

Lek said, "But—" He bit the objection off. Only Warriors carried blue steel, and Warriors fetched their own weapons. What Nandan had reported was obviously not impossible, just very, very wrong.

Pimchan continued. "Nandan took the kukri and waited to see its intended recipient, but some of the wrappers had blown away. The merchant claimed the wrapped packages belonged to other people who had asked him to deliver them to the capital. He said he didn't know who had sent the kukri or to whom it was going."

"He was lying," Nadia said.

Nandan rubbed the rune of discernment on the front of his shaven head. "I don't think so."

Tyana, who had no shaven head, no runes, but plenty of wits, agreed, and Pimchan accepted their testimonies.

Lek held out both his hands. "Let me see."

Nandan lifted an eyebrow. "How do you know I kept it?"

A snort from Nadia overrode the others' chuckles. "Of course you kept it. We know who trained you."

It no longer irritated Pimchan to feel gratified by the compliment of a domestic. Although honor was no more than her due, she had learned to value a heartfelt tribute, no matter what its source.

Nandan pulled a short knife with a curved blade from his tunic and laid it across the old man's palms. Runes curled along both sides of the blue steel.

Lek ran a finger along the runes, lips moving as he laboriously deciphered the old, enchanted words. He looked up, eyebrows raised and jaw loose.

"Yes," Nandan said. "I found a priest who translated for me. The blade is inscribed with a spell to find the royal heart."

Pimchan asked the obvious. "A weapon made specifically to kill the All-Father?"

Tyana said, "We commandeered a pair of temple horses and hot-footed it to the capital to warn him. We couldn't even get into The Invisible City."

Nandan rubbed his rune of discernment again. "We didn't know whether to leave a general warning, to leave a message detailing everything we knew—which, after all, wasn't much—or to leave no message."

Tyana said what Pimchan was thinking: "It wouldn't be beyond an overzealous underling to take our warning against someone we can't name as a veiled threat from us, and to have us arrested."

Nadia nodded in approval. "So you came here. Naturally."

Pimchan decided it would be beneath her dignity to point out that Nandan had come to seek advice from *her*, not from Nadia.

Lek had been studying the kukri all the while. Now he said, "You know, I think this was made by Akara." He passed the knife to Pimchan. "Feel the finish on the hilt. Look at the sheen on the steel."

Pimchan nodded and touched the blade, where a notch in the shape of a stylized cow foot was cut. "Look at the cho. The way it curls inward the slightest bit here and here."

"Ah, yes," said Lek. "It's his, all right."

Nandan sat forward. "You know this person?"

Pimchan waved a hand to the northwest. "On the other side of Brighttop Mountain. Two days' hard walk from here." She put the kukri on the table and pushed it toward Nandan. "This must never leave this compound. It must never be touched again, without the All-Father's permission."

"Making such a thing isn't like Akara," said Lek. "He would only do it under compulsion."

Somboon spoke for the first time. "Who could compel him?"

Pimchan said, "A question Nandan and I will go and ask. We leave tomorrow."

Lek wrung his hands and bowed over the table, signaling respectful disagreement.

"Speak," said Pimchan.

"If you go trumpeting your knowledge of what he's done, you could put his life in danger while most likely gathering no intelligence. If you go under false colors, you might be able to tease out some clue."

"Bah! Am I a diplomat?" She said the word as if it had a nasty taste.

The compound's entrance screen rattled and jingled as someone gave the special knock that signaled a message from the All-Father.

Everyone in the room rose, but Pimchan gestured them all down except Nadia.

"Answer," she said. "I'll stand by."

When they returned a few moments later, Pimchan held a letter. "The messenger said he was not to wait for a reply. Listen."

To my beloved Pimchan, fond regards.

Your humble friend begs you to disregard any rumor of threats to his well-being. He is secure as always, happy in his solitude. His hope is that you will grace him with your company again soon.

Ever yours,

Adhi Muluk Budiman, All-Father

Pimchan shook the letter. "Nadia, you've read my previous correspondence with the All-Father. Does this sound like him?"

Nadia cocked her head and narrowed her eyes. "It *sounds* like someone under constraint, instructed to write to a possible rescuer to persuade them he doesn't need rescuing."

Pimchan didn't miss the emphasis. "He isn't above trying to make me think he's safe when he's actually in danger. And he isn't above making me think he's in danger when he's actually safe."

Somboon said, hesitantly, "So he might be in danger, trying to tell you he's safe, expecting you to understand he's in danger? Does that even make sense?"

Pimchan said, "Would he expect me to understand all that? He knows I'm not a strategist! I'm a Warrior!"

She had an almost overwhelming urge to smash something. She wanted to stop the talking. She wanted to retreat to her practice arena and fight shadows until she trembled with weariness.

Then, she realized with dismay, she wanted to follow that with a warm bath and a soft bed. What sort of Warrior had she become, as keeper of a town, head of a household? Only years of training enabled her to control the inner Chaos the question raised.

Lek was bowing again, curse him! What now?

"Speak!"

"The only loose thread in this tangle is Akara."

"Yes!" Pimchan beamed at him as she considered which weapons to take.

"But we've agreed that thundering in, waving swords, would be a misstep."

"We have?"

Lek bowed again. "Yes, Mighty One."

Pimchan looked to Somboon for support. "Have we?" She turned to Tyana. "I don't believe we did, did we?"

"It was strongly suggested. Perhaps it should be considered."

Before Pimchan could refuse, Lek said, "I suggest a subterfuge."

Subterfuge was an acceptable Warrior tactic, so Pimchan nodded to him to continue.

"I suggest you pretend you've chosen to marry, and your groom is buying you a blue steel weapon for a bridal gift."

"Marry? *I*?" Pimchan remembered Somboon's annulled wedding to Isa with contempt. They hadn't loved one another. They had wed for... Oh, for many wrong reasons. The annulment was the only thing about it that was right. And she was to pretend to the same thing?

"Warriors do marry," Lek said.

"Who would I pretend to be marrying?"

In the ensuing silence, Pimchan was acutely aware of Somboon, seated across the table, taller than she and stocky, with dusty red-brown skin and short black hair that stood up all over his head like the spikes of an echidna. His strong brow curved down in a scowl over shining eyes and reddened cheeks.

"If you're thinking I would pretend to marry Somboon," she said, icily, "he's already been used so once before. No one is to suggest he be used so again. He is not a thing."

Somboon was, after all, Chief of Guards in the town the All-Father had given her; it was her responsibility to care for him as much as for any of her townspeople.

"Just this once more," said Lek.

"He doesn't mind," said Nadia.

Somboon's face grew redder than ever. "Would no one believe it? Is that the problem? Is it unthinkable that a Warrior would marry a humble guard, even a Chief Guard? Am I that unworthy? Am I that repellant?"

The outburst was so unlike Somboon's usual even temper, Pimchan gaped at him.

He clamped his jaw shut, teeth grinding on any further words that had made it as far as his mouth.

"You are not," Pimchan said faintly, feeling heat in her own face. "Very well. Lek, Nadia, make whatever arrangements are necessary for this farce. We depart as soon as possible. Nandan, you will stay here."

He placed his palms against the table, objecting.

Pimchan was no longer in the mood for discourse. "I promised this town I would never leave it unprotected. If I'm away, I require you to be in residence." She saw him cut his eyes at her, and said, "No, I don't intend to bind you here in my place while I return to the field. Just hold the town for me until I've done this thing."

Leave the town and return to the field. Her dearest wish, ever since the All-Father had installed her here. Now the very suggestion made her stomach clench. This was *her* town! *Hers*!

Nandan bowed acquiescence.

"I'm coming with you," Nadia said.

"You are not."

"But a bride needs an attendant!"

"She does," said Lek. "So does a groom."

Pimchan huffed in irritation. "Very well! Nadia will attend me. My Male will attend Somboon. I hope that is acceptable to everyone." Her tone made it clear she cared little if it wasn't.

She rose. "I'll be in my practice arena. I will not be disturbed."

Pimchan and Somboon carried full field packs, Nadia having her own cooking gear and dried food to deal with and Pimchan's Male supplementing Nadia with a burden appropriate for a sturdy eight-year-old.

"Your Male says he has concoctions against scorpion and snake bites," said Lek, "but I've also packed a powder to repel them. Dust it on your clothes and boots, and sprinkle it around your campsite. Not infallible, but it'll help. Wild cats, wild dogs, and monkeys, you'll just have to watch out for. And bears. And tigers and leopards."

"I have a spell for ghost fire," Pimchan reassured her Male, who looked more concerned as Lek's list grew. "I used it in the field, and never had beasts in my camp. And I was only one, while we are four. Beasts generally avoid the stink of humanity. It's a defense granted by Lady Chaos, who loves wild animals."

Pimchan's Female handed each of them a thin sash cut from the same piece of cloth, each with scarlet thread around the borders. "I was up all night, trimming these," she said, the dark circles under her eyes testifying to her claim. "Wear them like this." She draped one over Pimchan's Male's right shoulder and tied it at his waist on his left side. "Please."

They did as instructed.

Pimchan felt over-indulgent, following a slave's direction, but the Female did have a way with cloth, as her brother did with herbs.

Pimchan set off at a brutal pace. She had slept in her practice arena, wrapped in a cloak in the open. The sand was much colder and much harder than she had remembered. The stars and chill mountain air had not emptied her mind and settled her thoughts, as she had hoped. She had, uncharacteristically, found herself replaying the events and conversations of the previous day.

She had a vague feeling that she had been manipulated into something, but couldn't put a finger on any point at which she had not been the one to make a decision.

It was Somboon who had been coerced. No one had asked his permission to place him in jeopardy or to toy with his honor. It was no wonder he had been angry, and it was to his credit he had raised no objection, other than his protest that he might not be a believable match for a Warrior.

Was he a believable match? Could they convince Akara he was?

He was strongly built, in excellent physical shape, practiced in weapons and in street fighting, accustomed to keeping the peace or, if peace was disturbed, restoring and enforcing it. He had proven himself fearless in combat and clever at strategy.

She paused at the edge of the forest and looked around, expecting him to be apace with her. Instead, he was far behind, matching his speed to Nadia's, carrying Pimchan's Male on his shoulders.

Ashamed, and angry at being ashamed of not considering the welfare of domestics, Pimchan halted by a pool of clear water just inside the shade of the tree line.

"We will rest," she stated, as if she had her own reasons that had nothing to do with anyone else. "Nadia, cook food. My Male, spread Lek's powder." Monkeys screamed overhead and threw nuts and branches at them, but quickly lost interest and went elsewhere.

Nadia set up the hibachi and boiled some rice, adding greenery and roots she had gathered along the way. While they waited, she said, "We need to plan the wedding, in case anyone asks us about it."

"It's none of anyone's business," Pimchan snapped.

"Even Warrior brides want to share their plans," Nadia said. "It's only natural. If you get sour and terse anytime you're asked about your ceremony, you'll spoil the fiction."

After a moment, Pimchan nodded. "I wouldn't want flowers."

"Of course you would want flowers! You would want *special* flowers."

After another moment, Pimchan twitched a corner of her mouth and said, "White and purple orchids." She thought of her slave charges as orchids, the males purple and the females white. White and purple orchids were common on the heights of two of the Seven Sisters mountains, but no less precious for that.

"And you would wear white trousers and a purple tunic."

Pimchan made a sound of disgust. "I'm not a doll. I wouldn't dress to match my flowers. I'd wear my deep blue trousers and the long tunic with the silver and crimson trim."

"So that's settled," said Nadia. "Somboon, they might ask

what bride gifts you've collected. You let Isa keep the ones you brought for her, but you could *say* those are the ones you have for *this* wedding."

"No," said Somboon, "those would not suit a Warrior. Besides, I gave her a hair comb!"

Even Pimchan was surprised into laughter.

She listened with bemusement as Somboon said, "A Warrior would have a sword belt made from fine red leather studded with brass, and boots made of otter skin with soles of ironwood. For her tattoos, I would have a bottle of pure mineral oil perfumed with ginger flowers, a pot of bright indigo and another of scarlet cochineal. I would have a bracelet of gold, as broad as the blade of a sword and inlaid with protective runes in silver."

The list caused Pimchan's heart to beat faster. How could a mere layman imagine such perfect gifts for a Warrior who was also a woman? She cast a look of more admiration than usual at him, and found him staring at her, cheeks again red, eyes again shining.

With a lightning flash of insight, she understood that he wasn't improvising these items; he had them. They were purchased or ordered and were or would be tucked away, out of sight of his snickering Guardsmen.

And this was what they were always snickering about: That Somboon loved her, and she was oblivious.

What had she done, in pretending to be his bride? How could he have agreed? Was the thought of marriage to her so sweet, he was willing to play at it, in the absence of the reality? Was his loyalty to the All-Father so great that Somboon would open his heart and pour his deepest longing onto the ground on his behalf?

Pimchan held his gaze for long moments. Then she stood and said, "We need to move on."

She set a slower pace after their rest. Nadia walked by Pimchan's side, silent, for a wonder.

Was it Nadia or Lek who had told Somboon what she would like? She cut her eyes at her Household Overseer, who looked calm, serene, innocent.

Definitely Nadia.

They took four days to reach Akara's forge. Pimchan's Male manfully trudged along, attempting to keep a pace Pimchan felt was no better than a stroll, but his flushed face and wheezing breath so alarmed her, she slowed further. Somboon was willing to carry the boy, but Pimchan had no intention of fostering a weakling. Better to walk at his speed and teach him to walk than to push beyond his limits and teach him to be carried.

No more was said about the imaginary wedding, but Pimchan thought about it as she macheted the overgrown path, making as much noise as possible to warn off innocent predators. If she *were* to be married, how *would* she arrange things? Somboon lived in the barracks now. Naturally, he would move into her compound.

And what would he do? Chief of Town Security? He and Lek, together, could probably be quite inventive. Together with the Temple priests, they could probably make Mountain Cloud the most formidable stronghold in the region. But not *too* formidable. It would never do for the All-Father to feel she was consolidating any sort of power. She doubted he would consider her a threat to him, but it was always better to be circumspect.

When they exited the jungle, Brighttop Mountain filled their view, a slide of scree reaching down its side almost to the footpath. Pimchan turned to her left and passed between farmsteads, leaving it to Nadia, Somboon, and her Male to return any waves and acknowledge any obeisance.

At the outskirts of Silkmist Village, a swarm of children surrounded them, bowing and offering to show them the way to Akara's smithy, for why else would a Warrior come here?

Somboon paid the smallest of the urchins a coin and tossed a handful of copper clippings to the rest, raising a dust cloud of scrambling.

Akara's establishment was surprisingly spacious: a three-story wooden house with a stone smithy that ran into the living rock of the mountain.

Someone had obviously let Akara know they were coming, for he met them at his gate, bowing low. Pimchan forced herself to dip her head slightly in return.

A sheen of perspiration coated Akara's bony brow. "Greetings, Worthy One! I am Akara, of Silkmist Village. If you would condescend to enter, my slaves will see to your comfort. Your attendants have the freedom of the kitchen."

"I am Pimchan of Mountain Cloud and this is my bridegroom, Somboon of Mountain Cloud. My attendants have the freedom of your household."

Akara hesitated only a moment before he said, "As you say."

"My Overseer and my Male will supervise our refreshment."

"As you say, as you say."

Nadia led her protégé to the back quarters, where they would make sure nothing untoward happened to Pimchan's and Somboon's food or drink. They would then deliver the trays themselves, lest something unfortunate should happen between the kitchen and the table.

Pimchan and Somboon rested on pillows stuffed with eiderdown, across a well-polished table from their host. A long, slender wooden bowl of peanuts roasted in the shell sat in the center.

Pimchan, who was accustomed to relying on the runes of strength and speed tattooed on her shaven head, concentrated on the rune of discernment, which had been far from the first she had chosen to bear. Akara believed he was master of the situation, which frightened and exhilarated him. Pimchan suppressed a smile. If he thought his domestics were more than a match for hers, he would soon learn otherwise.

Akara made the traditional small talk. He tipped a mound of peanuts onto the table and smashed them open with his shoe. Courtesy demanded that they make no comment and show no reaction—a man may use what manners he pleases at his own table—but Pimchan and Somboon opened their nuts in the conventional way, returning their shells to the bowl, rather than blowing them onto the floor as their host did.

After inquiring after Pimchan's health and journey, Akara asked, "And how may I serve you?"

"You may serve my bridegroom," said Pimchan, daring to look directly into Somboon's face for the first time since she had guessed his feelings.

He looked back at her, his lips curved up in a gentle smile, but depths of sorrow in his eyes. He had no hope, yet he had supplied himself with gifts that would please her if there were any possibility of marriage. He would, she understood, be faithful to her for the rest of his life. He would live out his years married to *her*, no matter what *her* marital status might be.

He said, "I wish to buy my bride a kukri. It must be of your finest make. It must be inscribed with runes that make it especially effective when *she* wields it and especially *in*effective when an enemy wields it, assuming any enemy could take it from her."

Akara dutifully laughed at the absurdity of such a prospect. "I can do that."

A slender young woman dressed as a favored slave bowed herself into the room and indicated she needed to speak to Akara privately. He excused himself and stepped into the corridor.

Somboon and Pimchan sat silently, cracking and eating peanuts. Pimchan wondered what was taking Nadia and the Male so long.

Pimchan was cold—cold to her core, paralyzed with cold, lying on frigid rock in pitch black, a dank breeze cutting through her. A band of faint warmth lay across her body, from her right shoulder to her left hip. She concentrated on it, and the warmth slowly grew. She could move, but no faster than a sloth.

Fortunately, she didn't need to move quickly to cast ghost fire. Slowly, small points of blue light illuminated the air, showing darkness beyond and an uneven rock ceiling above. Too far aside for her to see where it led, was a circular hole in that ceiling.

She thought Somboon's name, but her tongue, throat, and lips couldn't move to form the sounds.

She managed a grunt. She heard a grunt in reply, then another sound from the same direction: "Izzizz."

Her body was engulfed in warmth. It was slight warmth, but in contrast to her bone-deep chill, it felt like a heated bath.

Gradually, life returned to her limbs, and her blood flowed at normal speed. She rolled onto her side.

Somboon lay next to her, only his chest moving as he breathed. His eyes were open, focused on her. He blinked. Beyond him, her Male sat up, yawning and tousling his hair into a greater mess than usual.

"Nadia?" Pimchan managed to say.

"Izzizz," the sound came again.

Pimchan levered herself to her knees, then to her feet.

Nadia lay on her side, curled up like a pangolin, left hand fisted around two of the clay beads of her necklace, beads made from the earth of the compound and connected, through some magic of Nadia's own making, to the compound's inhabitants.

"What's wrong with Nadia?" It was a measure of the Male's distress that he spoke without permission. Technically, that warranted punishment, but Pimchan approved of his concern for his superior.

"We were placed under a reptilian spell. Like serpents, our blood would slow in the cold. Then we were put here, where we would be powerless. So much for subterfuge." She stood under the hole in the roof and considered the long chimney leading from it to a metal grate. "These sashes your sister made for us counteracted the spell enough to rouse us. Your twin, it seems, has a touch of weaver's magic about her, and possibly some seamstress spellcraft as well."

Pimchan regarded her Overseer again. "Nadia moved enough to grip our beads, yours and mine, and she's passing what heat she has to us."

The Male prostrated himself at Pimchan's feet. "Make her stop! Don't let her die!" He seemed to dredge up a scrap of Nadia's training and said, "Please!"

"If I make her stop, we'll all be helpless again." Eyes back on the chimney above, she spoke her thoughts aloud: "How did they do it? How did they administer the spell? We ate nothing but peanuts we shelled ourselves."

The Male lifted his torso and squatted, as if in council. "They gave us peanuts, too, Mistress. They gave them to us in a bowl.

We cracked them and pulled them from the shells ourselves."

She remembered Akara's boorishness. "Our host smashed his with a shoe and blew the husks off the table. The spell was on the shells."

"A powder? A powder we ate?"

"It must have been." It unnerved Pimchan, how easily she had been taken, but the enchantment had been undetectable, one that didn't exist until it was active, and then it had been too late.

He scrambled up and looked around. "Mistress, can one of those flames follow me?"

"Grasp it and carry it with you."

He hesitated but a second, then wrapped his fingers, still padded with baby fat, around a ghostly flame. The blue light leaked between his fingers, bands of red glowing through his flesh.

She watched the light circle beyond Nadia and Somboon, around her, and back to where it had started.

"Our packs aren't here. Or yours and Somboon's weapons."

"Naturally."

"I brought something with us that might have helped. What do you think they did with our things? Do you think they're nearby?"

"What's the difference, boy? If we can't get to them, they might as well still be back at my compound."

The Male joined her under the chimney and stared into it. "Mistress, can you lift me up to that hole?"

"Am I an acrobat?" But she considered it. "We can make the attempt, if you aren't afraid." She was unsurprised when he cast her a reproachful glance. "Put the ghost fire on your head." She had been about to assure him that it wouldn't hurt, but he had already done as she said, heatless blue flame licking at his unkempt hair.

She squatted so he could climb on her back. She stood, lifting her arms so he could wriggle up to stand on her shoulders using her arms for support. Slowly and with wobbly care, he rose to his full height.

His feet flew from her shoulders and his weight was gone.

"Ha!" He had leaped and braced his hands and feet against the chimney's sides; keeping his arms and legs stiff, he inched up and up, the ghost light on his head casting a monstrous blue silhouette below.

He bent his head and pushed at the grate with his shoulder. The echoes of its scraping fell into the chamber as he gently shrugged it again and again until the top of the hole gaped open.

With a heart-stopping lunge, he threw his arms over the top and drew his legs after.

The newer purple mark on Pimchan's ribcage throbbed, and she knew the boy was exhilarated, terrified, breathless.

While he recovered and reconnoitered, Pimchan checked Nadia and Somboon again. Nadia was in the same position as before, but her flesh was almost as warm as Pimchan's. Somboon was alarmingly pale, and the faint blue cast to his lips was not the reflected color of ghost fire.

If their packs were not to be found, or they were found and her Male didn't have anything in his that would help, or he found something that would help but it came too late, would Somboon die? He looked as if he might die.

She knelt by his side. Then the Warrior did as she would have done for a companion in the field: She stretched her body upon his, warming it with her own, breathing against his left cheek, then his right, murmuring a spell of well-being into his ears. She bolstered the heat of her own blood with the heat of her fury at having no more powerful remedy, that such a man might die because she had led him into a danger she couldn't guard him from.

The voice of her Male echoed down the chimney. "I found them! I'm coming down."

She stood to catch him when he could no longer brace himself against the chimney walls, and came face-to-face with him, clinging to a line.

"I brought a rope," he said, unnecessarily.

"Where is my pack? My weapons?"

"They're above," he said. "I'll fetch them if you want, but may I try my herbs first?"

"Absolutely."

Whatever he used (it was bitter and stringent on Pimchan's tongue, but infused her body with freshness, as a warm rain does the earth), whatever words he mumbled as he administered it, it worked.

Somboon was the slowest to recover.

Nadia apologized to him. "I couldn't pass my warmth to all of you. The Male is the smallest, and my mistress is... my mistress."

"Of course," he said. "You chose perfectly." He didn't look at Pimchan, but he said, "I was protected."

There was nothing tender in his statement, only comfort for the guilt-ridden Overseer. Or was there an edge—just the hint of an edge? Not of tenderness, but of.... She felt her rune of discernment throb as she stared at him and he stared into the darkness beyond the ghost fire. He understood he had been honored by her treatment of him as a comrade, he resented that it was honor and not love, and he was resigned.

Pimchan thought better of him for his resentment. He was not a boy with a heart that would fill with tears until it burst. He was a man with a Chaos heart that could feel many things at once and find a balance.

But that was a matter to contemplate another time.

The space above was a larger rock chamber, with a wooden door fixed into one side. Chains clamped to the walls, floor, and ceiling spoke of its use. The rust and rock dust coating the ironware testified reassuringly to its *dis*use.

Somboon tried the door. "It isn't bolted. He trusted his spell and pit to hold us. I would guess this is a part of Akara's smithy, the part that runs into the mountain. Perhaps the house once belonged to a noble, and we're in the noble's dungeon."

"That makes sense," said Pimchan. "He's keeping us while he asks the person who commissioned that kukri what to do. So we need to be gone before he has a reply." *Finally! Something simple!* "I'll go first, then my Male, then Nadia, then you. We'll find our way out, then fight, if we must." She drew a sword for her right hand and a dagger for her left.

Somboon produced his short sword, a plain, workmanlike weapon of ordinary silvery steel, and the long club or short staff he called his "courtesy stick" because obstreperous townsfolk learned manners very quickly, under its influence.

Single file, they crept through the door and down a stone corridor, blue ghost light dying away in the glow of the corridor's torches. Regulated bustle and clang came from behind a stout wooden door. The smithy, no doubt.

Pimchan reached another wooden door. She lifted the latch and pushed the tiniest bit, revealing another torch-lit corridor, this one of wood.

Nadia whispered, "I know where we are, Mistress!"

The boy began, "This is—"

Nadia hissed a warning and he fell silent.

Pimchan admired Nadia's admonitory glare, recognizably modeled after her own.

Nadia continued, "This is the corridor we came down to go to the kitchen. The far door to the right leads to Akara's eating area."

Pimchan eased open a door at the end of the hall, revealing the empty entryway. She led her troupe silently across the tiled floor, and they emerged into the courtyard with fence, gate, path, and village beyond.

A woman called, "Ai! Master! Look! Help!" A stream of names and orders followed.

Pimchan had no intention of being chased down a village street by a bunch of domestics. She and Somboon, as if with one mind, pushed Nadia and Pimchan's Male into a corner of the yard and stood before them, their weapons ready.

Seven people rushed from the house. One man, not much taller than Nadia, brandished a cleaver; one man, twice the size of Somboon, hefted his smith's hammer; and five men and women in between waved various swords and knives. None of the weapons, Pimchan noted with satisfaction, were made of blue steel; they weren't totally lost to propriety.

Akara stood in the doorway, wringing his hands. "Just wait. Just for a while longer."

The smallest man gibbered, "She'll kill us! We kill her or die."

"No!" said Akara. "I forbid it!"

Underlings were expected to yield instant and unquestioning obedience. Pimchan would never dream of disobeying the All-Father, but her experience as a householder had taught her that lesser servants were not as steadfast as she.

Akara's menials, infected by fear, shifted their weapons to more offensive positions, shuffling their feet like a herd of water buffalo making ready to charge.

A cultivated voice from within the house said, "She won't kill you, idiot. You have my word."

The "idiot" drew back his cleaver and clumsily let it fly toward Pimchan. As it tumbled to the ground many inches from her feet, a streak of blue flashed from behind her, past the idiot, past Akara, to thud into a body in the entryway.

The cleaver-thrower shouted, "I told you so! Kill her!"

The attackers rushed forward, panic turning them savage. They were unused to fighting, which made them dangerous in their own way. If fighters knew their weapon and knew how to use them, it was possible to anticipate their attempts to block or land a blow. These amateurs swung wildly, desperately, as her townspeople had against a bandit incursion.

She opened a gash down one man's arm from shoulder to wrist. He clutched the flesh together and rolled in the dust, wailing.

Somboon, accustomed to keeping—or making—the peace among people who fought each other rarely, was more proficient at this sort of combat. His staff knocked the feet out from under the burly smith, whose hammer fell upon the toes of another attacker, putting him out of commission.

The battle, half slapstick, half horror, paused while the ambulatory wounded retreated, and four more servants crept out onto the field, clutching rolling pins and long kitchen knives. They cried out in dismay at the sight of their fallen comrades.

Perhaps it was all over. "Drop your weapons, all of you!" Pimchan shouted.

The cleaver-thrower waved a knife snatched from a fallen comrade, his face pinched with bitter resolution: "She'll kill us all, if we don't kill her first!"

She was afraid he might be right. At any rate, they weren't going through her to harm Nadia or the Male. She wished she could shove Somboon back with them and defend him, too, but his Chaos heart kept him at her side, giving his town's Warrior his best service.

Akara's servants, led by the cleaver-thrower, charged again, terrifying in their terror.

Iron-shod hoofbeats thundered along the path toward them, and battle shrieks ripped the air. Two mounted Warriors, dressed in ironwood armor and brass-plated tunics, with helmets shaped like snub-nosed dragon heads, plunged into view and vaulted their mounts over the fence into the yard.

The new Warriors steered their horses with delicate power among Akara's fighters, opening painful but not fatal wounds with breathtaking precision beyond even Pimchan's ability.

Akara's people dropped their weapons and fell to the ground, all but throwing themselves under the hooves of the new Warriors' steeds. They begged for mercy, scrabbling backwards toward the dubious protection of their prostrate master.

The mounted Warriors slid from their horses, facing Akara, and removed their helmets. They were each very small, and each had their snowy hair twisted up into flat knots.

Their backs were to Pimchan, but she recognized the shapes of the taller one's ears and the set of his shoulders.

She bit back her exclamation, not wanting to expose him to greater danger by identifying him.

"Rama!" the All-Father called. "Come forth!"

A slight but strong-featured young man in rich clothes nudged Akara aside and came into the yard, his left hand over his heart. He dropped his hand, revealing a dent in the bronze plates of his embroidered tunic. Although he grinned merrily, he bowed deeply.

The All-Father didn't return the bow. "As you see," said the All-Father, "your coup failed." Then he did bow, a quick head-dip. "But I am not entirely unimpressed."

The young man dared to look directly at the All-Father, still grinning. He winced and placed his hand over his heart again. Pimchan saw the glint of blue steel tucked into his waist.

She stepped forward, putting herself between the young man and the old. "Drop that kukri. Now."

He gingerly pulled it forth with two fingers and held it. "Do I really dare let it out of my hand? It nearly killed me, you know. Was it you who threw it?"

"It was I who ordered it left in my compound."

Pimchan's Male shot out of the corner where he had been stashed, obviously propelled by a Nadia-sized shove.

He returned Pimchan's frown with eyes that crossed as he defended himself, a sure signal that he was justifying misbehavior.

"I needed a weapon, and Nadia wouldn't let me take anything from the kitchen."

"So you took a Warrior's weapon I had specifically ordered left behind?"

"It was enchanted to seek the royal heart! How could it have been a danger here?"

"Ah! Ah!" The handsome young man tried to laugh, but every guffaw caused him to clutch his torso and twitch.

The All-Father shook a finger at him. "Now, Rama, you see the foolishness of taking the so-called unimportant people for granted. This slave boy was nearly the death of you. And that would have made me very unhappy, although it would have served you right."

Rama swung the knife between the fingers that held it. He cocked his head at Pimchan and smiled. "May I hand this to my father as a keepsake of the occasion?"

Father?

"You may drop it to the ground, as I told you."

He dropped it. The All-Father strode past her and picked it up. He examined it appreciatively and tucked it inside his armor.

"So let it rest next to my heart, as it was inscribed to do. Now, may we have some refreshment? We've galloped all the way from the court, with five changes of horse." He toed Akara, still prostrate. "Take your makeshift army and tend their wounds. If there's anyone left in the kitchen, have them prepare a repast."

"Nadia. My Male," said Pimchan. "Go see that all is done properly. Make certain everything is tasted in your sight." To the All-Father, she said, "Don't touch the peanuts."

Rama chuckled and held out both hands. "Come in and refresh yourselves, Father, Mother."

Mother?

Pimchan looked at the second Warrior more closely. It was, indeed, a woman, as lined and frail-looking as the All-Father, with eyes even sharper and brighter. Pimchan bowed deeply, and the All-Mother returned her bow, almost as deeply, a tremendous honor.

The All-Mother tucked a hand into the crook of Pimchan's arm. "You and your associate must come join us at the table. I've heard much about you."

Pimchan surreptitiously drew her dagger and held it under the table. A sideways glance at Somboon showed he had done the same.

The dusted peanuts had been removed.

The All-Father leaned across the table while his wife and son chattered in happy reunion. "Sheathe your weapons and be at ease. All is well."

Somboon obeyed instantly. Pimchan obeyed grudgingly. As she did, she felt a great release.

The All-Father nodded approvingly as he saw her finally understand that he always knew what he was doing, that he never stumbled into danger, that her casting herself into peril was correct, but that she wasn't rescuing him, she was following his unspoken lead. Like a Dependent piece on a carto board, he moved her and he valued her response and abilities.

He said, "When my son can outmaneuver me, he can have the throne. He's very nearly there. He coerced one of my finest bladesmiths into crafting a blue steel weapon that might have been my death, knowing it would be detected the instant it reached The Invisible City. Sadly for him, he failed to take Akara's household staff into account. I was warned. If I had not been, I might have looked for danger from within the Warrior ranks instead of from the junior ministers he promised to promote if they removed me from power."

Pimchan, aghast, imagined the fate of anyone attempting to lay hands on the All-Father.

"Oh, they wouldn't have tried to harm me, they would just have imprisoned us in our suite and given Rama's orders in our names until they could announce we had abdicated in his favor."

Rama and the All-Mother had fallen silent. The All-Father leaned back into his place.

Rama gestured to the All-Father's breast, where the hilt of the kukri gleamed in a shaft of sunlight. "How did that end up in the hands of a slave? And how did that slave end up here to throw it at me?"

"Thanks to my informant, the merchant you sent it by was intercepted by 'bandits.' They would have carried it until they came across a certain wandering Warrior. As it happens, he was on the spot at the theft itself. Of course, he came to inform me, but your ministers refused to let him in. If they had admitted him, *my* ministers would have refused him."

Pimchan thought she knew the answer but asked the question anyway: "Why?"

"Because, failing, your protégé would go to you for advice. If you didn't recognize the kukri's make, Lek would have, and that would have led you here. If you had been contained, my son would have thought he'd won, and my arrival would have disabused him of that misconception. If you had prevailed over whatever happened here—as you did—my son would know he had failed, especially when the two of us showed up."

"But," and this question, Pimchan did not know the answer to, "why did you not just send him a message that the coup had failed?"

"A lesson half-taught is a lesson unlearned."

Pimchan had the feeling that this aphorism was directed toward herself as much as toward Rama.

Nadia and Pimchan's Male brought in a platter of food and a tray of tea things.

The All-Father eyed Pimchan's Male. "This one, even I didn't expect. He stole and used a Warrior's weapon. I assume it wasn't found on him because it didn't occur to anyone to look for such a thing on such a person."

Rama lifted his shoulders apologetically.

The All-Father said, sternly, "This slave would have killed the heir to the land, if the heir hadn't armored himself."

Pimchan's Male prostrated himself and Pimchan felt her heart prostrate beside him. It would not be easy to face the Male's twin, to tell her that the boy had earned the ultimate punishment. She was too disconsolate even to resent feeling so deeply for mere domestics, or be angry with the life that had caused the word "mere" to seem inappropriate.

The All-Mother's voice cut into the discussion like a well-honed blade through flesh. "Since the weapon was commissioned by our son and the boy returned it to our son, there was no theft. Since our son had it inscribed with runes deadly to the royal heart, it was our son's own enchantment that nearly took his life, not this boy."

The All-Father cocked his head, smiling at his wife, and bowed to her.

She continued, "Since the boy disobeyed our Warrior Pimchan, the punishment for that is obvious. He must continue in her service until he learns proper behavior."

The All-Father objected. "That seems rather hard on our Warrior Pimchan. Ah, well, so be it. Rise, boy, and serve us."

They were all silent until they had begun to share food. Then the All-Father said, "I understand there is to be a wedding. We're all invited, of course."

Pimchan bowed deeply, forehead almost touching the table, to cover the jolt. Of course he knew the deceit they'd employed; that was to be expected. What stunned her was the sudden suspicion that it was he, through Lek, who had instigated it.

When Rama made a sound of surprise, she looked up.

Somboon sat bolt upright at her side, both palms on the table in objection, face glowing red as if heated in a furnace.

The All-Father, impassive as an idol, said, “Speak.”

“Your Warrior Pimchan lowered herself to pretend we were betrothed. It wasn’t true. It isn’t true. She would agree to the wedding if you pressed it, but I won’t.”

“Pimchan,” said the All-Father, eyes never leaving Somboon’s face, “what is he saying?”

Pimchan, heart thudding as heavily as if she had run far after winning a heavy combat, placed her hands over Somboon’s. “He says of course you’re invited. He says the matchmaker is always invited.” And, solemn as she felt, she couldn’t stop her smile.

TREE OF SOULS AND JEWELS

by Robin Wayne Bailey

Here is a classic-style fantasy with an unexpected ending.

Robin Wayne Bailey is the author of numerous novels, including the *Dragonkin* trilogy and the *Frost* series of novels and short stories, as well as *Shadowdance* and the Fritz Leiber-inspired *Swords Against the Shadowland.* His short fiction has appeared in many magazines and anthologies with numerous appearances in Marion Zimmer Bradley's *Sword and Sorceress* series and Deborah J. Ross's *Lace and Blade* anthologies. Some of his stories have been collected in two volumes, *Turn Left to Tomorrow* and *The Fantastikon: Tales of Wonder* from Yard Dog Books. He's a former two-term president of the Science Fiction and Fantasy Writers of America and a founder of The Science Fiction Hall of Fame. He's recently co-edited, along with Bryan Thomas Schmidt, *Little Green Men-Attack!* from Baen Books.

The city of Waylan-Rahn, a place of cheats and liars, thieves and worse, rose out of the desert sand under a cold full moon. The crude architecture of its high, cracked walls offered no welcome to strangers, nor even to those who lived within, as bricks and bits of stone were wont to fall at random upon those who dared walk too close or too carelessly under its shadow.

Two figures, one cloaked and hooded in black, the other all in white, rode across the dunes and down a slope toward the open gates as a light wind stirred the sand and set it to rattling like a nest of snakes. Some superstitious souls might have taken the sound as a warning, but the pair came on, undeterred. At the city threshold, no guard hailed or challenged them. Indeed, they saw no guards at all.

"Damn." The black-cloaked figure leaned forward and stroked the withers of his gray mare as the pair rode through the gates and forward. "I've smelled slop jars with better bouquet than these streets."

The second figure kept silent, but put one hand beneath a white cloak to grasp a sheathed dagger. It vibrated and purred like a wary cat. Green eyes narrowed watchfully, and the same hand moved up to push back the hood. Black hair, tied back with a silver cord, fell back over a woman's shoulders. A silver diadem with a single inset moonstone glimmered on her brow.

The rider on the gray horse followed her lead, pushing back his hood. His moonlit features were those of a young man barely out of boyhood, yet with a hardness to his angled jaw. He kept his voice low. "You have been here before, Samidar."

"How do you know?"

"Your secrets fall off your shoulders like snow," he answered. "I've learned to read you."

"Snow is an odd choice of words, given all this sand," she said. "Just stay alert, Kipling. Crime and vice are the coin of this city, and people would as soon cut your throat as the strings of your purse."

"If you fault my word-choice, critic, I will compose verse…."

Samidar waved him to silence and drew back on the reins of her stallion. "Dismount," she whispered.

Quick to obey, Kipling swung a leg over the gray's neck and slipped to the ground, one hand already on the hilt of the sword beneath his cloak.

Samidar allowed herself a spare moment to admire the boy's easy grace. *The man*, she reminded herself. In the past year, Kipling had grown taller than she. She pushed such thoughts aside, however, and again touched the small dagger on her belt. Its strange purring continued but did not increase.

Six men rushed out of a shadow-filled alley with weapons drawn. Their faces and blades were blackened and they advanced quietly, except for the shuffle of their boots on the sandy street and their mouth-breathing. At the front of the gang, a man ordered in gruff voice. "Strip and give us everything you've got, including those horses."

"Calmly, Kipling," Samidar said. "If he wants the horses, let him have them. She offered the reins of the stallion to the gang leader. "Take Ashur," she offered. "He's strong, but a very gentle beast."

The leader reached to take the reins. "He would have to be for a woman to ride him."

Samidar dropped the reins. Ashur reared suddenly and smashed into the six attackers, scattering them. At the same time, Kipling spun, and the weighted hem of his cloak struck at the eyes of the two men nearest him. His sword, however, did the real damage, and dark blood showered the sand.

"Wait!" Only two of the thugs remained standing, and both stepped back a little. One held up a hand and repeated, "Wait!"

Samidar tensed, and did not lower her sword. Kipling hesitated and looked to Samidar for guidance. Ashur nickered and shook his mane as he returned to his rider's side. "Wait for what?" Samidar said.

The attacker who had requested pause moved suddenly. His sword flashed up as he half-turned toward his companion. His stroke admirably perfect, he struck off his companion's head and sent it flying.

"I've been waiting for the right moment," he explained, looking to Kipling as he shook blood from his blade. "The bastard has been sleeping with my lover for months." He kicked the body and spat on it, then looked to Samidar. "Now, unless you feel a desperate need to do me in, as you have these others, I'll be on my way." He shrugged. "I never cared much for this lot."

"One moment," Kipling interrupted. "Before we let you walk away, we'd first have you strip and give us everything you've got."

The thug looked startled. "Everything?" he said. "I haven't got much. We were hoping to profit from…!"

"From us," Kipling interrupted again. He looked to Samidar. "Let's let him keep his trousers. I'm not certain I want to see him naked." He turned back to the thug. "Everything else, though, including your sword."

"My sword? But without my sword how will I dispatch my lover? He wasn't innocent in this business, you know."

"Love will find a way," Samidar answered. "Now, strip."

"Not the trousers," Kipling reminded.

The bravado faded from the thug's face as he threw down his sword and bent to unlace his boots. "I've done you no harm." He rose, hopping up and down on his right foot as he struggled to remove the boot on his left. "Don't slay me in my moment of awkwardness." When the boot finally came free, he stumbled backward and fell on his rump. He forced a smile as he wiggled out of the second boot. "I'm so embarrassed," he admitted. He fumbled at his waist band and tossed out a thin purse. Next came a small belt-knife. Finally, he removed his tunic and shirt and lay them aside in the street. Bare-chested and barefooted, he rose again. "Anything else?"

"I'd like to see how skillfully you can run," Kipling said. "Keep in mind you've terrorized our horses. They may give chase."

The thug turned as pale as the moonlight, glanced at his sword on the street, then sped off as swiftly as he could. The city's darkness swallowed him up.

Kipling smiled. "Well, he was a jolly fellow."

Samidar sheathed her sword and gathered Ashur's reins. "You're developing a mean streak," she said to Kipling. "Or a sense of humor. I can't tell which."

"I'm developing something else," he said as he collected the sword and the belt-knife. "An itch in the back of my brain, like something is watching us." He tied the extra sword to his saddle and put the knife into a pack. Then, leaning over the back of the Gray, he asked. "Why did we really come to this city, Samidar?"

"That itch in your brain," she said in a softer voice as she touched the purring dagger again. "You're becoming sensitive to the magic around you. You're not yet a warlock or a sorcerer, but in your time with me, you've learned things." She paused as she scanned the moonlit rooftops. The jewel in her diadem flashed. "Before this place had a name, it was known only as the City of Sin."

"Well-named, I assume." Kipling said.

"Now I'm drawn back again," she continued. "I don't know

why."

A large rock struck the ground near Samidar's boot. Another quickly followed, another near-miss.

"Children," Samidar said, gazing upward. "Along the rooftops."

The gray mare panicked and reared as a stone struck its saddle. Kipling ducked as the stone ricocheted toward his face. "Murderous little spawn!"

The air quickly filled with a rain of rocks and stones. "Take the horses and get into the alley," Samidar ordered. "It won't protect you for long.

Cursing as he tried to dodge the missiles, Kipling gathered the reins of both mounts. "What about you?

"Go!"

Kipling obeyed. Swiftly, he led their animals into the narrow alley from which their original attackers had emerged. Stones rattled the boards and clattered on the ground, but none made it past the alley's mouth. He leaned out as far as he dared to watch as the itching in the back of his brain became something fiercer.

In the street, Samidar knelt down. Her eyes burned suddenly with fire, not a trick of the light, but seemingly real red fire that flickered and danced over her face. The rocks and stones that continued to rain down all missed her, every one. She swept her hands over the sandy street, gathered up fists full of sand and threw it upward into the air. An unexpected wind rose swirling around her, carrying the sand higher and higher.

The night filled with a wild keening. A greater wind blasted through the city gates, bringing with it sand from the desert, a massive sandstorm that roared across the rooftops. The children screamed and ran for any shelter as the storm stripped skin from their bones.

The fire in her eyes faded. The wind died, and the sandstorm became still. Rubbing his neck, Kipling led the horses back out of the alley. "Barely ten steps inside the gates, and we've been attacked twice. Are you ever drawn to more pleasant places?"

Samidar didn't answer. Putting one hand on the hilt of the dagger, she whispered, "Listen."

The dagger no longer purred. Rather, a sound like distant terrified shrieking issued from it.

Samidar looked at Kipling. "You hear it, don't you? You hear Demonfang's cry?

"It's in my head," he answered. "It hurts."

"The city is permeated with magic," she explained, "and we just drew the attention of something ugly and powerful."

"This is the reason you were drawn here?" Kipling said quietly.

She nodded. "I think so. This has always been a place of sorcery and evil. The people reveled in their corruption and vice. But there is worse here now. Those children were not children at all, but soulless things."

"I confess, I feared you had slaughtered innocents." He swung into the saddle of the horse he called only the Gray. "The buzzing in my brain is making my head throb."

"You can turn it off," Samidar answered. "Just will it so." She climbed upon Ashur, and they began a slow ride down the street. From the corner of her eye, she watched the boy. *The man*, she reminded herself. She had found him as a boy, though, an awkward little thief about to meet his end. She saved him, and to her sometime annoyance, he followed her and had never since left her side.

A short scream from a candlelit window in a second-floor apartment caught their attention. A moment later, a head came flying past the open shutters and landed in the street just before them. A shirtless figure appeared briefly, silhouetted by the flickering light.

"Is that who I think it is?" Kipling asked.

"Love found a way," Samidar answered as they continued past. "Speaking of heads, how is yours?"

"The buzzing is there, but fainter," he said. "Now, I hear music."

"This way." Samidar gently tugged on Ashur's reins and led them down another darker street where the moonlight did not yet reach. When a man ran out of a doorway with a knife, she kicked him in the face and paused to make sure he didn't get back up.

"Are these people all insane?" Kipling whispered.

"Worse," she said. "Like the children, this man has no soul. I can feel his emptiness. Yet, he isn't mindless. He uses a weapon and attacks from secrecy, which implies intent, as well as strategy."

They rode on, and the music grew louder. A tympany of dumbek drums echoed among old wooden walls. The metallic clash of zills and tambourines kept pace. The twisting rhythms were alluring, infectious—hypnotic. When Kipling realized he was nodding his head in time, he jerked upright in his saddle and muttered a curse under his breath. With sure fingers, he loosened the knots that held the extra sword to his saddle and laid the blade across his lap.

"This music is…!"

"Intoxicating?" Samidar. "Listen carefully. The rhythms are interwoven with old spells and dark magic. Demonfang shivers like a caged animal at my side."

"To warn us?" Kipling said.

"Hardly," Samidar scoffed. "The dagger would devour us if it could."

The drums grew louder and wilder. The walls on either side of the street seemed to come alive, to inhale and exhale on the upbeat and the downbeat. The air pulsed suddenly with subtle colors. For a moment, caught off guard by the intensity of something she didn't yet understand, Samidar reeled. She grasped the horn of her saddle, squeezed with her knees and managed not to fall as she pushed back at the malevolent force. When she was free of it, she shot a look back for Kipling.

The boy was gone! Only the Gray remained, snorting and uneasy and riderless. A strangling gurgle made her look up in time to see her companion rising toward the rooftops, hoisted at the end of a rope by three moonlit men.

The sword he had carried on his lap lay in the road. Samidar stretched out a hand, and the weapon came flying into her grasp. When she opened her hand again, the sword flashed upward like a steel bolt of lightning to strike one of the three through the chest.

But one was not enough. The other two caught Kipling by the shoulders and hauled him over the edge of the roof and out of sight.

"Kipling!" She called his name twice and waited. When no response came, a cold hand closed around her heart. Seeing no quick way to the roofs, she gathered the reins of the Gray and stared upward for another long moment. Finally, she leaned forward and stroked Ashur's withers. "If anything happens to Kipling," she whispered into the stallion's ear, "if he is dead, I'll burn this city to the ground and bury the ruins." Ashur snorted and pawed the road.

She blamed herself for not being more alert, for letting ancient magic distract her even for a heartbeat. She listened to the drums again, the zills and tambourines so reminiscent of the dark, forgotten things that rumbled in the earth.

She felt the heat of her own rising anger. It inured her to the age-old rhythms, to the black magic that permeated the very boards and stones, the streets and alleyways and corrupted every soul within the city perimeters. She rode forward as anger turned to rage, following the music down one street and into the next. She felt the drumbeats on her skin, and the air swirled with mesmerizing colors. Samidar brushed it all aside.

The street opened into a vast plaza. Half-naked and less, women and girls danced impassioned to the music. The full moonlight shimmered on pale breasts and gyrating hips while men watched with drooling lips and hungry eyes full of vile intent. All around the plaza, naked and sweating drummers beat the rhythms on their dumbeks, on anything, bucket or barrel, that would cast a sound. Tambourines shook and zills flashed on the fingers of those who stood next to the drummers, who worked with them. And there were kalimbas and chipolis, as well.

The eyes of the musicians were turned up inside their heads, and whatever they saw was not of this earth.

"Stop them! Please, make them stop!"

Samidar gazed up at an open window of an apartment on the second floor that overlooked the plaza. A young girl stood there, crying and waving her hand to attract Samidar's attention. "You have to stop them!" she called again.

"Come down!" Samidar called back.

"I dare not!" the girl cried. "It's me they're after. They want me! If I come down, the town will take me, and evil will win!"

The girl recoiled from the window as she looked out over the plaza. "Oh, gods! They have him! An outsider—they're going to kill him!"

Again, Samidar felt the hand of fear. Rising in her stirrups, she stared outward, but could see nothing. She rose higher with consummate balance to stand on her saddle, and still she saw nothing. With a determined leap, she caught the rail of a balcony beneath the girl's window and muscled herself over that. She stared outward again—and gasped.

A gang of men, none with souls of their own, dragged a bound Kipling through the crowd and toward a tree that grew in the center of the plaza. His cloak and most of his clothes, as well as his weapons, had been stripped from him. All he truly wore was a rope around his neck.

"Another innocent soul!" the girl in the window cried. "Despair!

The members of the gang held Kipling in position beneath a tree limb and threw the rope over it. They meant to hang him. A trio of men hauled on the rope, and Kipling shot upward, kicking and twisting.

Enraged, Samidar reached toward the sky with clawed hands. Impossible clouds trundled over the moon, obscuring its light. Inside those clouds, lightning danced. "I'll give you rhythms," she shouted.

Crackling bolts stabbed downward. Dancers and musicians ran screaming as old rooftops exploded and walls shattered. The plaza filled swiftly with the stench of charred flesh. The onslaught did not abate as sweat began to bead on her face.

Casting aside her white cloak, Samidar jumped from the balcony. "Ashur!" she called, as she drew her sword. The black beast came to her at once, but she did not mount him. Swinging her blade, she charged into the crowd. They were all soulless; she perceived that now, although she couldn't explain it. But she held nothing back as she fought her way toward the tree where Kipling hanged. Men or women who got in her way or fought back, they all fell before her strokes.

Battle-trained Ashur stayed close to her, as well, and his hooves, teeth, and broad shoulders claimed as many.

Yet, even as Samidar fought and killed, she saw that no lightning touched the tree from which Kipling hanged. The air around it flickered and flashed and diverted every bolt, and the tree remained unharmed. Stranger yet, even though drummers and dancers vanished or were dispatched, the sound of the drumming intensified.

Some force attempted to repel her as she came closer and closer, but nothing could keep her from Kipling. "I am Samidar of Esgaria!" she hissed, announcing herself. "And I am Frost, handmaiden to Lord De'th, himself." Her eyes filled with inhuman fire. "And I am the Doom that came to Waylan-Rahn."

A line of men rushed to take station between Samidar and the tree. Ashur charged into them, scattering them like sticks. More rushed to take their places. Samidar cut them down, her hands and garments slick with blood. Now, the Gray, Kipling's mount, charged into the fray, fully Ashur's equal at breaking and maiming.

"This is madness," Samidar muttered to herself. She backed up a step and cleared a space. Ashur and the Gray came to her side. Her only goal now was to claim Kipling's body, and she was tired of those that stood in her way.

Again, she raised her hands to the sky, and she blew a breath upon them. The lightning dimmed, but the clouds remained, violently churning, to blot out the moonlight. A wind rose from nowhere, became a swirling mass of power, a serpentine tempest that tossed people like leaves or sucked them bodily into the sky. Their screams meant nothing to Samidar. Her way finally clear, she went to the tree. With a savage stroke, she cut the rope from which Kipling hanged and caught his body in one strong arm. Gingerly, she lay him down and removed the rough coil from his neck.

The drumming ceased. The insane magical rhythms faded

and withdrew. Yet, though she sheathed her bloody sword, Samidar did not let down her guard. The great wind swirled upward to form a churning vortex above the city, a maelstrom ready to answer her command.

She was still uncertain of the Power that had challenged her, but plainly its focus was the tree. Cradling Kipling's body in her arms, she rose. The fire softened in her eyes and they became normal again. "We are not done," she said softly, her heart breaking as she looked at Kipling's face. Then, she screamed it to the tree, as if it was a living thing. "*We are not done*!

Lightning continued to flicker in the thick clouds above, and a muted thunder rumbled in the slowly swirling maelstrom. Except for these, silence hung over all. Samidar carried Kipling across the plaza, stepping over wounded men and dead. Ashur and the Gray flanked her, and none of the few remaining survivors dared to offer more trouble.

She reached the street from which she had previously emerged and glanced upward. The light in the second-floor window still burned, but more dimly, as if someone had shielded it or moved it further away.

"If there is a way up," she said in a clear, low voice, "tell me what it is."

After a long moment, the young girl appeared in the window. "No one can get up," she answered. I barricaded everything, even tore out some of the stairs."

"I got up once before," Samidar reminded. "I mean to get up there again. Don't keep me waiting."

The girl crept out onto the narrow balcony. "But why?" she asked, her voice plaintive. "Just leave the city while you can. You don't know what is happening!"

Ashur reared and slammed his hooves against the building walls with such force that boards broke and the small balcony shivered. The startled girl stepped back again.

"We intend to find out," Samidar answered. "Besides, I need a place to shelter my friend. Your apartment seems safe."

The girl came out onto the balcony again. She looked distraught. "Is he dead then?"

Samidar glared.

The girl bit her lip. "Then wait. The course is not easy, but if you promise your protection, I'll come down."

Samidar kept her silence, determined to promise nothing in this dark city until she knew to whom she was making such a pledge. The girl hesitated, her fear palpable, but she turned and went back inside. A moment more and the candlelight began to move. Then, the apartment went dark.

The Gray nickered. Samidar looked over one shoulder and then turned. Out on the plaza, the few survivors began to move in her direction. The maimed and crippled began to crawl, pulling themselves forward over the dead, over the sand and stone. Faintly, the throb of dumbeks and tambourines commenced again.

The girl had said they were coming for her.

At her side, the Demonfang shivered in its sheath.

"Be quiet," she whispered, and the blade obeyed.

As gently as she could, she tossed Kipling over one shoulder and drew her sword. The flickering of lightning in the clouds intensified, and the wind began to blow once more.

The girl spoke up from the shadows behind them. She held her candle close to shield the small flame, and it lit up a heart-shaped face with frightened eyes. "Come at once!" she whispered. "It's me they want! Come on!"

"The horses…," Samidar said,

The girl interrupted, her eyes widening as she stared across the plaza. "You can bring them a little way inside. It may hide them. But there is no route to get them upstairs. Please, hurry!"

Samidar gazed once more toward the plaza. The sight of the advancing wounded unnerved her. She had seen many strange and horrifying sights. None quite like this.

"Come!" the girl whispered again. Samidar turned and saw only the movement of the candlelight. Sheathing her sword, she hurried to catch up. Down a twisting maze of alleys, the girl went, always looking over her shoulder, scared as a hunted doe. Furtively pushing open a door, she beckoned. "Leave your horses here," she said. Then, she went to another door and pushed it carefully open. "This was once a tavern. The owner smuggled liquor and other things through a series of tunnels below. Now, the tunnels serve my needs."

Samidar stared warily through the door and down the steps. "If you plan to lose me down there, you should know that darkness and I have a first-name relationship,"

"I saw what you did on the plaza," she answered. "We can share first names, too. Mine is Calynda N'Sol."

She led the way down the old stairs, holding her candle in a manner so that Samidar could also see.

"That sounds like a Rhianoth name," Samidar noted.

"I am not from here," Calynda affirmed.

As they progressed, Samidar noted how the tunnels became filled with refuse, broken furniture, and trash. She took care not to bang Kipling's head or hands or any part of him and picked her way along carefully. The girl, Calynda, obviously knew the route and any of its pitfalls by heart.

"The clutter is mine," she admitted to a question "Something about the magic that possesses everybody—it makes them hate clutter. Clutter confuses them. So, I've dragged everything I can find into these tunnels."

"Including the slop jars," Samidar observed.

They continued the rest of the way without speaking. The tunnels were as twisty as the alleys above, but more claustrophobic and dangerous. Without warning, Calynda stopped and set her candle down. Neatly camouflaged by all the refuse, a ladder lay. Calynda lifted it and positioned it in a specific manner against the tunnel wall. She climbed it with sure movements, although her skirts threatened to entangle and trip her. She fumbled with something unseen, a latch or a lock, and a door well above Samidar's head swung quietly open.

Calynda descended again and took up the candle. "I dare not let its flame go out," she whispered. "I have no way to make more fire, neither the skill nor the knowledge."

"I could teach you," Samidar answered as she followed Calynda up the ladder with Kipling on her shoulder.

Calynda shrugged and giggled, the first such sound Samidar

had heard from her. "I would just forget your lesson," she said. "I'm a very stupid girl.

Samidar doubted that. Yet, she was distracted. Demonfang was alive again and purring. It sensed something, and she sensed it, also. For some small time, since descending into these tunnels, she had been aware—of something. On an impulse, she put one hand against the wall. Was its imagination or did she feel movement? She wasn't sure, so she leaned around the edge of the ladder and put her ear to the wall.

With a gasp, she lunged backward. Her foot slipped on a rung, and she nearly dropped Kipling. Only Calynda's steady hand at the top of the ladder saved Samidar from falling. But falling—where?

She wasn't sure anymore if the tunnel had a floor or a ceiling or even an end. The ladder seemed to reach up and up and down and ever down, stretching into eternity. Time and space lost meaning, and all she knew was that *something* pulsating within the wall or very near on the other side of it had spoken her name!

But there was Calynda to save her. "Warrior!" she called, knowing no other name for Samidar. "Warrior!" That was enough. Samidar grabbed hold of the sound of it and regained her focus. The tunnel became just a tunnel again and the ladder just a ladder. Still, she climbed with speed and urgency until she reached the top rung and emerged into the cluttered hallway of an old apartment building.

The girl held up her light. "Be careful of the stairs," she warned. "I've booby-trapped several of them. Even I don't remember which, so just be careful. Stay to the edges, and if something creaks, get off it."

Calynda went first, and Samidar took care to note where the girl placed her footsteps before she followed. When they reached the top, the girl grabbed a rope that ran smoothly through a hook in the ceiling. With an effort, she hauled up the entire staircase and tied the rope to a rail.

"I would have helped," Samidar said apologetically.

Calynda interrupted, "You have your burden."

Samidar looked into Kipling's face, observing traces of the

sorrow and fear and disbelief he had felt in the last moment before the noose took him. He had expected to be saved.

"He's no burden," Samidar said. "But I need a place to lay him down and make him comfortable. I have unfinished business."

"My room is down this hallway," Calynda said. "Please place your young man upon my unworthy bed. It is soft and clean."

Samidar studied Calynda, recalling that she had not trusted the girl at first and wondering when exactly that had changed. The girl was a contradiction, so child-like, yet obviously capable of surviving in the face of great evil. "You're very kind," Samidar said, and Calynda's face lit up at the compliment.

Calynda inclined her head and touched Samidar's cheek with a fingertip. "So are you," she said. "Your eyes shine with kindness.

That caught Samidar off guard. She did not think of herself as kind. In fact, the idea chilled her. She went to the balcony and looked up. Lightning still snaked through the clouds, and the wind made a soft moan. "You said they were coming for you, that these people wanted you." Samidar turned toward Calynda. "Why?"

Calynda looked puzzled. "I honestly don't know."

"I think you do," Samidar said. "You are not quite what you seem. Your candle burns, but it doesn't burn down. Your bed and your floor are free from dust, yet it hangs everywhere in the air. The desert night is chill, and you have no fireplace. Yet, your room is warm."

Calynda hesitated as she rubbed her cheek and looked toward the carnage in the plaza. "I have never known the body of a man, nor the pleasure of a woman," she answered, tears welling in her eyes. "I've never been loved, so I loved all." She looked down at her feet and wrung her delicate hands. "I have a small power. I used that to help others, sometimes to heal, sometimes to nurture. For that, people loved me back, after a fashion, and I was content.

"But this city has always been corrupt, and corruption festered in the hearts and souls of the people who lived here.

That corruption inevitably formed a seed, and that seed took root and grew. The citizenry—every man, woman, and child—gave themselves to it and were changed. Those few who resisted were seized and fed to it, as your young man was."

Samidar stared down into the plaza, which was still a place of carnage. Her gaze went to the tree. In the back of her mind, she heard its primitive music.

Calynda's voice became plaintive again. "Don't let them take me,"

Samidar released the clasp of her cloak and let the bloody garment fall to the balcony floor. "I won't," she answered. "Watch over Kipling. I will be close by."

Jumping up, she caught the eave of the roof and swung outward. For an instant, it seemed that she would fall, but she curled her body as she continued to swing and twisted herself until she landed cat-like on the roof's edge.

She folded her legs and her hands as she sat down. It didn't look much different from any other tree, but she knew better. She felt its roots growing deep into the earth, burrowing beneath the city into all its corners. She had felt those roots in the tunnels as they gnawed at the city's foundations. Those roots had looked back, too, seen her and called her name. Even now, she felt them digging and burrowing ever deeper, not just under the city, but reaching all the way down to its original home in the bowels of hell.

Calynda N'Sol was a witch with limited ability, a minor white witch who tried to help her friends and neighbors. Samidar closed her eyes as she reached for understanding. Calynda was not just a minor witch. The tree didn't want her for that reason. Calynda had never known a man or woman in carnal fashion. She was an innocent. For that reason, the tree desired her, to feast on that innocence, to corrupt her. But without even knowing it, Calynda was using her meager power to hold the evil—and the townspeople—at bay. She protected her home.

The drums began to sound again. In the plaza, people came out as if nothing had happened. They ignored the bodies in the sandy street and all the wounded. They beat their tambourines and zills, shook the chipoli. And danced naked with abandon.

Yet, as they played and danced, every hungry eye turned toward the apartment, toward the last innocent in all of Waylan-Rahn.

Samidar drew a deep breath and let it out. When she looked to the tree again, she saw it with new eyes. A veil fell away as the tree revealed itself to her, every branch and limb budding, not leaves, but jewels of all kinds, and trapped writhing at the heart of every jewel, a tiny, eternally damned soul.

Her senses might have reeled, but instead she thought of Kipling—another innocent. A surge of anger strengthened her. Let no one say otherwise, anger had its place.

"Ashur," she whispered. Over the crazy percussion in the plaza, a new sound was heard, a crashing and breaking of wood, the loud battle cries of the black stallion and its mate. Ashur and the Gray charged through the street and stood position directly beneath the apartment.

Samidar swung down from the rooftop to the balcony.

"Go now, Calynda, by the most direct route to the street below. Mount the Gray and ride as fast as you can out of the city. Ashur will go with you and keep you safe."

"No!" Calynda wore a look of terror. "I dare not go! They're coming for me, and I have to stay. I'm only safe here in my little home!" She ran into her kitchen and seized up a large knife. "This is the end," she cried. "I feel it! But they will not take me—never! I will deny them!"

"Don't!" Samidar shouted. But the mad rhythms of the drums surged upward like the charge of an army. Samidar felt the onslaught like a blow to the back of her skull. The tree meant to take her, too.

Calynda called to her. "Warrior! Thank you for showing me strength." She plunged the knife into her belly and drew the sharp blade upward. "Now, I am free. No more fear, Warrior. No … more … love." Calynda sank to the floor.

Samidar knelt down and cradled Calynda's head. "No, Calynda," she said. "I love you."

Calynda reached up weakly. "You are kind, Warrior." The

light faded from her eyes, and her breathing stilled.

Samidar screamed in rage. Kipling dead. Calynda dead. Now it was Waylan-Rahn's time to die. She went out onto the balcony. "Run," she whispered to Ashur, and the black stallion reared before it raced away with the Gray following right behind,

The tree was defiant. The jewels that served it in place of leaves shimmered with insane fire, and the thousands of souls trapped inside danced and laughed, just as the empty flesh in the plaza danced. Samidar felt the tree's power bend toward her, felt the trees roots digging and crawling beneath the city and the earth, but now those roots reached out for her.

Standing on the balcony, Samidar spoke in a normal voice. "I promised you that if you harmed Kipling, I would burn this city to the ground and bury its ruins."

No more words, no pronouncements. Samidar's eyes flared with unnatural fire as she stretched out her arms to the clouds above. Blue lightning crackled between her fingertips. In the sky, lightning shot across the heavens. She caught it and hurled it straight at the tree. More lightning pounded downward. Rooftops exploded and caught fire. Flesh burned, and the stench rose amid screams and sighs of ecstasy.

She began to sweat and her skin gleamed. Yet, she did not weaken or falter. She fanned the flames with intense winds and drove the fire through streets and alleys, from one quarter of the city to the next. The city walls crumbled from the heat and collapsed while on the plaza bolt after sizzling bolt stabbed the tree until its great trunk exploded and the light went out of every single jewel.

And still Samidar stabbed it with lightning until she found the tree's heart, until that also exploded.

Deep in the earth, the roots stopped digging.

For a long moment, Samidar stared, her body shaking as she observed her handiwork. Then, she went to Kipling and took the boy up in her arms again. The apartment began to smoulder and fill with smoke. She carried Kipling into the hallway. Fire was already licking at the broken staircase. She didn't care. She walked into the blaze, then out into the streets, finally through the burning gates.

She wore the flames like a cloak as she passed into the desert, and the fire did her no harm.

Wrapped in his own black cloak, Kipling woke. The desert moon shone above, along with a few bright stars, and a gentle wind kissed his face. As he stirred, soft lips brushed the back of his hand. Nearby, Ashur and the Gray nickered. He sat slowly up.

"What happened?" he asked, his gaze locking on Samidar and on the burning ruins of the city behind her. "I thought …."

"You were." Samidar leaned closer and kissed away his words before he could speak them. "I couldn't save you from hanging, Kipling. But Lord De'th and I are old friends. He owes me many favors. I collected one of them tonight."

"Thank you," he said as he took her hand in his.

She pulled back. "Don't thank me yet," she answered. "No one crosses that threshold without being changed, and De'th will forever have his hand on you. You won't always welcome my intercession."

She shifted her position on the sand, folded her legs and her hands in her lap. The desert dunes rolled up like a wave, wave upon wave, and they buried Waylan-Rahn deep until no trace of the city remained to ever be discovered.

Kipling watched, his turmoil visible on his face as he took her hand again.

Samidar did not resist this time, but squeezed his finger. "I was not the one summoned to this city, Kipling," she explained. "You were the one. Your destiny begins here. And I have a gift for you. She unfastened the belt around her waist and held out Demonfang in its silver sheath.. "As this was given to me long ago, I give it to you. Never draw it from that sheath unless you mean to kill with it. It is older than time."

Kipling looked at her. "What am I?

She brushed back a strand of his dark hair and flashed a rare smile. She loved him in so many ways.

"That is for you to find out."

CONTROVERSIAL KNOWLEDGE

by Jane M. H. Bigelow

When I was seven, I wanted to be a librarian when I grew up. I had no idea just how dangerous that job could become.

Jane M. H. Bigelow wrote her first story in crayon. Since then she's published poetry, short stories and short nonfiction on such topics as gardening in Ancient Egypt. She has also published a fantasy novel, *Talisman*. Several of her short stories appear in the Darkover anthologies, including this year's *Citadels of Darkover*. She's currently working on a fantasy suspense novel with the working title of *The Body Under the Bed*.

History and mythology, travel and gardening, all influence her fiction.

Jane is a retired reference librarian, a job which encouraged her to go on being curious about everything. She lives in Denver, CO with her husband, Robert, and two spoiled cats, Shiraz and Thunderpurr.

"This touches me too nearly. I cannot leave it to others. I need those books here, where I—and only I—control the use of them." Prince Radulph didn't raise his voice. He didn't move from his bog-oak throne, inlaid with silver that glinted in the late afternoon light. He merely stared.

Ysolde, Guildmistress of Archivists, tried not to flinch. The Great Audience Chamber's echoing expanses of stone were intended to make subjects feel small.

It worked.

Wouldn't it be better to give in to His Highness' demands? Defying a Prince was always a risky business. Her stomach clenched at the thought of just how miserable he could make life for her and for the Guild. As the final victor in a generations-long war, he was not known for his delicate conscience.

Yet she dared not. Ysolde wasn't even sure it was possible to remove the records from the Sequestered Collection of the Guild

House. Each of them had its own place on shelf or scroll-cubby, and troubles came if that order were disturbed.

And if it could be done, what then? Left unwarded, what plagues and battles would be let loose? Ysolde raised her eyes to the throne, and immediately looked back at her own feet.

Come now, be brave.

Her guild had a long, honorable history of scholarship and preservation. *And few know of some of the texts we preserve.* They had been called upon in matters of disputed succession, where there was always the chance of being murdered by one displeased side or another during the several-sided struggles that finished with the current king's seizure of the throne. This was not more frightening than those days, surely?

But then I was a young girl who ran here and there with books, with ink and pens and paper. I was happy to do so, rid of the crawling unease of sorcerous studies. I had no responsibilities, only duties. She tucked a wisp of salt-and-pepper hair back under the band of her hood.

His Highness tapped one arm of the throne. He was a tall man, thickly-muscled still; he'd used the two-handed sword in his battling days. His hairline remembered the pressure of a helm. "Madame Archivist?" His voice would have carried over an entire battlefield, she felt sure.

Ysolde felt light-headed at what she must say next. "I regret, your Highness, that I can't do as you ask. It has always been our honor to assist the Prince or Princess..." she faltered. He had not been over-fond of his aunt, for all that she kept the Norwegian claimant off his land during his boyhood.

He laughed. To her relief it sounded like genuine amusement. "Whoever the prince may be?"

She cleared her throat. "We would loan the books to you if we could, Your Highness."

"What's the difficulty? I will send as many soldiers as you like to guard them, a sorcerer or two to cast wards around them as they travel the league or so from your archives to my palace, and have them gently and carefully placed in the room I've had created for their short stay with me. Come, I will show you the room." He heaved himself up, shouted to the sleepy page leaning against the far wall, and strode down off the dais, to a low door in the wall behind it. Obediently, Ysolde followed. *The room isn't the point, Your Highness.* There was no point in saying it, and no chance to do so.

Down a narrow hall bare of tapestries, up a staircase whose treads were worn uneven by many feet, along another hallway, and they stood in a scholar's dream of a room. It was a half-tower; its three outer walls each had a large, well-glassed window. Between the windows and at intervals around the room, were set metal-backed niches for candles. The two interior walls were lined with bookcases. A table, light enough to be moved easily, stood in the middle of the room. A wooden chair with arms stood by it. The plaster smelled new; the room as a dustless as anything in this city could be.

A narrow line of green around each window, and the faint prickling sensation as she walked through the door, said that elementary wards had already been cast.

Ysolde sighed. "It's a beautiful room."

"Why so sad, then? Your books will be quite comfortable here, my lady."

He meant that for flattery. Guildmistress she was, and proud of the honor, but she had no claim to be called Lady. Would he believe that she could do without it quite nicely?

"Because the books, ungrateful creatures, would *not* be comfortable here. You smile to hear me say it, Your Highness, but they are," she grimaced, "aware, in a sense. The first archivist really did construct the first archive around them, and they must stay there. Even within the archives, they can't be moved. It is inconvenient. We would dearly love—but Your Highness will not care about that."

"I care about getting those books." He put his head to one side. "I will tell you something that is to go no farther."

"I am honored."

"Her Highness is with child again."

Her Highness had been with child three times. Early or late, they had come to nothing for the poor lady. After each failure, more attendants were brought in, more magical wards added. Her chief *sage-femme* had committed suicide after the last time. "I wish her health and happiness, Sire. We all admire and love her." That was true. Her Highness was an excellent Princess, gracious even to her inferiors. She had founded two schools for orphan children, and stocked them well with books.

"Thank you, but good wishes aren't what I need. I know why my sweet lady has lost three children, and it isn't going to happen this time. I need those books."

"Perhaps Duke Henry could come to us? The books will not allow themselves to be copied, but he could make a precis." As the second son, he'd received training in magic. Ysolde thought he might have made a good scholar, had circumstances been different.

Prince Radulph's face grew cold. "No, I cannot and will not send anyone down there to your Archives, most especially my brother."

Ah. *This is awkward.* "Your Highness, shall I deny him access the next time he comes to us?"

"The *next* time?"

"Yes, sire."

The Prince's lips tightened. Ysolde knew he prided himself on his spy service. "Which rooms did he visit?"

"The medical collection, and," she did flinch now, *that look must be what his enemies see in battle,* "the Sequestered Rooms."

"When did he last visit you?"

"Your Highness, it was over two years ago, in the late fall; a little later than this, I believe. I can consult our records to give You a more precise answer, if You wish."

"No need. I remember full well that Her Highness lost our child on the first day of winter. He has visited other times?"

Ysolde's stomach clenched. "Highness, we knew of no reason to deny a royal Duke! His own lady was with child each time; we thought nothing of it. The books in the Sequestered Rooms do hold counter-spells of beneficent intent, which is why we've lately granted some access. I gave him the blessing to enter and to leave, thinking no harm—" *I'm babbling. Quiet, Ysolde.*

His Highness waved her fears aside. "No, you would not. But I must and will have those books in my hands and out of his. He continued, "Our best sorcerer swore there was a stench of dark magic about the *sage-femme's* death, under all the chaos of self-harm. You have some training in these matters yourself, I believe?"

"A little. Certainly dark magic has a scent. Visible talismans may be made invisible, but the smell cannot be smothered." She grimaced. "Some of the Sequestered Rooms reek of it. "

She shook herself free of the memory. "Truly, for your own safety and that of the city, the books must not leave."

"They would, what? Burst into flames?" He chuckled.

"Oh, not the *Codex de Pulvis*. It would crumble into dust. The difficulties would arise for anyone who breathed the dust."

He looked disconcerted. Then he shook his head. "And there are similar problems with the other books I wish to see?"

She smiled. "Oh, it isn't always anything drastic, Your Highness. Sometimes the pages simply lose all their ink."

He looked at her sideways. "If it was ever there."

"According to the records of Gunther of Hesse, the ink may be found as a drift of powder lodged in the crease of the pages. It's *there*."

No earthly use to anyone, but it's there. At least, I've never found a spell to turn it back into the forms of letters again. In times of confusion, there was always someone who thought they could take advantage of that confusion to smuggle out a sequestered book. They were wrong.

Ysolde continued, "No, if you wish to see them—and I really do advise against it, sir, they are neither trustworthy instructions nor reliable sources—you or your agent must use them where they are. You are welcome to the best comforts we can provide. If those are too humble—"

"I don't need comforts. I need to have this one simple demand met. Go home, Madame Archivist, and turn your mind to finding a way to fulfill it."

"Yes, Your Highness."

She did go home, knees shaking, through the darkening streets. She wasted no time trying to think how to meet his impossible demand. Rather, she sent new orders to all Guild members, both those who lived within the house and those who lodged nearby. The Controversial Knowledge collection was once again closed to all researchers, as it had been during the wars. She doubted there would be many complaints; the collections were not well-known. Her assistant, Hawyss, was to use her discretion as to which complainants were given appointments with Ysolde herself.

At least Duke Henry's out of town right now. Maybe Prince Radulph would tell me how long his brother will be gone. I'd know how much time I have to work with—unless the Duke sends someone else to do the deed.

She also had her Captain send guards to each of the Sequestered Rooms. That seemed wiser than trying to get the Sorcerer's Guild to set any more spells of protection. It had taken weeks of negotiation and flattery to obtain the one she had. Briefly, she was tempted to try doing it herself. She certainly had the reference materials, and some training—enough to know the gulf between reading a spell and casting it. No.

Days slid by, uneventful save for one researcher who had counted on having access to the Controversial Knowledge collection. Ysolde considered telling Captain Arden to cut back on the night patrols.

Somewhere between midnight and dawn of the seventh night, her maidservant wakened her. She shivered in spite of the thick wool shawl she'd wrapped around her. "Guildmistress, I'm so sorry, but it's Captain Arden, and he said you said you wanted to know if anything happened, at any hour."

Ysolde yawned. "No need for apologies," and she climbed out of her bed.

"He says it isn't a panic, Guildmistress."

"I doubt that anything less than the Mongols at the gate would alarm old Arden. Is he here?"

"Yes, Guildmistress."

Ysolde delayed long enough to pull on a work-dress and house-shoes. For another moment she stood, head to one side, before her secretaire. Unlocking it, she took a pair of fine linen gloves, and relocked the small desk.

Captain Arden bowed and doffed his hat to Ysolde as she entered her antechamber. Stocky, gray-haired, he had the reputation of being the calmest man in all the little armies of the City. "The catch-spell you had laid on the room worked a treat, Guildmistress. I picked him up like a wee mouse."

"Has damage been done, Captain?"

Captain Arden chuckled. "Not to us, Guildmistress."

"I think it's one of the locals," he said as they made their way to the Controversial Knowledge rooms. "Hard to say when he's all shrunk up like that, of course."

Shrunk up, indeed. A terrarium held a tiny figure less than a handspan tall, cowering between a euphorbia and the pond that kept the entire little world moist.

"Hope you don't mind me borrowing yon plant box without asking," Arden said. She assured him that she didn't.

The terrarium had been a gift from a grateful patron. Ysolde would rather have had the price of it for the Guildhouse, but it did have enough silver in the metal that joined the glass panes to thwart any number of escape spells.

The figure retreated into the middle of the terrarium, but not before Ysolde recognized him. "I think you're right, Captain. I would have expected better of one of Karroll's guild."

A book bound in supple leather lay splayed open on the floor. "Sorry to leave that lying there, but I wasn't sure I should touch it," Arden said.

"Wise man," said Ysolde as she pulled on her gloves. Arden stepped back to where he could watch the terrarium and the Guildmistress at the same time.

One page was folded back on itself where it had hit the floor. Ysolde smoothed it and squinted a little, reading the crabbed script by candlelight—and slapped the book shut. She held her breath a moment to let the dust disperse.

She could feel the book's agitation through her glove.

Someone had begun to use it; someone had drawn on its power. The sorcerer now confined in a terrarium? Ysolde hoped it could be no one else. A glance reassured her that the prisoner still sat quietly in the terrarium. Most of the plants in there bore thorns, many of them poisonous.

There was a gap on the shelves, but she dared not use it. Two of the volumes which could not be shelved next to the book in her hand now flanked the open space.

No one had ever seen the books move, but none of the very few who entered these rooms would deny that books were found on different shelves than where they had been left. Thick cross-indexed volumes of notes specified which ones must be kept apart. Finally, after shifting most of the books on that rank of shelves, she could safely replace the volume between two collections of questionable folk cures.

Steam rose from double-walled pitchers of exotic coffee and, for the more traditional guild members, mulled ale. Plates of pastries perfumed the air with cinnamon and cardamom. There was even a small jar of oranges preserved in sugar. Cold chicken and a small round of cheese were provided as well.

It might have been an ordinary Guild meeting, except for the grim expressions on the faces of the dozen people seated in the room—that, and the fact that the sun was barely appearing over the rooftops of nearby houses.

A raised stand in the middle of the table held the terrarium. The tiny figure within had seated himself on a shelf fungus and stared out glumly.

Ysolde took another swallow of coffee. She was beginning to like its bitter taste, and already liked the way it substituted for lost sleep.

A young, slender man frowned as he dusted crumbs of pastry from his front. "Can he smell the food in there? It seems unkind..." he trailed off as several people glared at him.

"He tried to steal books, Gerald."

"Do we know that?"

"What else would a sorcerer be doing in the Controversial

Knowledge section in the dark of the night?"

"They *will* try the dark of the night," commented the oldest Archivist.

"No," Ysolde cut in, "he cannot smell the food, nor can he hear much of what we say. Let's just make sure of that." She picked up a quilted warming-cloth from beside an empty pastry plate, and covered the terrarium. "That should muffle our voices sufficiently."

Immediately, a plump woman in green said, "Once again, I must ask why we have these volumes sequestered? Has anyone reexamined—"

"Hawyss, child, they're sequestered because they're dangerous. That doesn't change," snapped the oldest Archivist.

"Better to destroy them," said a voice from the far end of the table. "No need then for guards, and no more midnight alarms."

Ysolde had to speak twice to make herself heard over the well-worn argument that erupted. "Archivists! Librarians! Your kind attention, please."

Silence fell.

"I think we'd best leave the large philosophical questions for later. I called you here at this horrible hour (and I do thank you all for attending) to ask your counsel on whether we should return the sorcerer to his guild."

Hawyss half-choked on her pastry. "You can't be serious!"

"As a professional courtesy. It was a trap-spell cast by a member of the Sorcerer's Guild that protected us from this man."

"And it caught one of their own?"

"Possibly working without their knowledge, since he lacked the counterspell."

"Probably," commented the guild member who wanted to destroy the books.

"They won't like that," Hawyss purred.

"Indeed," said Ysolde. "And they *will* like our calling them, rather than the Prince. We may need another favor from the Guild of Sorcerers someday." *Possibly quite soon, if I can't devise some way to protect Her Highness and the books at the same time.*

"Yes, Guildmistress," said Hawyss, "Let us tell Guildmaster Karroll that we've found his strayed spell-caster."

Hearing no objections, Ysolde closed the meeting. Gerald lingered as everyone except Hawyss filed out. He folded the warming cloth back and peeked at their captive.

Ysolde nodded to Gerald. "Very well. You may try to feed him."

Gerald frowned. "He's so small! Maybe some chicken cut up fine, and part of a slice of bread? And to drink...Hawyss, have you a spare thimble?"

She snorted. "God's toenails, Gerald, he's not a pet! He's lucky to have anything to eat. Let him gnaw on some hard cheese, since he's about the size of a mouse."

Ysolde couldn't quite suppress a laugh. Gerald glared at them both and set about chopping some leftover chicken. He wrapped it in a scrap of bread, opened the top of the terrarium—and dropped it, swearing. Blood welled from a puncture in his hand.

Ysolde heard a scrabbling sound like a mouse trapped in a cup. "Plague!" She grabbed at the manikin as it swung itself up over the glass and slithered down the other side. She was too late.

It set off running for the edge of the table. Hawyss lunged forward, half-full tankard in hand. The figure dodged behind the coffee pot. Ysolde ran around to the opposite side of the table; the manikin zigzagged towards the end. Gerald ran for that.

"Tha wouldst," cried Hawyss, and slapped her tankard upside-down over the fleeing figure. She waited briefly, then retrieved a soggy little man who wobbled on his feet.

She laughed. "Many a man's dreamed of having more beer than he could drink! In wi' thee," and she dropped him into the terrarium. He landed just beside the bread and chicken.

Ysolde slammed the terrarium shut hard enough to crack one pane of glass. She shook her head at Gerald. "Have Mistress Eleanor look at that wound. I know it's small," she went on, talking over his attempted protest. "No wound from a sorcerer can be neglected."

She flung a towel over the terrarium and bound it firmly with a length of bookbinder's cord. "Journeyman Gerald, your pet will have to make do with the water in the pond, there."

The Master of the Guild of Sorcerers and two assistants arrived before mid-day. Ysolde chose to receive them in her office with only Hawyss and, at his earnest entreaty, Gerald to assist her.

She allowed Guildmaster Karroll to remove his sorcerer from the terrarium himself. With a few murmured words, the Guildmaster restored the man to normal size. Soggy and leaf-strewn, smelling of beer and something rotten, he blinked silently.

Karroll turned back to face the Archivists. "Guildmistress Ysolde, I thank you for your great courtesy in allowing me to reclaim this member of our Guild. We hadn't seem him in some time. There are several reasons why a Sorcerer may disappear, though none of them is admirable. He was never formally expelled." Karroll's mouth stretched in a thin smile.

Of course. Thus they still have authority over him. "We owe you thanks for your excellent trap spell. Will you grant me one more favor?"

"Possibly."

"We need to know who sent this man. It seems extremely unlikely that he came purely at his own wish."

"Master, no!" hissed one of Karroll's assistants. "You can't allow this outsider—"

"I...can't?"

"M-my humblest apologies, sir," sputtered the assistant. "But surely—"

"Surely, the Guildmistress has a right and a duty to know."

He turned to Ysolde. "You vouch for your assistants?"

She did. Gerald positively glowed with delight. Ysolde could only hope his soft heart wouldn't lead him to say anything unfortunate; this was likely to get unpleasant.

"And I for mine, *and their obedience.*" Karroll let silence stretch. "Edward," he finally said.

"Yes, Guildmaster."

"How came you to be in that place, Edward?"

"It wasn't my idea, Guildmaster!"

More silent waiting. Ysolde allowed the whisper of a laugh to emerge. No, being in the terrarium had surely not been this renegade's idea.

Karroll spoke clearly, carefully. "At whose bidding did you enter those rooms?"

"Bidding, Guildmaster? I work at no man's bidding. I took a contract *sub rosa*." Edward picked leaves from his doublet, keeping his eyes firmly on his task. "A prisoner has a duty to escape. A sorcerer who takes a contract in confidence must keep that confidence. I have done only what my oath allows."

Ysolde avoided looking at Karroll. Heaven send she never had to deal with such a subordinate, especially in front of others!

"I release you from the obligation of confidentiality, Edward. You may speak the truth before these Archivists, whose Guildhouse you have invaded."

Edward avoided meeting his Guildmaster's eyes. "Sir, I swore an oath to my client. Only the client can release me from it."

"You swore an earlier oath to me, which takes precedence."

Ysolde heard a cart creak by in the street below. There came a soft rustle of cloth as someone in the room shifted position.

Karroll's beard rasped against his doublet as he shook his head. "Edward, you know I can compel you."

No answer.

Gerald leaned forward. "Don't hurt him! Please, sir," he added as Karroll gave him a sideways look.

"Don't be a fool, boy. Pain's an indirect and unreliable method. I compel."

Karroll stood between Edward and the Archivists and made a few swift gestures. Edward gasped, choked, and said, "Duke Henry."

Ysolde stifled a groan.

For once, there was no argument over what to do. They must go themselves and wait upon His Highness as soon as he would receive them. Ysolde sent a messenger ahead to beg Prince Radulph's immediate attention on urgent and private matters.

The Oldest Archivist was left in temporary charge of the archives. Gerald and Hawyss got the dubious privilege of accompanying Ysolde to the castle. Karroll and his two assistants bound the renegade sorcerer with silver-laced cords, hobbling him to allow only a short step.

As it turned out, he was the only one who *didn't* walk up the steep streets. The Guild of Archivists owned a small closed wagon for transporting books; pulled by a mule from the nearby livery station, it served well to transport a prisoner.

Outside the Guildhouse, Ysolde braced her shoulders against the drag of the woolen tunic and the chain of office. The counterweight on the chain had been an excellent idea, but right then she felt as though it was pulling her over backwards.

She stepped carefully as they walked up the zigzag road to the castle. Aldbrough had been fought over and through three times during the wars, and cobbles made good sling-stones. Avoiding turned ankles or soaked shoes (better not to ask, soaked with what) required careful attention.

They entered the castle through the northern forecourt. It was the smallest of the castle's entryways, and rumored to be haunted. Four cousins of the current Prince had been slain there, trying to defend his grandfather. Even at mid-day, frost still slicked much of its stone paving and glittered on the heads of the prancing horses that stood to either side of its gate.

Here they offloaded their prisoner. "Unbind his feet," ordered Karroll after Edward had nearly fallen full-length. He'd dragged one assistant sorcerer to a bruising stumble against the stairs in the process.

The entire group muddled its way into one of the Prince's smaller audience chambers. Its walls were hung with tapestries showing fanciful beasts, and its two fireplaces blazed with newly lit wood. There was just room for the royal armchair, a long narrow table up against one wall, and two additional chairs.

Prince Radulph took one look at the mixed group and raised his hand. "Wait."

He went himself to the doors to the even smaller

antechamber. "Check again to make absolutely certain there's no one waiting to see Us," he instructed the guards. "If there is anyone, send them away, not to return until summoned. You may tell them that any other course will incur my severest displeasure. You yourselves will stand guard at the *outer* doors."

Sorcerers and Archivists milled uneasily until His Highness returned and seated himself in the armchair. "What is this urgent matter?"

They sorted themselves out with Ysolde and Karroll standing nearest the Prince. Hawyss and Gerald stood behind and to either side of Ysolde; Karroll's two assistants stood to one side of him, flanking Edward.

Prince Radulph began. "To what do We owe the pleasure of seeing the two of you in the same room yet not in conflict? Your message, Guildmistress, told me little."

"I crave Your pardon, Your Highness. To write a full report—"

"Which We would have now."

And so, as briefly as she could, Ysolde told him what had occurred. The Prince's mouth tightened when she spoke in passing of notifying Karroll.

"His was the clever trap-spell that allowed us to seize the would-be thief," she said, nodding to Karroll. He looked as though he could have done without the compliment.

"Hm," said the Prince, with narrowed eyes. "Guildmaster? Tell me briefly why you did a considerable favor for someone We had believed was your rival."

Karroll hesitated. Ysolde realized that she was holding her breath. Even she knew the Prince's reputation for crushing any hint of conspiracy. She had no wish to find herself sent to the Northern Marches.

"Gladly, Sire," said Karroll. "Although we wish that the volumes in question did not exist, they do. In order to protect our homeland, we will protect the books and help to keep them sequestered."

Radulph nodded, with the air of a man reserving judgement.

Karroll continued. "Your Highness, we released Edward

from his oath of confidentiality to his ill-chosen client."

Tactfully edited, thought Ysolde.

"And discovered that his client was Duke Henry."

Prince Radulph's brows drew together into one solid line. "Sorcerer? Is this true?"

Ysolde heard a faint twang, like a lute string snapping. Edward wriggled from between his guards and flung himself forward. "Your Highness!" He lay on the floor, gasping like a landed fish. "Mercy!"

The Prince gestured; Karroll's assistants pulled Edward to his feet.

"Highness, I swear to Heaven, I did not know."

"Did not know what?"

"Sire, I didn't know that he had ill intent."

"You thought that there might be a *good* reason for stealing books from the Sequestered Rooms?"

Ysolde hoped to Heaven that His Highness never spoke to her in that coldly reasonable voice.

Edward swayed on his feet. "Merciful Lord,"

You hope, thought Ysolde.

"I—he told me that he needed to work against Your enemies, that he'd almost got what he needed when his assistant was denied the use of the collection. He swore he'd see the books smuggled back in, Highness!"

"What a sweet, trusting nature you have," commented His Highness. "I wonder, is there any truth in the tale?" He turned to look at Ysolde.

"There is this much truth: I closed all access to the Controversial Knowledge sections the day that Your Highness summoned me to Your presence."

Karroll slid his eyes sideways at her. Hawyss gasped, and put one hand to her mouth as if to block some risky words. His Highness gave Ysolde a just-visible nod and something that might almost be a smile.

Yes, Sire, I kept Your confidence.

"And one week later, you catch a thief. That's time for a messenger to reach my brother on the Northern Marches, and for that messenger to return. Guards!"

The sudden bellow made Ysolde jump. Even Karroll recoiled in his seat, and Gerald clutched his hands together.

Two guards marched in—not, Ysolde noted, the same two who had been ordered to watch the door. Prince Radulph waved at Edward. "This one, to a warded cell. Try for one with rats."

Karroll raised one hand. "With respect, Sire,"

"I hate statements that start out, 'With respect.'"

"Forgive me," Karroll persisted.

Valiant man, thought Ysolde.

"But better not have rats. Nothing living that could be made an ally."

"Even in a warded cell?" Radulph shrugged. "If you say so, Guildmaster. You should know. He's your man."

Karroll paled.

Edward tried to drag his feet as the guards hauled him away. "Guildmaster, please! Master Karroll, don't you remember—"

"Nothing that I remember can counterbalance this." The Guildmaster turned his back.

Edward's despairing wail echoed through the closing door.

"And now," said the Prince, "I would know—"

The doors to the Prince's audience chamber were flung open without warning. His Highness half-rose from his seat, frowning thunderously—and rose the rest of the way, followed by everyone else in the room.

"Am I to have any say in this?" demanded a light, high soprano voice. Princess Margery strolled into the room, accompanied by a tall young woman in a plain gown. The Princess's pregnancy didn't yet show in the floating, high-waisted silks of court.

All well enough, thought Ysolde, *for those with plenty of silver for firewood.* She felt over-warm in her layers of wool and linen, but that would just have to be endured. *Not a bad problem to have, this late in the year.*

"My dear! You shouldn't have disturbed your rest."

"Then someone had best provide me with a chair."

Gerald recovered his wits first. "Your Highness," he

murmured as he dragged his own chair over to the royal couple. "It's quite comfortable, really, Your Highness," he assured her.

Princess Margery inclined her head graciously as she sank onto the armless chair. Her attendant moved to stand behind her.

"What a lot of people you have at this meeting about me," she commented.

Prince Radulph made extensive introductions. Princess Margery could have posed for an allegorical picture of Patience.

When all of that was done, Her Highness asked, "What have you decided thus far?"

"Very little, I fear."

Not even the fate of a man. It seemed unwise to ask what would become of the renegade sorcerer.

"We have only just received valuable information from Guildmistress Ysolde and Guildmaster Karroll."

"I am in good time, then. How fortunate that I didn't nap this afternoon."

Prince Rudolph sighed. "My dear, as your Prince and as your husband, it is my duty to look after your welfare."

The Princess nodded. "Yes, of course, my dear. I appreciate your anxious care. I simply wish to contribute my own thoughts on the matter."

No reasonable person could argue with that. The Prince was renowned for his reasonable qualities; they had been essential in his settling of the long wars that had ravaged his principality. That, and his strong sword arm.

Prince Radulph sat silent, head to one side. Ysolde became aware of a frantic wish to untangle a bit of hair that was snagged in the embroidered band of her hood, but restrained herself.

Princess Margery continued, "Whatever else is decided, whether or not you gain those volumes from the Archives..."

One of Radulph's rings thunked against his chair as he grasped the arms tightly enough to turn his knuckles white.

Didn't know she knew, did you? Oh, I like our Princess better than ever! It was a great struggle not to laugh.

"I do not wish to have any evil spells used in guarding me or the child. It might bring ill luck to the baby."

Ysolde noticed that the Princess didn't mention possible ill luck for herself.

The Princess turned to look at Karroll. "Might it not, Guildmaster Karroll?"

"There is that possibility, Your Highness," Karroll said softly, "These things are linked in ways that not even the wisest yet understand."

Prince Radulph glared. "And why was I not told this?"

Karroll blinked. "Highness, you did not ask."

No one said anything, not even the Prince.

Karroll coughed drily. "Your Highnesses, I beg leave to return to our Guildhouse and await your instructions. We will be happy to add whatever spells of aversion or protection we may, but this is not our quarrel. We have no need of such dangerous volumes. We keep the knowledge as it should be kept, passed from one trusted adept to another, and not all guild members are trusted equally."

Ysolde demanded, "And when plague strikes a besieged city, and no one's spells or treatments will cool the fevers, how many trained adepts do you lose? How much of that precious knowledge?"

"I do not need advice from a failed sorceress."

Ysolde forced words past the anger that clawed at her throat. "I did not fail. I chose to leave. You may consult your own records—oh, no, you don't believe in them, do you?"

"We believe in doing, though that does require more courage than sitting quietly in a room and never leaving it again."

"Oh, there are perils in our work, too. Sometimes people break in during the night!" As soon as the words were out of her mouth, she wished them unsaid.

The Prince's face went purple. The Princess rose from her seat and hurried to his side. "My Prince, please—"

He looked at her, and the dark tide receded. "Don't worry, Margery," he said, as though they were alone in the room. "If court rivalries and politics haven't done me in yet, then these quarreling fools won't." He patted her hand.

"Guildmistress," interrupted the Princess. "Guildmaster."

Both bowed to her.

"Are there no *protective* spells in the knowledge that you both hold?" She gestured to Ysolde.

Just this once, she would gladly have passed up the honor of speaking first. "Your Highness, there are, of course. We have a good medical collection also, and would be delighted to share both with your Mistress of *Sage-Femmes* if you wish."

"Excellent. She is most knowledgeable, but no one can know all."

Ysolde saw several people shifting in their seats. "I beg the indulgence for a few words more, if Their Highnesses agree." That wasn't just *politesse*. The idea wasn't quite clear in her own mind yet.

The stately pace of royal consultation and agreement gave her time to think. It *should* work. If the Guildmaster Karroll agreed. If the Prince could be persuaded. If Duke Henry would walk into the trap.

Permission was given, though the Princess stretched her back in a way that said it had better *be* just a few words.

Ysolde smiled at Karroll. "You said, Guildmaster, that we went into our rooms and never left. What if someone did just that?"

He looked at her as though she had lost her mind. "That seems unlikely, Guildmistress. The natural need for food, water and, ah, sanitary facilities—"

She smothered a laugh. "Oh, we have all those! But think you: What scholar hasn't felt the need to follow up a reference, and track down the reason for a difference between that account and the previous one? If the scholar is speaking with people, there's an end to it eventually. People get weary of talking. Some of them die. Eventually, as you say, the scholar must do—must at least report, in writing or by speech, the results."

Karroll nodded. "Yes, that's so." Irrelevant, his voice implied, but true.

"But the scholar using books can go on indefinitely. A spell of obsession would only have to intensify something that already exists."

Ysolde gazed modestly at her toes. "Even after the great losses in the wars, we have thousands of books, and hundreds of scrolls. Most, I blush to admit, have not been properly indexed."

Prince Radulph shook his head. "Guildmistress, it sounds to me as though you've just suggested that I allow my brother to become fantastically well-educated in the Dark Arts."

Karroll sat silent. Was that a faint hint of a smirk? Never mind.

Ysolde protested, "Highness, no! If the spell causes him to wander endlessly from one source to another, never making the connections between them or understanding the contradictions, then he will not have increased his knowledge. A man with a head full of jumbled facts is not educated; he's confused. A properly cast spell will keep him too busy ever to make those critical judgements."

The Princess laughed. A faint smile showed briefly on the Prince's face.

"And you wish me to allow this experiment—assuming that the Guildmaster can even create such a spell?"

"Oh, yes!" Karroll leaned forward in his chair. "As my colleague says, it's merely an intensification of an already-existing desire. Preventing the *connections* between one source and another is a pretty problem...some forgetting overnight, perhaps... Guildmistress, do you mean to keep him there all the time, nights and days alike?"

So, I'm a colleague now and not a failed sorceress? "That would be safest in some ways."

"Isn't his absence going to be rather noticeable? His wife, for one, might wonder what had become of him."

"It isn't an affectionate marriage," said Princess Margery. "Also, she avoids Our court as much as a Duchess can. Give her a respectable reason for his absence and she'll be well content to live without his company."

"We wouldn't have to keep him ensorcelled forever," said Ysolde. "Just until the baby's safely born, and through the first year."

"Until he's seven would be better," objected Karroll. "At

seven, a child can be protected by its own wards in addition to those of its parents."

Hawyss asked, "Can a royal Duke really just disappear for over seven years?"

"Perhaps a Seeming could be cast," suggested one of Karroll's assistants.

Prince Radulph shouted them all down. "We have not yet decided to keep Duke Henry resident in the Archives for seven days, let alone seven years! You wish me to somehow lead my devious, scheming brother into a trap. We speak here of my nearest brother, Duke Henry. The one I'm quite certain is somehow working spells against my beloved wife, possibly by his own hand."

"That may be a bit of a challenge," Ysolde admitted.

"He'll do it," said Princess Margery. "All you have to do is make him believe he's deceiving you."

"Hah! True, my sweet lady." Radulph sat thinking while the silence stretched thin in the room.

The Princess turned to Ysolde. "Perhaps the Archives could be seen to receive a donation of volumes about which you will say nothing?"

"Oh, yes," Ysolde agreed. *But if we tell no one...*

"And I will whisper the news in secret to a lady of my household, who has a cousin in your brother's household to whom she owes favors." Her smile was sweet and bland as a child's posset.

Prince Radulph shook his head briskly. "My clever wife! Very well. I'll call him home from that inspection of the northern ports. The journey shouldn't take him more than two days, if he leaves some of his baggage to follow."

He turned to Ysolde then, and the amiable husband of a charming lady vanished. A man who'd won his throne by battle, scheming, and—some said, but very quietly—assassination, stared at her. "Get Our brother into this clever trap of yours within two days of his arrival in Our city, or I will come and take those books. No, don't bother reciting the dangers again!"

Ysolde obeyed.

"And if any harm comes to Her Highness—if she so much as trips on a stair—then I will send the guards for you. In fact," he turned to Princess Margery, "Stay away from stairs."

"My lord, I must have some exercise! The *sage-femmes* say—"

"Are the Royal Hallways not long and spacious?"

She shrugged, though her brows drew together for a moment. "Indeed, my lord."

The Prince rose; all save the Princess popped to their feet.

"Go, then, and see to my commands."

As the two groups left, the Sorcerers' Guild gave Ysolde the same distance as they would a suspected victim of the sweating sickness.

Only Ysolde, Arden, and the Oldest Archivist saw Guildmaster Karroll arrive, though he came at mid-day. Only Ysolde accompanied him into the Sequestered Collections.

Ysolde opened book after book in what looked like a random selection. Not every volume was given a trickle of dust-colored powder down the gutter. He chose a different place in each chosen book to place it.

He saw her puzzled stare. "Duke Henry's no fool—and if it isn't Duke Henry, then he'll use someone else with a good mind. There must be no pattern to alert them."

"You're quite sure this won't actually damage the books?"

"Not nearly as much as their being hauled off to the Palace would damage them and all the rest of us."

Duke Henry beat the Prince's estimate by half a day. Proper ceremonies of reunion were observed.

The next day, Ysolde waited.

She stood in the narrow garden that lay between the Archives and the alleyway, wondering just what she was going to do if Duke Henry didn't take the bait soon. She still had most of a day left. The Duke might arrive. If he didn't, then the Princess—oh merciful Heaven, was the Princess still in good health? Surely she would have heard if it were otherwise? Why should she have heard? There'd be more important—but the Prince had sworn he'd come for her if any harm befell—and he would, he made no idle threats.

Ysolde paced the paths of the garden, brushing past stands of winter-killed herbs. Finally weary, she seated herself on a bench in the sun, near the back gate that led to the river path. The bustle of the city was faint.

Sprays of rose hips brightened the southern wall. As she stared at their red defiance, she thought for the first time that she could lose this struggle. The rest of Aldbrough would lose with her. With luck, she'd be dead before the worst happened.

Well, if that was to happen she must at least warn the resident guild members of just how dire the situation had become. It was growing cold. Time to go in.

As she came in the back door, the Oldest Archivist ushered Duke Henry in through the front. Taller, slimmer than the Prince, he still had a full head of hair. He wore finer clothes than the Prince himself; the curled toes of his shoes were tethered with fine chains to golden knee-bands. His heavy perfume of vetiver and rosemary overlay an older, ranker scent.

He nearly tripped over those elegant long toes when he first saw her. "Ah, Guildmistress! How kind of you to welcome me! Forgive my arriving all unannounced. I didn't wish to bring the entire panoply of a court visit."

She swept him a curtsey. "How kind of you to honor us with a visit so soon. I trust that our Oldest Archivist has taken good care of you thus far. Now, please, come and take some refreshment."

"Honored Guildmistress, the only refreshment I wish is to visit your collections. It is so delightful to be back in civilized lands."

And so they went up the narrow stairs that led to the Sequestered Rooms. At one low doorway, she hesitated.

"You do recall, Your Grace, that I cannot vouch for the reliability of the Controversial Knowledge collections."

He raised one ducal eyebrow at her. "Yes, Honored Guildmistress. I'm not a neophyte scholar, you know. I choose what subjects to pursue."

"Blessed be your studies." She stood aside to let him enter.

TROUBLE FOLLOWS HER

by Jessie D. Eaker

Trouble can take many different forms.

This will be Jessie Eaker's ninth story in the *Sword and Sorceress* volumes. A native of North Carolina, he currently lives in central Virginia and has been there so long he's lost his southern accent (much to his wife's disappointment). When not writing, he talks to the cats, reads, and works on his ever-growing list of things to fix around the house. "Trouble Follows Her" is a prequel to his new novel series. You can learn more about the series and his other works at JessieEaker.com.

"Would you look at that!"

Risten ignored the loud whispers which came from the side of the road. Two old farmers abruptly halted mid-chat to gawk—their heads tracking her progress as she walked by. They were trying to be subtle in their discussion, but obviously didn't know how to talk quietly. Risten kept her head high and trudged on, pretending not to hear. Because, if she decided to hear them, she might take offense and draw her sword. Then things would get ugly. And she was not here for that. Besides, she could understand their amazement.

It was because trouble followed her.

Risten was obviously of high station. Although dusty and splattered with mud, she wore a royal guard uniform, and had not one but two fine swords: one high on her back and the other swinging at her hip. Some whispered she looked like a minor noble bravely returning from some far off battle.

Yet what followed her was in sharp contrast to that image. In fact, it was obvious Risten was trying to ignore what was behind her.

A chicken.

The red hen, head bobbing and clucking to herself, followed three steps behind—striding along as if she owned the road itself. She might pause and peck at some pebble or some unfortunate insect, only to scurry after her escort to regain her regal position in the procession.

Much to Risten's embarrassment, there was little shortage of gawkers as the setting sun encouraged most of the honest townspeople to scurry home. Risten glanced at the bird following her. Of all things to be cursed with, why was it a chicken? She hated chickens!

She faced forward, trying to ignore the trouble behind her and set her eyes for what trouble might lie ahead. Rumors were a group of bandits had made this town their home, and after dark had been harassing the town's people. They had even threatened the town's elder. Risten frowned. She knew without a doubt the thievery was the result of a false king now sitting on a stolen throne. The rightful heir would never have allowed this.

Risten's eyes perked up at the sight of the town's only tavern—her steps becoming a little quicker. Her dry mouth remembered it had been days since her last ale. Maybe some good would come out of this after all.

A man and woman standing outside the tavern watched in amusement as Risten paused before the entrance to scoop up the hen and tuck her under her arm.

"Must be a real royal bird," the man commented, which earned a snicker from his companion. Risten gritted her teeth and stepped inside.

The interior was smoky and filled with mostly men talking and laughing. A few eyed her as she entered.

"Hey! Take that chicken outside!" yelled the proprietor.

Risten's head swiveled to glare at him as her other hand moved to rest on the hilt of her sword. The noisy banter inside subsided as the two exchanged a tense stare for several heartbeats. Risten finally dug in her purse and produced a shiny piece of silver, which she flipped in a high arch toward the proprietor. It caught the lamp's light, sparkling brightly as it tumbled end over end through the air. And every eye in the room followed it. One gasped. It was a silver royal—easily more money than the establishment saw in a couple months. The proprietor snatched it out of the air and then pointed to a table in the corner.

The banter in the room slowly resumed as Risten seated herself with her back to the wall and placed the hen in her lap. The bird surprisingly decided it was time for a rest, fluffing up its feathers and closing her eyes. It clucked softly to itself. Risten snorted. Travel must be hard on chickens too.

The ale came a moment later, delivered by an older woman who looked to be the proprietor's wife. She set the mug down and with it a piece of bread and cheese. Risten mumbled her thanks, intent on the ale. To her surprise the woman slid onto the bench beside her.

"Are you a royal guard?" she asked. "We don't see many of those pass through here." She leaned an elbow on the table, a friendly smile on her face.

Risten sighed in delight after draining half the mug. "Ex-royal guard," she said, wiping her mouth. "I guess you could say I was kicked out."

The woman leaned forward. "I thought once you made it to the royal guard, you were in for life."

Risten nodded. "So did I. But things changed. I was in the king's personal guard. Assigned to the princess actually."

The woman's mouth made a big "O" in understanding. No doubt the news had reached even this backwater by now—of old King Xernow's murder, the blaming of his only daughter, and her immediate execution. Or so said the rumors. The old king's son now sat on the throne.

The woman glanced to Risten's hand, which was gripping the mug so tightly her fingers were white. Risten gave an embarrassed snort and took another swallow. "Let's just say the new king didn't value my services."

The woman laid a reassuring hand on her arm. "I'm so sorry to hear that." She leaned closer. "But it's not the end of the world. I can introduce you to someone who would greatly value your services." She eyed Risten's swords. "If you know what I mean."

Risten sighed and looked around the room. The silver coin had definitely gotten their attention. Greedy eyes were already glancing in her direction and sizing her up. The clientele here looked rough—hardened might be a better description. To not align oneself with the leaders would be asking for mischief.

"Thank you for the kind offer." Risten pointed to her lap. "But I have to take care of my chicken."

The woman paused with her mouth open, not exactly sure how to respond. She rose, deciding not to press her case. She patted Risten's arm. "If you change your mind, let me know. Just don't wait too long."

The lady stepped away and went to talk to her husband, returning a moment later with another large mug. Risten slowly sipped it while watching the last of the day slip away. She seemed oblivious to the customers exchanging course whispers and trying hard not to look her way. Risten was pretty sure one or two would try to lighten her purse while she slept.

It was late when the proprietor's wife stopped by with yet another mug. Risten asked the woman about the privy and was pointed out the back door. She stood, and with her chicken clucking under her arm, stepped outside.

She found a well-worn path, lit by a full moon and a single beaten up lantern, which led to a small stall of the usual shape. Risten was impressed it had a door and a roof. The chicken squirmed under her arm so she put the hen on the ground and went inside to do her business.

As she emerged, she found a group of twelve men surrounding her—their shadows long and menacing in the dark. Risten blinked at them in surprise. It wasn't supposed to be like this. They were supposed to attack her when she laid down, not when she went to relieve herself. This was going to be a little much for even her to handle. The men pressed too close—she had no room to maneuver, little alone pull her sword. And they knew it too.

The one in front of her wore a fine hooded cloak—something a well-to-do merchant might wear. This was in sharp contrast to his scruffy boots and the worn clothes of the others flanking him.

Risten gave a nervous chuckle. "I'm sorry for taking so long. I didn't realize there was a line." She leaned forward slightly. "You haven't seen my chicken, have you?"

The robed man just grinned. "It ran off when it saw us coming. Seems the bird is smarter than its owner. Now do us all a favor by handing over your purse and your swords. We don't see many silver coins around here."

Risten pursed her lips and considered what to do. There were just too many of them to fight effectively. They could easily rush her and pin her against the privy. She looked around. What she needed was a distraction.

And where was the stupid bird?

Suddenly, the sound of flapping wings came from behind and above her. Risten craned her head around to see the shadow of a hen sitting atop the privy's roof—the light of the feeble lantern barely reaching her. The hen flapped her wings hard, raised her head and crowed to the full moon. It almost sounded like a battle cry.

Risten breathed an anguished sigh. "Oh no."

The chicken began to glow, softly at first, then brightening into a nearly blinding blue light. A murmur broke out among the men. They all tried to take a step back.

"Sorcery!" someone gasped.

The glowing form of the chicken began to change, its legs growing longer and its body elongating into a distinctly human figure. Suddenly, the glow faded, leaving behind the shadow of a young woman. She reached down and grabbed the sword off Risten's back.

"Now!" shouted the young woman.

Risten smiled.

The group's slight retreat gave her room to draw. Risten's sword appeared in her hand and she leaped forward—dealing blows left and right, whirling and spinning in the dance of one long-trained to the sword. The shadow of the young woman leaped down and attacked the crowd on the other side. She hung to the edges of the group, expertly using the shadows to her advantage. And while unclothed and not nearly as adept as Risten, she held her own against the untrained bandits and ensured none escaped. Until finally, all were down—except for one.

The robed leader of the group tried to flee but Risten blocked his exit. He tried to back away, but froze at the sharp point digging in his back. Risten stepped forward and freed his purse, hefting it in her hand.

He fell to his knees. "Your moves... I've seen one before... you're a blasted sword-master," he spat. "There's only ever been one woman who made that rank."

Risten cocked an eyebrow in surprise.

He continued. "You're Risten Brightmare, the personal bodyguard to the princess. Or was before she was executed."

A female voice called out from behind him. "Only I wasn't. Instead I was cursed by my brother right after he murdered Father. Cursed to transform forever into random animals."

With a look of shock, the man looked back over his shoulder at the shadow of a woman, her face hidden in the dark.

She continued. "And what better way to get my kingdom back than by robbing the bandits my brother encourages."

Risten dealt with him in one quick blow.

After collecting all the purses from the fallen, the princess took them, as well as the leader's robe, and vanished into the dark. Risten used the opportunity to find the road out of town. The full moon provided enough light to follow it. If they were careful, they would reach the next village at first light. The king's guard, who was chasing them, would find the bandits on the morrow. While under orders to hunt them down, they were good men and would deal with what was left of the bandits appropriately.

A little while later Risten was joined by a figure wearing a long cloak—the same one the men's leader had worn. They walked in silence for a bit.

"You gave the money to the elder?" Risten asked.

The princess chuckled. "He was most surprised to receive a late night donation. He was so grateful he gave us half the plunder to keep for ourselves. We now have enough to search for an answer to my curse."

Risten glanced in her direction. "Your hair-brained scheme almost got us killed."

The princess snorted. "You're just embarrassed a chicken saved you."

Risten stopped and glared at her. "You did not save me."

"Did too! If my crowing hadn't struck fear into their hearts, you would have died."

Risten leaned back and shouted at the stars. "Mother of the Creator, you are so much trouble."

The princess started walking again forcing Risten to follow. "I would have you know, I am not trouble all the time."

"Really? And just when are you not?"

You could hear the mirth in her voice. "When I'm a chicken."

Risten just groaned.

MANY TEETH

by Deborah J. Ross

A young lady wants to hire you to escort her on a quest to find her father, a noble amateur naturalist who went missing while searching for a place you don't believe exists. You're really not that crazy, but... Do you know where your mother is?

Deborah J. Ross is an award-nominated writer and editor of fantasy and science fiction, with over a dozen novels and five dozen short stories in print. Recent books include *Thunderlord* and *The Children of Kings* (with Marion Zimmer Bradley); *Collaborators* (Lambda Literary Finalist/James Tiptree Jr. Award recommended list, as Deborah Wheeler), and *The Seven-Petaled Shield* epic fantasy trilogy. Her short fiction has appeared in *F & SF, Asimov's, Star Wars: Tales from Jabba's Palace, Realms of Fantasy,* and *Sword & Sorceress*. She's edited *Lace and Blade, Citadels of Darkover*, and other anthologies and novels. Her work has earned Honorable Mention in *Year's Best SF,* and nominations for Gaylactic Spectrum Award, the National Fantasy Federation Speculative Fiction Award for Best Author, and inclusion in the Locus Recommended Reading and *Kirkus* notable new release lists. She has served as Secretary to the Science Fiction Fantasy Writers of America (SFWA), the Board of Directors of Book View Café, and the jury for the Philip K. Dick Award. When she's not writing, she knits for charity, plays classical piano, and studies yoga.

The messenger led the sword-for-hire, Karan, by a circuitous route through the city's cheaper district to one that featured better quality inns, places where the ale actually tasted good and the accommodations were clean and insect-free. Finally they arrived at a compound whose unassuming but robust gate opened into an immaculately swept courtyard and the main buildings beyond. When they entered, a liveried groom was just leading a fine dappled gray lady's palfrey toward the stables. At the main building, they were greeted by a man in matching livery, visibly armed and, Karan judged, quite competent. The corners of his mouth moved downward slightly as his gaze flickered across her worn shirt and vest, the patched trousers tucked into boots that had been re-soled several times. She'd long been of the opinion that it was a good thing to be underestimated on the basis of clothing; no man could purchase the incomparable steel of her blade.

The understated richness of the parlor furnishings would have done the Palace credit. Karan wondered, *Who is this patron, and why does he want to hire me when he could afford an entire squadron of mercenaries?*

The inner door swung open and a young woman entered. Karan's first impression was of a lioness suddenly finding herself in the midst of a fancy dress ball. The gown was of silk, the hair set with pearls and tiny winking gems. But the skin was sun-browned, the cheeks innocent of rouge powder, and the expression one of determination.

"Leave us," the young woman said to her attendant. Once they were alone, she approached Karan. "Please, let us sit together."

Karan lowered herself into a chair, choosing one that put her back to the nearest wall.

"I'm Estelle Rockland, and my father is Sir Henry Rockland." When Karan looked blank, Estelle explained that he was a founding member of the Royal Society of Naturalist Adventurers.

"Never heard of it," Karan said.

"There's no reason you should. I'm not sure anyone cares who they are or what they do, beyond their own membership and the Lord of the Keys, who supervises the royal charters. For the past twenty-five years, my father has been on a single-minded quest, and now he's gone missing. I want you to find him."

"Tracking down errant lord-naturalists is not the sort of work I usually do. Doesn't sound like there's much need for a sword. You'd fare better with someone accustomed to finding missing people."

"That's the point exactly," Estelle said. "This is no *ordinary* search. I cannot undertake it by myself. I must have protection, and I am assured you are the best. I promise you, your wits as well as your sword will be required."

"And the payment?" Karan asked, half-hoping it would be paltry enough so that she might walk away with an unsullied conscience.

Estelle named a sum so generous that Karan would not have to work for several years. Besides, she liked the look of her prospective employer, the sun-browned skin coupled with the level gaze and straightforward speech. She'd wager Estelle had not spent all her years in a bower, embroidering pillows. And she knew a thing or two about wayward parents.

"And where might we look for your father? What was his destination?" she asked.

Estelle shook her head. "I will not tell you that until we have a contract. You agree that even if you do not accept this commission, you will not divulge what I'm about to tell you?"

"I have a feeling nobody would believe me if I did."

"My father still has a bit of his former reputation to protect, and I would not have that taken from him by idle chatter. You see, you are quite correct. No one would believe you. Just about everyone will conclude that you—and he—are quite mad. So hear me out before you walk away."

"I'm listening."

"My father's destination was Jökull."

"Jökull? The land beneath the northern volcanoes? Home of the ice giants? Please. That's a child's tale. It's no more real than Hy-Brasil or Lemuria. It doesn't exist."

"My father believes it *does* exist, that there is an island of ice volcanoes far to the north of the Frozen Sea. He mounted an expedition based on references he's accumulated over the decades, some of them very obscure. I know because I helped him translate them." She sighed. "Now I fear the worst."

That seemed the likely conclusion for anyone haring off to such a dangerous region as the Frozen Sea. "What inquiries have you made?"

"None of his contacts in the arctic archipelago have heard from him. I know what you're thinking—an elderly man, a scholar, embarking upon such a hazardous quest. But this would not be his first venture where few others dared. He's explored Afrique as far south as the Black River. He's documented the Painted Caves high in the Gopal Range. He knows how to prepare, and he hired the best bodyguard he could find."

"It's a fool's errand."

Estelle's chin lifted and her mouth set in a stubborn line. "Nevertheless, I will go after him. Are you too cowardly to accompany me?"

Karan stirred in her seat. "Cowardice has nothing to do with it. Good sense and a desire to keep living, with all my limbs reasonably intact, does."

"Is the fee not adequate? Your boots have seen better days, and from what I have heard around the district, it's been a long time since you've had steady work. You *need* this job."

"And words like those will not induce me to take it." Still, Estelle's determination renewed her curiosity.

"There is another reason why you must agree."

"And what is that?"

"My father is not the only member of that expedition in need of rescue. My father's bodyguard was none other than One-Eyed Wanda."

The name hung in the air. Karan's mouth dropped open. How many One-Eyed Wandas could there be in the world, especially ones who hired on as bodyguards?

Mother mine, what have you gotten yourself into?

Estelle had already reserved space on a riverboat that would take them to Port Town. A friend of her father's knew of a ship venturing on the Frozen Sea, one that might take on passengers as it hunted the horned whales.

Estelle didn't know much about organizing a polar expedition beyond what she'd read in her father's notes, so it fell to Karan to make lists of necessaries: medicine kits, gear for fishing and trapping, lightweight cooking vessels, concentrated food, water sacks, and the like. Some of this, boots and warm clothing, they would get in Port Town, but the rest must be stowed in durable packs.

The journey down the river to Port Town went smoothly. The boat captain knew her business, and the currents kept the vessel moving smartly along. Although Karan was not normally gregarious, she found in Estelle a pleasant and undemanding traveling companion. The younger woman cheerfully shouldered her portion of the load whenever there was lifting or shoving or carrying to be done, never complained about the food, and often left Karan in privacy.

Karan took advantage of the lulls to practice her sword skills. She could handle the short, wide blades that were in widespread military use, using her own coordination to compensate for the roughness of balance. Very few of them were truly well-made, just serviceable. Not so the light, elegantly curved blade that was her prized possession. The desert-forged steel rippled in rainbow patterns, its edge as sharp as any razor. Just to pick it up sent her heart singing; the sword was so perfectly balanced to her hand, so responsive to her will, it practically moved itself. To use it properly required constant discipline. The deck was piled with crates of goods, but she welcomed the challenge, for she'd fought in even more confined circumstances.

After one such mock battle, dodging adversaries around corners and leaping over various obstacles, she became aware that Estelle had been watching from the shelter of a doorway.

"You're good," Estelle said.

"You say that as if you're surprised."

"Not surprised, for I knew your reputation. The legends about you are true."

"Not all of them, I hope."

"I met One-Eyed Wanda, you know, before she and my father left. He was skeptical until she showed him what she could do. She took on six of the finest fencers in the *salle* and finished them in less than two minutes. I've never seen anything like it, but I do believe you are her match."

"I'm better," Karan muttered under her breath. She picked up the towel she'd set out and wiped first her blade, then her face.

In truth, she didn't know whether she was better. Different, certainly. Still young enough to use her agility and suppleness instead of Wanda's brutally crafty style that assaulted the minds of her opponents as well as their bodies. They took different sorts of risks, she and her mother, so it seemed best—safest—*sanest*—to go their separate ways. Yet to venture into a part of the world no one had ever seen—to brave dangers beyond imagination—to become a legend, a very wealthy legend if she survived—yes, that would appeal to One-Eyed Wanda.

And, Karan had to admit to herself, it held no small amount of fascination for her, as well.

In Port Town, they located the *Elsie Mage*, on which Estelle had booked passage. Like other whaling ships, it was unlovely but sound. The captain referred them to his chandler, who sold them clothing and other items suitable for an arctic voyage. Karan had been correct that the prices, quality, and suitability were much superior to what they might have found inland. She went looking for an additional pair or three of able bodies, reliable and willing to work hard. A little exploration of the dock district led her to the right sort of tavern. She nursed an ale while assessing the other patrons, and finally approached a pair drinking at corner table, their backs prudently to the wall. Both had visible facial scars but not too many, a few white hairs but not too many, weather-tanned skin, and they took occasional sips from their tankards, suggesting moderation and relative sobriety.

"Evening, gents," she said, hooking a stool with one foot, pulling it close and settling on it.

"Karan Wanda's-Daughter," the older greeted her with a nod and a lift of his tankard.

The two men, Verron and Stape, were long-time partners. They'd joined the army about the same time, and resigned rather than continue their increasingly poor chances of surviving against younger men when brute numbers meant more than experience and common sense. Karan liked what she heard, and proposed to hire them for a respectable fee and indeterminate length of time. She described the work as likely not involving much actual fighting but a good deal of camp management for an arctic expedition. Stape had grown up in a northern village where it snowed half the year.

Last-minute arrangements concluded, the *Elsie Mage* set sail for the Frozen Sea and the feeding grounds of the horned whales. As soon as they cleared the breakwater, Karan discovered that the ocean was entirely different from wide, placid river. The captain assured her that there was no storm, only the usual rough water in this stretch of ocean; with a grin, he went on to add that the farther north they went, the higher the waves.

"And the heftier the whales!" the captain said.

Karan took the captain's advice and remained on deck as long as she could tolerate the cold, keeping her gaze fixed on the horizon. Estelle joined her, swathed in furs and apparently unaffected by the constant movement. Verron and Stape spent most of the journey below, much to Karan's satisfaction. One-Eyed Wanda, she reflected, would have balanced on the railing, laughing at the waves.

The whaler took them as far as a fishing village on the largest in a chain of volcanic islands. Lord Rockland's notes indicated his intention to land here and then hire a smaller boat to continue northward. The only accommodation to be had was a space on the floor of the headman's house. The place reeked of fish and whale oil, but the food, trenchers of fish stew sopped up with chewy rye bread, was plentiful.

The headman remembered the Rockwell party and remarked with considerable disapproval that they had bought a boat instead of hiring a knowledgeable guide. He presented his cousin's brother-in-law, a fisher noted for his far-faring ways. His name, as close as Karan could make out through his heavy accent, was Aimik, which she gathered meant *wahlruss*, although she had no idea what a *wahlruss* might be. At first glance, Aimik's boat looked dangerously flimsy, no more than a frame of bones from the horned whales, covered with *wahlruss* skins, stitched together and heavily oiled. There were no sails, only paddles. Between Aimik and Verron, who turned out to be surprisingly adept at fitting irregular bundles into crevices, they got everything loaded, everyone onboard, and set out.

The skin boat slipped through the waves. Estelle sat to the front of the craft, occasionally consulting her father's notes before re-wrapping them in oiled cloth. Aimik, the two men, and Karan took turns by pairs paddling. Aimik had protested in his broken Common Tongue that this was men's work, until Stape spoke quietly to him, and thereafter Aimik called Karan, "Long Blade Woman."

"That's Long *Bloody* Blade Woman," she'd responded.

After a time, they came to a mist so dense and white that it turned the entire world into a veil of ice that obscured the sun. Frost formed on exposed skin. There was no way to tell direction. Aimik wanted to turn back, exclaiming, "Crazy air! Crazy water!" Only after Karan unsheathed her sword and reminded him of his agreement did he relent.

They kept paddling, one stroke after another. Karan's breath rasped in her throat and her arm muscles burned.

Stroke.... stroke...

"Look!" Estelle's cry pierced the haze of numb endurance. "Look there!"

Karan lifted her head. Ahead the fog was clearing to reveal an immense iron-gray volcano. Clouds wreathed the upper peaks.

They soon drew close enough to see a gap in the mist through which they glimpsed a bay, its waters azure and cobalt, ringed with beaches of black sand.

Without warning, the skin boat lurched. Karan's first thought was an unusually choppy wave. Verron yelled, "Whale strike!"

Aimik tucked his paddle neatly along the bottom of the craft and brought out a harpoon set in a throwing stick. The end of the spear trailed a rope. He crouched, balancing as the boat rocked wildly.

A curved black shape broke the watery surface. Aimik hurled his harpoon to catch the whale as it breached. The harpoon arced through air as the sea creature rose up—and up—and up—

That's no whale!

Karan had only an approximate idea of how big a whale

might be, but she was certain they were roughly cylindrical, round in the middle and tapering on both ends, with flippers instead of arms. The beast now towering above them had a long, snake-like neck ending in a triangular head and jaws full of teeth.

The harpoon missed by a hair, due to the undulating motion of the creature's neck. It towered over them for a moment, its eyes huge and glaucous. Karan wondered if it was contemplating snatching one of them from the boat, but then it dipped its head and dove back into the water. They all sat, astounded by their luck, all except Aimik, who was busily hauling his harpoon back by its dripping rope.

Aimik indicated by gestures that they were to get themselves to the relative safety of the bay as speedily as possible. Everyone leapt to obey.

"What *was* that thing?" Karan asked as they sprawled, still breathless with exertion, on a stretch of soft black sand. The skin boat lay beside them, where they'd managed to drag it before collapsing.

The men shook their heads. Aimik grunted something she didn't understand.

"I believe it to be a species of pleiosaur—an extinct aquatic reptile," Estelle said in between gasps. "My father collected a few fragmentary specimens—teeth mostly—but he corresponded with a colleague in Armgard. They had the angle of the skull wrong, though."

She went on, chattering about the atlanto-occipital joint or some such, but Karan's thoughts had already gone off in a different direction. She'd never heard of such a creature as the one they'd narrowly escaped, but clearly Lord Rockland had and that was why he'd come here. One-Eyed Wanda, always in search of another wild adventure, could not have resisted. The only question remained was what *else* was out there. Harpies? Manticores? Dragons? Wyverns? A basilisk or five?

Sitting up, Karan voiced her question aloud. "I need to know what we'll find on this island." *Besides a pile of bones.*

"I truly have no idea. I'm as surprised as you that such an

animal still exists. I only hope my father had the opportunity to observe it."

Rising, Karan turned to scan the beach. The sand extended a considerable distance from the water's edge, lightening in color. Tall grasses waved in the breeze, obscuring the dunes that lapped the stark volcanic slopes of the peak forming the island. Although it was difficult to make out, it looked as if something had been dragged through the dunes.

Rockland's boat?

"That way," Karan said, pointing.

"No go." Aimik crossed his arms over his chest. "Stay with boat."

"We don't know what we'll find out there," Karan argued. "We might need you."

He gestured toward the interior. "Demon home. Eat all. No go."

After several rounds of "No go, crazy runs after crazy," Karan accepted that Aimik would not leave his boat.

Shouldering their packs, the rest of the party headed inland. Something the size of their own boat had been dragged through here. They found the boat itself in a cluster of huge-fronded ferns, turned bottom up. Lifting one edge, they saw paddles, carefully arranged beside oilskin packs. By the drifted sand, it had been there for some time.

It took Karan and her party the rest of the day to reach the bottom of the volcano itself. The light dimmed to a twilight glimmer. A sense of unease had been growing in Karan's mind. When Verron offered to gather downed wood for a fire, she squashed the idea.

"It's safer to tread lightly," she explained, "than to attract attention to ourselves."

The men grumbled as they set up camp, just quietly enough so that she could pretend she hadn't heard them. Estelle, on the other hand, was enchanted with everything from the unfamiliar stars to the plants underfoot, to the palm-sized woodlouse she unearthed when she moved a decayed branch.

"I don't care whether it's a new genus of *Isopoda*," Karan

said, "or one that's extinct. I don't want it crawling over my face when I'm trying to sleep."

"But—"

"But if you are so enthralled with the bug, *you* can stand first watch."

"It's not a bug! It's a crustacean, and the only ones extant today are aquatic bottom-dwellers—"

Karan rolled on her side, her back to Estelle. If Lord Rockland were anything like his daughter, it was a miracle he'd survived this long. Just as she was drifting off, she heard a long piercing shriek, so distorted she could not ascertain the direction, only that it came from somewhere in the vicinity of the peak.

Eventually she drowsed, waking to see eyes glinting at her in the half-light. Her fingers curled around the hilt of her sword, but the eyes kept their distance, fading into the shadows.

The next morning, they headed for a notch in the slope of the volcano. The trail forked, one branch ascending sharply. At the crossroads, Karan spied a mound of water-smoothed rocks. The uppermost stone bore a whitened mark, possibly scratched with a knife, shaped like an arrow pointing toward the notch.

"They must have left this as a marker," Karan said.

Estelle picked up the marked stone to reveal a second scratching that resembled the letter *p*. "It's Father, all right. Look, he's used the Greek letter *rho* for Rockland."

With the extra weight of the packs, their progress was slow. Karan had learned to pace herself on mountainous terrain, but she knew better than to push her companions. They all needed to be alert and ready to respond to any threat.

Finally they reached the lowest portion of the notch. From there, the trail dipped and then dipped again, disappearing into a vertical fissure in the volcanic wall. Here they halted to rest and drink from their stores of water. Karan fashioned a torch from a truncheon that Stape had carried all the way from Port Town and a strip torn from one of her old shirts.

Karan stoppered her waterskin and strode through the opening. Estelle followed closely, and then the men, by the sound of the footsteps on the pebble-strewn slope. The torch cast a wavering light on the rounded stone walls.

Estelle pointed at one of the walls, where a charcoal arrow and the letter *rho* indicated one of two forks. "Look, Father's left us a guide."

Time dripped on as they made their way ever downward. The tunnel dipped, then flattened out. Hazy golden light showed at a distance. As they approached the opening, the air grew noticeably warmer. The skin on Karan's face, which had felt brittle with cold, softened. She breathed more deeply, inhaling a faint scent of flowers.

They emerged onto a ledge overlooking an enormous valley as lush and humid as any jungle. Low-lying clouds cloaked a ridge of low hills in the distance. A flock of bat-like flying creatures took off near the bottom, gliding into the distance.

The air grew warm and sweet as they descended along the forested slopes. Karan recognized horsetail ferns, but much of the vegetation was unfamiliar to her: huge-leafed shrubs, sedge-like grasses, and trees that might have been ferns or palms, or both.

After a time they rested and stripped off the outer layers of their clothing. Everyone was thirsty from exertion and increasing heat.

The soft earth of the trail carried many tracks. Some of them were small, like tiny deer, others so flattened Karan could make nothing of them, but still others, overlaying the smaller ones, were clawed and three-toed, as long as Karan's forearm.

"Demon," Verron muttered, echoing Aimik's words, but Estelle examined the tracks excitedly.

The overhead light dimmed to gray twilight, and they paused for a rest. The air was filled with strange trumpetings, distant ululating cries, raucous calls, and once a scream so eerie it made Karan's guts quiver and her heart pound. She scolded herself: One-Eyed Wanda would not be intimidated by mere *noises*. Nevertheless, she wished she dared light a fire, even though she knew how foolhardy that would be. As she sat her watch, she thought she saw a flicker of orange through the jungle growth but could not be sure.

Late the next day, they came across another camp, or what was left of it. Long-dead ashes and half-burned green wood lay scattered in a haphazard manner, as if something large had kicked over the small fire. The surrounding greenery had been trampled in places, smaller palm-like ferns uprooted, and a swathe of bark ripped from the trunk of a tree that resembled a laurel. A further search turned up splatters and smears of black, dried blood.

Estelle scrabbled around in the undergrowth where the blood spatters were thickest. She held up the cap to a fountain pen. "It's my father's! I'd know it anywhere. Oh, he will be livid to have lost it. His pockets will be splotched with ink."

"That," Karan remarked dryly, "will be the least of his worries. At least we know they got this far." *And that they encountered something big and bad.*

Before she could say more, Stape drew her attention. He'd been searching on the opposite side of where Estelle had found the cap, a little ways off through the broken ferns. With a look he indicated that he'd discovered something serious. Karan went over with as little fuss as possible; she knew what she'd find. She'd seen men dismembered or gutted or so drenched in blood as to be unrecognizable, but she'd never come across one so shredded. Bits of desiccated skin and hair, mingled with gouts of coagulated blood and fat and intestine in a circle of trampled vegetation. The only recognizable object was a boot, a single boot, with the foot still inside. The ankle bones had been gnawed clean.

Karan picked up the boot, turning it this way and that. The leather was thick and of good quality, although scuffed and stained, and the heels had been reshod. "Don't let Estelle—"

"Don't let me what?" Estelle stood at the edge of the flattened area. She held her hand out for the boot and studied it. When she glanced up, her face was ashen but her expression resolute. "This was not my father's, if that's what you're thinking. It's too big. He has rather small feet and hands. Nor do I believe it was your mother's, as it's too wide for most women's feet."

Karan forbore commenting that One-Eyed Wanda was not *most women*.

"You were correct in warning us to not camp along a game trail," Estelle said.

"What happened here?" Stape said, walking up and gazing at the carnage. "What did this?"

"Something fairly large—" Estelle began. "Oh god, I probably *knew him*. I mean, Bertrem was practically Father's disciple, they'd worked together so long—I've known him since I was a child—and Evren, he came, too—but maybe it was someone he'd hired in Port Town—" Estelle broke off, visibly struggling against the tears that welled up in her eyes, spilling down her cheeks.

Karan stared, caught off guard and unnerved. She could face many dangers, but a weeping young woman was beyond her skills. Yet she must do something. She could not just stand there when Estelle was in such obvious distress.

Stape stepped forward, holding out his arms. Estelle hesitated for only a moment before throwing herself into his embrace and bursting into sobs.

Karan returned to the main part of the camp, where Verron had continued the search for more bits of evidence. He'd found the fountain pen itself and a cooking pan that had been squashed flat.

Although the day was fading toward twilight, they pressed on. The land rose and spaces opened up between the strange large-boled trees. At last, just as Karan was on the brink of calling a rest, they came to a thickly wooded overlook.

A vista opened up before them: a wide valley, more meadow than forest, with lakes and streams surrounded by wetlands. Enormous beasts, several tons at least, moved across the landscape, long-necked and ponderous. A flock of brightly colored winged animals took off from the water's edge. Wonder swept through her, and awe. She had no names for these creatures, fantastical living beings unknown to the outer world.

The treetops directly below Karan rustled. Another huge

beast, twenty feet long from snout to tail and striped like a tiger, broke from cover almost directly below her. It had been waiting, so still and silent she hadn't noticed. It ran on two legs toward a flock of camel-sized bipedal grazers, which immediately bolted. Feathered tail extended, the predator launched itself at the scattering herd. It knocked several from their feet before closing its massive jaws around the neck of a straggler. The entire kill, from the first movement to the final crunch of a severed spine, had taken only a couple of minutes.

As quietly as they could, the human party retreated the way they had come. Estelle had stuffed all her fingers into her mouth and was shaking like a leaf. It was some time and even more distance before they felt safe enough to find a place to rest.

The next morning a sense of discouragement settled on the camp. As long as they had been following the trail used by Rockland's party, there was a chance they might catch up. It was unlikely Rockland's party would repeat their mistake of camping along the trail. Karan hesitated to break up her own group to search more widely. Calling out Rockland's name struck them all as suicidal.

Karan noticed that Estelle looked quieter and sadder as the discussion went on. The younger woman had been largely quiet, other than giving the names of the creatures they had seen the night before.

"You know your father better than anyone," Karan said. "Where would he have gone after the attack?"

Estelle shook her head. "I have no idea, beyond that I don't think he would have turned back—" which had been Verron's suggestion "—voluntarily."

Wanda, he would have relied on your advice.

One thing was sure, Wanda would never have run from a fight, even if it was with a gigantic tiger-striped, feathered allosaur. She would have pushed on until she'd achieved her goal.

"Was there something in particular on this island your father was after?" Karan asked Estelle. "Or would just setting foot here and seeing these creatures have been enough?"

"The stories of Jökull tell of many wonders, most of them too fantastical to be real. But on the other hand, I would not have ever imagined I would see a dinosaurian in the flesh. In the center of the island, legend has it there is a well that leads through the Earth's crust to a land of winged beings composed of molten gold and living gems. Father had little interest in the monetary value of such things, but I can't see him leaving this place without trying to find them."

Karan, satisfied, nodded. "Then our path is clear."

They made their way back to the valley, on alert for any sign of the tigerish allosaur. Compared to the previous dusk, the valley and wetlands were quiet, almost empty except for the ponderous sauropodians and some more distant rhinoceros-sized ceratopsids with huge bony frills extending over their necks. Their passage did not go unnoticed, as the largest of the sauropodians trumpeted a warning but did not pursue as they hurried away. A herd of pony-sized hyracotheres, spotted like fawns, scrambled to their feet where they had lain hidden in the sedge grasses.

"I guess the allosaur hunts at dusk," Verron remarked.

Karan noticed how Estelle had moved closer to Stape and slipped her hand into his. If it brought comfort and calm, she wasn't going to object.

What with crouching down in the grasses at any movement in the herds, it took them most of the day to reach the far end of the valley. They felt safer once they'd reached the line of bushy, flowering magnolias, and here they made camp.

With the next brightening of the light, they moved on to beyond the strip of forest and began to climb again, this time to an ashen cone within the larger caldera of the island. A flock of winged pterodactyls circled overhead. As they climbed, the vegetation thinned. Panting, they looked at last down on the crater, in the center of which stood a structure like a circular stone well.

One-Eyed Wanda stood, legs braced, atop the wall of the well. A pterodactyl with a viciously sharp beak and a wingspan easily her own height banked, angling in for an attack. Her sword sliced through the membrane of the leading wing. Shrieking, the creature back-flapped wildly. It managed to gain altitude although it was listing badly. Above, a dozen others wheeled and screeched.

For a heartbeat, Karan could not move. She'd forgotten the grace and deadly speed of her mother's sword technique. Wanda had been a force to reckon with as a young fighter, but over the decades she'd developed skill, balance, and sheer bloody-mindedness as her physical power waned. Now Wanda shifted her stance as another pterodactyl glided in. The narrow edge gave her little room in which to maneuver.

Why doesn't she fight from the ground?

Wanda wielded her blade in a circular stroke, using momentum to cut off the tip of the beak and the fragile wing bones. The pterodactyl tumbled through the air, spraying blood, and landed almost on top of Wanda. In the tumult that followed, Karan glimpsed two men, one of them elderly, peering out from the well. Wanda had positioned herself to shield them from attack.

Karan looked for a way down, and noticed steps carved into the inside of the crater, weathered but passable. She rushed down them. By some miracle, she kept her footing as the eroded rock crumbled under her boots. She sprinted to Wanda's side.

"What the hell are you doing here?" Wanda said, as together they fought off the first pterodactyl she'd wounded, which had circled back for another attack.

"I could ask you the same thing," Karan shot back as another pterodactyl dove toward them, then veered off as she slashed at it. "Oh, hell—"

Estelle had reached the well and was leaning over it, helping her father to climb out.

Within a few minutes, however, the battle was over. Those uninjured pterodactyls that could still fly flapped away. The bodies of half a dozen littered the space around the well.

"Did you think I wouldn't come after you?" Karan said.

"Will you two stop nattering and help me with my father?"

Estelle said. "Evren's here, too, and he's hurt."

Between them, Verron and Stape hauled the two men out of the well. Karan, pointedly turning away from Wanda, knelt beside the wounded man. Cuts, some of them deep and oozing, covered his face and one shoulder, and he looked to be on the edge of shock. Karan made him lie down while she wiped away the worst of the blood and bandaged the deep slit at the base of his neck. Meanwhile, Estelle had been interrogating her father about his own condition, in between scolding him in a tone, both loving and imperious, that Karan wished she could use on her own mother.

"We need to leave this place as soon as possible," Karan said.

"No, no," Lord Rockland protested. "We descended only a short distance into the *omphalos*. Having come this far, and at so great a sacrifice, I refuse to turn back without having achieved my objective, which is nothing less than possession of the Fount of Wisdom."

"Those flying monsters will be back," Karan said. To emphasize her point, she drew out her chamois and wiped the blood off her sword. "We beat them off this time, but who knows what other, even more dangerous things are out there?"

"Surely we will be safe with two such swordswomen to guard us," he replied.

"Father, your life isn't worth it, no matter what the treasure," Estelle said, taking his arm and gazing pleadingly into his eyes. He scowled at her.

Karan wanted to smack him. "Your daughter risked her life to come after you. You may throw yours away on a foolish quest, but I will not allow you to throw away *hers*. This place is no better than a killing field. We mustn't be trapped here."

"I agree," Wanda said, as if that settled the matter. "Lord Rockland, you promised to follow my orders concerning your safety. We are leaving. Now. No more discussion. Stop this nonsense and get yourself up those stairs."

Karan didn't know why she should be astonished at his instant obedience. This was One-Eyed Wanda at her most tyrannical, after all. And she was right.

Wanda turned to the wounded man. "Evren, can you walk?"

"Aye." He clambered to his feet. His color wasn't as good as Karan would have liked, but they had no time to waste. Already a lone pterodactyl, perhaps a scout for the flock, appeared overhead, hovering on the air currents.

They went back up the steps, Verron helping Evren, and headed back to the magnolia forest.

"You didn't have to come after me," Wanda said to Karan as they walked side by side.

"You didn't have to get yourself in such a scrape."

"We were doing just fine until just before you showed up."

"Really, Mother? We found the remains at your camp. Whose brilliant idea was it to set up on a game trail?"

Wanda turned her blind eye to Karan as she gazed beyond the last line of trees to the meadow, shimmering in the overhead radiance. Karan noticed for the first time that her mother's hair was more white than dark, and even the dimmer light could not soften the wrinkles. She felt her own heart beating, fast and strong, and her throat closed up.

"We'll need to cross the valley as rapidly as we can," Wanda remarked, "preferably at midday."

"We saw the allosaur. How would you fight such a thing?"

"Did I teach you nothing about strategy? Your sword's a bigger tooth than any of them have, so make it part of you, an extension of your will. Move from your center, don't let its size make you overreach yourself. Watch how it moves, where it's off-balance, where it's vulnerable. Thing's got hamstrings, same as anything else, and it's not that fast. Can't pivot like we can. Bigger they are, the harder they fall. But..." And here Wanda's voice dropped in pitch and she turned to face Karan full-on. "It's not the big ones you have to worry about."

It's not the big ones you have to worry about. Wanda's words rattled around in Karan's mind as they set out the next morning. It wasn't full light yet, but would be soon, and Karan judged the risk to be worth it. Evren, the wounded man, had emerged from his shock and could walk with a hitch. As for Lord Rockland, he still muttered about the prize he was leaving behind, the discovery that would seal his reputation as a premier naturalist forever.

"Fat lot of good that would do you if you're dead," Estelle remarked."I promise you, the Society will be properly impressed by your reports of extinct saurians and botanicals. I saw you making notes and sketches last night."

They began moving across the valley, skirting a spit of wetland and its margin of horsetail ferns. The grasses grew to head height in clumps, making it difficult to survey the terrain. Their roots formed hillocks, perfect for tripping over. They discovered, too, that burrowing creatures had left holes everywhere. Stape stepped in one and went down hard. He grabbed his ankle, smothering a groan. Estelle rushed to his side. He got to his feet with her help and stood, gingerly testing his weight on his ankle while leaning on her shoulder.

Before they could move on, Wanda signaled everyone to hush. Karan focused on the sounds beyond the faint rustle of the grasses in the breeze. At first she heard nothing, but then—a crackling, a snapping of a stalk and silence, as if something were treading in a stealthy manner.

Karan slipped her sword free. Wanda did the same.

Karan took the lead as Wanda whispered directions to the others, putting the weaker members in the middle. The two injured men could not walk smoothly, but lurched along. Lord Rockland had no notion of how to step carefully, but at least his complaints had dwindled to an occasional *hrrumph*.

Karan wished she could get a good look around, to see how far they were from the overlook and the hills beyond.

They went on a pace... two... three. Then stopped. The rustling sounds did the same, only this time, perhaps because Karan was listening so keenly for it, she detected several sources converging upon their position. She wished she knew how far they had to go—should they make a break for it, praying they'd reach shelter before whatever it was caught them?

They went on, step by nerve-wracking step, until the

vegetation ahead of them thinned out to reveal a stretch of open space dotted with clumps of dwarf horsetails and barberry shrubs. Beyond it, dirt gave way to rock, rising sharply, in places vertical. Best of all, the base of the trail was defensible, up against a solid face of stone, which meant that Karan and Wanda could hold off their stalkers until the others scrambled to safety.

Karan stepped to the side, catching Wanda's eye and indicating that they would guard each flank while the others made for the hill. Wanda nodded, a sharp jerk of her chin, and took up position on the other side.

"Go!" Karan commanded.

Estelle took her father's arm, while Stape propelled Evren forward. Verron paced them, his sword ready.

Together they surged into the open space. Karan and Wanda tried to keep the others moving in a direct line, instead of swerving between the brushy clumps. The two of them could have covered the distance quickly, but it was slower going with the injured men. Lord Rockland was clearly doing his best, but Karan heard his wheezing over the sound of their footsteps. Behind, the grasses swished as if a storm were bearing down.

"Come on, Father!" Estelle cried. "Almost there—you can do it!"

The overlook loomed closer now, with still no sign of their pursuers. Each moment, each step, brought them closer to escape.

Where the tall grasses extended a short distance to one side, the stalks parted and a two-legged reptilian form burst forth.

The creature was easily ten feet long from snout to the tail held stiffly horizontal, its feathers of muted greens providing perfect camouflage. The light glinted off its dagger teeth. Muscular hind legs armed with wickedly hooked claws churned the earth as it charged directly at Wanda. And Wanda carried her sword low as she ran.

"Behind you!" Karan screamed, just as the creature leaped.

Almost faster than Karan could follow, Wanda spun around. Her sword flashed upward in a curved arc. The point penetrated the animal's belly at the peak of its trajectory. The creature impaled itself as it plummeted, colliding with the ground. Wildly it thrashed, its tail whipping from side to side. Blood sprayed in every direction.

Karan skittered to a halt, not daring to approach for fear of getting caught in the monster's convulsions. "Mother!"

Wanda rolled to her feet behind the downed beast. Blood drenched her torso. "Go! Get out of here!"

As she spoke, a second and then a third... and then a fourth hunter emerged from their grassy cover. Like the first, they were coated in green and gold. Two veered off, angling toward the rest of the human party, while the largest, head lowered and teeth bared, advanced toward the two swordswomen. Estelle screamed.

Just then, Wanda went to one knee, biting off a cry of pain. Karan saw then that not all the blood had come from the creature. Maintaining her grip on her sword, she slipped her free hand under Wanda's arm and hauled her to her feet.

There was no point in asking if Wanda could fight, and no breath to waste. Karan pulled Wanda back, trying to give them more room. This put them closer to the others, backed against the solid rock face, too far from the trail to run.

"Let me go," Wanda snarled. "You'll be the death of us both."

Karan shoved Wanda behind her, facing the hunter. Taking a wide stance, she lifted her sword over one shoulder in a two-handed grip, poised for a spiraling stroke. For a long moment, the two faced off, woman and reptile. The creature bobbed and dipped, but did not close with her. Its head swung toward its fallen pack mate, now still. Perhaps it was assessing the threat. It turned back to her, mouth gaping wide, and hissed.

"So you've got teeth?" Karan snarled. "I've got one, too. Let's see whose are sharper."

The next attack came not from the front but from one of the other hunters, dashing in from the side. Karan whirled, bringing her sword down in a diagonal path. Her blade caught the side of the beast's head, sliced through the meaty jaw muscles, and bit deep into its shoulder. For a horrific moment, the blade caught there, snagged on bone. The weight of the creature almost jerked the sword out of Karan's hands. Then the blade came free in a gush of blood.

The wounded hunter scrambled away and a second rushed forward, gathered itself, and hurled itself into the air. It brought its hind legs, with those vicious, hooked claws, up and out. Karan tucked one shoulder and rolled. The claws missed her by a hair's-breadth. She came up, pivoting to face the beast. It wasn't built to spin around quickly, and she was. Even as it turned, she closed the distance. Steel sang, parting hide and feathers and flesh as if they were silk. The creature went down with a deafening wail. Karan stepped in, following up her attack—

—and saw, almost too late, at the very edge of her visual field—

—a flash of motion, a green-yellow body speeding toward her—

She turned, but slowly, too slowly, caught as she was between two attackers. The one she'd just wounded had recovered and was bearing down on her. It was closer, and maddened with pain. But if she turned, she would leave her flank open to the second—

The second who now went flying sideways. Its body slammed into the ground, skidded, and came to a halt, shrilling and wheezing. Wanda surged to her feet beyond the writhing body. Her upper body gleamed red. She dug the point of her sword just below the hunter's ribs, leaned her weight on it, and shoved. Bone and muscle resisted, and then the blade slid home.

Karan whirled back to face the remaining hunter. Her breath rasped in her throat. Sweat trickled into her eyes. The creature skittered backward, turned, and limped back in the direction of the tallest grasses.

The smell of the blood, not to mention the carcasses, was sure to attract scavengers. And with three wounded, they were in no shape to fight off anything with teeth.

Wanda was trying unsuccessfully to pull her sword out of the hunter's body. After shooing the others in the direction of the trail, Karan wrestled the sword free.

"I can manage," Wanda said as Karan slipped one shoulder under her mother's arm. "Leave me be. Don't stop for anything—not even to clean your sword."

"But didn't you always say to—"

"Not now!"

No one argued about the need for haste. Evren slipped and fell once, but Verron caught him. Estelle, surprisingly agile on the steep slope, helped her father over the worst parts. They were all out of breath by the time they reached the top.

The trees and undergrowth were too dense to push through with any speed, but within a short distance, they came across a trail that might be the one they'd followed.

Karan led the others along the gentle downward slope. They were going to have to stop sooner or later, to rest and tend their wounds. Just a little farther, she told herself, just a bit more distance between themselves and the valley with its hunters.

She froze, signaling a halt with her free hand. Although the trail stretched before her, empty of obvious threat, something was wrong. The leaves of the brushy trees were too still, and there was no sound other than the beating of her heart.

A tall shadow moved in the gloom of the forest. She saw it then, the bulk of the body, the massive head. The tiger stripes. The eyes set below bony, protruding ridges.

The teeth.

Slowly, with the intent grace of a stalking predator, the allosaur moved from its hiding place. It loomed over her. White feathers grew in pale, parallel lines down one shoulder. From its throat came a thrumming sound that approximated a growl.

For a long, agonizing moment, Karan gazed up at the allosaur. Despite the warmth of the day and the heat streaming from her body, she shivered. She wanted nothing more than to run and cower in hiding, but she could not give up now, after all they'd been through. *Wanda* would not back down.

She took a step forward, bringing her sword up in a diagonal angle across her body.

"You want a fight?" she screamed, her voice raw and manic.

"Come on then! Have at it!"

Snout extended, the allosaur lowered its head. Slit nostrils flared wide as it inhaled, then again and again. It was *smelling* her. Not just her—the hunter blood on her sword. In the humid air, it hadn't had time to dry. Her pulse yammered in her ears, but she held firm.

With a snort, the allosaur drew back, returning to its previous upright posture. One deliberate step after another, it disappeared back into the forest. Branches crackled and leaves rustled with its passage. Once they could no longer hear the allosaur, the entire party gave a collective sigh of relief.

"I told you it wasn't the big ones you needed to worry about," Wanda said.

"So you did."

"*Now* you clean your sword."

Aimik grinned broadly when the entire party stumbled onto the beach. They were all filthy and exhausted, but none of the wounds had gone bad. Karan divided the party between the two boats. Stape's sprained ankle did not impair his fitness to paddle, so she put him with Aimik, Lord Rockland, and Estelle, who looked quite pleased with the arrangement. That left her with Evren, who appeared to be a taciturn soul, Verron, and Wanda.

They set out, with Aimik leading. Even once they had passed the worst of the surf into slow, rocking waves, Wanda was uncharacteristically silent. Karan tried not to stare, but her mother looked pallid—that could be from the pain of her wounds—and thoughtful, which she couldn't explain. The ocean wasn't *that* interesting.

At Port Town, Lord Rockland insisted on the best of everything for the entire party: soft beds, hot baths with perfumed soap and thick towels, *more* hot baths, massages and nurses and musicians to entertain them as they dined on roast meat and wine. By this time, it was clear that Estelle and Stape were thoroughly enchanted with one another, and Lord Rockland was too excited about the monograph he planned to publish to notice or care.

He'd had his life's biggest adventure and lived to tell the tale.

Verron and Evren took their pay and went their own ways, while the rest of the party accompanied the Rocklands to their compound in the city.

Karan and Wanda settled into quarters at one of the better inns, intending to enjoy clean linens and decent ale while their purses were still fat. They sat together in the common room, nursing their drinks and looking at everything except one another.

Finally Wanda set her tankard down with a sigh and stretched, her joints popping. "I'm getting too old to be traipsing halfway to nowhere and back, fighting off monsters. I've been thinking of retiring while I still have both my hands."

Karan stared. Until that moment, she'd been sure that her mother would die as she'd lived, taking on the worst the world could throw at her and giving as good as she got.

"I was thinking," Wanda went on, "that if I pooled my takings with someone else, together with what I've saved, I might be able to buy a place like this."

"You'd lay down your sword?"

"Nah. Hang it over the mantle, someplace handy. Y'know, just in case the rowdier sort decide to make trouble."

Karan had no doubt that the "rowdier sort" would be attracted to any place that Wanda owned like flies to honey—but they would quickly learn manners. She had no idea of what to say about her mother becoming an innkeeper.

After a long moment, Wanda said in a deliberately and dangerously casual tone, "Are you in?"

It took Karan a dozen heartbeats to understand. Then, astonishingly, something akin to joy swept through her. They'd argue, of course, at times loudly enough to send half their patrons running for cover, but they'd also cover each other's backs and never want for a roof against the rain.

She could think of no better way of preventing her mother from taking off on another hare brained, monster-ridden adventure.

It was only after they'd shaken hands on the deal that Karan realized that being partners meant Wanda would keep an eye on her, as well.

THE NIGHT WARD

by Steve Chapman

I've been waiting for years for Shada to start working with other people, instead of trying to save the world all by herself.

Steve Chapman is a learning science professional who writes genre fiction in his somewhat elusive spare time. He lives with his wife, daughter, and sailboat at the New Jersey shore. This is his ninth appearance in *Sword and Sorceress*.

Orange flames danced beneath the cold night sky.

Shada raced across snow-dusted rooftops. Below four wights marched toward the burning building, to meet its fleeing inhabitants.

She flung a glass sphere at the first of the walking corpses. It shattered against the head, oil splattering its hair and tunic. The wight ignored it, intent on the family of five. Shada tagged the second, the third—and then she was out of time.

She leapt from the roof, Dolu sticks in hand, yelling to draw the wights' attention.

The ploy was too effective. Before she had her balance the first was on her. She pivoted and let its claw rake her arm. That stung, but she was protected. Her tights were threaded with iron twine, impervious to the wight bites and scratches that first killed you then reanimated your corpse as one of them.

Two others flanked her. If they got hold of her the iron twine wouldn't matter. They'd just eat her face.

So it was a good thing her friends weren't far behind.

An arrow struck a wight's shoulder. The arrow was on fire, and then the oil slick wight was too.

Aaron—on the roof—targeted each wight with flaming arrows. Claude burst from an alley bellowing like a berserker in a bear trap, giving the wights plenty of warning. Annabeth leapt from a roof she didn't need to be on and nearly twisted an ankle.

Shada huffed in frustration—the Court Kids never *listened*—but the wights were on fire and couldn't do much damage as the Kids shattered their limbs.

She ducked through the melee, intent on the enormous fourth wight closing on the family. Without oil its dead flesh hadn't ignited.

Shada's sphere crashed against its face, oil splattering. The wight turned. It was a warrior, seven feet tall, white bone showing through decayed flesh. She was out of Aaron's range. She had to get in close to ignite the oil, where she risked getting pulped.

The big wight grinned.

A flaming arrow punched through its thigh. The fire died, but the wight limped.

Shada wasn't sure if she was more excited to gain an edge or that Aaron had gotten around to practicing his distance shots.

The wight ran.

Shada pursued. Warrior wights were rare and deadly. Taking it off the board would save a lot of lives.

"Shada—no!" Dockerty blocked her path. He was out of breath, glasses perched on the tip of his nose.

She skidded to a halt. "I can finish it."

"By yourself?" Dock was ringleader of the Court Kids, disaffected children of powerful nobles who'd taken to Vaska smoking, black marketeering, and other petty crimes. When the wights first attacked, Shada had protected them. They'd wanted in. Much as she'd hated to admit it, she needed help.

But Dock didn't fight. A self-proclaimed 'thinker and cynic,' he was eighteen, just a year older than Shada, but talked down to her like a decorated general.

"What do you think I did before you miscreants suited up?"

"Nearly died a lot." Dock's exasperation steamed his lenses. "Sit on your death wish. Wait two minutes and someone can back you up."

Shada didn't wish for death, she just wasn't afraid. "In two minutes that wight is gone. Tomorrow night it could kill dozens."

"You can't save everyone—or every hypothetical."

She didn't know what that was, except the end of her patience. She darted around him.

"Come back!"

She'd be back once the wight was down. Dock said Shada had to act like a leader; that had to include ignoring him.

Civil war had come to St. Navarre in the guise of walking corpses. The man known as the Consul, once King Sisco's right hand, now attempted to take his crown. The wights were his weapons. Sisco's troops struggled to adapt their tactics. So Shada, the King's last-born, least favored, most likely to throw a punch and get confined to her chambers child, had taken up the task.

The wight lowered itself into a sinkhole.

Shada approached. Light glowed below. The wight was trying to pull the arrow free.

She dropped a lit match into its oil-soaked hair and jumped down, landing on the knee of its bad leg. Bones snapped. She hit it with a Dolu stick then delivered a spin kick to its face. The wight went down. Fire ate through it.

Shada stood in a dilapidated, torch-lit room dominated by a fallen chandelier and overgrown with vines.

Something flew at her. She batted away a plum-sized green sphere.

"Nice reflexes, Princess." Tall and muscular, the Fae woman wore a short dress of leaves.

A Fae assassin; they were expensive. Shada felt a flush of pride. She must be hurting the Consul badly.

She dropped her sticks, hands empty in challenge. "Whatever the Consul's paying you, it won't be worth it."

Shada had fought Fae. They were fast. She was faster.

The woman nodded, accepting. She spun forward into an open palm strike. Shada blocked it easily.

It felt like she'd been hit with a building. She flew backwards, her arm numbed. The woman was impossibly strong. An icy jab of fear cooled Shada's insides.

She got up and threw a footsword kick. Vines appeared between the woman's hands, snagging Shada's ankle. The assassin pulled her off her feet and flung her across the room.

Shada landed face down in the fallen chandelier. The assassin's knee dug into her spine.

"The Consul said you'd come to me." The woman twisted Shada's wrist behind her back. "That you pursue your own extinction as avidly as the wights."

Big words; that sounded like the Consul.

"I'm Lady Gilead. You may have heard of me."

Lady Gilead was a campfire tale of Verdigris forest, a Fae assassin possessed by a Green Man, a woods demon. Instead of fighting the demon Gilead worked with him. She had the Green Man's strength, powers, and appetite for human suffering. Shada felt only slightly better about getting her ass so profoundly kicked; she was in deep trouble.

She shifted her hips to twist free—

"My Green Man hungers for your torment." Gilead wrenched Shada's wrist, breaking the bone with a sickening snap.

Shada gasped in pain. The woman's strength was obscene.

Gilead rolled her over, pinning her arms above her head. Vines poured from the assassin's mouth, opening Shada's jaw and tunneling down her throat. She gagged. Panic flushed her body, and then terrible, shooting pains. She saw double: Gilead and the demonic presence, drinking down her agony.

Dockerty leapt down the sinkhole, brandishing a dagger. Shada had never been happier to see his annoying face.

The assassin tripped Dock, stabbed him with his own weapon.

Vines burrowed *out* of Shada's stomach, turning her white outfit scarlet.

A flaming arrow just missed Gilead. Aaron lined up another through the sinkhole. Claude jumped down, then Annabeth.

Gilead ran for a tunnel.

Shada's eyes closed.

Shada woke by slow degrees.

She lay upon a hard cot. The air was cold, tiny ghosts of breath issuing from her mouth. The dim room was thick with shadows. A bedside table held herbs and ointments. Five other cots lay empty.

She felt warm and spent, as if a fever had broken but not entirely faded. Her mouth was dry, her eyes sticky.

She sat up. She wore a sleeveless black shift, the sort you're given at a healing space. A chill passed through her: she remembered Lady Gilead…

She extended her arm. Her wrist turned. Everything worked. The cuts were gone from her stomach. But there was a faraway ache to each movement. She'd been mended by a powerful healer. Her fog, like the fever, was an aftereffect of healing. But where were the healers?

She tried to stand. The stone floor chilled her bare feet. The damp air was too cold for her tiny shift, but there wasn't even a blanket to be seen.

She smelled the sea. Was she in the caverns beneath the city? She'd heard stories about a secret healing space below the Citadel, where illegal magics saved lives St. Navarre couldn't afford to lose: the Night Ward. She'd thought it a tall tale.

But where was everybody? Had Dockerty been too far gone to heal? She needed to find a wrap, and slippers.

The door led to a stone corridor. A few lonely glowstones provided unsettling, monochrome light. She stepped in something wet: blood. A wave of fever passed through her. She needed to lie down, to rest. But she felt the low pulse of danger everywhere. Something had gone wrong here.

The passage opened into a vast rotunda, floor and ceiling open at its center. An enormous statue stood there, a slice of its torso visible. An iron railing circumscribed the open space. She leaned over it, peering upward. The figure's full height vanished into darkness. She dropped a loose stone over the rail. It hit bottom with a splash.

Shada circled the rotunda. Stone doors, each marked with a quarter moon emblem and a ruby, were set into the outer wall. Stairs curved along the perimeter, up and down. It felt more like a cathedral than a healing space.

She nearly tripped over a body: a young man in a healer's smock as ravaged as his corpse. He was still warm. Whatever killed him was close.

Her heart beat wildly. She had no weapons and a fever. She had to find an exit *fast*.

She took the nearest passage. It led to a room similar to where she'd woken but this one was stocked with… instruments.

An iron chair and a breaking wheel. Knee splitters, a head crusher, and a rack. The back wall bristled with spikes. A sunken iron tub filled with liquid. She tossed a ceramic bowl in. It dissolved.

An acid pit; where was she? No healer kept a roomful of industrial-strength painmakers at hand.

She turned to go. The corpse from the rotunda blocked the doorway. Blank eyes found her. The jaw worked up and down.

This was a newly risen wight.

It attacked, teeth gnashing to tear out her throat. It could have bitten her bare arms or legs. That would have killed her, turned her. But it was still learning.

Shada's kick drove the wight back, but it nearly grabbed her foot.

She retreated; it was a mistake. The wight backed her against the spiked wall. She wanted to scream. She wanted her iron twined tights and an oil sphere.

The wight lunged. She caught its wrists. It wasn't large but had the uncanny strength of the undead. It forced her backwards, her feet slipping across the cold floor. Jaws snapped at her face. A spike stung her leg.

She twisted to one side, letting the wight's momentum carry it into the spikes.

She stepped back, checking her arms and legs; no bites or scratches. The wight pulled itself off the spikes. One had transfixed its left eye, adding to its striking appearance.

Shada had no fire. She had to use what was at hand.

It charged.

She rolled backwards with it, putting her feet into its gut, kicking out as they went over, launching it into the acid. She scrambled away from the deadly, hissing spray.

The wight rose, extremities liquefying, then sunk back into the pit like a noxious dab of cream in a horrendous soup.

Shada shuddered; her fever spiked. She realized she was leaning on a brain-encrusted head crusher and stumbled for the exit.

A second wight appeared. She threw a side kick.

Dockerty screamed and ducked into it. "Why are you attacking me?"

"I thought you were a wight." She helped him up.

"Do I look like a wight?" He looked paler than usual in a black shift like hers.

"I was just attacked by one. I'm a little on edge."

Jumpy, he looked around the room.

She pointed to the acid pit. "Dissolved it."

Dock adjusted his glasses and took in the painmaking devices. "I'd have gone with the knee splitter."

Shada resisted the urge to hug. Court Kids were too cool for hugging. "Where are we? What's happened?"

"Beside me getting gutted because you didn't listen?"

Fair enough; Shada expected to live that down never. "Your crap knife skills might have contributed."

Dock laughed. He must be terrified; he never laughed at her jokes. "We both needed serious healing. I couldn't wake you or find anyone. I went looking."

"And found empty creepy place, bodies, wights, torture gear?" Shada shivered. "What is this place?"

"The Night Ward. You know it?"

"Secret healing space beneath the Citadel? We were hurt bad." Saying it made her feel queasy, like she'd already died.

Dock seemed like he wanted to add something. Probably something about her greedy family hoarding resources.

"A wight must have got in," he said. "Some staff fled, others died. The Ward locked down to keep the infestation out of the Citadel. I saw a lot of bodies. They're all gonna rise."

"We're trapped in an abandoned bunker with a ton of

wights?" Shada fought down panic. "How long until they open the doors?"

"Standard procedure is a week. Let the infestation burn itself out."

Once the wights killed the living they'd turn on each other: end of infestation. But first they'd scour every room for live meat. A week was a death sentence. Shada felt dizzy. "There's no way out?"

"Not unless you can destroy a wight army without fire. You got your death wish."

"I don't want to die." That had been obvious when Gilead was killing her. But Shada had put herself—and Dock—in terrible danger. "With this horrible stuff, I just feel like I have to run right at it."

Dock looked interested. "Why?"

She didn't know.

"There has to be a way out." Shada shook off the fever. "Let's find it."

Passing back through the rotunda, Dock stopped at the railing. "You really don't know this place?"

"You said it's the Night Ward."

"And you, the King's kid, don't know what that means?"

Shada remembered she couldn't stand him.

Dock moved close. For a shocked moment Shada thought he was trying to kiss her, which would have earned him another kick in the head, but he pointed up. The statue had *horns*. It was a Kjenga fire demon, a humanoid with the curved horns of a ram.

"The Night Ward isn't for healing," he said. "It's for cleansing demons. We were healed in the Citadel. They brought us down here to cleanse us of Green Men."

Shada had never heard this. "Why is it secret?"

Dock met her gaze. "Shada, back when we used to mess with you, it was because I thought you were in on stuff like this."

She couldn't parse what he was talking about.

"But you're not. You're not in your father's inner circle or part of his plotting." Dock faced the moon-marked doors.

"You're not stupid. You haven't asked the questions because you don't want the answers. Like, why would St. Navarre keep its possession ward a secret?"

Shada recognized the crescent symbols as spatial wards—and she understood. Shock, fury, sadness; each came and went. Dock was right. She should have known. She touched the cool stone. "They're kept in here?"

He nodded. "Eight cells on each level, eight levels."

Shada's heart pounded. Some possessions couldn't be cleansed. You had to kill the host to end their suffering. But some hosts, like Gilead, gained abilities. They could be weapons. Only a small section of the Night Ward was for cleansing. The rest was for experimentation. Behind these doors, held by the moon wards, were the possessed.

"How do you know about it?"

"My brother Theo stumbled into an old shrine on the cliffs. A Kjenga latched on to him. They couldn't get it out. Theo begged us to kill him. But Dad agreed that he could be 'used.' That's how our family got so prominent. Lucky us. I was twelve, a smart little bugger. I snuck down here to kill Theo. That went as well as you'd expect. Dad bartered for my life. I started smoking Vaska and grew up to be the upstanding citizen you adore today."

Shada felt for him. No wonder Dock had a rotten attitude. "I'm sorry."

He shrugged it off. "We're about to die anyway."

Shada' shame turned to purposeful anger. St. Navarre needed to get out of the torturing possessed children business. "What was your plan?"

"I was *twelve*."

"You were just as annoying then, I'm sure." Shada's head was buzzing. "Tell me."

He rolled his eyes. "The researchers use personal talismans as protection from the demons while they work. I nicked one. I was going to open Theo's cell, kill him."

"What stopped you?"

Dock slapped the ruby. "The doors are sealed by bloodstone.

Unless your blood's in the stone, the door won't open."

The Citadel used bloodstones for security. They opened for Shada because blood*stones* followed blood*lines*. Her blood read as her father's.

"I've got an idea." She inspected the ruby. "We're not dying here."

"Hello children." Lady Gilead appeared and tossed a green sphere. "Sorry, but you so are."

Spores exploded in Shada's face.

Shada woke on a cot.

Her wrists and ankles were trussed to its corners. Knives and clamps filled the table beside her. Painmaking devices surrounded her.

Her breath came too fast. The leather straps were thick and tight.

Dock was bound on the next bed. "This woman *really* hates you."

Gilead didn't hate Shada; she'd been paid to kill her. But the Fae was no normal assassin. Her Green Man gave her power beyond her own skills. In return she fed it the suffering of her victims. Gilead was a monster.

"I'll get us out of this," Shada said. "I promise."

"How?"

She had no idea.

"I've never failed to kill a mark, Shada." Gilead locked the door behind her. "My demon was furious when I retreated. His appetite, once roused, must be fed. But a little improvisation and here we are."

Gilead fastened a clamp around Shada's calf. The iron was cold, the divots sharp.

"Green Man's waited days for you." Gilead tightened the clamp to the point of pain. "We'll make it up to him with these horrendous toys."

"How did you get in here?" Shada had to stall. "What happened to everyone?"

"The Consul's a clever man. He knew they'd bring you here.

Easy enough for the possessed to get in."

Gilead placed a clamp above Shada's left elbow; pulled it tight. The divots found a nerve. Shada gasped.

"He gave me a wight's claw to scratch you; make you a wight. But to feed Green Man, I have to kill you myself. So I scratched a Guardsman instead. He died, turned, and starting killing everyone else." Gilead was proud of her improvisation.

Shada seethed. The Consul's machinations were again slaughtering his own people.

Gilead scooped an iron ladle of acid. "The lockdown allows me an uninterrupted evening of torturing you to death."

"You don't have a mark for Dockerty."

"Your friend's discomfort will increase your suffering." Gilead dribbled acid on Shada's shift. "More for Green Man."

Drops ate through the fabric and bit at Shada's belly. It barely hurt; this was theater. It bought Shada time to think.

She was surprised to find she wasn't terrified. She was scared, sure. But she was breathing normally, thinking clearly. That was interesting.

She felt a new clarity. She wasn't terrified because she *wanted* to be here. As a child she'd been frightened by the world's violence but—if she was honest—also thrilled by it. The Citadel had been her cradle. There'd been assassination attempts, kidnapping plots, poisonings. The world was broken. She'd discovered a gift for violence; the only honorable use that gift was against the broken world's horrors.

She wasn't stupid. She'd understood enough not to ask the questions until she was strong enough to survive the answers. As a child, knowledge of the Night Ward might have broken her.

But there was a cost—a shame—to her years of willful ignorance. Now she could handle the truth it wasn't enough to confront her world's wrongs: she had to run right at them.

And in Gilead's use of the painmakers she saw something she could use.

"The Consul *is* a clever man," Shada said.

Gilead's blade traced the underside of Shada's arm.

She shivered at its touch. "His plan allowed for your

survival—yours doesn't. I wouldn't have thought I'm worth your life."

"You're not."

"Then put down the knife. You're not going to hurt me."

Gilead brushed Shada's cheek. "Sweet girl, you're making this worse."

"You've created dozens of wights. The lockdown will last a week. Starving wights will scour every inch of this place looking for food."

"A week?" Gilead blinked.

"It's standard." Dock's voice shook. "Ensures the wights kill each other."

Gilead gripped Shada's arm; thumb found nerve. Shada felt as if her shoulder had been set ablaze.

"Maybe your Green Man could beat them." She ignored the pain. "But you can't access its powers. That's why you need painmakers, why you aren't using vines. Is it because there's no greenery here?"

The sinkhole room had been overgrown. Here there was only stone.

Gilead nodded.

"Great improvisation, except the bit where you created an army of hungry wights and locked yourself in a bunker with them. How are you at fighting wights, Gilead? Because I'm the best. I'm your only hope of surviving this."

Gilead tightened the leg clamp. Shocks of pain ricocheted up Shada's spine.

"Get us out and we'll finish our business then." Gilead turned the clamp again. "Betray me and I will tear you apart."

The pain made Shada's eyes water. She smiled anyway. "Deal."

Shada moved through a seven point exercise, punching and kicking. Her muscles warmed, her reflexes improved.

"You can't fight wights in a threadbare shirt." Dock was still overwrought.

"It's a shift." Shada had no intention of doing so. The chance of a scratch was too high. “Shirts come with pants.”

Gilead just watched her.

“I miss pants.” Dock sighed. “What’s the plan?”

Shada was working out the details, where devils lurked. “We need fire.”

“There’s nothing flammable down here because—”

“Because the Night Ward’s stocked with fire demons.” Shada turned, kicked. “Which suggests an approach. I can open Theo’s cell. Where do we find talismans?”

“There’s a safe upstairs. But it’s got a bloodstone lock.”

Shada met Gilead’s unnerving gaze. “Here’s the plan.”

Theo’s cell was on the top level. A ruined dome hung over it. The Kjenga statue glared, it’s curling horns each the size of an elephant.

Shada’s breath steamed the safe’s bloodstone. An iron panel clicked open and her heart broke. Her blood would open every locked door in the Night Ward. Her responsibility for it couldn’t be clearer.

Inside were bracelets of sea blue crystal.

“Kjenga fire burns hotter than natural fire but seawater stops it cold.” Dock slipped a bracelet on his wrist. “That’s why there’s a deep seawater pool at the bottom the rotunda. Wearing this, it’s like you’re encased in it. You’re protected from the demon’s fire and its strength.”

Shada and Gilead each took one.

Dock would wake Theo. Shada would lure the wights. The demon would burn them. Then Dock could free his brother.

Shada opened the cell. A tall, nude man stood within. His eyes opened.

“Theo.” Dock pushed past her.

“Little brother?” Animation seeped into Theo’s face. “You know, when I asked you to kill me I meant then, not six years later or whenever you got around to it.”

Dock stopped dead. “I tried.”

“I’m joking.” Theo grinned. “Look at you, all grown up and you finally got a girl to hang out with you.”

Shada felt a second presence like Gilead's green man.

Theo's dark eyes found her. "Princess Shada. You two make a cute couple." He stretched, muscles rippling. "But matching outfits is never a good idea."

Fire poured off Theo.

Shada felt a flash of heat as flames engulfed the cell. If not for the bracelet the flesh would have been stripped from her bones.

The fire faded. The walls were scorched black.

Theo laughed. "Talismans, sure. But you should have seen your faces."

"Fight the demon, Theo." Dock was shaking.

"I've been here six years. There's no Theo, no demon. We're one thing. I appreciate the rescue but I'm also keen to feast on you."

Dock's eyes turned cold. "Get the wights," he told Shada.

She brushed past Gilead. The assassin's gaze never left her. She wouldn't wait until she recovered her demonic strength; the moment Gilead felt safe she'd attack.

She slipped down spiraling staircases, descending around the enormous statue. At its waist she spied a trio of wights.

"Hey!" She felt stupid waving to corpses. "Guys!"

She darted back to the next level. As she'd hoped, the noise brought more. Four wights came from her left. She raced to the next staircase, her pursuers forming a posse.

On the next level she picked up five more. She ran for the nearest staircase, leapt the first steps—and saw nine wights coming *down* it. She jumped off, back into the rotunda, the wights from below on her heels. She sprinted past the central railing, aiming for the next staircase, but three more cut her off.

Shada skidded to a halt. Thirty wights flooded the rotunda, blocking every stairway.

This was bad.

The first wight reached her. She dodged and kicked and smashed its skull open on the iron railing. A second; she rolled it over her hip, over the railing, into space.

This didn't feel bad. It felt awesome.

She leapt on top of the railing and then across the dark chasm, landing in a breathless crouch in the statue's open hand. Two wights followed. She kicked them off.

More wights jumped to the statue, hanging on with their uncanny strength. Shada scrambled up the statue's arm, finding purchase in the weathered stone. Wights followed, clambering up the statue like insects.

Shada climbed. Her muscles ached but her heart sang.

From the demon's shoulder she leapt back to the railing. Wights followed. More poured up the stairways.

She ran at Theo, the wight army right behind her.

The world burst into flame.

Shada was thrown backwards. Wights were immolated in midstride. In moments every walking corpse was reduced to ash.

Shada lay on the smoking floor, unhurt but stunned.

"You used me." Theo was annoyed. "I want out."

Dock, holding a knife, came close. "I can do that."

Theo punched him in the face and tore the bracelet from his wrist. Dock scrambled backwards.

"Don't need demon strength to punch." Theo crushed the crystals. "Show me the exit or Dock burns."

"It's locked down." Shada struggled to stand. The room spun.

"You're lying."

"The doors are barred," Gilead said.

"You're possessed." Theo hadn't realized.

Gilead stared at him. "What have they done to you?"

Theo's laughter sounded like sobbing. "Taken me apart so many times I can't remember."

Dock stared. Shada felt a sorrow indistinguishable from shame. She tried to blink away her dizziness.

"Fine; I'll burn everything," Theo whispered. "Everyone."

"The doors open in seven days," Gilead said. "We wait. In the meantime—"

She kicked Shada's unsteady legs out from under her, stripping the talisman from her wrist.

"You get him." Gilead shattered Shada's talisman. "I get her."

"I've no interest in waiting." Theo flashed his grin at Gilead. "Give me your talisman. Let's *all* burn."

On the floor, Shada caught Dock's eye. She motioned to the statue. His eyes widened. But they didn't have a choice.

"They broke your mind," Gilead said to Theo.

"Years ago."

Shada and Dock sprinted for the rail.

Theo flamed on. Shada felt heat on her back, saw orange light reflected in the statue's eyes. She vaulted the rail, fire pouring over her head, and fell.

They hit the water hard, but it was deep. Shada swam to the surface, pulling Dock behind her.

At the pool's center Kjenga hooves rose from a circular base. A foot of water covered moss-coated stone.

The flames around the statue's head threw hellish light downward, shadows of the curling horns outlined on the water. Theo's fire was coming.

The seawater would protect them, but Shada's pursuer would arrive first.

Gilead hit the pool then burst from the water, knives in both hands. Shada blocked and dodged, her feet uncertain on the slick rocks. Gilead slipped. Shada kicked at her wrist. One knife fell. Gilead slashed at Shada's throat. She turned. The blade sliced her shift. Gilead tossed a green sphere. Shada kicked it away, but it was a distraction.

Gilead tackled her. Shada gasped, swallowing water. Gilead got on top of her and forced her underwater.

The Consul was definitely getting his money's worth.

Shada grabbed the assassin's wrists. She pulled Gilead's hands away so she could raise her head to breathe, but couldn't buck her off.

"How many have you broken like that boy?" Gilead's thumbs jabbed at Shada's eyes. "The Consul thought you had a death wish. Maybe all you wish is to see justice done."

Shada didn't wish to die. She wished to be the girl who destroyed atrocities like Gilead, like the Night Ward. That meant taking terrible chances.

The fire overhead grew brighter, dropped closer.

Gilead broke from Shada's grip with unexpected strength. With a shock Shada realized the rocks were covered with green lichen.

"Green Man's coming." Gilead pushed her back underwater. "Only question is whether you drown before I regain the strength to crush your skull."

She wasn't kidding. Gilead's hands wrapped around Shada's head, squeezing. Shada held her wrists, but Gilead had grown too strong to restrain. Shada couldn't breathe, could barely think.

The fire—beautiful, terrible—burned through level after level.

With her talisman Gilead would survive. She'd kill Dock, the Court Kids. Shada couldn't see a way out.

A gambit appeared in the flames. Shada timed the falling fire, waited, then bit Gilead's thumb.

The assassin's death grip relented. Shada slipped sideways, kicked up and locked her legs around Gilead's neck.

The assassin squeezed harder. Shada's temples throbbed. She made a show of trying to snap Gilead's neck between her knees, but she knew the only way she could beat her demon was with another.

Gilead saw the descending fire reflected in the water. She didn't care—she had her talisman.

Shada ripped it from her wrist.

Gilead tried to duck underwater but her throat was trapped between Shada's knees. Shada had the angle, the leverage. She dropped her legs just beneath the surface, keeping Gilead's head above it.

Fire hit water. Shada felt the heat along her body.

Gilead shrieked. Her hair burned. Her flesh melted. Her white skull turned black and crumbled to ash.

Shada rolled off the platform into deeper water as the Night Ward burned.

Shada and Dock climbed endless blackened stairs.

Dock, for once, was quiet. Fair enough; he had less

experience than Shada in being stabbed, burned, drowned, beaten up, and falling from heights. The fire had swept through every level. Theo had destroyed the Night Ward.

They found him just outside his cell.

His remains hung in the air, a floating mannequin of ash. Dock gave his brother a final hug and the ash dispersed, coating him, dusting Shada.

Hours later the main doors opened and Guardsmen flooded in. Shada finally procured a blanket and slippers, and a Guardsman to escort them back.

"What will happen?" she asked him, "Now the Ward's destroyed?"

The Guardsman chuckled. "This happens sometimes. Have to replace equipment, supplies. But the subjects are behind charmed doors, safe from fire. Things will be back to normal in a month."

Shada felt like she still had vines in her stomach. The Night Ward would go on.

Dock didn't look surprised.

"You knew?"

He shrugged, his arrogance gone. "The place's been running a long time. Makes sense it would be Kjenga proofed."

"I have to stop it." But Shada felt so tired.

"I understand your run-right-at-things deal." Dock straightened his glasses "But most horrible things—wights excepted—can't be burned down in an instant. It takes time, patience, strategy."

Shada had none of those things. She had punching. Also kicking.

"My whole life," Dock said, "I thought fighting this stuff was for suckers. Better to zone out on Vaska. Maybe I was wrong."

"What's changed?"

"I never thought someone like you—one of *them*—could also be one of us. We should be thinking about more than wights."

The spiraling stone staircase delivered them into the warm glow of the Citadel. Shada was home.

She realized that she wanted to burn it all down.

A ROSE BY ANY OTHER NAME

by L.S. Patton

Clara can find more than enough problems in the small village she lives in. She really doesn't need to go to the royal court to find trouble.

This is the fifth story L.S. Patton has written for *Sword and Sorceress*. She read this anthology series growing up and has enjoyed being a part of it. She works as a biochemist in Indianapolis where she lives with her husband, cat, dog, and horse.

Something happened three days ago. The Enchanted Forest had huddled in on itself, like some giant murmuring creature. I'd never seen it do anything like that before, and I had no idea what it might mean. I'd spent hours yesterday sitting on my favorite rock in my shielded area within the Enchanted Forest and didn't see anything different about the patterns to the magic there, except that it seemed more withdrawn somehow. It wasn't something I could explain. So I did what I always did when I needed information: I went to the inn.

Karen's inn was a large building on the village square and served as the town's main gathering spot. Anyone coming through town stayed there, and anyone wanting to gossip about anything hung out in the common room. I spent my fair share of time there, but I didn't usually show up three days running. Our town wasn't the largest, so this slight change in my schedule was at least as interesting as anything else that was happening and people were starting to wonder what I was doing. Unfortunately, I wasn't sure what I was looking for, I just knew something wasn't right. Being clueless appeared very similar to being mysterious to an outside observer, so I wasn't surprised to see a much larger crowd than usual as I pushed open the door. I was surprised to see Alex; I'd been planning to run by his farm after my stop here since I hadn't seen him in a couple of days. I wondered if he'd come to the inn to see me.

He was sitting at my usual table, and waved his glass of cider at Karen when he saw me push the door open. She flapped a hand at him and headed toward our table with my drink. As I slid into my chair, I noticed people glancing at me out of the corner of their eyes. I surreptitiously looked down; travel through the Enchanted Forest required walking through clouds of unformed magic, which occasionally coalesced into spells. I had been observing the formation of these spells since I took up temporary residence in the Forest, and had even developed some new magical theories from my observations that I had published in a couple of magical journals. Since no one would believe a small time hedge witch like me would have magical breakthroughs, I'd been using the pseudonym the Enchantress of the Forest. While melodramatic, the name kept the curious from interfering too much with my regular life. The townspeople thought my double life was endlessly entertaining, and often made up stories about the Enchantress in their spare time. They didn't tell any strangers my secret identity, though. My souvenirs from the wild magic in the Forest, such as my retractable claws from last week, were the most likely way for someone to notice that I was the Enchantress, but I didn't have anything like that happening today. The people looking at me today must just think I knew something. I wish I did.

"So, Clara, you figure it out yet?" Karen asked me as she plopped my drink down and pulled out a seat at the table.

"Maybe it's nothing," I said, not very convincingly. I certainly wasn't convinced.

"You wouldn't be this jittery about something if it was nothing. If you think something weird is going on, it probably is. My guess is Tom's screwed something up again." Tom had left our village to go to the schools of magecraft and now served as a mage at the castle. Despite his training, he seemed to screw up more than he got right and he always ran back to our town when he'd done something boneheaded enough that he needed to get out of the queen's sight for a while. I don't know what happened when he was at the capital, but when he was in town I usually cleaned up his messes, including changing him back into a human when his trip into the Enchanted Forest had turned him into a goat. It was a mystery to me how anyone ever thought he was competent, and I also suspected that whatever was happening might involve him. I wasn't ready to pick up and go to the capital on the off chance this was Tom's fault, though.

"I'm sure we'll hear what's going on soon enough," Alex said. "Anything that has you this jumpy must have affected more than just you and the Enchanted Forest, so someone should know something."

The door to the inn crashed open, and it was a testament to the extent of the rumors going around that only half the people looked at the man in the doorway; the other half of the patrons looked at me. "Hey!" shouted Karen, with all the ire of an innkeeper whose door was being abused. She didn't finish, though, because by that point we had gotten a look at the man in the doorway.

He was haggard: he looked like he had been walking along the dirt roads for days. He had road dust in the wrinkles of his face, and he was a uniform brown from his knees on down. The look in his eyes, though, was the worst. This man had seen something terrible and desperation and helplessness radiated off him. His clothes looked like they had once been a nice uniform; a servant, perhaps, in one of the fancy houses the nobility had in the capital. And I knew he had come to tell me about what it was I had sensed.

"The Enchantress," he blurted out and then paused, as if everyone else was completing his thought with him. Luckily, Karen never bothered to listen to full sentences.

"She lives just over the line into the Forest," said Karen, carefully not looking back at me.

The man slowly collapsed to the floor, still right in the doorway. "She must come...there's no one left. She's needed in the capital." With that, he pitched onto his back and passed out. The silent inn suddenly erupted with noise.

"Clara?"

"What's going on?"

"Is this what she's been sensing for the past few days?"

"What do you think happened?"

"Do you think something's wrong with the queen?"

Obviously, none of us had any answers, but that didn't stop the questions. Those who were best at wild speculation got started, and it looked like the beginning of a busy evening. I looked over at Alex. "You ready to get out of here," he didn't ask. I nodded, and he offered me his hand. I took it and we headed out the door. Someone had lifted the messenger to a nearby table, and he was surrounded by a ring of speculators.

It was much quieter outside, though my mind was whirling. I might not know what the problem was, but, combining the magical disquiet I'd been experiencing and a man searching for the Enchantress, I knew something bad was happening. I'd never had much power, but I had learned some good new ways to accomplish the same things with less magic from my observations in the Forest. Since then, a few people had begun searching me out to help them with magical problems, and I was starting to develop a reputation as a powerful mage, though in reality I was more efficient than powerful. I'd never even gone to the academy.

"So will you leave tomorrow?" Alex was apparently not thinking along the same track as me.

"What?"

"Well, they need magical help, even if we don't know the details yet. Aren't you planning to go?"

Okay, he was thinking along the same lines as me, he'd just gotten farther. And if there was something I could possibly do, I had to try. I had the impression that something terrible had happened, and I wouldn't forgive myself for hiding here if it was as bad as I suspected.

"Tomorrow? I don't know...I need to see what that man has to say. I should get some herbs together, but I think I have most of that in my storeroom at home. I could probably leave tomorrow..." I trailed off uncertainly. How to prepare for something that terrified a man when you had no idea what it was? I didn't really know.

"Do you think you'll need to bring Margot?" Margot was Alex's magical cow, and she was the reason I'd set up shop in the Enchanted Forest to begin with. She absorbed all magic from an area, cleared it of spells, and concentrated the magic into her milk. If you drank the milk, you gained the power. I'd hidden her away to keep her from the unscrupulous since she could bestow unimaginable power. Now that she lived in the Enchanted Forest her milk was always quite magically potent.

"I...I don't know. I don't have a lot of power of my own, and if it's a spell that's done this, she could certainly help. If it's as bad as the messenger implied, though, then it's probably the work of a powerful mage. If he got hold of Margot, it would greatly increase his power; we probably can't risk it." I'd kept her safe from the power hungry by keeping her hidden away and secret.

We walked in silence for a few more moments, contemplating what might have happened. "Would you like company? I can't do magic, but I can keep an eye on you while you do. It seems like you might need someone to watch your back," offered Alex.

Alex and I had been almost dating for a while. It would look like things were going somewhere, then one of us would get busy and we wouldn't know quite where we stood. I didn't know if he was suggesting he come along as a sign of romantic interest or if he really thought I needed backup, but it couldn't hurt to have someone along. And I was interested too.

"Sure, I'd like that." About this point we reached my house and bid each other good night. Alex said he'd meet me at the inn at noon with horses and food. So I only needed to figure out what magical supplies I might need for the trip.

The next morning, I had gathered up all the herbs and spell components I could think of, and was at my hideout in the Enchanted Forest. I'd built it while experimenting with the Forest's magic, and it was a whimsically built stone edifice. If I could hold the building materials in place for long enough to say the spell, I could turn those materials into stone, so there were lots of impractical arches and curving corners. I usually stayed here a night or two a week, so it was more of a clubhouse than a home. The one part I did take seriously, though, was the basement. Concealed in the floor there was a stone slab that could be slid to the side to access a dirt stairway down into a small cellar. On shelves in the cellar were thousands of cheeses that I had made from all the milk I had gotten from Margot since we moved to the Forest. I had not found a good way to dispose of them, so I had been keeping them hidden here. I had eaten a couple of them previously, but even a tiny bit gave you so much power it was hard to control and even harder to know when you were about to run out of it. It was nearly as dangerous as it was powerful, and it was very powerful. I grabbed ten of them and hid them in the inner pocket of my jacket. If I wasn't going to bring Margot with me, this was the next best thing.

I patted Margot as I left my hideout and headed to the inn to see what I had gotten myself into. I figured that I'd given everyone enough time to gossip so the townspeople would let me have a conversation with the messenger.

Judging by the number of people milling about the square, the inn was probably still packed. Our village was small enough that an exciting messenger was big news, regardless of what he had to say. I pushed open the door, and saw a crowd of people by the bar. Assuming that the crowd hid the messenger, I headed that way. Liam gasped when he saw me approaching the huddle, which caused about half the group to turn to see who was here. Upon seeing me, they opened a path to the messenger, who was in fact in the center of the crowd. More and more people noticed my arrival and moved aside, until I was standing alone in front of the messenger. He stared at me in confusion.

"Can I help you?" he asked.

"I'm the local hedge witch...I'd like to hear the news you brought. What happened?" I hoped that that was enough of an explanation to justify the attention I was getting. Maybe he was still rattled.

"It's the castle. The queen's castle has been cursed. There's some sort of magical barrier around it. We haven't been able to contact anyone on the inside in three days. All the royal mages are trapped in there with her, so Duke Gillingham has called for all the remaining mages in the kingdom to come to the capital to try to remove the curse."

"Duke Gillingham is the queen's second cousin," Olivia piped up helpfully. Which was lucky, since I had no idea who he was. "He says the Duke's holding court in Wainsbridge until the curse is removed. Too scared to stay in the capital, I say." Apparently the inn's regulars had pulled the whole story from the messenger already.

The messenger stared daggers at Olivia. "His royal highness has removed to a sensible distance while the threat is assessed. But that's beside the point. Where is this Enchantress? No one's been willing to tell me all morning, and I need to get the message to her so I can move on to finding Lord Bentworth."

"I can pass the message along; I work with her sometimes, and I know how to get to her passage within the Forest. She's not particularly fond of strange visitors."

The messenger looked skeptical, but decided that interrupting an Enchantress who didn't want to be disturbed was probably more trouble than it was worth. So he nodded as regally as he could in his dusty clothes. "Then I will continue on to find Lord Bentworth. It is imperative that all mages are brought to the capital at once. Is there someone here who could loan me a horse? Mine went lame yesterday, and the news must get out quickly." I faded back into the crowd as people started helpfully suggesting other people's horses and which would be the best for the journey.

Cassie trotted smoothly along, and although Alex had assured me she was a calm and steady horse, it still looked like a long way to the ground. I didn't ride horses very often; I usually just walked around the village. Hedge witches didn't really make enough to justify keeping a horse. I'd gotten more used to riding over the course of the two day trip, but my saddle sores were now agreeing with my nerves that walking was a better way to travel. Unfortunately, I didn't think we could spare the time.

As we approached the capital, I saw a dark, nebulous cloud rising up out of the center of the city, instead of the expected castle towers. That must be the barrier the messenger had spoken of. I looked over at Alex, "Are you ready for this?"

He smiled back at me, "I'm not the one who has to do anything here; I just relax and prop you back up when you keel over from exhaustion." He reached over and squeezed my hand. "You'll do just fine. You go check it out, we'll think about what we can do, and if you have an idea you'll try it. If not, we'll find Duke Gillingham and see if there's another mage at the capital with a plan and help him. Or her." Despite the fact that I'd spent most of the ride up today discussing how this was my plan, it was reassuring to hear it again.

We winded our way through the streets and up the hill at the center of the city. With each lurching step upward Cassie took, I felt my stomach sinking lower. This was big magic. I was a small time hedge witch with a few cool tricks and illusions of grandeur. What was I even doing here? We passed the last row of fancy houses, and then all we could see in front of us was the shifting fog.

It should have reminded me of the Enchanted Forest: magic in constant motion, so strong it was slightly visible to the non-magical eye, and blinding to me, with my proclivity for magesight. I'd always made observation of magic my specialty, and this seething mass in front of me was almost too intense for me to observe. I felt something touch my leg and started, thinking the magic was spreading toward me, but it was just Alex. "Sorry, I was just examining the barrier. What do you see?"

He looked over toward where the castle should have been. "Just a sort of haze...I can't really look at it too hard, but I can't see the castle in there, either. What do you see?"

"...I'm not sure yet. I'll have to take a closer look." I slid off of Cassie. "Um, this may take a while....should we look for a better place for you to wait? It's not going to be very interesting."

"This will work just fine; I'll move the horses over here out of the road. Do what you need to do, and I'll keep an eye on the mundane world." I nodded, and looked back over at the barrier. It was mesmerizing, and I stepped closer to get a better look.

There was a pattern to the shifting fog, which felt foreign after all my time in the Enchanted Forest. Every time a dark tendril would snake out, it would turn and move along the face of the barrier, then grow additional, shorter tendrils along the face. A new tendril would appear just above where the last one had started. It reminded me of something...I took a couple steps left, then a half step right. I sharpened my magesight even more, giving myself the start of a headache. And then I saw it. Branches of magic, growing out of the ground and curving up toward the light, sprouting thorns as they went. A bramble of magic growing and regrowing from particular spots in the earth, forming a barrier around the castle. I sat down to take a deeper look at the workings now that I knew the structure of the spell.

I was glad Alex had made stew, since that meant I didn't choke myself to death trying to eat it as fast as I could without bothering to chew. Alex looked a little worried, but I was still too hungry to care. I had spent seven hours staring into the barrier, and the effort involved had left me ravenous. When I came back to myself, all I could think about was food.

"So, um, did you learn anything?" Alex ladled more stew into my bowl. Bless him. I should probably stop eating long enough to answer.

"Yes. It's like nothing I've ever seen before; usually mages use magic to create physical objects in our world, or to make standard shapes, like a sphere around something to shield it, or a ring to keep people out. This is a complex shape made of magic, patterned after a plant. It's using the growth pattern of the plant to keep the spell constantly moving and changing without guidance from the mage. It's an amazing idea, really. Plant growth patterns are so complex they might as well be completely random, so it'll be nearly impossible to predict exactly what it will do next." That was enough talking to get Alex to let me finish my stew; he looked pensively over at the barrier. I scraped my bowl clean, finally starting to feel full.

"I think the mage must have a plant attached to the spell as a template. If we detach that, it should stop the shield's motion, and possibly destabilize the entire spell. In order to serve as the pattern, it will have to be magically connected to the barrier, so we should be able to follow that connection to find the plant template," I yawned hugely.

"You're exhausted. This part of the city seems deserted, so we should be able to sleep here and look for your plant thing tomorrow." He patted the sleeping rolls, which he had apparently put out while I was eating. I was so tired I crawled into mine without even considering the fact that I was sleeping on some fancy noble's lawn.

The next morning, I roused Alex out of bed to circle around the castle and see if I could determine where the plant might be connected. We led our horses and chewed some jerky as we walked sunward around the palace. So far, I didn't see anything magically connected to the barrier, but we were only halfway around. I was feeling less optimistic than I had been earlier; we hadn't found the connection. Could I just not see it? What would I do if the plant was within the barrier? Then I saw a thin line of cloudy grey magic, slipping along the ground into the city. I stopped dead. Cassie snorted, disturbed from her almost doze as she walked at my side. "What is it?" Alex asked.

"I see it, Alex...there's a connection that leads into the city. We need to see where it goes." With that, we took off into the tangle of streets.

The streets quickly became smaller and more tangled, and sometimes we couldn't follow the thread directly as it cut through houses and shops, but it moved in a straight line so we were always able to find it again. Until, suddenly, I couldn't see anything. It led right up an inn, but I couldn't see it coming out on any of the nearby roads.

"This might be it; I don't see where the thread continues. Hold Cassie while I check." I thrust the reins at Alex and slipped into the stable yard of the inn. The horse stalls were behind the main building, and I walked along them. There was no magical thread extending from the back wall of the inn, so the spell must stop somewhere inside.

"What're you doing in the stables? You aren't staying here." The stable boy eyed me with obvious suspicion, but I suppose I had been staring intently at walls.

"We're planning to, though; are there any open rooms?" The boy looked at me like I was even crazier than he thought, which was saying something. I remembered how deserted the city had looked, and realized he probably had a point. "Our horses are out front." At the mention of horses, the boy perked up, and headed toward the front of the inn to deal with something he knew how to handle. He grabbed the horses from Alex, who looked at me inquiringly. "We're planning to stay here tonight. This is where the spell thread ends. Let's get some rooms, then hopefully I'll be able to snoop around and see what's going on."

The inn had three stories: a common room and kitchen on the first floor, guest rooms on the second floor, and the attic appeared to be used for storage and space for pallets if the inn was too full. It did not appear full today, as the only thing I saw moving on the third floor was a spider, and she looked like she'd been undisturbed in her web-building for a while. I came back down to the second floor, and poked my head into Alex's room. He was going through the saddle bags, sorting things into piles that could be packed back away or things we would need tonight. He looked up as I came in. I sat down on the far side of the bed from his piles.

"Nothing upstairs. My guess is it's in one of the other guest rooms; I didn't see anything in the common room, so I'm guessing it snakes up from the kitchen, so any of the four rooms at the back could be our target." We, of course, were in the two rooms at the very front of the building. "I'm not sure how to figure out which room it is, though. I can look for the magic in the rooms, but without being able to see the walls it's hard to tell which room is which.

"What if I hold something magical and go stand in front of the different doors? Then you could judge the distance between my magic object and the spell."

"Alex, that's a great idea! When did you learn so much about magic?"

"Well, I have been spending a lot of time with a very good Enchantress recently." The look he gave me made my cheeks heat up. "I try to pay attention. Do you have something magical for me to hold? I'll plan to stop in front of each of the doors"

I leaned across the bed and kissed his cheek, then grabbed a hairbrush and settled in cross-legged on the bed. I filled the brush with a touch of my magic, then passed it to Alex. His hand dropped down from his cheek and he took the brush and headed into the hallway.

I closed my eyes to focus, then expanded my magesight to encompass the inn. I saw a few small charms on the first floor, probably in the kitchen. Presumably charms to keep food fresh, start fires, etc. Most kitchens had a few of those. I saw the thread snaking up, and expanding when it hit a room on our side of the hall. I saw the magic in the brush pause three times, then a fourth time right near the spell thread. The thread wasn't the only thing in the room, however; there was a very bright spot, probably a pack, and a large shape that was moving. A mage.

I opened my eyes as Alex reentered the room. "The mage is there."

I could see the worry in his green eyes. "What do we do now? You've never fought an evil sorcerer before. This doesn't seem like the time to learn, with all you were saying about how brilliant he was last night."

I chewed on my lower lip. "I suppose we could try to tell someone, but I think we need to know more first. It seems obviously related to the barrier to me, but to a mage not used to using magesight, there's no obvious connection. We're either going to have to get proof or I'll have to disable the spell, and either way I think that means going in there."

"This doesn't seem like a good idea. All we know about this mage is that he's very powerful. I have no magic and can't help you in a magic duel."

Alex was making a lot of sense, but without some sort of

proof we had nothing.

"Look, why don't we wait a little and see if he goes down to lunch, then scope out the room? Once we know a little more, we can take it to Duke Gillingham and the mages he's gathered," I thought back to how quiet everything had been in the streets. We'd walked most of the way around the palace and hadn't seen anyone else working on or near the barrier. Maybe there were no gathered mages.

Alex nodded reluctantly. "I guess that makes sense. I'll go down and get lunch when he does so hopefully we'll know what he looks like too."

"Be careful."

"Right back at you." The bell tolled 11:30, and we sat in silence, me watching the mage with my magesight, thinking about what we were planning to do. I hoped it worked. I reached out and grabbed Alex's hand, and, judging by how hard he squeezed my hand back, he was nervous too.

An eternity later, the mage began to move. I sat up straight, and Alex met my eye. "He's heading down?" I nodded, and watched as the mage descended to the first floor. I gave Alex's hand one last squeeze, then slipped out the door.

I didn't see anyone as I walked down the hall, and the knob turned easily under my hand. I opened the door and looked into a room that was the mirror of my own. The bed was up against the wall on the right, window straight ahead, and small table with a chair to the left. A full pack was on the bed, glowing gently in my magesight. Leaning against the wall by the table was a staff, and I could see the grey swirl of the spell around it. I stepped closer, and saw the staff was covered with small thorns. They matched the thorns I'd seen on the shield spell. I slipped further into my magesight, trying to confirm that it was the template for the spell. I could see the grey threads of the spell spooling out of the staff, and a single thick tendril feeding into the staff, powering the template formation. There was something else in the staff as well, something subtle. A failsafe of some sort? Something to prevent me from severing the thread to the spell? I focused my magesight on the staff as hard as I could, but still couldn't distinguish the magic inside it.

I glanced back at the door; I didn't have much time, and while I could probably sever the thread anywhere along the line, I didn't want that to trigger something much worse. I reached into my pocket and pulled out one of my magic cheeses. I'd put it there as a precaution and I'd never tried to use it to intensify my magesight, but it seemed worth a shot. I took a small nibble, then refocused on the staff. I felt the surge of power through my veins, and the fuzzy, poorly defined something in the staff suddenly snapped into focus. The fuzziness resolved into a pulse of energy up the center of the staff and descending along the upper layers of the wood. Along the paths the nutrients would have followed when the staff had still been alive. It probably wasn't part of the spell, but instead a residue of magic from the tree the staff had come from. It had been quite the tree, judging by the amount of magical residue.

"Well, you're not what I expected," said a voice from behind me. I whirled around, and the lights from the pack on the bed and the power of the person in the door almost blinded me. I blinked back tears until I could see a woman in the doorway. Her iron grey hair was pulled back in a braid, and she was wearing a long green robe. Her hands were on her hips, and she looked annoyed that I was standing there gaping like a fish. I kept suddenly getting flashes of magesight even though I'd tried to turn it off, which was distracting. "You're not just a common thief, are you? That would be distressing. There are thieves everywhere these days. No, you were staring at my staff." She walked across the room and closed her hand over it, thorns and all. "You must have followed the spell. I was beginning to think no one in this godforsaken country had eyes."

This was not at all the response I had expected, though I was thrilled that I wasn't expected to fight a magical duel. That would not have ended well. Maybe we could just discuss what was going on like rational adults? It seemed worth a shot. "Yes, I was trying to find who had cast the spell on the castle, and was looking for the template for the thorn bushes. I believe you're holding it."

"The Staff of Selion." She held it out for me to admire. "Of the Grove of Selion, which can only be welded by the Guardian of the Grove. I'm impressed you've gotten that far, given how pathetic the attempts of the mages inside the castle are. They can't even seem to communicate with me, and I've been trying to get their attention. They just seem to be blowing up bigger and bigger things. I don't know what they think that will accomplish."

"Why are you trying to talk to them? And why did you put the shield up in the first place?"

"Some idiot stole a flower from one of the trees in the Grove. As its Guardian, I both protect the trees and prevent them from being formed into more magical artifacts, as was done in the Lost Ages. As such, I track down every twig that is removed. But a flower, with all its potential for life and birth? That's especially dangerous. And the idiot not only stole it, but wore it in his buttonhole all the way back to the castle, bragging about the theft. I have several good firsthand accounts of his appearance. I set up the barrier to hold him in place while I came to get him and the flower, but no one in there seems capable of communicating with me so I can tell them to hand him over. It's difficult enough to communicate through the spell; I can't pinpoint him with any accuracy, and I can't afford to lose him."

This story reminded me too much of similar stories over the years, and I felt my stomach sink. "This idiot...dark brown hair down to his shoulders, about 5'8", bit of a paunch? Wearing clothes much too fancy for traveling?"

Her eyes sharpened, and she really looked at me for the first time since she'd started her story. "Who did you say you were, exactly? You seem much better informed than I expected." Her voice hardened.

"No one in particular; a hedge witch from a village a couple days ride away. But Tom grew up in my village, and the story has all the earmarks of one of his idiot ideas." I paused, realizing I was going to have to admit my secret to help resolve the situation. "I'm also known as the Enchantress of the Forest."

Her eyes widened perceptibly. "Ah! That explains how you

found me. I've seen your work; it's quite impressive. Perhaps you have a way to get the attention of those on the inside? I'd rather not hold the castle captive for too long; that sort of thing always gives rulers ideas."

"No, but I might have another solution. If you'll follow me to my room?" I led her down the hallway and opened the door to find Alex, looking stricken and holding a long knife.

"You're okay! I saw her head back upstairs, but I didn't know what to do. I'm so glad you're okay." He crushed me into a hug, and stiffened when he saw the mage behind me.

"I'll explain later, but I think she's just after Tom." Alex, who was also familiar with Tom's antics, found this to be a reasonable explanation.

I riffled through my magical supplies and pulled out a vial containing a single lock of hair. "After Tom's last several debacles, I felt the need to be prepared." I held the hair out to the Guardian. "This is a lock of hair from the man who stole the flower. I assume it's enough that you won't lose him, even if you bring down the shield."

Her eyebrows rose. "He does things like this often? Never mind, I don't want to know. Yes, with this I can pull him to me with enough drama to prevent thefts for the next decade."

My conscience wasn't thrilled with turning Tom over to an angry unknown sorceress, no matter how much he deserved it. "May I ask what will happen to him?" My fingers closed around the vial. "He's an idiot, but we did grow up together."

"The key is to discourage additional theft, so I tend to be more lenient than some past Guardians. I will strip him of his magic, but do nothing else to him." It honestly seemed like more of a chance than Tom deserved. I handed the vial to the Guardian.

"Will you lower the barrier now?"

"Yes, of course, but we need to set everything up first. I'm not just going to take him and slink away. I need an audience too, so everyone knows I created the barrier and that I can protect my Grove. Half of having power is knowing when you need to show it off and when to keep quiet about it."

"So we should have Clara gather Duke Gillingham and some other mages." Alex had apparently been following things pretty closely, despite missing the first part of the conversation.

"Perfect. Clara, you can break the barrier, which will be my cue to appear, grab this Tom and the flower, and leave dramatically. Your boyfriend seems pretty good at this."

Break the barrier? I thought I could, given a little time, but I really didn't want to have to do it in front of an audience. I'd never even tried something like this before. But knowing I just had to cut the thread to the template, it didn't seem impossible. I was the Enchantress of the Forest, after all.

"Okay, that should work," I said.

"Also, you'll have to change into something a little more dramatic. Torn elbows are not really as imposing as you might think," the Guardian scowled disapprovingly at my grubby clothes. I guess I'd have to do some shopping; dramatic wizard robes were not in my repertoire.

"Oh, she has something appropriate," interposed Alex. I looked at him in shock. "I had them made for you once you became the Enchantress; it seemed like you would need them sooner or later."

"Well, that's settled then. I'll go finish my lunch while you get the Duke and I'll wait for your signal. They're at the Hall of Justice, by the way. I was afraid I was going to have to try to talk to them myself." She sailed out of the room and back down the stairs.

In my new robes I did look like a powerful mage, and Duke Gillingham had sent me with a sizeable entourage while I took down the barrier. He wasn't willing to come himself, though. We circled around the castle until I saw where the thread attached, then I got off Cassie and approached the barrier. I held my hands up dramatically, and severed the line with one swipe of my power. The line dissolved into smoke, and the barrier froze in its last position. I had worried that cutting off the template wouldn't dissolve the barrier, and apparently I was correct. Luckily, I'd also finished my magic cheese from yesterday, so I had enough power to shoot a blast at the base of the nearest barrier bush. I formed the energy into the shape of fire, hoping that magic-fire could burn magic-bushes. From learning spells in the Enchanted Forest, I had lots of practice making spells look like the shapes I wanted.

The blast knocked me from my feet, and flattened my entourage as well. As I pushed myself up onto my elbows, I saw it was working. My spell was burning the barrier, leaving an opening through which we could see the castle. I sagged in relief.

A puff of smoke at the opening dissolved to reveal the Guardian holding her staff. "I have come to collect that which was stolen from me. Come here, thief." She closed her hand, and stood still as a statue. After five minutes that seemed an eternity, Tom stumbled out of the castle with most of the rest of the inhabitants on his heels. He still had a flower in his lapel. "You took that which I guard." She plucked the flower, and slipped it into her pocket. "For this theft, I will strip you of your magic." As she opened her hand, my magesight flickered on again for a second and I was nearly blinded by the sorceress' spell. I blinked back tears. The Guardian frowned and opened her hand more emphatically. A stream of small trinkets flew from Tom's pockets to the air in front of her, then dropped to the ground. "You have no magic. These charms are the only magic around you." She looked over at me. "I thought he was supposed to be a mage?"

Tom opened his mouth, but only managed to sputter. He looked around wildly, as if hoping someone would intervene. I stared at him with my magesight, and, with his charms gone, I couldn't see any magic on him. He must have been using premade charms whenever he claimed to be doing magic for years.

"Magic, reveal thyself!" the Guardian intoned, and the trinkets and several of the people from the castle glowed a gentle red. Based on my sleeve, I was glowing as well. There was no hint of a glow from Tom, and several of the other mages from the castle gasped.

"Tom, how could you?" asked a young woman with the

group from the castle, and burst into tears.

"Of course I have magic! Everyone knows I'm the best mage in the capital," Tom became even more frantic. The looks of shock on the onlookers' faces were fading into scowls and head shakes. The Guardian turned slightly and nodded at me before she slowly faded from sight.

Everyone started talking at once, and I figured I had fulfilled my part, so I passed out on the grass.

I escaped the hubbub of the capital as soon as I could, which was several days later. Alex had stayed with me, for which I was forever grateful, and had run interference when I couldn't take it anymore. He'd been strangely silent on the way back, though. We put the horses out in the field on his farm. I reached over and put a hand on his arm.

"Alex? Penny for your thoughts?" He put his hand over mine.

"It's all just a bit much...I'm glad you finally have recognition as the Enchantress, but I'm wondering how much that will change things."

I had been thinking about that on the ride back as well. "I don't think too much. I've definitely established that I don't want any part of court, and people think I'm too powerful to cross if I want to live in a tiny village. I may get a few more petitioners around here, but I think I can mostly do what I want. Powerful mages are entitled to a little eccentricity." Alex searched my eyes, then leaned in and kissed me. I closed my eyes and kissed him back.

"I definitely think you should stay in this tiny village. People would miss you terribly if you left."

"People?"

"Me. I'd miss you so much, I'm not sure I can let you leave now." He kissed me again.

Some time later, I stowed my magical supplies back in my hideout and went to check on Margot. My magesight was still turning on unexpectedly, and it did so again as I came up to her.

And something must have changed when I amplified my powers, because I could see, clear as day, the tiny shunt of magical energy inside her. I'd never been able to pick out anything before, but now I could see soft runes lining her stomachs and udder. They were very subtle, but having seen them I could remove them. Turning her into a normal cow would mean that I didn't need this elaborate setup to protect her any more, and I wouldn't have to worry about her falling into the wrong hands. On the other hand, I was starting to feel like I knew enough magic to protect her and myself if needed. If I could break the shield of the Guardian of the Grove, surely I could take care of a cow. At least for now. I'd let the future worry about itself.

GUIDANCE COUNSELING

by Michael H. Payne

I've always loved Cluny, the squirrel sorceress. I hope that Michael will continue writing about her.

Michael H. Payne's short stories have appeared in places like *Asimov's SF* and the Writers of the Future contest collections while his poetry has shown up in *Silver Blade* and the Rhysling Award anthology. His novels have been published by Tor Books and Sofawolf Press, and his webcomics get updated Monday through Friday. He works at the local library, sings and plays guitar at the local Catholic church, hosts a Sunday afternoon radio program at the local university, and both writes and helps curate My Little Pony fanfiction for *Equestria Daily* and the *Royal Canterlot Library*. Check hyniof.com for links to various bits of it all.

No matter how often she scented it, the sour-salty stink of Crocker's fear still managed to curl Cluny's whiskers. "It's just—" Crocker's pace slowed as they reached the third floor landing of the cold and echoing back stairwell at Powell House. "We should probably tell Magister Gollantz," he murmured for what had to have been the seventeenth time that morning.

Very pointedly not digging her claws into the hem of her pocket along the front of Crocker's robes, Cluny also managed not to roll her eyes. "We'll be fine," she said.

Shtasith, stretching from shoulder to shoulder across the back of Crocker's neck, puffed twin gusts of steam through his scaly nostrils. "As much as it pains me to agree with the simian, my Cluny—"

"*What?*" She craned her head back to stare at the firedrake. "Magister Watts is one of the finest practitioners and theoreticians teaching at Huxley! Sophomores like us who aren't in Powell House don't usually stand a chance of getting on his schedule, and what happens? He sends us a note asking for a meeting!" She had to shrug. "And yes, we've been on different sides during certain debates that have come up over the past year, but—"

Crocker snorted. "You mean the way he insists a familiar is less valuable to a wizard than a sturdy pair of boots? Or d'you mean the way he thinks non-sapient animals deserve better treatment than familiars because animals show that they know their proper place by not talking back? Or d'you mean the way he was the loudest voice demanding I get set on fire when everybody thought I had two familiars?"

Cluny almost sent the tiniest possible jolt along the link the three of them shared, but that would've been the exact *opposite* of helpful in this particular discussion. "I mean that we can't ignore him and hope he'll go away." And because she was almost certain their conversation was being monitored, she fell back onto the cover story they'd put together to hide the truth about their unprecedented relationship. "Of course, you're the wizard here, Crocker, so the final decision on what we do is entirely up to you." She fixed her gaze on him in what she hoped was a meaningful fashion.

He blinked down at her, then his eyes went wide and shifted from side to side as if looking for eavesdropping spells. "Of course," he said, a swallow convulsing his throat.

She nodded: he really was getting better at picking up her hints. "But remember," she went on, "there's nothing really bad Magister Watts can do to us that won't get him censured by half the faculty. And if he maybe wants to clear the air between us, that's all for the good, don't you think?" Switching her gaze to Shtasith, she brought out the argument she'd thought up to use on him during the walk over here from Huahuo House. "We've turned enemies to allies before, and it's always made our position stronger in the end, hasn't it?"

The resistance of her familiars hummed at the link they shared like a musical note almost too quiet to hear. Then Crocker sighed, and their collective flow of power smoothed out. "That's why we keep you around, Cluny," he said, stroking his thumb through the fur between her ears. "We all need a little dose of squirrel sense every once in a while."

"Indeed," Shtasith said quietly, then he whapped the flat side of his barbed tail against the dark curly hair above Crocker's ear. "Make haste, therefore, simian! We ought not to keep the magister waiting!"

"You, on the other hand—" Crocker flicked a finger through the spikes along the side of the little dragon's head. "I'm pretty sure any random burlap sack full of acorns would prove just as useful around here as you do." And he started up the next set of stairs.

"Ha!" More steam gusted from Shtasith. "Any self-respecting sack of acorns would refuse to work under the conditions through which I'm forced to suffer!"

Smiling, Cluny settled back and let the sound of their bickering wash over her. Yes, her guys could get a little annoying now and then, but not even her parents' nut farm felt as much like home as this pocket did these days.

They quickly reached the fourth floor, and Crocker pushed through the door into the hallway outside the rooms of Powell House's resident mage. That was something Cluny had always admired about Magister Watts—maybe the *only* thing now that she thought about it. Yes, he was one of the most powerful and influential wizards in Pel Laugos, but he'd remained RM here, living and working with upcoming students of sorcery, for more than a hundred years. And while the philosophy of life and magic that he passed on to those students was one that Cluny found to be largely abhorrent, still, she couldn't help but send a little grudging respect in his general direction.

Crocker plodded across the industrial gray carpet to a door that was only distinguished from the others farther down the hallway by the sign on it: *Cyrus Watts, Resident Mage.* That sour-salty stink rustled Cluny's whiskers once more. "Last chance to run for it," Crocker muttered.

Cluny let herself sigh. "Do you want *me* to knock?"

"Fine." Blowing out a breath of his own, Crocker raised a hand and tapped softly.

"Enter!" a thin voice called from the other side, and Cluny's resolve failed: a few flicks of her ears and whiskers set several low-level defensive spells to humming around the three of them.

Not that she was worried, of course, but, well, everything they'd been through during their frosh year—not to mention the whole adventure two weeks ago just getting Esteemed Tadon and his wizard to finally start listening to each other—it had all taught Cluny the importance of being prepared.

Squaring his shoulders, Crocker took the doorknob and turned it, pushed the door open, and carried them all into a short corridor. A similar door stood closed at the other end, but what drew Cluny's attention were the twelve identical wooden coat racks spaced evenly along the walls—six on each side, none of them holding a coat or a hat or any other article of clothing that she could see.

"Straight ahead, Sophomore Crocker." Magister Watts's voice had always rubbed Cluny's fur the wrong way, like he was setting a trap with each word and waiting to gloat when his listeners fell in. "I've attuned my defensive spells to the ones you've just activated so you should have no difficulty walking my little gauntlet."

"Thank you, sir," Crocker called back. He swallowed loud enough for Cluny to hear it, then made his way toward the other door as gingerly as a cat crossing damp grass.

Concentrating, Cluny could just make out lines of force weaving back and forth across the hall and among the coat racks, but whatever spells might be spinning along those threads proved too subtle for her to untangle. Shtasith hissed quietly above her, and Cluny gave a swallow of her own, all the assurances she'd been dishing out to her familiars a few moments ago echoing a little hollowly in her head.

But they passed the last pair of coat racks without anything exploding or even bursting into flame. Cluny hadn't felt a single prickle against the edges of her defensive spells, either, and she couldn't help wondering if the trap this time had been that there really *wasn't* a trap...

Stepping up to the door at the end of the corridor, Crocker

reached for it—

And *then* everything exploded, the walls whisking away with a whoosh that struck Cluny like a gust of sudden wind. Gasping, she gaped at the room now surrounding them, an office nearly as large as Magister Gollantz's. Packed bookcases lined three of the walls from floor to ceiling, but in all her life Cluny had never seen a more meticulously arranged and perfectly aligned collection, each shelf highlighted by the sparkling geodes and dust-free figurines and little water-filled jars with creatures swimming inside that served as book ends. The wall ahead seemed to be just a giant window, and even though the curtains were drawn, light poured through so sharply, Cluny had to squint.

"I *suppose* that will do," Magister Watts said from somewhere within the wall of light, Cluny's eyes adjusting till she could make out a large, carved-oak desk just in front of the window. A slight shadow behind the desk resolved into the scarecrow-thin figure of the magister himself, his elbows resting on a blotter pad and his fingertips pressed together in front of his hatchet-like nose. "Come in, Sophomore Crocker, and sit. There's a matter we need to discuss."

"Yes, sir," Crocker more hiccupped than said, but Cluny was glad that he retained enough presence of mind to stump the rest of the way across the room to the simple, square-back chair that faced the desk.

More details emerged from the brightness as Crocker settled himself, the desk completely empty except for a thin wooden post with a small crossbeam at the top sticking up near Magister Watts's right elbow. Perched on this stand, the slightest possible barn swallow cocked her head, Eulalie so gray and wispy, Cluny always thought she looked like a ghost.

"I'll get straight to the point," Magister Watts said, sitting back in his chair. "Your brother, Captain Lionel Crocker of Her Majesty's Navy, has recently become engaged to Crown Princess Alison, has he not?"

"Captain?" Crocker blinked. "Isn't Lionel a lieutenant?"

Magister Watts's eyes narrowed. "I'll not be played for a

fool, Sophomore Crocker."

"*You*, sir?" The shrug Crocker gave was so small, his shoulders barely moved. "I'm the fool, I'd hafta say. I mean, not even knowing what rank my brother is?"

Shtasith's sigh sounded like a winter wind through a broken casement. "The news outlets reported your brother's promotion from lieutenant commander to captain a good two weeks ago."

"Huh." Another blink, and Crocker nodded. "Well, good for Lionel. He deserves it."

The following silence filled the room almost to overflowing, the magister's eyes still narrow. Then Eulalie shook herself on her perch, and Magister Watts shook his head. "All that aside," he said, his voice somehow even drier and crisper than before, "Princess Alison is recruiting for a new personal mage." His eyebrows practically crackled. "You were aware of *that*, I believe?"

"Yes, sir." Crocker slumped a little behind Cluny, and she couldn't keep from slumping a little herself. She and Crocker and Shtasith had been right there at Crocker's family estate when Beatrice Elaro, Princess Alison's former mage, had tried to kill Lady Hesper, the unicorn who was the temporary dean of Huxley's Healing Arts Department, after Hesper had petitioned the princess to become the department's permanent dean. And considering how hard Magister Watts had fought last month during his unsuccessful effort to get even Hesper's temporary status rescinded, Cluny couldn't imagine this conversation heading anywhere good.

"Well." Magister Watts's thin lips twitched, but it looked to Cluny more like an involuntary muscle contraction than a smile. "Then you'll see, I think, why you're the perfect person to convince Hesper to send Princess Alison her résumé."

Cluny managed to keep her gasp from becoming audible, but Shtasith's rang out like a bugle call. "*You?*" the firedrake shouted. "Suggesting *this?* You've opposed Lady Hesper at every conceivable turn! How can you possibly—!"

"Sophomore Crocker!" Magister Watts's sallow complexion was quickly reddening. "I did not invite you here to bandy words with the specimens of your peculiar menagerie!"

Crocker's slump straightened. "Sorry, sir." He stood. "But if you're gonna talk to *me*, then you're gonna talk to *them*. We're a partnership—you might wanna look that word up someday when you get the chance."

"You miserable little snip!" Magister Watts surged to his feet. "I'm offering your precious Hesper a way out of this unconscionable situation she's created—the only *possible* way out, as a matter of fact! It disgraces the entire wizarding profession to have that animal scampering about, pretending to run a school at this university! That she has ensnared certain weak-minded but powerful individuals into supporting her cause, I cannot deny, but—!"

Eulalie gave a single chirp from her perch, but it pierced Cluny's ears like a dart. She felt Crocker wince behind her, and Magister Watts froze, his mouth still open. Then he drew in a breath, touched a fingertip to Eulalie's head, and said in an almost normal tone, "You're correct as usual, my pet. I'm letting my passionate nature once again overwhelm my reason." Something close to an actual smile creased his face. "Wonderful creatures, aren't they, Sophomore Crocker? As extensions of our will, familiars are truly incomparable."

Cluny's fur wanted to bristle, wanted to send her leaping into a hover above the magister's desk so she could tell him in great and studious detail just how wrong he was in everything he thought about the wizard/familiar relationship. But instead she tightened her grip on the hem of her pocket and said, "Crocker? Maybe we should sit down and hear what Magister Watts is actually proposing?"

Crocker didn't move, the usual quilt-soft warmth of his magic around hers as itchy as a cheap woolen blanket.

Magister Watts's face tightened for an instant, then that tricky sort of sharpness came into his gaze again. "What was the phrase you used in the stairwell earlier, Sophomore? 'A little dose of squirrel sense'?"

Another moment of silence, then Crocker slowly settled himself back into the chair, Magister Watts doing the same into his. "In short," the magister said, "I will guarantee not a single voice raised in opposition from any member of the faculty or staff here at Huxley should Hesper apply for the position of Princess Alison's personal mage. I and others of my coalition are even prepared to write glowing letters of recommendation that we ourselves will read aloud to any board of inquiry or Parliamentary committee in support of the proposition." A whiff of his usual sourness came back into his scent. "She is, in fact, ideally suited to the job, and as it will get her off this campus, it's a winning solution for all."

"Huh." Crocker folded his arms just below Cluny's pocket. "She's really got you rattled, hasn't she?"

The magister's jaw clenched. "I've said my piece." Standing, he held out a finger, and Eulalie flapped from her perch to settle on it. "That a squirrel seems to understand while you don't, I think, speaks volumes for your own mental acuity, so let me give you the advice you toss so freely at others: listen to your familiar." He shrugged. "Or whatever that creature is to you." Fire flared around the hand without the barn swallow in it. "You can show yourself out."

The air swirled, Cluny's whiskers prickling, and she caught a haughtily narrow-eyed glare from Eulalie as the walls of the little corridor slammed back into place around them, Crocker still sitting in the chair facing the closed door.

"Thank you, sir," Crocker called out, pushing himself to his feet. "So glad we could have this little chat," he mumbled too softly, Cluny thought, for any spell to have picked up.

Still, she kept all her defensive measures simmering as Crocker turned, marched them back to the other door, and pushed it out of the way. None of them said a word till they'd descended the stairs and left Powell House, the scattered clouds of a late October Saturday morning weaving patches of blue across the sky and puddles of sunlight across the flagstones.

"The willow?" Cluny asked when she felt they were safely out of range. Looking up, she saw both her familiars nod, so she flexed her claws and carried them away to their favorite spot in the depths of Eldritch Park, the semi-wild woodland at the center of campus.

The sky vanished behind the branches that suddenly spread overhead, the mossy scent and quiet trickle of the little stream behind them stroking Cluny's whiskers. His boots squishing, Crocker stepped forward, brushed aside the branches of the big willow tree, and ducked through. Cluny leaped from her pocket, landed in the slightly damp dirt, and scampered over to the stone she liked to perch on when they were all in here.

Shtasith, however, threw himself from Crocker's shoulder and began dashing in circles around the entire clearing below the willow's canopy. "The base ignominy!" he shouted in his nasally little voice. "I announce that that human has hereby taken sole possession of the spot at the top of my list of those to whom I am sworn to demonstrate the joys of immolation!"

Cluny sighed. "No setting anyone on fire, Shtasith," she said more out of duty in this case than anything else.

"He is arrogant!" Shtasith swooped and spun. "He is conniving! He is insufferable! And most infuriating of all?" Diving toward where Crocker was settling himself against the base of the tree, Shtasith pulled up, folded his wings, and dropped like a black and gold dagger onto Crocker's knee. "He is absolutely correct!"

"What?" Crocker blinked at the firedrake. "You think Hesper should go work for Princess Alison?"

"Of course!" Green and blue sparks began flickering in Shtasith's solid black eyes. "Can you not envision the pageantry? The princess bedecked in white and gold, Lady Hesper prancing along at her side like laughter made visible?" His mouth went sideways, and he smacked his tail against Crocker's thigh. "But I forget that I'm speaking to one who possesses less imagination than the average potato."

With a snort, Crocker poked a finger at Shtasith's chest. "Y'know what I don't hafta imagine, Teakettle? The way Hesper's face just plain lights up when she talks about teaching classes. And you don't hafta imagine it either 'cause I know you've seen it the same as I have."

Batting a wing at Crocker's hand, Shtasith turned to Cluny

just as she'd been afraid he would. "Surely, my Cluny, you can see how important this would be to our cause. After Jorvik declared himself to be her familiar, Lady Hesper became a mage in all but title. So if Princess Alison were to bestow upon her the crown's seal of approval—"

"I know, I know." Cluny didn't try to stop her tail from frizzing. "But Crocker's right, too. I mean, we all heard Hesper pretty much turn down the offer—she even suggested the princess consider us, remember? And after how hard she fought in the Academic Senate to keep her position here..." She sighed. "It would be so great if she wanted to do it. But I don't think she does."

Branches rustled all around, but behind her, two quiet chimes went off, the first one higher than the second. Cluny's ears twisted, and she looked over her shoulder at the willow's drooping skirt. She'd heard that sound before, hadn't she?

Another pair of chimes, and Crocker covered his face with his hands. "What do they want *this* time?" he groaned.

Through the veil of leaves, Cluny could see a silver bubble the size of a pumpkin bobbing slowly in place: a calling sphere, she realized, a very expensive sort of communication spell that wouldn't respond to anyone except the party it had been sent to find. The only other one she'd ever seen had drifted into their dorm room last year so Crocker's parents could yell at him about his adventures giving the family the wrong kind of publicity, so... "Do you want us to go?" she asked.

He shook his head. "This'd be doubly awful without you guys." Blowing out a breath, he rose to his feet, Shtasith taking wing to land on Crocker's shoulder and wrap his tail gently around the back on his neck. He took the three steps from the willow's trunk to its canopy so slowly, the bells went off two more times before he even got there, and when he reached for the sphere, his frown made Cluny think of her father back on the nut farm when he had to head up into the treetops to deal with walnut blight.

"Okay." Crocker tucked the sphere under his arm and moved back to his seat among the willow's roots. "Smiles, everyone."

Cluny leaped from her stone to scramble up into her pocket and gave as big a grimace as she could manage while Crocker set the sphere on his knees and poked it. "Hi!" he said, his voice dripping with phony cheerfulness. "You've reached Crocker, Shtasith, and Cluny! We can't come to the sphere right now, but if you leave a message—"

"Terry?" a male human voice said, and the bubble's silver surface cleared to show the genuinely smiling face of Crocker's older brother. "If you were any more of a nut, Cluny would've cracked you open months ago."

"Lionel!" Crocker sat forward, everything about him brightening. "How are you? What's going on? And why didn't you tell me you were a captain now?"

Somehow, Lionel's smile got even more genuine. Tall and lean and laughing where Crocker was more squat and chubby and self-effacing, Crocker's brother rubbed Cluny's fur very much the right way though he'd never actually scratched her behind the ears, she realized with a start. She needed to look into fixing *that* situation sooner rather than later...

Shtasith puffed from Crocker's shoulders. "Forgive him, Captain. Your brother's keeper I may be, but alas, he maintains a certain level of stolidity that even I cannot penetrate when it comes to matters outside the realm of his studies."

"Hey, now." The image of Lionel raised a finger and shook it. "No 'captain' here, Shtasith. We're all family, right?"

The fiery tendrils that connected Shtasith's magic to hers did a giddy little dance, and Cluny had to force herself not to giggle. "Of course, Lionel!" the firedrake crowed. "I fear our mutual simian's stolidity is somewhat catching."

Crocker flicked Shtasith in the head again. "So c'mon! Spill! What's up? Or are you chasing me down with a calling sphere just to hear the Teakettle's latest comedy routine?"

Lionel shrugged. "You gotta admit: he's pretty funny."

"What's that?" Crocker grabbed the sphere in both hands and shook it. "I think you're breaking up. Maybe you better call back."

"All right! All right! Sheesh!" When Crocker set the sphere

back down, Lionel was trying to look annoyed, but Cluny could see that it was another form of banter. "If you're gonna be like that, maybe I *won't* invite you and your friends to the ceremony tonight."

Shtasith practically flowed down the front of Crocker's robes. "It's a secret wedding, isn't it? You and Crown Princess Alison are to declare your loving vows before a privileged few beneath the silver light of the autumn moon!" He sighed, and Cluny could almost see little hearts spinning in the steam he vented.

"Uhhh, no." Lionel's blank expression was almost as funny as Shtasith's dreamy one. "Ali's gonna be officially pinning my captain's bars on me aboard the *Undaunted* while five dozen or so of the realm's biggest wigs try not to get seasick even though we'll be as thoroughly docked as the ship's ever been." His nonchalance became just a little bit forced, Cluny's whiskers prickling. "We thought maybe the three of you might like to attend along with, say, Lady Hesper and her new familiar."

All the dreaminess left Shtasith's face, but Crocker clapped his hands. "Well, yeah! Sure! That'd be great! I mean, we'll hafta check with Hesper, but I'm sure she—"

"Forgive me," Shtasith said, a rumble in his voice. "But might there be a pretext underlying this gracious invitation?"

Crocker snapped a glare down at Shtasith, but Lionel just gave another little shrug. "One thing the navy's taught me is to embrace efficiency. We'd love to see you guys, and if Ali can make her pitch to Hesper at the same time—"

"What?" Crocker's glare became a stare when he aimed it at his brother. "You...you mean the princess's search for a personal mage? That's what this is all about?"

"No, Terry." Lionel suddenly looked more like Crocker than Cluny had thought possible. "It's about having my brother and his two nearest and dearest there when I take a big step forward in my life. And if Ali also gets a chance to ask Hesper to join her court, that's a plus, isn't it?"

His forehead ever so slightly wrinkled, Crocker didn't say anything. So Cluny did. "Can I ask, Lionel: how many times has the princess offered Hesper the position?"

"Officially, she hasn't." Even through the filter of the calling sphere, Cluny could feel the intensity of Lionel's gaze. "She broached the subject just after Beatrice was arrested, then again when Hesper had recovered enough to leave Mom and Dad's place. Hesper said she'd think about it, but that was two months ago, and all the other candidates Ali's been looking at, well, none of them are unicorns, are they?" A bit of his smile came back. "Ali's not big on intrigue and drama, so if Hesper says no, then we don't need to let anyone know we even asked. But if she says yes, then we can start wheels turning to smooth over some of the major rough spots before we—"

"Magister Watts," Crocker said, shuddering a little. "We just talked to him, like, five minutes ago. He said no one in his coalition—whatever *that* means—will oppose Hesper becoming Princess Alison's mage. He even said they'd write letters of recommendation for her."

Lionel's eyebrows went up, and Cluny could almost smell his thoughts cascading like a waterfall. "That could be either good or bad," he said after several heartbeats.

Crocker sighed. "Let's call it good for now and move on." He straightened against the willow's trunk. "So you send us an invitation with where and when and make sure it's got a 'plus one' on it. We'll tell Hesper what's really going on, and if we show up tonight without her, that'll be a straight-up 'no.' If she's with us, though, that'll mean either 'yes' or 'maybe,' and the princess can take it from there."

Shtasith was blinking at Crocker. "You know how I dislike it, simian, when you force me to revise my poor opinion of you."

Cluny had to giggle, Crocker poking Shtasith's scaly side and asking, "That sound good to everyone?"

His gaze flickered down to Cluny's, and she gave a tiny nod as Lionel answered, "That'll be great, Terry, and I've already got the invitation set to drop right out of the sphere when I end the call." His smile came back full force. "It'll be great seeing you all tonight, too, no matter what else happens."

"You, too, Lionel," Crocker said, his voice firmer than it had been all week.

The image of Lionel raised a hand, swiped it sideways, and the sphere popped to reveal a card with gold-embossed lettering. Shtasith grabbed it with his front claws before it could even begin to fall, but Crocker, clearing his throat, took it between his thumb and forefinger. "*I'm* the social director around here, Teakettle." He looked down at Cluny. "We should probably call Hesper before we pop into her front room, right?"

"Ah, yes." Shtasith's steam this time was greenish and smelled of overripe cabbage. "Behold our social director."

Another giggle, and Cluny twitched a pulse from her whiskers into the aether along the twisty little path she'd come to know so well from the messages she and Hesper had been sending back and forth all summer.

The pulse returned almost immediately, a scent of lilacs and a golden glimmer at the corner of her eye telling Cluny that Hesper was bidding her good morning and asking her how she was. Cluny took a deep breath of the little glade beneath the willow and puffed it along the link.

Again, the reply came back quickly: the sound of happy clapping and a fleeting taste of hastily gobbled oatmeal across her tongue. "Actually," Cluny barely had time to say before the greenish light out by the stream went all spattery like a beam of sunlight had somehow squiggled through the branches to shine directly onto the flowing water, "they're coming over here."

The silvery specks flocked together, settled to the rocks, and became Hesper, as delicate as a snow-white yearling gazelle, her golden horn spiraling from her forehead. A black cloud drifted up from her, though, swirled and grew to at least twice her size before solidifying into Jorvik, the barghest's fiery eyes flickering, his tongue lolling from between too-sharp teeth in a canine smile.

"A marvelous idea!" Hesper declared, her voice tickling Cluny's ears like sweet crystal bells. "Saturday in the park!" Trotting forward, she nosed the willow branches aside, and the whole area underneath took on a warmer glow. "I was just remarking to Jorvik that, other than our Tuesday night salons, we weren't getting out and about nearly enough."

Jorvik loped in behind her, and the squirrellier parts of Cluny's brain jittered as usual at the sight of the big smoky wolf monster. "My innate honesty," he said, his brogue somehow both lilting and growling, "compels me to report that Her Ladyship was in fact splayed despondently across her red satin cushion and lamenting the ennui that was enveloping the very core of her being at the thought of having no classes today."

Hesper turned narrowed eyes on the barghest. "As a former familiar myself, Jorvik, I know that you have an obligation to puncture your wizard's ego whenever it needs puncturing. In certain cases, however—"

"Well, now." Jorvik sat back on his haunches. "Are you finally prepared to properly call yourself a wizard, Milady?"

Somehow, Hesper's eyes got even narrower. "You know as well as I do that the current political climate here on campus is not at all conducive to me using that term."

"Oh, aye." The growl behind Jorvik's words became much more pronounced. "Or rather, I know that you've a fear of laying claim to what you've earned."

"Ummm..." Cluny unleashed her most ostentatious teleportation spell, puffing herself away from Crocker's pocket in a crackling shower of sparks to plop down into the dirt beside Hesper and Jorvik with a burst of cotton candy scented smoke. "That's actually what we'd like to talk to you about."

"Really?" Hesper looked down her snout at Cluny and gave a dainty sneeze that dispelled every trace of candy scent. "You'd also enjoy discussing my fears, Sophomore?"

"Not your fears," Cluny said, gesturing with a claw for Crocker to come forward. "Your hopes, maybe, or your dreams."

She heard him scoot up behind her. "There's a party tonight for my brother," he said, and the invitation drifted over Cluny's head in the surprisingly solid light of his levitation spell. "Princess Alison wants us to invite you to come so she can ask you to become her personal mage."

Hesper's ears flicked, but she didn't say anything; her hornglow just took the card, Jorvik towering up to peer over her shoulder. Cluny watched both their eyes move as they read it, realized she was holding her breath, tried not to make a big whoosh when she blew the breath out, ended up making a weird whistling noise instead, and—

"I see," Hesper said, still looking at the invitation.

"Excuse me?" Jorvik flowed around her like a fog bank and resolidified in front of her with an eyebrow arched. "As a relative newcomer to this particular section of the Mortal Realm, I might be misunderstanding the situation, but this all strikes me as worth a bit more of a comment than 'I see.'"

"Does it?" Hesper's light had become as cold as winter stars. "Then perhaps you shouldn't flaunt your ignorance."

Jorvik's hackles rose, Hesper's horn lit up, and Cluny's whiskers frizzed at the touch of a teleportation spell.

"Wait!" Cluny jumped forward, pressed her paws to Hesper's fetlock and kept her gaze fixed on the unicorn's narrow eyes. "Hesper, please! We're your friends here! We want to help! It's a big decision, sure, but—"

"No." Tight and flat, Hesper's voice had nothing of bells left in it. "It's not any sort of a decision at all. Because I can't leave Huxley."

"Truly, now?" The sharp and pungent air around Jorvik made Cluny imagine a thunderstorm trying to hold its lightning in. "It's a fine gig: I'll not gainsay you that. But Hesper! Mage to the future Queen of Pel Laugos! You'd be in a position to—"

"No!" Hesper shouted it this time, then squeezed her eyes closed, her other forehoof gently touching Cluny's paws. "The future of Pel Laugos," she went on more quietly but through clenched teeth, "is *here.* The wizards Huxley trains will guide the realm no matter who's on the throne. So how can I abandon them to Watts and his stultified cronies?" Her eyes opened shimmering, their anguish tightening Cluny's throat. "How?"

Unsure it would help, Cluny offered the first answer that came to mind. "Magister Gollantz and Magistrix Ippolitov and the other good professors will still be here. But only you can be the princess's mage."

"And," Shtasith offered, "the Court Mage maintains a certain statutory authority over Huxley's operations. Few in the past have exercised that authority, but it does exist."

Behind her, Cluny heard Crocker shift where he sat in the dirt. "Change is always scary. But, well, sometimes scary's good." His shrug was almost loud enough for Cluny to hear.

Hesper blew out a breath and patted Cluny's paws. "Thank you, all of you." The invitation drifted in front of her again, and she nodded at it. "I suppose I should hear the princess out at least. So, sophomores, I'll see you at seven at my place." She stood and turned. "Jorvik? Come argue with me."

"A pleasure, Milady." A fiery wink, and he puffed into a cloud of smoke, wafting away in the direction of the silver sparkles fading to green outside the willow's canopy.

"Well, then," Cluny made herself say after a moment. "We'd better get our homework finished."

Which was normally her favorite thing to do, of course, but just before noon, Crocker, beside her at their desk working on his own paper, tapped her page and asked, "I thought ameliotides *did* contribute to priozine production."

Cluny blinked up at him, blinked back at her assignment, winced at the complete gibberish she'd been writing, and called for a study break. They had a leisurely lunch downstairs in the Huahuo House cafeteria, then fell into a bout of hoverball with a group of other students.

Neither she nor her guys were very good at the game—Cluny always found herself worrying so much about defense that she never took any actual shots; Crocker's aim was so bad, the only points he ever made were completely accidental; and Shtasith seemed to think every sport was a blood sport. But it filled a couple hours with laughing and shouting and running around, and Cluny still had time to rewrite the page she'd lost control of earlier before it was time for them to wash up, get dressed, and pop over to Hesper's house.

The gentle mid-autumn evening draping down from the trees that surrounded the little cottage off Berryman Lane gave a restful air to the place, and while the unicorn and the barghest stood on the front porch waiting, Cluny had known them too long to be fooled. Hesper tap-tap-tapping the wooden deck at one end of the porch and Jorvik's cloudiness roiling soundlessly at the other showed that their argument hadn't resolved anything. Even Crocker apparently noticed, not clapping his hands or spouting any sort of joking comment as he carried the three of them up the little path from the sidewalk where they'd appeared.

"So," Cluny said since *somebody* had to break the silence. "Are we all still going?"

Hesper's sigh seemed to come all the way up from her fetlocks. "Yes. But only to insure domestic tranquility." She shot a glare at Jorvik.

He just got to his paws and padded across the porch, his blank expression very out of place on his usually lively face.

Another sigh from Hesper. "Have you the invitation, Sophomore?" she asked.

"Yes'm," Crocker replied, and Cluny felt one of Hesper's sweetly compact teleportation spells enveloping her. The dark of the quiet cul-de-sac whisked away, and Cluny blinked at a flood of magelight, winced at a burst of voices and a blare of trumpets. Empty pavement spread out to their left and right, crowds of people standing behind the glowing yellow filaments of a security fence and flashing camera pods at them.

The air crackling at her whiskers, Cluny hung on as Crocker turned, a line of Royal Guard soldiers interspersed with mages facing them from in front of a long wall of steel and cement so heavily enchanted, it felt like a hand pushing against Cluny's face. In the wall past the soldiers, a gate stood open, sparks dancing along its every strut and bracing, a red carpet running up the walkway through it.

A shiver iced Cluny's spine. Hesper had just teleported them more than a thousand miles, straight from Huxley Grove to the Admiralty Gate at Port Lomax, with barely a flicker of her horn. And still the unicorn pranced as light as dandelion fluff toward the center of the guard line, Jorvik padding along behind. "Come along, Sophomore Crocker," she called, her voice once again all butterflies and daffodils. "I expect someone among these fine constables will wish to see our invitation."

Crocker lurched forward, but an older woman stepped from the center of the line, the insignia on the sleeves of her purple robe telling Cluny that she was one of Queen Dorothy's personal mages. "No need for that, Magistrix Hesper," the woman said with a smile and a bow. "We were told to be prepared should you and Esteemed Jorvik accompany Sophomore Crocker and his ensemble."

"Thank you." Hesper gave a bow of her own. "We've not met, Magistrix Falco, but the stories I've heard of you inspire the best sorts of thrills and chills."

Cluny swallowed. Her senses still ringing from the light and the noise, she hadn't recognized Luciana Falco: not just one of Queen Dorothy's personal mages but *the* Court Mage of all Pel Laugos. So what was she doing out here with the guards at the front gate?

Waiting for her possible colleague and successor, Cluny realized, and that made her swallow again. She'd also called Hesper 'magistrix' rather than just 'lady' and had given Jorvik the proper title for a senior supernatural familiar, but Cluny barely had time to register those facts before Magistrix Falco was directing that penetrating gaze toward her. "Sophomores Crocker and Shtasith and Cluny," she said, and Cluny's throat went so dry, swallowing seemed like a distant memory. "I've heard a great deal about you from a variety of sources."

"Sorry, ma'am," Crocker mumbled, his face downcast.

Shtasith, however, slid from Crocker's shoulder into a gentle hover before Magistrix Falco. "There are few humans to whom I've honestly said this since arriving in the Mortal Realm, Magistrix, but it is an absolute honor and privilege to meet you." He bowed his long snaky neck.

Shaking away as many layers of shock as she could, Cluny managed to bow from her pocket, and the wink she got back from Magistrix Falco made her wonder if Magister Gollantz had shared Cluny's secret with the sorceress. But then Magistrix Falco was spreading her arms, honey-colored lightning flashing from her fingers. "With your permission," she said, "I'll take us directly to the festivities aboard the *Undaunted*."

"That would be lovely," Hesper said. "I know Jorvik was very concerned about a long walk ruining his pedicure."

"Ah, yes," Jorvik rumbled, the first words he'd said all evening. "We barghests are such slaves to proper couture."

Everything flashed, Magistrix Falco's spell nearly as silken as Hesper's, and Cluny found herself blinking at the masts and rigging of the large ship that had sprung into being around them, the sails furled and bound up so the night sky showed clear and starry overhead. To her left—or to port, she supposed she should say considering where they were—a pier glowed under much softer magelights than had struck her at the front gate, and the darkness to starboard held nothing but a string of shining spots that she guessed marked the breakwater separating the naval base from the rest of Lomax Bay.

Ahead on the ship's foredeck milled a chattering crowd of fancily dressed people—humans and humanoids, mostly, elves, gnomes, dwarves and such—but the prickling of her whiskers drew her attention to Princess Alison at the front of the group, her Royal Prerogative shimmering invisibly. Forcing her focus to widen, Cluny saw Crocker's brother looking very handsome in his white uniform at the princess's side as well as Lord and Lady Crocker, self-satisfaction practically a scent around them. Here and there among the folks standing and moving between the buffet and the bar, Cluny also recognized a number of faces she knew from the gossip magazines Shtasith pored over every week.

Shtasith sighed behind her, and it was all she could do not to start giggling. A flap of dark wings in her peripheral vision, though, snapped her attention to a screech owl gliding onto Magistrix Falco's shoulder. "Ah," the owl said in a smooth baritone. "Our unofficial guests of honor."

Part of Cluny wanted to leap away from that curved beak and those attentive eyes, but the rest of her wanted to lean into the owl's crisp aura. Themistocles was probably the most famous familiar in all of Pel Laugos, and the thought that she might be able to talk with him—

The deck jostled then, and several things happened at pretty much the same time as far as Cluny could tell: a gasp cut through the murmuring of the guests; a silent magical crackle rose from every mage and guard on deck; and a roar bellowed from the darkness. Something long and sinuous and glimmering wetly lurched upward just off the ship's starboard bow, and when it roared again, sharp spiny teeth shone in the magelight from a mouth gaping nearly as wide as one of the buffet tables.

Magistrix Falco vanished from their side with a piercing whistle, and blasts of sorcery plastered the thing, no sort of sea serpent that Cluny recognized from the various bestiaries she'd read when Shtasith had first come into her and Crocker's life. None of the magic seemed to bother it in the slightest, either, its flailing head smashing down against the purple and red energy shield that had just now sprung up around the entire front part of the ship.

It squirmed, shrieked, and smashed again and again, the ship jouncing to send food and drink spilling and splashing across the deck despite the shock absorbing elements Cluny could see in the shield spells. That meant the creature had to be magically enhanced, and with no eyes, no spines, no scales, the more she looked at it, the more she thought—

"It's a worm!" she yelled, not sure who would hear with all the shouting, crashing, and screaming. "Some sort of enchanted annelid!" Praying to the Squirrel Mother that no one would notice, she cast an analysis spell. "The magic's so tangled, I can't tell what's at the base! Something powerful and—!"

"Yes," Hesper said, and the word hissed as sharp as a dagger. "I see it now. That's pain magic. It needs healing."

Cluny looked down, saw Hesper's horn flare as golden as the sun at midday. "With me, Jorvik!" she shouted, and the two of them burst from the deck to the area above the masts where Magistrix Falco and the other mages were spinning their defensive and offensive spells.

Another bash rocked the ship, Crocker crying out and almost tumbling sideways. "Fool!" Cluny heard Shtasith yell. "Employ levitation, or we'll be over the rail!"

Crocker raised shaky hands and started sketching a spell, but Cluny couldn't look away from Hesper and Magistrix Falco,

Jorvik floating behind them as a cloud darker than the night sky, Themistocles flying in circles around the group.

Magistrix Falco gave several whistles, and the blasts bouncing off the worm's skin from the mages on the deck all solidified into beams, wrapping around the worm not far below its head and stopping its upper portion from moving. It gave another roar, then Magistrix Falco thrust a hand toward the creature, a narrow purple tube of light spinning away from her fingers and stretching toward the worm's unnaturally massive jaws. Hesper, hovering beside the magistrix with Jorvik's cloud surrounding her, touched her horn to the tube, and golden sparkles rushed up it just as the tube brushed the worm's snout.

The worm's cry cut off, and Cluny could feel relief flooding the air like a cool breeze on a scorching day: Hesper dispersing the pain magic at the core of the transformation. Magistrix Falco's other hand came up, made a quick jerking motion, and the whole gigantic monster vanished, the sorceress unraveling the rest of the thing's enchantment so neatly, Cluny wished she'd been taking notes.

Then Themistocles was swooping forward, catching something in his claws, looping back with it to the others. A quick telescope spell zoomed the scene in, and Cluny watched the owl drop an oddly shaped but regular-sized worm into the little clear pouch Magistrix Falco was holding up.

After that, the ceremony itself, conducted on the dock rather than the ship, passed in a bit of a blur. Princess Alison pinned Lionel's bars to his uniform jacket while applause spattered from those dignitaries who'd decided to stay—quite of lot of them, Cluny was surprised to see—and when the princess then thanked Hesper for her quick assistance and asked if she'd consider becoming her personal mage, Cluny was again surprised, both that Hesper instantly said yes and that the announcement also got applause. The few frowns among those watching, Cluny figured, would lead to stories that either Hesper or the princess had staged the attack just to give the unicorn the job, but that didn't bother Cluny.

What bothered her was knowing who'd *actually* staged the

attack.

Fortunately, folks started exiting soon afterwards, and Hesper sought them out where Crocker had taken a position that Cluny couldn't help noticing was as far from his parents as possible. The unicorn was smiling, but her mane looked more than a little frazzled when she reared back and wrapped her forelegs around a startled Crocker. "Thank you all so much!" she said, stretching just a bit to touch a kiss to Cluny's cheek. "I still don't know about this, but I do know that you were right: I'm the only one who can do it."

She dropped to all fours, stepped back, and Cluny noticed a young man dressed in royal purple robes beside her. "This is Magister Mutembe," Hesper said. "He'll be seeing you home. The princess has asked me to assist in the investigation, but Jorvik and I will be calling upon you soon. Good-bye!"

Magister Mutembe took the trip back to Huxley at a more reasonable three hops, but Cluny was too busy putting a plan together to pay much attention. So as soon as the young mage had vanished into the night outside Huahuo House, Cluny said, "We've got one more stop to make."

"Huh?" Crocker asked.

"Please, my Cluny," Shtasith murmured. "Far be it from me to be the voice of reason among us, but—"

But Cluny was already raising her paws, was already popping them to the fourth floor of Powell House, was already picking at the impressive array of defensive spells around Magister Watts's office till she had a hole just large enough for her to squeeze through. "I'll do the talking," she said, setting the three of them down in front of the magister's desk, the window behind it dark now though the little jars on the bookshelves were glowing just enough to layer thick shadows over the walls and floor. "But be ready for anything."

Directing their combined magic, she deflected every injurious spell the room's wards hurled at them but let the silent alarms ring. Three, maybe four minutes, this went on, then she felt the space above the desk's chair warp, Magister Watts appearing in a dark red smoking jacket with Eulalie glaring from his shoulder. "There are those," he said, his words even more clipped than usual, "who would consider breaking into a professor's private office to be an offence worthy of suspension."

"True," Cluny said. "But then there are *also* those who would consider an attack upon the crown princess to be treason." She aimed a claw at the empty spot she'd already noticed on the end of the third bookshelf up in the second case to her left. "Or am I mistaken that you seem to have lost one of your little sea creatures, magister?"

"I see." Magister Watts was focused on Crocker, his anger fading from hot to cold against Cluny's whiskers. "And you've come alone to confront me about my alleged misdeeds, Sophomore? Or do you wish to argue that a gigantic worm could somehow threaten a party guarded by a dozen of the finest mages in the realm?"

"No, sir." It took some effort for Cluny to keep her tone steady, especially when the magister's gaze only darted down to meet hers before returning to Crocker's. "No confrontations. No arguments. We just thought you'd like to know that we're paying attention."

He opened his mouth, closed it, cocked his head, and lowered his gaze once more to Cluny's. "An excellent quality in a student," he said, and his thin lips pulled back into something that might've been a smile. "A pity you're not one, Miss Squirrel."

"My name's Cluny, sir." She gestured to her guys behind her. "I'll be at Huxley as long as Crocker and Shtasith are, and I'll be the one talking to you if it ever turns out we need to again."

"Indeed?" He bowed shallowly. "Then I shall look forward to many such fruitful discussions." Flicking his fingers, he shrugged. "Or 'nutful,' I suppose, would be a more appropriate adjective." With a yawn, he began fading into the darkness. "You can show yourself out, Sophomore Crocker. Or do you need a forest creature to do that for you as well?"

Silence for a long, long moment, then Crocker clicked his tongue. "So. We trash the place?"

Shtasith hissed. "You have but to say the word."

Sighing, Cluny just wanted to curl up somewhere warm and dry and not have to think for as many hours as she could manage. “What we do is keep our eyes open,” she said. “But for now, let’s go home.” And since Magister Watts was undoubtedly listening in, she added, “Please, Crocker?”

He pulled in a breath and blew it out. “I suppose.” She felt his power drawing on hers, straightened a few segments of the teleportation spell he was constructed, and let him carry them all away.

IN SMALL PACKAGES

by Mercedes Lackey

Swords may be impressive, but sometimes a dagger is much more useful, and the greatest heroincs start young.

Mercedes Lackey graduated from Purdue University in 1972 with a Bachelor of Science in Biology. This, she soon learned, along with a paper hat and a nametag will qualify you to ask "would you like fries with that?" at a variety of fast-food locations.

She had always written from her early teens and developed this hobby by writing fan-fiction for various amateur magazines. In the 1980s she met both Marion Zimmer and C.J. Cherryh, both of whom helped mentor her from amateur into professional writer. Her first book was published in 1985. Misty is approaching 100 books in print, and her foreign editions include Russian, German, Czech, Polish, French, Italian, Turkish, and Japanese. She is the author, alone or in collaboration, of the Heralds of Valdemar, Elemental Masters, Secret World Chronicles, 500 Kingdoms, Diana Tregarde, Heirs of Alexandria, Obsidian Mountain, Dragon Jouster, Bedlam Bards, Shadow Grail, and other series and standalone books. A night-owl by nature, she is generally found at the keyboard between 10 PM and 6 AM. For more information, see her website: www.mercedeslackey.com.

"What are you doing to that poor, innocent dagger?" asked Paul. "I thought you were pleased with Can Opener." "Can Opener," being, of course, the dagger in question. All of Vickie Nagy's other classmates in the swordsmanship class at St. Rhiannon's School had given their weapons impressive names, like "Adamant" and "Vigilant." Vickie had protested that weapons were tools, and there was no reason to give a tool a name, but when the others had insisted, she had named her dagger "Can Opener" and her sword "Tire Iron," and nothing would sway her from those decisions.

At the moment, she had the dagger on a stand on her magical

workbench in Paul's room. It was in Paul's room, because Paul had more space in his room than he needed. He had one of the four round tower rooms on this floor of the dormitory building. Like Paul it was preternaturally neat. All the windows filled it with light regardless of the time of day, and he had chosen to leave it painted the way he'd gotten it, warm tan walls with a stenciling of cream geometrics. Vickie didn't actually live here at the school, so she kept her workbench here, and because after that little incident where she bespelled his room to give the people who were going to trash it exactly what they had coming, no one ever bothered Paul *or* his room.

The dagger rested lightly on the two wooden, silk-insulated holders, squarely in the middle of a heavily-inscribed marble slab, and scribed into the slab around the holder were circle after circle of runic inscriptions all enclosed in a final, plain, silver-inlaid Closing-Circle. Vickie normally worked magic with minimal equipment, given that she was able to see magic as equations, and could take old spells apart and create new ones on the fly. But sometimes she went old-school, with censors and candles, and chants, and this time she was trying something new and wanted every possible reinforcement she could manage.

Paul, who also understood magic as numbers, eyed Can Opener dubiously. "I am not touching that," he declared.

"You shouldn't," she agreed, getting down at eye-level with the dagger and staring at it intently, looking for flaws in the equations before she made them permanent. "I should rename it 'Fisher King'."

"For the never-healing wound?" Paul replied, his black brows furrowing as he, too interpreted the magic that was there. "Why would you *do* this? Make a weapon that inflicts wounds that never heal?"

"Because sometimes you need something like that," she replied absently.

"For *what?* Cutting off the heads of a Hydra? Hydras are myths!" Paul protested.

"Are you sure?" she replied, and straightened. "Okay, maybe not fighting a Hydra," she conceded, tugging her brown knit shirt into place. “But there are metahumans my parents come up against that can heal themselves instantly and I’m pretty sure there are magicians out there that can armor themselves with spells that do the same thing. You see any flaws or loopholes?”

He shook his head, and nervously combed a hand through his raven hair, pushing it back off his forehead. “No.”

“All right then.” She sketched several signs in the air, the dagger glowed an eerie blue for a moment, then the glow faded. “That makes it permanent.” She picked it up carefully by the hilt and sheathed it in its proper home. Once again, dagger and sheath glowed for a moment, then faded.

“Do the teachers know you did that?” Paul asked, as she wrapped dagger and sheath in a silk scarf and put the bundle into her backpack.

“The teachers don’t know half of what I do with my parents, and my parents want it that way,” Vickie countered, and patted the backpack, feeling pleased with herself. “This is my ace. Big bad guys will look at a pint-sized girl with a puny little dagger and think I’m insignificant. Good things come in small packages.”

She shouldered the backpack and headed out, directly for the portal in the courtyard that would take her home. She was one of only three students at St. Rhia’s who didn’t actually live there. “See you tomorrow, Paul! Thanks for letting me use your room!”

Paul nodded, but as she turned to leave, she heard him mutter, “Not just good things. Lethal things.”

The moment that she came through the portal into the basement of the house in Virginia, she knew something big was up, because her mother was waiting there, dressed in what Vickie knew was her “traveling suit”; a tailored, yet slightly loose cotton twill blazer and matching slacks in a charcoal gray just a shade off from the Classic Black FBI Agent Suit everybody thought of when they thought “FBI Agent.”

“Where are you going?” she asked, “And am I coming?”

“Upper Michigan, I’ve packed your bag and called the school and yes,” Moira Nagy replied, deftly confining her mass of scarlet curls into a bun as she turned away from the portal and headed for the basement stairs. "This is going to be a long op, and we'll need you to keep the comms from blowing up on us."

Vickie followed her mother up the simple wooden stairs, her heart already racing. "What's the op?" she asked as Moira opened the door into the kitchen.

"Your father has the details, but it involves kids, a cult and the ECHO metas couldn't crack it, probably because whoever is running the cult is good enough to produce first-class cloaking spells." Moira pushed open the door into the living room; sure enough Vickie's two suitcases—one with clothing, the other with "working supplies" stood at the door with her mother's identical cases, the only difference being the color of the bag-tags. That meant Alex Nagy was already in the car.

A moment later, her bags joined her father's single bag in the back of the van. "Coach or do we actually get the plane?" she asked her mother without hope.

"We actually get the plane," her mother replied as she hopped in the back. Vickie suppressed a cheer. "Not many commercial flights where we're going, and Autumnal Equinox is coming up fast, so we're on the clock."

Vickie got in behind her father and all the *yes!* that she'd been feeling, knowing they were going to get the FBI private jet they shared with other special units drained away. She didn't yet know what it was her family was facing, but the mere fact that it involved the Autumnal Equinox was bad. This was the time of year when Light began to lose its fight against Shadow, when Darkness began its long winter siege of the Earth and all its creatures. Now, this was not necessarily a bad thing. Unfettered growth was as bad as unfettered death. All things had to be in balance, after all, and life in the spring, in everywhere that was not the tropics, required the cold sleep of winter.

But if something strengthened the Darkness at the crucial moment when the world tipped into the decline into winter....well, that meant that all things of Darkness were strengthened. Or—and potentially much worse—a magician would use that yearly tipping-point plus some special blood-sacrifice, as a way to add unstoppable momentum to his own power. And that, of course, was Trouble. A little trouble—well, they wouldn't be called in on something that looked like a "little" trouble. A great deal of trouble, now...well, that was what they were there for.

Here in Virginia the leaf-turning hadn't really started yet, but up in Maine, where St, Rhia's was, it was at its peak. Vickie felt sad that she was going to miss it; autumn was her favorite season up there. "Where are we going?" she asked from the rear seat, as her father deftly maneuvered the van through rush-hour traffic.

"Upper Michigan," he said shortly. Her mother handed a paper-clipped set of papers back to her without comment. Vickie's eyes widened at the top one. *Well, it's not every day we have to find a Senator's daughter.*

She knew better than to ask anything from her mother and father; her father was using every bit of his werewolf reflexes to move a van through traffic holes two sizes too small for it, and her mother was deep in her own briefing papers.

This evidently started out not at all routinely. The thirteen-year-old daughter of the Junior Senator from Michigan had been stranger-kidnapped out of her bedroom at midnight. The screen had been pulled out and the window levered open without anyone in the entire house waking up—including the family dog sleeping in her room. Nobody in the FBI could find an explanation for that—there were no traces of gas in the house, or drugs in their bloodstreams, but one of Moira's magical contacts had been able to get as far as the driveway and reported back that the entire house reeked of magic.

And why *this* girl and no other? Well, the contact was local to the area, and it was well known that the Senator and his wife were good Catholics who came from huge families, that the daughter was Number Seven in their tribe of girls, and the contact quickly established that her mother was the seventh daughter of *her* family...as was her grandmother.

That was enough to warrant a long-distance call to Moira's personal hotline. In essence, this time the case to bring in Division 39 had been established backwards, even before the FBI had been on the ground a day. It was Moira who had gone to the Director, rather than vice versa, and laid out the evidence.

This...was actually a good thing. Less than 24 hours had passed since the girl had been taken, and they were already on the way. Usually by the time they got involved, there were already bodies, the trail had been muddied, and the FBI metahuman division had been called in with nothing to show for it.

The bad thing, of course, was this was September 19. Three days to the Equinox. Not a lot of time.

On the other hand—if whoever took the girl knew nothing about Division 39, the four of them would start out with an advantage.

But don't count on it, she reminded herself. *Count on everything possible going wrong. The timing is on their side, whoever they are.*

The jet was kept on a small private airfield next to the training facility at Quantico—so at least they were mostly going in the opposite direction of traffic now.

She finished skimming the briefing papers, but there wasn't much there that applied to her. The first bit of this was going to depend on her father's nose, her mother's Sight, and her godfather's tracking skills.

So keep the comms running, watch and learn.

Her godfather, Raven Stormdance, was waiting beside the stairway into the tiny private jet. Division 39 shared it with Division 5 (FBI Metahuman), Division 6 (FBI Metahuman SVU), the special taskforce of specialist profilers, and whatever bigwigs couldn't bear to travel commercial. "I've loaded the gear," he announced as they got out of the van and her father handed off the keys to the waiting ramp agent who'd park it at the hanger for their return. By now the sun was on the horizon, but they'd be chasing it; figure three hours in the air, and they'd be touching down not long after eight or nine local time. "There's a rental waiting." Now he looked at Vickie. "Have you got your license yet?"

She didn't grin, because this really wasn't a situation that allowed for grinning; instead she nodded. "Last week. Although Mom did some document-fu and it says I'm eighteen, not fourteen."

Raven rolled his eyes. He didn't approve of lying. Moira shrugged. "She's a good driver, and it'll save us time." Vickie scrambled up the stairs, her parents and godfather followed.

The pilot did not bother with seatbelt announcements. He started rolling as soon as the stair retracted, and it was up to them to get their asses planted and buckled up before he aimed the nose of the plane for the North Star.

"We're setting down at a private airport just outside Newberry. That's on the edge of the Mackinaw National Forest," Raven told them. "Odds are, that's where our vic was taken, but I could be wrong. There's lots of land in private hands around the Forest that's just as wild. Not a lot to choose from in the way of lodging, but our people on the ground out of Sault St. Marie got us a reservation of two adjoining rooms at the 'Pine Grove Lodge'." He grimaced. Vickie didn't blame him. "At least it has a kitchenette. Given the hours we're going to put in...."

Vickie sighed, but...this was part of the job. She was support, after all. "If we spot any kind of an open store with food on the way there, I've got you all covered," she promised. She just wished they'd had time to load some food into the plane.

Huh...maybe...

There was a galley in this thing, after all.

As soon as the plane leveled off, she headed for the galley and started rummaging, while keeping an ear on the conversation in the cabin. There wasn't much she could contribute to, other than one thing...

"Mom?" she called out during a pause. "You guys might be out there long enough my protection spells on your rigs run out. Remember that old-school thing we used to do? The spirit slates?"

"Good idea, kitten," her mother replied. "But what can we pick up at short notice to use?"

"If there's a store, I'll see if I can find something," she

promised, and finished packing food in a trashbag. Bread, cheese, cold-cuts. The all-important coffee, and filters. Cream and sugar. That would hold them for twelve hours, and then she could get to a real store that would be open. "Anyone want a sandwich?"

There were no open stores, except a *Liquor and Beer, Bait* that otherwise had no name. The Pine Grove Lodge was exactly as expected. It boasted *Clean Rooms.* It was two-bedroom cabins with kitchenettes, built of peeled logs. There were room dividers between the two double beds with silhouettes of deer, and pictures of men fishing on the walls. The beds bore blankets woven with "Indian" designs. There was a radio in each bedroom. No TV. A dial phone.

They left Vickie to stow the food from the jet and the little extra (milk, snacks) they'd gotten from the liquor store in the kitchenette. Then she sat down to wait with her class books, which were, of course, still in her backpack.

She didn't expect her parents to be back as soon as they were. Her mother was fuming and muttering imprecations in Gaelic under her breath. She went straight to the shower, which was her usual go-to when she was angry.

"You didn't find any tea in there, did you?" her father asked.

"A few tea-bags. Might be enough to calm her down," Vickie replied, gesturing at the kitchen counter where she'd left coffee, teabags and sugar packets. With her father busy making tea, with a balky electric burner and a kettle that looked old enough to collect Social Security, she turned to her godfather.

He shrugged, unperturbed. "She is mostly angry on my part," he said. "The local agents turned us away from the scene with some words about 'not needing any help from drunk Indians.' In the morning they will be very unhappy, there will likely be demotions, and possibly pay-cuts. And none of it matters because we have a good trail leading down the road into the National Forest. That is the good news. The bad news is that in the morning we will need to buy camping equipment and head into the National Forest."

Vickie groaned inside. *Crap.*

There were phone calls to the Director in the morning, and her mother led the way to the SUV with a cat-ate-the-canary smile on her face.

The parents left her at the tiny grocery store while they went literally across the street to the "Sporting Goods" store that actually catered mostly to hunters and fishermen. While Vickie looked over the stock and the middle-aged clerk who was probably also the owner eyed her with deepening suspicion, she made some mental calculations about how much four people were going to eat in four days and began looking for whatever was going to be light to haul around, filling, and didn't make you want to spit it out at first bite. For a while she was resigned to the fact that they were going to be hauling sacks of cans across thousands of acres of wait-a-minute bushes.

And then she turned a corner and hit pay-dirt. Off in what looked like a forgotten wire rack all by itself next to the soda machine were three cut open cardboard boxes displaying foiled bags of freeze-dried meals specifically for camping, and it looked as if no one had ever bought a single packet out of them. Without a second thought except profound relief, she picked up all three of the boxes, dumped them in her cart, and went looking for something to cook them in, just in case the 'rents forgot you needed stuff like that. She filled up her cart with other essentials, and on a hunch, went back to check the microscopic "toy" section.

Aha. As she had hoped, among the paddleballs, rubber balls, wooden and metal puzzles, were five or six of those "magic slates," cardboard with a heavy coating of wax and a grayish sheet of plastic over it. You were meant to write or draw on the plastic sheet with a stylus, pressing it into the wax enough that what you'd scribed there was visible, then "erase" it all by pulling the sheet up. Those would do for her "fallback" comms.

She wheeled the overflowing cart to the counter. The clerk frowned. "How you expect to pay for all that, Missy?" he asked.

She'd come prepared, since her parents had known from

experience she'd never get away with using the "company" credit card. She opened her wallet and pulled out five hundred-dollar bills and slapped them on the counter.

His eyes bulged—then he reached for the phone. "Do your parents—" he began.

She pulled her FBI ID out of her jacket and slapped that on the counter too. Fortunately it did not give her age. "Are we done here?" she asked dryly.

"You—" he began, looking from the ID to her and back again, because the picture on it was unmistakably *her,* but his brain clearly could not handle the cognitive dissonance between the ID and her youth.

"How do you think I infiltrate high schools?" she said into the silence.

Well, he'd clearly seen enough TV for that to be an explanation his brain accepted, so he rang up the purchases and gave her her change. There wasn't much. Those freeze-dried packets were pricey. But in her mind, worth it. Besides, if the Bureau was going to force her to camp, they could bloody well afford to pay for some decent chow. "Can I borrow the cart?" she asked as he handed her the last paper bag full of groceries. She didn't wait for his answer, just wheeled it out the door and to the (thankfully) giant SUV the Bureau had supplied for them.

The 'rents returned with a loaded-down flatbed cart and an attentive clerk from the store across the street just as she tucked away the last grocery bag in the back well out of the way, leaving room for the mounds of stuff they would have to buy. "Please tell me you got something to cook with," she said, eyeing the pile of nondescript boxes on the flatbed.

"Not my first rodeo," her father reminded her, as he and the clerk began stripping the goods out of their boxes and packing them professionally into the SUV. A moment after that, Raven returned with his own cart from the hardware store and went through the same routine.

The cardboard boxes were neatly dismembered and folded up into tight little rectangles to use later for kindling. Groceries got transferred into duffle bags bought for the purpose, shopping bags folded and added to the cardboard, and they were on their way. *I'm just glad Mom packed for me,* Vickie reflected, as they headed out of town.

For a while, it was Moira doing all the tracking, as they followed a blacktop road to a gravel one, then a gravel road to a dirt track. Then "I've lost the trace," her mother said, and they slowed to a crawl, and Raven got out and took over, reading the dirt track for signs of another vehicle's passage. Probably—no—almost definitely—looking for the marks of an exact set of tires, which they would have seen last night at the crime scene.

They'd lost a couple of hours back there packing up their things from the motel and again as they shopped. By now it was noon, and Vickie passed around more sandwiches she'd made this morning from the last of the bread and cold cuts.

Aside from this dirt track, this was deep forest, all of it ablaze with color. This increased Raven's difficulties because the track was covered with fallen leaves, and to be honest, was as opaque to her as magic was to mundanes.

Time crawled as slowly as the SUV. Insulated by all the steel and rubber, Vickie couldn't "read" the ground any further than a hundred feet, and she didn't have Raven's permission to use him as a channel. She felt as if she ought to be tensely concentrating on the kidnapped girl, but the simple fact was, she was bored, and wished she dared get out one of her textbooks to study. Finally, as the light faded, Hosteen stood up and waved to her father to stop, then came to the driver's side window. "I'd like Vickie to come out here and see if she can sense anything," he said, and looked past Alex's shoulder to her. "What's your range now?" he asked.

"Ten miles," she said confidently, as she opened the door, stepped out and put her hand on the ground.

And stood up almost immediately. "Nothing but us and forest for ten miles in any direction," she said with disappointment. And knowing what was coming next, she added, "Can I sleep in the car?"

The freeze-dried stuff hadn't been half bad, and the SUV had been a *lot* more comfortable to sleep in than the cold, hard ground. She still didn't understand how her parents could stand camping. Raven, she understood, but her parents? It made no sense...

They continued to follow the track at a walking pace well into the morning, and about once a mile she got out and searched the earth around them for signs of anything that wasn't forest and wild animals. And about mid-morning, she got it.

That was when they made a more permanent camp, used the radiophone in the SUV to update Headquarters, and proceeded on foot, all four of them clad in hunter-camo, insulated coveralls. At least they were warm, because despite the exertion, Vickie was all too aware of how cold it was. By mid-afternoon, they were perched beneath an overcast sky, on a rocky outcropping of exposed boulders, looking down at—what for all intents and purposes was a pristine meadow.

That's not what Vickie's Earth-magic told her, however.

"There's...a lot of stuff down there," she said, frowning with concentration. Moira peered down at the meadow through a pair of binoculars, all of her bright red hair tucked out of sight inside a brown stocking cap. All of them were flat on their bellies, behind the cover of some tall grass and weeds. "I can't tell how many people it is, because it's all concrete and steel. Mostly steel. And it goes underground. In fact, there's a lot of it that's underground."

"How in hell did anyone build a complex here in the middle of a National Forest without anyone noticing?" Moira demanded. "And why?"

But Alex had wriggled back from the edge and taken out some old maps from inside his jacket. "Because it was in the 50s, it was the government, and they've abandoned it because they can't sell it." Moira and Raven joined him; Vickie stayed where she was, trying to unravel what must be the mother of all concealment spells. He spread out the map on the ground and stabbed at a spot with a finger. "Abandoned missile complex."

Raven grunted. "That makes altogether too much sense."

"Well," Vickie said, as the equations of the concealment field danced before her eyes and she looked for a loose end to pull on. "I'll tell you what else makes sense. When they abandon those places, they pull everything technical out of there, no matter how old and outdated. They're bare except for mechanical stuff." She looked over her shoulder again. "Whoever took the girl is probably relying on things like tripwires and physical or metaphysical guards rather than lasers and motion-sensors."

"We can take them," Alex said, confidently.

"We don't know how many 'them' there are," his wife pointed out sharply. But her father had already taken a tiny flashlight and a featherweight black bag made of ripstop nylon out of his pocket. He pulled the bag over himself and pulled the drawstring tight from inside. A few moments later, a 180 pound wolf emerged. The flashlight replicated the exact spectrum of moonlight, which was all that Alexander Nagy needed to shapeshift into his wolf form by daylight.

He shook himself all over, padded over to the edge of the bluff, and inhaled deeply, closed his eyes, and did it again. Then he looked down at them, and pawed at the ground.

"Seven," Vickie counted. "Shouldn't we wait for backup?"

Moira scowled. "Those idiots from the local office don't believe us. They're still questioning the neighbors. Even if you ran back to the car and called it in, Headquarters would have to call their superiors, who'd have to override what they're doing. That's a good two hours wasted. Then, even if they come, they're five hours away, and nightfall is in three. By the time they get here, we'll be collecting a corpse, and the Lords of Light only know what these people have planned for the power they are going to release. Your father's right. We can take them."

Vickie's stomach knotted. "All right then. Let's get you wired up, and I'll put a camouflage spell of my own on you." She took the headsets out of her backpack, and out of their protective bags, and activated the spell that kept them insulated from Moira and Raven's magic. "You've got six hours," she said handing them over, then fitted an earpiece to her father's head. At least he didn't need insulation; his transformative power involved a lot less magic. Then she handed over "Magic Slates" to the two who were still human. "Backup," she said. "Once you get inside, if you have to go hunting down in the silo and launch control area, the signal might not reach outside here."

Then she took thirty minutes she honestly didn't think she had to place a light-bending spell of her own on the two humans as well. Wonderful thing about understanding magic as math; three months ago she'd worked out the equations to tell light how to bend around something; if you looked hard now at the place where her mother and godfather were, you might see a faint shimmer where the light hadn't bent perfectly, but you had to know what you were looking for.

At least they could pretty much count on the enemy *not* having infrared detectors.

"We're counting on you to stop anything coming up that track," Raven's voice said from the apparently empty air.

And then...they were gone.

OK Vickie, they're counting on you to stop anything coming up that track.

Of course...it might not come up that track. She reached for the rifle; beggars couldn't be choosers and the best he'd found at the shop was a hunting rifle with a scope that none of them had yet had a chance to try. She had her father's Glock, Raven's shotgun, and Can Opener.

"Penetrating the perimeter," came her mother's whisper over the radio, as the sun began to sink towards late afternoon, casting long shadows into the meadow. *"Alex was right. This is an old missile base. The buildings are a wreck though, I think we'll have to head down inside."*

"Look," Raven Stormdance interrupted. *"The silo to the far back right. It's open. And I just had an unpleasant thought. A silo is a perfect place for a magic circle. And all that steel—"*

"Will contain and funnel the magic released by a sacrifice into anything they place across the top," Moira responded.

"Or worse, what if the girl is meant for a vessel instead of a sacrifice? That same silo will channel every particle of dark force they invoke straight into her."

There was silence on the radio. *"Then we'd better get a move on,"* Moira said grimly. *"Raven, can you pick the lock on this thing?"*

There was a snort. Vickie managed to hear the *click* as he spring a lock—presumably on the entrance down into the silo complex below. "Keep talking," she urged, her eyes not just on the track, but glancing over the air above her, and as much of the meadow as she could. *But with the camouflage spell on, would I even see something coming in from the other side at all?*

"Infiltrating," Moira responded. *"Long staircase down, badly lit. Dim li—om—are—"* And then there was nothing but static.

Vickie swore. In English. And her mother didn't respond. She scrambled for the Magic Slate. *Lost you,* she wrote, and erased the words.

Finally. *10-4.* A little of her anxiety eased. At least they all knew they were out of comm-reach now. And at least they were all in touch with each other down there.

But a sound like the sky tearing open riveted her attention up and to the east, where a personal jetwing was coming in—fast.

INC! she wrote on the Slate, and brought the rifle to bear on the growing target.

Jetwings were fast, but they weren't exactly maneuverable, especially when coming in for a landing. She had enough time to calculate a simple spell on the fly, slam it on the bullet in the chamber, fasten her gaze through the scope on the fuel-tank on the back of the wing and pull the trigger as the bulky man wearing the wing touched his feet to the ground.

Go where I send thee! It was a simple variation on an ancient spell that went back to *at least* the Middle Ages, meant to be used with an arrow.

It was equally effective when altered for the faster speeds of a bullet. A fraction of a second after she pulled the trigger, she watched the fuel tank erupt in a blossom of fire, and the sound of the explosion echoed across the meadow.

YES! she thought in triumph.

Triumph which died when he came walking out of the fire-cloud, shrugging off the burning wing.

Crap. He's a metahuman. There was not so much as a glimmer of magic power about him, so he had to be a metahuman, and he was either invulnerable, or he regenerated damaged flesh quickly.

Through the scope, she saw him scanning the area, looking for the sniper that had shot his tank. And felt a chill run down her back as his eyes seemed to look right through the scope back at her. He'd spotted her. And he started walking towards her, his pace leisurely, the growing smile on his face nothing less than overt sadism.

And she was the only thing between him and the team.

The rifle had a ten-round magazine and she unloaded it into him as fast as she could aim and pull the trigger. At least some of them hit him; she saw him react to the impact, but he still kept coming.

She jumped to her feet, dropping the useless rifle. *Up here is no place to fight him. I need room.*

The thought was the mother to the deed.

She jumped.

To him, she probably looked like an insane flea as she leapt, tumbled, twisted, spun, and ricocheted her way down the slope. It probably looked like a series of uncontrolled spills and falls that somehow always ended in miraculous landings.

He probably had no idea he was watching an expert level parkour traceur. *This...* she thought, skidding her soles along the surface of a boulder..*isn't even...* and her feet hit the next one down, and she threw herself into the air in a somersault...*a medium...* that ended as she came down in a controlled tumble in the space between two more....*course.*

She hit the ground running, drawing her dagger at the same time, charging towards him. His grin turned into a bellow of laughter. "What? They send a kid with a pin to take me?" He drew back a hand the size of a cast-iron skillet to smack her out of the way. "What kinda—"

She ducked under the blow, slashing his wrist as she passed under it, turned on a dime, and launched herself at his back.

While he stared in shock at the bleeding gash in his wrist. He whirled at the last minute to intercept her; she had to change her target from his hamstring to his hand, taking care to slash and not stab. His bellow of startled pain rang across the meadow as she put the still-burning wreckage of his jetwing between them. "Not such an easy gig, is it?" she taunted him. *I know his type. A merc who's coasted on the fact that nothing can hurt him. Even now, he still doesn't believe it...*

"When I squash you like a bug they'll pay me plenty!" He screamed, oblivious to the fact that both his hand and wrist were still bleeding freely and showing no signs of stopping. She'd never be able to get a hit on a major vein or artery—

—but she didn't need to.

In the course of ten minutes, he was literally covered in bleeding, shallow cuts. In fifteen he was panting. In twenty, he was having trouble getting his breath.

In twenty-five, she managed to cut a hamstring. And then she sat down in the grass, well out of reach, and watched him slowly bleed to death. It wasn't a pretty death. But it was her doing, and she felt she needed to own it. And when he was dead, she cleaned her knife on his shirt, careful not to touch the blade at all herself, and slipped it into its protective sheathe.

Then wiped off as much of the blood as she could, and sat down to catch her breath and wait for the team.

A whisper of feet through the grass—and the sight of an unconscious girl in floral pajamas floating in mid-air with a large gray wolf pacing beneath her—told her they'd succeeded. She jumped to her feet and quickly unraveled the concealment spell she had put on them. Raven had the girl. Her mother was staring in shock at the dead metahuman.

"What—" she began, then shook her head. "Never mind. Debrief later. There might be more coming."

"Roger that." Vickie sprinted and leapt back up the bluff; her father kept pace with her in wolf-form, her mother and Raven alternately climbing and handing up the sleeping girl to each other. *That's not a normal sleep,* she thought, as she gathered up everything they had brought with them. *Mom must have put her out. Easier that way.*

Alex burrowed his way into the bag. Moira fished for the flashlight, then closed the bag around her wrist. The bag convulsed, Moira shoved the coverall into the bag, there was some thrashing, then Alex emerged with the garment pulled up to his waist. He finished dressing, took the girl from Raven, and flung her over his shoulder in a fireman's carry. Vickie slung the rifle over her back and they all broke into a ground-eating lope, heading for the car. And she explained what had happened.

"Are we going to call this in?" Vickie asked.

"Yes," her father replied. "That concealment is going to fade out in a few hours. We were in luck, the seven I smelled were spaced out all over the complex. We took them out one at a time, although a couple of them gave us a good fight. They weren't expecting me." He flashed her a grin that could only be described as "wolfish." "No silver bullets."

"It was worse than we thought," Moira added. "The setup we found—not only were they planning on expending the power of this child's death to summon something, they were going to let it inhabit her body."

Vickie's whipped her head around to stare at her mother as they ran. "What the actual—frack?" she gasped.

"We think they had a long-term plan involving the Senator himself, or the access he and his family had to DC," Moira said grimly. "But we're going to call this a kidnapping and blackmail plot."

Vickie was glad she was running; it made it easier to shake off the chills.

"We're going to get to the car," her father said. "We're going to haul ass out of here, because I do not know if they had any other backup muscle, magical, metahuman, or conventional, and I don't care to find out."

"Well, while we're hauling ass, I'll get on the radiophone and boost it all the way to HQ," Vickie panted, shifting the rifle on her shoulder so it wouldn't jounce so hard on the bruises she hadn't realized she'd collected on her butt.

"Good plan. There's the car," her father said. "Forget the

camping gear. If the boss wants it collected, he can send someone to collect it. Raven—"

But her godfather was already dashing ahead; and by the time they reached the SUV he'd spun an expert half-donut and had it facing the right way. Moira flung the girl into the back; Vickie jumped into her seat, and Alex piled in on the other side, Between them they managed to get the unconscious girl strapped into the middle and then held on for dear life as Raven accelerated down the primitive track like a moonshiner with Revenuers on his tail.

Back at Pine Lodge. Vickie lay flat on her back on her bed, trying to decide if she liked the "massage for twenty five cents" or not. Given the general stickiness of her situation, her mother ceded the first round of showers in the two bathrooms to her. By this time tomorrow, they'd be on the jet back to Virginia.

Day after that, she'd be back at class.

I wonder what the other kids would think if they knew what I'd just done. Even Paul only knew that her parents were FBI and that they periodically pulled her out of class to "help them with their equipment." He had no idea about the rest of it. He probably thought she spent all her time safe in the back of a van.

No one that she knew of at St. Rhia's had ever hurt someone, much less killed him, except maybe one or two of the teachers.

At that point, the sheer loneliness of her situation overwhelmed her, and as the bed stopped shaking, she turned over on her side and started to sob into her pillow.

Out of nowhere, she felt the bed settle as someone sat down beside her. And her mother took her shoulders and pulled her up so she could sob into the towel wrapped around her mother's hair.

"I know," her Mom said softly. "I know, kitten."

And she did know, of course. How could she not? She and Dad had been doing this for years before Vickie was even born. Things they couldn't even talk about with colleagues at the Bureau, because the very fact that magic was real and powerful and dangerous was something that was a very closely kept secret, even within the Bureau.

"It's hard. It's impossible sometimes, or it seems like it," Mom murmured, holding her close. "But you can always come to us. You're not alone. And someday, if you're really lucky, you'll find someone you can share all this with. Someone you never have to keep secrets from. And until then, you have us."

She nodded, unable to speak, throat raw and nose clogged. Mom was right of course. There was always the family.

And...maybe someday...

DEATH MOST ROYAL

by Jonathan Shipley

Life is never dull for an exorcist.

This is Fort Worth writer Jonathan Shipley's tenth appearance in *Sword & Sorceress*. Since last year, he has taken his writing into international venues by presenting his short stories to several literature classes in Karlsruhe, Germany, and speaking on science fiction at the 2018 World Building Conference in Graz, Austria. For this tenth and final S&S story and his 97th short fiction publication, he writes again of Jenna the Exorcist, who this time must solve the political mess of a royal succession gone sour through assassination. Jonathan maintains a web presence at www.shipleyscifi.com where you can find a full list of his publications.

A bump in the road jolted Jenna awake in the carriage. Early morning light streamed in the curtained window and in the distance, she caught sight of the golden spires of St. Kyre's.

"Finally." She murmured to herself. It seemed like forever, but it had only been two days since the carriage arrived at the Northern Commandery to carry her brother and her to King's City. The message had been signed by Trayn, her Knight-Protector already in the city on business, but it carried the unspoken weight of a royal summons. Probably from Prince Mikhail, Knight-Commander of the order and Trayn's comrade-in-arms. The question was why any royal would summon a north country exorcist when he had the Exorcist-General himself right there in the palace.

She glanced over at her brother Herrin sleeping fitfully across from her. He was young for his role as exorcist's assistant and looked even younger asleep like this. But then again, she was young to be a Church exorcist. But she had the talent and that was what the Office of the Holy Exorcism needed in this kingdom of haunted byways.

She let her younger brother sleep a while longer, but shook him awake when they rolled under the city wall and onto the cobblestone streets. He yawned groggily and looked out the window. "Saint Kyre's already," he mumbled, catching sight of the cathedral's dome. It was part of a huge palace complex with palace on one side and episcopal offices on the other with the great cathedral of Saint Kyre connecting both around a great courtyard.

After rolling through the courtyard, the carriage came to a halt in a smaller service court with stables and exercise yards. The courier atop the carriage swung down to open the door. "We'll be entering the palace by a back way," he told them. "Your presence is not to be common knowledge."

Of course not, Jenna thought as they dismounted. *Why choose simple when convoluted is an option?* She stamped her feet to revive numb legs, then followed the man through a series of passages built into the palace walls. As they emerged into an austere anteroom, the courier said, "Your assistant remains here."

"What? Why?" Herrin protested.

"We'd best do as we're told—for once," Jenna advised her brother. "King's City is not the place to be overly independent." A political hellhole was a more apt description. She'd been here once before and hated the morass of lies and intrigue.

With a final nod at her brother, she let herself be ushered into the next room. It was shuttered and dim, but she instantly recognized Trayn with his clear, blue eyes and square jaw as he stood waiting to receive her.

"Thank Kyre you came quickly," the knight said.

"Let's hope that you have more answers than..." Jenna trailed off as Trayn meaningfully cleaned his throat and nodded toward the central table where a second figure sat.

"Your Highness," Jenna said with a quick curtsy. Tall and regal with flowing blonde hair, Prince Mikhail was a commanding figure, even in the semi-dark.

"Exorcista," the prince replied, rising to greet her. "As time is precious, let me come to the point straight away. The king has been in ill health for some months, but now he is comatose on his deathbed and is not expected to rally. The High Council is already assembled from throughout the kingdom to oversee the transition of power. But my father has not named either Theo or me as heir, and there will be anarchy without an official successor."

Jenna kept her expression neutral, though her thoughts were racing. Who was this Theo? And what did the prince want of her in this highly charged situation? Was she expected to contact the spirit of the comatose king to clear up the succession? But she could only talk to the dead. So was she to summon the spirit of the king when he was dead... but that was unthinkable. The Exorcist-General would never allow it. Her mandate was to clear dark, unsettled spirits that plagued hundreds of haunted corners throughout the kingdom. Bringing back a beloved sovereign who had died peacefully in his bed would violate all precedent and invite a backlash from the populace and Holy Mother Church itself. The line between exorcism and necromancy was fine at best, and this was a Church that still burned witches.

Trayn touched her arm. "Jenna?"

She turned, startled. "Yes?"

"You were a thousand leagues away. Mikhail asked if you would help in this stormy time."

"I'm sorry to have wandered," she told the prince. "My mind was indeed a thousand leagues away. But before I pledge anything, I have to ask what it is you want of my talent. This is a situation that borders on both treason and heresy."

The prince frowned. "How so?"

"Bringing the king back from the dead would—"

"Merciful heavens, no!" he snapped in alarm. "That would be the very last thing this very tense situation needs. I concur that the Church would call it heresy and the Crown would call it treason. That is not at all what I am asking of you."

"Then please explain," Jenna urged. "I will help as I can, but not blindly."

He hesitated, then nodded. "Fair enough. But this is not to

leave this chamber. While not treasonous nor heretical, this is murderous. I have in fact told no one, not even my good friend Trayn, for fear of the walls might hear and betray me. But you, I hope, can discern any such leaks before I start."

Jenna stifled her automatic "no," to think this through. Detecting spies and prying ears had nothing to do with exorcism per se, but on the other hand, there was no spy more effective than a dead one. She turned to her companion. "Where's Dwarf, Trayn? He came south with you to King's City, did he not?"

Trayn nodded. "He did, but spends his time about the city, no doubt doing some ghostly peeping around dance halls and bawdhouses. And I'm relieved to be rid of his cold breath on my neck. You know how irritated he becomes with me since you're the only one to see and hear him."

"This Dwarf is a ghost?" Mikhail asked.

"The same that we picked up last time we were in King's City," Jenna answered. "With your permission, I need to summon him back from wherever he has wandered. He is the best of informants."

"Then by all means," he nodded.

Jenna opened her satchel of tools and drew out the ritual silver knife. The only bread she had in the satchel had gone stale, but it would have to do. Drawing the knife across her palm in a shallow cut, she let a few drops of blood drip onto the hunk of bread. She closed her eyes to concentrate. "Spirits who have passed Beyond, grant my petition. Let the one we call Dwarf hear this call and return posthaste to my side."

He opened her eyes and counted heartbeats as she waited. When she reached twenty, she felt the temperature dip in the room. A moment later, a short, stocky figure appeared hazily before her. "About time," it growled. "I've been stuck with Sir Stupid for far too long." Dwarf and Trayn only got along because Trayn couldn't hear Dwarf's opinions. "And to make it worse," Dwarf continued, "it's been Sir Stupid and Prince Stupid both. You'd think they're of the age when lusting and wenching would be rampant, but no, the two of them are like sexless monks, plotting the future in dark chambers as though..."

"What does he say?" Trayn asked. "I know he's here because I felt the sudden cold."

"He says both of you need more of a sex life," she said absently, still listening to Dwarf's rant. Then her eyes widened. "Oh, I'm sorry, Your Highness. I should not have repeated that. I wasn't thinking."

Dwarf droned on. "...you'd think they'd at least go at with each other when no one else is around, but no—"

"Please, Dwarf. I need your help. In a palace full of spies and secret ways, I need to know if we are being overheard in this chamber. I know you can make a circuit of the walls, through the walls, and find this out for me."

"In exchange for what, prithee tell?" the ghost snorted. "A half-hearted thank you."

"If we come through this well, Trayn will take you wenching with him," Jenna promised.

"I will not!" Trayn sputtered. "I'll not have that Peeping Tom on my shoulder."

Dwarf gave a deep chuckle. "It was worth it just for the expression on Sir Stupid's face. Now try that with the prince as well."

"I value my life, thank you very much. Now that you're sufficiently amused, will you check the walls?"

With a final chuckle, Dwarf faded out and the sudden chill in the room faded with him. "A most interesting and unghost-like ghost," Mikhail commented. "From hearing one side of the conversation only, he sounds exceedingly randy?"

"Always," Trayn snorted.

"But he's a very powerful spirit who has been of enormous help in difficult situations," Jenna hastened to add, then paused as Dwarf reappeared.

"Secure here, though lots of hidey-holes," he said, "but I'm feeling odd things elsewhere in the palace. I'm going to take a look." He was gone.

"Dwarf says we're secure at the moment, but you may want to speak quickly. He indicated that odd things were happening close by."

"So be it," Mikhail nodded. "My mother the Lady Antaria, mistress to His Majesty, is dead." Trayn gave a start as Mikhail continued. "Undoubtedly assassination. She was a political manipulator of the first order and had a hand in everything regarding the king and the succession. That she is dead while he lies dying is no coincidence. Exorcista, you need to summon back my mother's spirit."

"How have I heard nothing of this?" Trayn demanded. "Why is the palace not abuzz with this news?"

"No one knows," Mikhail said tightly. "I found her dead in her bed three days ago and have allowed no one else in the chamber since. Officially, she is ill with grief over the King's coming demise, and my personal guards at the door deter all visitors. It is important, nay imperative, that her death be kept secret."

Jenna exchanged a puzzled glance with Trayn. "I don't understand your reasoning, Your Highness," she said. "We should move with discretion, yes, but secrecy is hardly—"

Mikhail interrupted her with a quick gesture. "You fail to grasp how central my mother was in the succession issue. I have no doubt that she knows things directly from the king's lips that no one else knows. She would know if he signed a Writ of Succession and possibly where that Writ is. With my half-brother Prince Theo and me both claiming a disputed throne, that document could determine the future of the kingdom when the High Council convenes tomorrow."

"Yes, but—"

He slammed a hand down on the desktop. "Exorcista, this is royal politics at its most vicious, and not even the dead are immune to manipulation. Once my mother's death is known, the race would be between exorcists to summon her spirit first. I have no idea how that plays out in the spirit realm. Do you?"

Jenna slowly shook her head. Exorcists were scattered so thinly throughout the kingdom that two were seldom in the same town. But with the Exorcist-General's Office part of this very complex, the situation was different here. The whole concept of conflicting summonings of the same spirit was unknown territory.

"I think I finally understand," she finally said. "Exorcist against exorcist would be bizarre, but whichever exorcist has access to the body will have the advantage." She took a breath. "Highness, I feel very tense about this. My instinct says to do this quickly before the wind changes."

"Agreed." The prince stood and beckoned. "Come." He strode across the room and out the door.

Outside the chamber, they picked up a disgruntled Herrin and continued down a broad corridor. There would be questions upon questions in this summoning, she thought as they walked. The prince obviously was focused on the succession and the kingdom's political future, perhaps to the exclusion of any other concerns... to the exclusion of grief, even. But Jenna was drawn to the more obvious question for Lady Antaria: Who killed you?

At the next turn, they passed through a heavy wooden door, and the character of the hallway changed immediately. Where it had been spare and utilitarian, now it looked palatial with benches upholstered in silks and portraits on the wall. Given that every organization headquartered in the huge complex, she guessed that Mikhail's workroom was within the commandery wing for the Knights of the Retribution.

A few more turns and the corridor broadened into a grand thoroughfare. Ahead she could see an ornate double door with guards on either side. As she watched, the door opened and a personage in healer's green emerged to pass out of sight into a side corridor. The king's chamber, she guessed, where their monarch lay comatose. She glanced at a second, closer doorway where guards were also stationed. This would be the Lady Antaria's chamber.

"Inside, quickly," the prince murmured as he signaled the guards to let them pass.

Jenna hurried inside and wrinkled her nose at the all-too-familiar odor of decay. Since no one had been allowed in this chamber since the death, no attempt had been made to mitigate the smell, and she automatically reached for the nearest tabletop where a bronze candelabrum loaded with beeswax candles stood waiting. At her touch, the wicks burst into flame. Then she grimaced and looked to Prince Mikhail apprehensively. But his attention—thankfully—was elsewhere. Lighting candles was a small and innocent bit of magic that made her candle-centric life as an exorcist easier, but technically she shouldn't have been able to do it. Trayn and Herrin were used to these little expressions of her witchblood, but in the eyes of Inquisition, witchcraft was witchcraft. She would have to be more careful here in King's City.

"How did she die?" Trayn asked the prince in a low voice.

"There were no outward signs," Mikhail answered, "so I'm assuming one of the subtler poisons that leaves no trace. It would best fit the occasion."

Jenna tried to ignore the fact that he seemed to know a lot about the subject, but then, poison had always been the favored method of royal assassination. As the burning beeswax lightened the odor of decay, she approached the bed with its sheet-shrouded form. But as she reached for the sheet, she paused. Something was off in the feel of the room. She focused her heightened senses on the chamber around her, testing this way and that. "What do you *not* feel?" she asked Herrin.

He frowned and glanced around. "No cold spot. This chamber isn't haunted."

"Yet a sudden, unquiet death almost always causes a spirit to linger." She turned to Mikhail. "Under what circumstances, Highness, would the Lady Antaria's spirit have simply passed on after death?"

"Under *no* circumstances!" he snapped. "My mother cared more about the succession than her own life, and death would not have altered that." He gave Jenna an intent look. "You've met the woman, Exorcista. I defy you to disagree with my assessment."

"I cannot, Highness," she said. The Lady Antaria had been both ruthless and obsessive in her dynastic ambitions. "But I say to you—there is no spirit in this chamber."

"Then she is probably elsewhere in the palace, probably spying on her political enemies. You yourself said that the dead made the best spies."

Jenna shook her head. "Highness, Dwarf is an ancient spirit and not human to start with. The newly dead are invariably confused, often unaware that they are dead. Even those with unfinished business need time to adjust after death."

"Then what?" he demanded. "She most definitely had unfinished business and would not have passed on. So regardless of where her spirit is, you can summon it, can you not?"

Jenna mulled that without answering. She could try, of course, but she had a strong intuition that nothing would follow expectations. But she gave Herrin a nod and proceeded to unpack her implements—salt, the stale bread that she had not renewed, thick votive candles, and her silver knife for drawing the all-important blood that spirits craved.

When the salt circle was drawn upon the parquet floor and the candles lit, she paused again. "I think," she said slowly, "that we all should sit within the circle."

"Too confining with all four of us," Trayn pointed out. "Perhaps better if the prince and I withdrew to an out-of-the-way corner."

But Jenna shook her head. "This isn't for the summoning... it's for protection."

"From what?" Trayn and Mikhail asked in unison.

"I don't know," Jenna admitted, "but there is a strange feel about all of this."

In the end, they all huddled together inside the salt circle as Jenna and Herrin began the summoning ritual. "Spirits who have passed Beyond, grant my petition," Jenna intoned as she pricked her finger to let three drops of blood fall onto the crust of bread. "Let the shade of the recently deceased Lady Antaria come to us who have questions for her."

As before, she counted heartbeats as she waited. Twenty was a standard length of time. But the count passed twenty, then thirty, before she felt a change in the room. The temperature dropped like a stone as a stiff wind whipped suddenly around them. And behind the wail of the wind came a chorus of distant shrieks.

"What is that sound?" Mikhail asked in a low voice.

That shook Jenna's concentration. "You can hear that? The shrieks?"

"We all can, Jenna," Herrin said. "This summoning is manifesting beyond the spirit plane."

"It sounds like the screams of the damned," Trayn interjected. "And getting louder." There was the sudden ring of a sword being pulled free of its scabbard, no mean feat in the confined circle. "Break the link, Jenna!"

She tried. "Spirits of the Beyond, we bid thee farewell. Leave the living behind and return to your own realm." The screams grew even louder.

"Jenna!" Herrin shouted above the din and pointed at the bed. The body of Lady Antaria shuddered and rose to a sitting position, the sheet falling away as she moved. The face was pale and sunken, but the eyes glowed with a yellow fire. The stench of decay became overpowering.

Jenna plunged the silver blade deep into her palm to let the blood stream forth. "The Gate be closed!" she yelled at the top of her lungs. "By the Blood of Life, I expel the dead from Beyond!"

Like a great inhalation, all sound was sucked from the chamber, leaving dead silence. The lady's corpse fell back to the bed with a plop and lay unmoving.

"Help," Jenna gasped, sitting in a growing pool of her own blood.

There was a scramble around her, then a searing, hot pain against her palm. She blanked for a moment, and when she opened her eyes, Trayn was wrapping her hand in strips cut from the bed linens. The bleeding seemed to have stopped, though her hand ached to high heaven. "Oh, it hurts," she murmured.

"Twice cauterized in candle flame," Trayn said, looking at her with danger behind his eyes. "That was a deep cut."

She looked around at the company. The prince and Herrin were on their feet, but still within the salt circle. Mikhail shared Trayn's deadly gaze of a soldier under attack. Putting aside her immediate pain, she quested with her other senses and found no trace of malicious intent in the chamber. She waited and quested again to be sure. "Whatever was here is gone," she announced hesitantly. "We're safe—for the moment. But what the hell was that?"

"Hell seems to be an apt description." The prince nodded grimly toward the bed. "That wasn't my mother, rather a demon straight out of hell. I'm ready to be quit of this chamber."

A chorus of 'ayes' followed that. Trayn helped Jenna to her feet, escorted her to the door, and they were down the corridor at a fast clip. Mikhail leaned closer. "I realize, Exorcista, that you need rest to recover, but I need your presence by my side right now. Rest will have to wait."

"I understand," Jenna nodded. "But a hearty stew would be appreciated."

When they reached the prince's workroom in the commandery, Mikhail gave a flurry of orders to his adjutant before plopping down behind his worktable. He, Trayn, and Herrin seemed inclined to share a flagon of wine, which held little appeal to Jenna. In her experience, the way to make a bad experience even worse was trying to deal with the dead while drunk. And this experience didn't need to get any worse.

As she sat in an easy chair before the hearth, she tried to sort out what the hellish summoning meant. She dozed at least once before hot food arrived to revive her, but after eating heartily, was finally ready to talk. The others took their cue from her and pulled chairs close to the fireplace. The three of them seemed more relaxed, so apparently the wine had succeeded in its task.

"It was a trap," she said without preamble.

"By whom?" Mikhail's eyes narrowed dangerously.

She shook her head. "I have no answer to that. But I can tell you that the trap was aimed toward an exorcist, designed to be triggered by a summoning."

"Why would you be the target—" Trayn began.

"I probably wasn't the target. More likely his Highness. But I was the trigger mechanism, so my presence here in King's City is known."

Mikhail frowned. "But how? Only my adjutant knew I was sending for you."

"Either a good spy or a good guess," she shrugged. "The connection between thee and me is known, and you, Highness, are a dangerous friend at the moment. Didn't the Inquisition just try to hang Trayn for sorcery because of your close friendship? "

"The Inquisition." Mikhail drew out the word grimly. "The Lord Inquisitor is the chief advocate of my half-brother as Heir to the Throne and no friend of mine. He was also the chief adversary of the Lady Antaria within the King's Council."

"The Lord Inquisitor has a dark reputation within Holy Mother Church," Herrin added. "He's known to be much too interested in power and not above assassination."

"Well said," Mikhail nodded. "This could be but one more assassination attempt from his hand. But the method perplexes. The Inquisition has nothing to do with the dead or exorcisms."

Jenna leaned forward. "This was something else entirely. Necromancy—I'm sure of it. The Office of the Holy Exorcism does not tolerate techniques such as we saw in that chamber."

"At least, not officially," Herrin added in an undertone.

"The nature of the trap means one more thing," Jenna continued. "Someone else knows that the Lady Antaria is dead, and used it to their advantage."

The prince shook his head. "But only I knew and I told no one until you arrived. And the chamber has been sealed."

"You're forgetting one person, Highness. Her murderer."

That brought a sudden grimness to the room. "Dwarf," she said suddenly. "He should have felt the energy of a hell-gate being opened. Why has he not returned?"

"Perhaps he found something even more interesting," Mikhail suggested.

Jenna's hand moved toward her pouch. "I should summon him."

Trayn interposed himself and moved the pouch out of her reach. "Don't even think about such a thing. You've lost far too much blood for a summoning."

"But we need to—"

"I'll do it," Herrin said. "I know the ritual was well as you do, Jenna. Let me try."

There was nothing to argue. Herrin did know the ritual and she had lost too much blood. But she shifted her position to watch closely as he unsheathed her silver knife. He slashed his palm lightly and let the drops of blood fall to the floor. "Spirits who have passed Beyond, grant my petition," he called. "Let the one we call Dwarf hear this call and return to my side."

They waited. Nothing happened. No sensation of coldness.

"You forgot the bread," Trayn finally pointed out.

"You have no right to criticize," Herrin shot back and glanced at his sister. "Should I try again with bread, Jenna?"

"Blood alone is usually sufficient to bring Dwarf," she said. "But I thought I smelled something for a moment when you summoned."

"Smelled?" Mikhail repeated. "Like the decay of a corpse?"

She shook her head. "Not the stench that came upon us in your mother's chamber—that's revenants, not ghosts. And this was nothing like that, just something that came and went quickly. And that's significant," she added, "because there should be no smell when summoning."

"I thought I caught a whiff of something as well," Trayn said and glanced at Herrin. "Another attempt, perhaps?"

Herrin squeezed a few more drops from his palm and repeated the words of summoning another time. Jenna closed her eyes to focus on the smell. There it was again, very familiar. When it faded, she opened and eyes and found Trayn staring at her quizzically. "Salt?" he suggested.

Yes, salt. She nodded and closed her eyes again to think what that might mean. Salt circles were very much a part of summonings as a protection against angry spirits. But Dwarf was friendly, not angry. Then her breath caught. Friendly towards them, perhaps, but not so friendly if someone else summoned him. But why would he not come back? Possibly because he couldn't.

"He may be trapped inside a salt circle," she told the others. "Salt would have the power to hold him for a time once he was summoned."

Herrin shook his head. "How could anyone else summon

Dwarf, Jenna? No one except the three of us—pardon, Highness, the four of us—knows he even exists."

"Excellent point," she agreed. "So not summoned, but what?"

"Trapped as you were trapped," Mikhail declared decisively. "And likely by the same hand with a talent for such things. I would be most interested where in the palace this circle lies. The location of the circle may be informative as to the perpetrator. I'll lead a troop of guards myself to find it."

"Out of the question, Mikhail," Trayn said firmly. "You're a target and need to stay here behind swords and locked doors. I'll go—perhaps in the guise of an exorcist's robes to confuse my intent."

Jenna looked from Mikhail to Trayn, each with the same robust build toned from years of training. "Trayn, you look like what you are—a warrior-knight. You would never pass as a priest of any sort. It takes a priest to look like a priest." She glanced pointedly at the thin, scholarly figure of her brother. He nodded agreement.

"But a map of this maze you call a palace would be helpful," he said.

She slept again, and it was dark outside when she woke in the workroom. "It's been hours—any word from Herrin?" she called to Trayn, who sat near the prince's worktable. The prince himself was nowhere in the room.

He crossed quickly to the hearth. "Nothing yet, but there are many rooms to investigate. Mikhail has passed the word among his guards to watch for unusual behaviors in certain quarters."

"Which quarters?"

"Oh, the Office of the Inquisition, the Office of the Holy Exorcism, courtiers' chambers—all those with the most to gain in a contested succession."

She wondered belatedly if sending Herrin out alone was as stupid as it now sounded. There seemed to be danger everywhere. "Where is the prince, by the way?"

"He had an idea for tracking this adversary by another

means. He's inventorying salt in the kitchens."

That sounded harmless, but probably wasn't. "You let him go?"

Trayn nodded. "The kitchens are friendly territory with guards already stationed there. With assassinations so common, the royal family maintains tight control over what they eat."

Her eye wandered to the surface of the worktable that was set out for a chess game, half played. Trayn had tried to teach her the game, but she was a weak player. "The two of you are playing chess?" she asked, trying to keep her voice neutral. At a time like this, it seemed frivolous.

"What—no," he said quickly. "This is how Mikhail thinks through his political strategies. Notice how all the bishops are on one side and all the knights on the other? That's no accident. He is plotting his next move after the loss of his queen from the board."

The Lady Antaria, Jenna realized. "Which side has the king?"

"Neither. Each side has *a* king, not *the* king, who is beyond the politics of the moment. Mikhail represents for his side and he's guessing either the Exorcist-General or the Lord Inquisitor is the opposing king."

"Not Prince Theo? And why have I not heard about this half-brother until now?"

"Because he's only nine years old and lives sequestered here in the palace. Unlike Mikhail, Theo is legitimately born, which strengthens his claim to the throne, but he is also only a child while Mikhail has experience as a commander and popularity as a leader."

"Why aren't the brothers working together?" she demanded. "That seems only common sense in a time of crisis."

Trayn sighed and shook his head. "Unfortunately Prince Theo is only a pawn in this game and has been very isolated since his mother the Queen died. Mikhail isn't even sure where the boy is at the moment. He was spirited away when the king's health failed. Theo's taking the throne would require a regency, and whoever was named regent would be incredibly powerful.

The Lady Antaria, however, argued that a regency would weaken the kingdom and that only her son could be the strong leader the kingdom needed. The debates were bitter, in council and out. What do you think, Jenna? Could the Exorcist-General be behind all this?"

She gave a short laugh. "I've met the Exorcist-General perhaps two times in my career. I may work for him, but I don't know his mind and certainly not his politics." She gave her companion a narrow look. "Would you be willing to try another summoning with me?"

"If you didn't need my blood, you wouldn't even be asking. Of course, Jenna. Are you trying again for Dwarf?"

She shook her head. "No, the Lady Antaria." As he drew back with a frown, she quickly added, "Just her spirit, nothing that would bring the revenant. To function, that trap needed the presence of the corpse itself."

"But why chance it?" he asked. "If the other summoning didn't work, she has obviously moved on."

"No, not obviously," Jenna argued. "Because her chamber had been set as a trap, it wasn't a fair summoning to start with. And I agree with the prince that the lady's spirit would be inclined to linger for the sake of unfinished business. Murder victims routinely do, and she has more motivation that most. If she is lingering, I may be able to contact her even at a distance from her body."

"Onward, then," Trayn said and drew his belt knife.

He shed the blood; she said the words. No spirit answered the call. "And that answers that," she said grimly. "Did you smell it?"

"I confess the sting of the knife distracted me. The salt smell again?"

"Exactly," she nodded. "I'm guessing the same salt circle is holding both her and Dwarf. And there can be only one reason in her case—to keep her from answering a summons. This has to be the work of another exorcist, or even several exorcists working in concert. I'm guessing the Exorcist-General has shifted his allegiance against Mikhail."

The door opened and Prince Mikhail strode into the chamber as she was saying this. He grimaced as he took in the words. "Then I shall deal with him when it comes time."

Jenna grimaced. She hated to think what that meant. Royal politics were always bitter, and a contested succession would be royal politics at their worst. "Any luck tracking the salt, Highness?" she asked to set aside grimmer topics.

"Some," he nodded. "A great deal of salt has been requisitioned in unsuspicious amounts over the last half year. Always for a particular storage vault in one of the far cellars underneath the cathedral itself. I know of no Church ritual that requires quantities of salt, so this gives me a starting point. I'm leaving immediately."

"I'm much recovered and coming with you," Jenna said, rising shakily to her feet.

"Not wise, Jenna," Trayn warned.

"But necessary as I'm the only one who can see the trapped spirits. And there's also the matter of my missing brother. I cannot sit idly by."

"Decision?" Mikhail asked, looking from one to the other.

"I yield, though I'm in the right," Trayn shrugged. "The Exorcista can be most willful."

"Then it makes sense for the Exorcista to investigate the vault while I provide a distraction. All eyes are on me anyway, so that shouldn't be hard."

They formed an expedition with ample guards fore and aft with a few unlit torches for the cellars, and the three of them in the middle, Jenna leaning heavily on Trayn for support. They took a very public way to the cathedral at the center of the complex, making no attempt to hide their progress. Mikhail had chosen, in fact, the processional hall that ran straight from Throne Room to St. Kyre's that the monarch used on state occasions. To all appearances, the prince was heading for the cathedral to offer midnight prayers for his dying father, and that's the way they would play it.

But as they neared the grand doorway that opened to the cathedral, Jenna had a disturbing thought. "Highness," she murmured, "what else besides this storage vault lies below the cathedral?"

"Just the crypts," the prince said.

"*Just* the crypts?" she repeated, dismayed.

"Yes, the vault in question lies within the crypts, which are usually locked and empty—why do you hesitate?"

"Since we are dealing with someone who can animate revenants, burial chambers are the last place any of us should go."

"Ah," Mikhail nodded. "Point taken. You'll need all swords down below."

"Mikhail, no," Trayn said firmly. "Your part in the plan is to create a distraction above while some of us slip in the crypts below. You need to hold to that. Send two guards down with us, but more than that will attract attention."

"Only two?" Mikhail asked with a frown.

Exactly what Jenna was thinking. A full complement of knights would be most welcome in a crypt full of revenants, if that was what they faced. But she trusted Trayn's judgment.

"You need to make the grand entrance with entourage as planned," Trayn continued to argue. "Three swords will suffice."

The prince acquiesced. She and Trayn hung back as Mikhail and his guardsman formed up at the side door to the cathedral. The guards pulled their cloaks over their sheathed swords in an effort to look as peaceable as possible, then on cue, opened the grand doors and followed the prince into St. Kyre's.

Jenna crept forward to peek through the still open doors. The prince and his escort were progressing with full pomp down the center aisle to the altar, flanked by a knot of priests. It wasn't an ideal time to take in the details of the kingdom's grandest ecclesiastical structure, but she did notice the vaulted dome soaring far overhead and the rows of large spiral-twist columns that marched down each side of the space. But more than anything else, it was the scent that overwhelmed her senses. The air was redolent with sandalwood incense burning in dozens of censers hanging from the ceiling.

She pulled back to a side hall where the three knights were

waiting. Trayn produced a heavy iron key and opened an unobtrusive door. A narrow spiral stair was built into a corner cubicle, and they followed it down to the cellars. "This seems suspiciously unguarded," Trayn commented in a low voice as he paused near the bottom to light his torch, then unsheathe his sword.

"That loudly suggests an unnatural trap in the crypts," Jenna murmured back. "But revenants are slow of movement. We need to move quickly—hurry in, break the salt circle, and hurry out."

They regrouped at the bottom of the spiral stairs, every knight with a sword and torch at ready. The air was heavily scented, and she took a careful sniff. More sandalwood. A storage bin by the foot of the stairs seemed to be stocked with blocks of sandalwood to be grated down to shavings for the censers. Big pots of shavings stood along the wall, ready for use in the cathedral above.

Then she heard a reluctant click and turned as Trayn unlocked a second door to the crypts proper and threw it wide open. All was dense darkness beyond. Trayn stepped inside, flanked by the two knights with swords drawn. They held their torches high as he unlocked a smaller door to the vault itself. She moved in beside them, senses questing for things that moved in the darkness of the catacombs. She sensed a few unquiet spirits as was common in places of burial, and something darker and less common beyond, but they hadn't yet triggered a trap. She calmed herself with her own words: *hurry in, break the salt circle, and hurry out.*

Then as Trayn opened the vault door and pushed his torch inside, her heart sank. Not a salt circle. This was nothing she had ever encountered before. The floor of the vault from wall to wall to wall was glazed in crusted salt. The shock clouded her senses for a moment, but as she calmed her thoughts, she saw wisps of apparitions inside.

"Dwarf," she called softly.

One of the tattered shapes floated toward her. "It's a damn salt cell!" a grizzled voice grumped. "That's old, old knowledge. Anyone knowing how to use salt cells to trap spirits ought to be centuries dead and gone."

"You're not alone, Dwarf. Who else is trapped in here? Antaria?" The other spirit was tattered like one long dead. "Milady, who killed you?"

"Yeah, the dead lady's not doing so well," Dwarf muttered. "The salt eats away at us and she's been here longer."

"Then how do I break the confinement?" Jenna demanded urgently.

"A gallon of blood ought to do it," Dwarf rumbled.

"Jenna, hurry," Trayn murmured from the door. "I thought I heard something moving out in the catacombs."

"Revenants, Dwarf," Jenna said quickly. "How many are there and what's the best way to fight them?"

"They can be hurt by iron or steel, so Sir Stupid could hold them off with his sword as long as he cleanly cuts off the heads and doesn't waste time stabbing. As for how many—I spotted six on the way in, but there could be more."

"Probably six revenants—go for the head, not the heart, if they come at you," she called over her shoulder, then turned back. "What about fire?"

"Slow going but they will burn, if that's what you're asking."

She shook her head. "No, for the salt. I know that salt itself doesn't burn, but it can melt. Is that enough to break the binding spell?"

Dwarf gave a shrug. "If melted salt is enough different from true salt."

"Trayn, a torch," she called. "Hold it against the floor until the salt crust melts away."

He stepped in and touched the flame to the salted floor. The spot where it touched turned a smoky orange. But just that one small spot.

"This will take forever," she muttered to herself. She took a deep breath and found herself breathing the heavy scent of sandalwood again. The storage bin. Then her thoughts came together in an idea, and she ran from the catacombs to the bin. The blocks were useless to her, but the wood shavings were tinder waiting to happen. She grabbed one of the big pottery jars, started to run back, when a wave of dizziness overcame her. Too much, she realized and slowed her pace to a walk. Back inside, she began spreading the wood shavings over the floor. There was just enough to cover the floor of the small vault with a shallow layer.

Trayn turned back from watching the darkness just as she finished. "Ah, incense. To make a deadly situation smell sweeter. We need to leave, Jenna." The *swoosh* of a sword in motion sounded in the darkness beyond him.

She nodded. "Then less talk and more lighting the shavings, if you please. Sandalwood burns slowly, but over time it should melt the salt beneath it. Dwarf, I fear we must leave you like this. Both of you come to the prince's workroom as soon as you're free of the salt."

"And we're out of time," Trayn said and abruptly swung at a shambling shadow just entering the ring of torchlight. "Back to the corridor." The other knights were already backing as they swung at the approaching shadows.

Jenna dashed out of the catacombs, then stopped to fight back another wave of dizziness. Behind her, she heard several more slashes, then the iron door slamming shut. When she turned, Trayn was locking it again.

He took a few breaths, sheathed his sword, then turned. "Well done, comrades. Success for the moment, though we leave the catacombs of the kingdom's highest cathedral infested with revenants."

"Not ideal," Jenna admitted. "But these are creatures of necromancy beyond the scope of any normal exorcism. A battalion of knights with torches and sharp swords may be as good a solution as we can muster."

"Necromancy implies a necromancer."

She nodded. "I know. We have a necromancer and a murderer at large."

"And if he—or they—return to find the vault a mass of burning sandalwood?"

She couldn't resist. "I suppose he'll be incensed." Close encounters with death always made her silly.

The journey in reverse was deliciously uneventful. Their escort of two joined the prince's entourage at the altar, signaling Mikhail that his prayers could conclude. Then the whole group of them made their way to the commandery wing. Along the way, Jenna reported to the prince what had transpired. His eyes grew cold as he realized not only had his mother been murdered, but her spirit was meant to wither away in a salt cell. But he said nothing.

It reminded her that Mikhail was a killer as well as a friend. Trayn also, if she extended the thought. By profession, the Knights of the Retribution were all killers. In a world where the dead stayed dead, strength of arms would have settled the question of succession. But that was not the world they lived in. And out of nowhere, she sympathized with nine-year-old Prince Theo, caught between his half-brother's cold-eyed knights on one side, and a necromancer on the other.

Her thoughts wandered to her own missing brother, his absence feeling like a nagging itch behind her eyes. She did not believe Herrin had fallen to the revenants because he was searching elsewhere than the crypts, but he could have fallen captive to the Inquisition. A cleric among clerics should not have aroused suspicion, but these were not normal times. Still, he was good at passing unnoticed. But why had he not returned?

By the time they arrived at the prince's workroom in the commandery, she was physically fatigued but ready to face the hard issues. She accepted mulled wine and sat sipping it for a few moments. Then she asked, "Highness, what will you do if your opponent does the unthinkable? We are now sure he has a necromancer in his camp capable of raising the king when he passes."

Mikhail's face flushed with sudden anger. "He wouldn't dare."

"Assume he might."

He was just working himself up to an answer, when she suddenly shushed him. An apparition was shakily forming. "Dwarf?"

"What's left of him," the ghost grumbled. "Blood and plenty

of it, if you don't mind."

"Would the kitchens have a calf or deer carcass on hand that they could drain of blood?" she asked the room.

"Cow blood!" Dwarf spat. "You offer me cow blood!"

"I suppose so," Mikhail returned uncertainly. "They are constantly feeding an army of courtiers."

"Then please send a guard to make that happen, Highness" and to Dwarf, "It's a dire situation, so please make the sacrifice and return when your strength is sufficient. We're evidently fighting a necromancer."

"What tipped you off—the walking dead?" Dwarf snorted and faded out.

Mikhail frowned. "If I can prove the Exorcist-General has fallen into dark sorcery, Holy Mother Church will have to support me."

"*If* it is the Exorcist-General," Jenna pointed out. "The salt cell in the crypts was a complete surprise to me. I would swear the Office of the Holy Exorcism does not have the knowledge to create something like that. Likewise the revenants. They are proof of necromancy, not exorcism."

"A catacomb full of revenants is definitely proof of something," Trayn shrugged. "Let the High Bishop take a look beneath his own cathedral before choosing sides."

Mikhail slammed a sudden fist against the table top. "By Kyre, yes! The High Bishop will be furious and may stand with me after all. His opinion will carry much weight in the High Council tomorrow. Unexpectedly, these revenants may be good for the cause."

"A good revenant?" Trayn repeated doubtfully.

As he spoke, Jenna felt the nagging itch behind her eyes. Odd because it was both unpleasant and familiar. But she never had headaches as a child—that was Herrin. Why was she feeling his headaches?

"Blood!" she called abruptly into the conversation. "I'm being summoned."

"The necromancer?" Trayn muttered, drawing his sword.

She shook her head. "Herrin, I think. Just a drop of blood on the floor." As he complied, she intoned, "Blood to blood and flesh to flesh. Show me."

The workroom grayed out and she was hovering in a dark space. Before her, two figures huddled around a candle. One was slicing a fingertip and intoning as the droplets fell toward the candle. "Herrin?" she called.

The figure with a knife raised a pale face to her. "Jenna, thank goodness. I didn't know if you would hear, but I had to try something. We're hiding in the cellars under the Inquisition wing but are hopelessly lost. There are priests hunting us, and it's only a matter of time before they find us."

"Who is that with you?" Jenna asked. Her own voice sounded hollow and distant... like a spirit's.

The other, younger figure raised its face, and she had a jolt of recognition. She didn't know the boy, but she knew the face. "I found him locked in an Inquisition cell. The Lord Inquisitor is the one to fear because he has a necroma—" Herrin began. Then a chasm opened and sucked her into darkness.

Jenna opened her eyes to the workroom, Trayn and Mikhail hovering over her in concern.

"An attack?" Trayn demanded. "Why did you call to Herrin?"

"I found him," she said with effort. She felt like the life had been squeezed from her. This was no way to communicate—probably why it wasn't taught. "My brother found your brother, Highness, and they are hiding from the Inquisition because the Lord Inquisitor is your true enemy. Dwarf, are you back yet?"

A stocky, sullen-looking figure materialized, still licking his lips. "I'm still feeding, if you don't mind."

"But you look worlds better," she insisted. "You have to find Herrin before the Inquisition does. He can't see you but will recognize your cold hand on his shoulder and will follow you to safety. He's in the cellars under the far wing—and please, keep him far away from the crypts."

"And a pitiless taskmaster you are," Dwarf grumped and faded out.

"There, done," she sighed. "Dwarf will bring them back to

safety. That's assuming, of course, that Prince Mikhail has more of a heart than an Inquisition dungeon."

Mikhail stepped back with a frown. "A heart?"

"Yes, we both need to welcome our brothers, Highness. This madness over the succession must end."

Trayn put a hand on her shoulder. "Jenna, don't get involved in the politics. It's a fight to the death for the Crown. Either Theo dies or Mikhail does."

"I'm already dragged into royal politics and not happily," she shot back. "This conflict has already descended into sorcery and necromancy and will only get worse. The kingdom needs a united royal family to survive this. It's the simple truth any idiot can see... Highness." She finished with a belated honorific.

"Madness," the prince snorted. "If you knew politics, you would know the royal family has never been united."

"But out of the mouths of innocents, Mikhail," Trayn interjected. "There are few in the kingdom who would not rally to the side of the princes united. And we do have revenants under St. Kyre's. What better villains in this piece?"

"There still might be civil war," the prince pointed out.

"But only a small one, and the Knights would so enjoy a small civil war."

Jenna was glad Trayn was taking up the argument because she felt herself descending into exhaustion again.

Do not sleep yet, Exorcista. The whisper was faint but insistent in her half-asleep head.

She opened her eyes, trying to place the voice. Trayn was still arguing with Mikhail by the window where the first light of dawn as creeping across the sky. But it wasn't one of their voices anyway. A woman's?

She roused herself enough to quest the room with her senses. Ah, a very dim presence near the prince that hadn't been there before. "Lady Antaria?" she asked.

The conversation at the window ceased instantly. "She's here?" Mikhail asked.

"Barely. A very weak presence."

"She must have blood," Trayn said, drawing his dagger.

"Mine, then," Mikhail said. "Blood speaks to blood, you said earlier." He took Trayn's dagger and crossed over to Jenna to offer her his palm.

She understandably hesitated. Drawing royal blood was heavily discouraged. But he was right, a blood connection would be the strongest link. She lightly cut at his palm and let the drops fall.

"Blood to blood and flesh to flesh," Mikhail intoned, remembering the earlier incantation. "Come to me, Mother."

The spirit of the lady solidified more than it had any right to in its tattered, faded state. "My son," she whispered, and he gave a start.

"I hear you, Mother."

The blood bond must be very strong, Jenna noted in surprise. This didn't happen often. It was why exorcists were needed to commune with the dead.

"I fought for you to be crowned, you and only you," she continued, "but I was wrong. From beyond the veil I see now that I wasted my time in constant intriguing. Listen to the Exorcista, my son. It is what your father the king has wanted—his two sons united. He planned for Theo to be king after him and you to be regent, but I was a fool and opposed the plan. I hid the Writ of Succession within my own chamber—a secret panel in the window alcove—and that murdering Inquisitor never found it. Be smarter than me, my Mikhail..." She faded out completely.

Mikhail turned to stare out the window, his expression unreadable. Jenna made an effort to shift out her chair to give him privacy, but he forestalled her with a quick gesture. "Rest, Exorcista. I'll be leaving at first light to hunt up the Writ of Succession and present a most unexpected succession plan to the High Council. It's a solid plan, I must admit, and with the backing of both Council and Knighthood, it should reduce the Lord Inquisitor's options to a fast horse out of the city."

She saw Trayn raise an eyebrow in her direction as he crossed over the fireplace. "For one new to the game, you have done exceedingly well."

She shook her head. "It took all of us. And you know there will be a price to pay for running Dwarf ragged."

Trayn gave a long sigh. "Wenching with a haunt on my shoulder—aye, I know. But much better than a revenant." He gave a snort. "Good or elsewise."

Jenna felt a surge of silliness after the long night. "The only good revenant is a dead one."

TO WOMEN GO

by Helen E. Davis

Helen E Davis is an author of Science Fiction, Fantasy, and—usually by accident—occasionally horror. Her short stories have been published in *Sword and Sorceress*, *Mutation Nation*, and *Abyss and Apex*. Her novels are available at Amazon.com. She was born in the deep South, moved to Ohio, married and raised children, and keeps caterpillars for pets. She also knits.

To Women go
The child and womb
Hearth and hold
Crop and loom.

The world was pain.

Sharp pains embroidered the dull, constant ache from Gynth's shoulder, and occasionally a white-hot pain coursed down her arm. The floor pressed against the blooming bruises on her legs, and her head pounded from exhaustion—but she could not lie down. She sat, back against the inner wall of her hut, bolstered by her husband's spare saddle on one side and a bag of raw wool on the other. The shadows of tree branches, laden with unopened seed pods, crept past a stain on her wooden floor. Bees hummed beyond the open window; a dog yipped and snapped at a flea. Soon night would bring an end to this endless day, but it would bring an endless night, and then another endless day.

Stupid, stupid, stupid.

Yemen, her daughter, had bound Gynth's injured arm against her body and seeped herbs in wine for her, but the pain blazed through it all. Her second daughter, Adril, had brought her bread soaked in milk, but her stomach twisted at the thought of eating. Flies buzzed around the untouched bowl, but she was in too much pain to brush them away.

Stupid.

There were things which needed to be done: goats and mares to be milked, turnips to be dug, this awful, dirty floor to be swept. None of those things cared that she could not move. And yet, who would do these things for her? Her husband, with the other men, were away trading wool for beads and silver bells, and her daughters had households of their own to care for. The other women of this village—no, she would not stoop to that. She would have to rise and do her work.

She struggled to bend forward, to push off the wall, and gasped as a new wave of pain shook her arm.

Not right now.

Stupid, stupid.

The rock had been in the same place it had been for years, so why hadn't she stepped over it? Why had she fallen while carrying water from the well, spilling her morning's efforts? And why had she sprawled before all the other women of the village? Especially now that her husband had taken a second wife? Even as Yemen and Adril had helped her up and led her home, snickers had followed them.

"Here's your water," Decendes announced as she walked through the open door, a leather bucket in her hands. The matriarch of the village was tall, like all the Grasslands Women, and her only acknowledgement to her age was the white hair pulled back in a braid. Her green eyes were still clear and her knee-length sapan, woven in clashing red, green, and yellow, stretched tight over ample hips and shoulders. She dropped the bucket in the corner of the hut, letting the water slop over the rim. "No doubt you'll want to waste it on that tree of yours."

It shelters my hut. And you enjoy the shade as well.

Her tree, the tallest thing on these grasslands. She had brought the seedling from the mountains, packed with the cooking pots and bedding for her bridal house, when she had come to be married. She nurtured it beside her own children, as they all grew tall and strong. But while her daughters flourished and started families of their own, the seed pods withered and fell unopened.

She sighed, then saw the cool water still dripping from the rim of the bucket. “Please, will you please give me a drink?”

“Of course.” Decendes found a cup, stared into it. She wiped it with a cloth from the table, filled it from the bucket, and set it down on Gynth’s injured side. “Is there anything else you want?”

“Did anyone find my amulet? I think it fell off when I tripped.” As she spoke, Gynth eyed the cup and thought how to reach for it with her good hand without jostling her injured shoulder. Maybe she would wait for Adril to move it.

“I don’t think anyone looked for your trinket. Yell if you need anything.” Descendes walked out.

As with the tree, Descendes made it clear that she thought Gynth’s protection against wandering fezrai to be a useless mountain superstition. Gynth leaned her head back against the wall and listened to chickens clucking on the other side, unaware of their eventual fate.

“I’ve milked your cows,” Hentatia announced as she walked in with a butter bag. The matriarch’s niece hung it beside the door and gave it a few hard punches. Not quite as tall as Decendes, she was thicker, with hard muscles beneath her golden-brown skin. She always wore a long knife, could hold a sheep for shearing, best any man at swordplay, and was extremely fond of punching the butter bags.

Good milk wasted on butter. Gynth preferred cheese. “Thank you.”

“You’ll need help dyeing and spinning your wool.” She pointed at the two stuffed sacks beside Gynth. “I’ll put those in with my own.”

Gynth eyed Hentatia’s blue and orange sapan, then glanced down at her own undyed tunic. “It can wait. I’ll be fine, soon. Very soon.”

“There will be snow before you can work the spindle.” Hentatia glanced out at the late summer afternoon.

“Mountain women heal quickly.” And she would rather have her daughters’ help rather than any Hentatia could give.

“Of course.” Hentatia’s disbelief rang through the words. “Let me know when you want me to take care of your wool.”

"I don't—" She bit back the words. "Did anyone find my amulet? It must be there by the path."

"I wouldn't know. You don't need it, here." Hentatia swept out the door, panicked chickens protesting behind her.

Gynth closed her eyes. With the pain in her shoulder all but blotting out the dryness of her throat, she drifted into a grey haze. Adril wouldn't be long, would she?

"You haven't eaten a bite of your dinner!"

Gynth opened her eyes to see not her daughter, but Lulanie, the matriarch's younger sister. Her face was too thin for her nose, her eyes too wide for her face, and her white-streaked red hair too sparse to stay in a braid. Her red and blue sapan was stained with mud, and she threw a dirty sack against the wall. Was every woman in the village making an excuse to come in and gawk at her? "I'm not hungry."

"Oh, you'll have to eat to get strong again. I dug carrots and turnips for you—enough to last you for a few days. Why don't I fry a few—I have fresh spices and peppers to throw in."

Hot spice on her parched throat? She wanted soft cheese. "I don't need…"

"It will be no problem at all." Lulanie swept out the door, pounding the butter bag as she went.

As the woman's shadow receded, another approached. Adril, at last? But then the swollen belly of her husband's new wife, protruding between the top and bottom of her sapan, came through the door. The rest of Miscordia the Orphan followed, proudly bearing her burden before the older and no longer fertile wife.

The girl gave the butter bag a quick poke. "Are you going to make me the blankets for my baby?"

"You may use the blankets my children had." The ones, of course, that her daughters had not taken for their own children. "They're in the trunk."

"I was hoping my baby would have new ones."

Of course her baby would have new blankets. Descendes and her entire household was weaving new cloth for the girl they had rescued from a wrecked village to the south, raised in their own household, and presented to Gynth's husband for a suitable second wife. Gynth's efforts had gone towards her own daughters, not this upstart who already had a better house, a better bed, and a better crib than she ever did. "I will make you one when I can."

And it will be tan and brown, proper colors for a baby.

Miscordia poked the butter bag again. "You'll have to hurry. You haven't even started yet."

"Leave her alone, Miscordia." Yemen, a baby on her hip and a toddler chasing her heels, pushed past the girl. She set a dish down on the table, then turned and hit the butter bag so hard that it bounced off the lintel. She was tall like her father, with his red hair and green eyes, but her child had Gynth's lighter hair and grey eyes. "It's true, you haven't eaten your food."

"I'm not hungry." Even if she could have reached without pain, or scraped the bowl with only one hand. "But I want something to drink."

"You need to eat." Yemen set down the baby and gave it a crust of bread to chew on, then took away the fly-infested bowl. Squatting beside Gynth with a plate of mashed—something, she took a spoonful. "Here."

"No!"

"I feed a toddler." Yemen poked the spoonful in.

Turnips, spicy and over-salted, of course. Gynth tried to turn her head, but Yemen did not stop spooning in the mush until it was half gone. Then she rocked back on her heels. "That will do for now. Here, drink this."

Gynth could smell the herb-infused wine. "That didn't work."

"I made it stronger. You'll sleep now." And she held up the cup so that Gynth had no choice but to drink.

She had thought being fed like this was the worst indignity of all, but then she saw shadows beyond her door. The others were out there, listening, laughing silently. With her good hand, she pushed the cup away. "I've had enough. Go."

"I'll check back on you later." Her daughter rose, picked up her children and walked out, not even bothering to hit the butter bag.

Gynth stared up at the rafters, where dried herbs and onions hung from the beams. *I would give anything to be free of this.*

The tree's shadow stretched out as the sunlight turned golden, then red. A seed pod fell, scattering the chickens and dogs. The world softened and dimmed, fading into the hum of crickets, taking the pain with it.

Gynth found herself standing before her tree, and the tree was with the other sacred trees of her mountain home. Just beyond, thc ground dropped away to show the long valley between the peaks to the west, a valley filled with forested hills and deep river bottoms. An owl hooted, off in the night shadows, and a fox barked. Sweet summer flowers and ripe apricots, moss and green trees, the spice tea perfume of opened seed pods—these scents and others swirled about her.

There was also the tang of recently burnt land—every mid-summer the women of the village would gather to burn the ground beneath the trees, to drive away the twisted fezrai that lurked there, gnawing at the roots. Once, when she was a child, a tree had to be cut down, carried far away, and burned, to drive away the fezrai within. And now her tree was here, in its place.

Here also was healing and safety. She remembered that she had wanted to come here to bear her children, within the shelter of the trees, but it had been too far for her to travel. Here—did this vision mean that she should come here now?

"You are in pain?"

She turned to face the speaker. He was—he had to be the guardian here, though he was not what she had expected. She had thought that the Guardian of the Grove would be a woman, fair as the people of the heights—but this man had wild, dark hair and cat-slit eyes. Strong muscles filled out his shirt, tunic, and woolen stockings—the dress of her own people.

Gynth bit back homesickness. "I fell, and my arm—is useless."

"Here." His fingers caressed her shoulder. The pain drifted away.

She raised her arm—it went up in a smooth motion. As her hand turned from side to side, she could feel strength flow back into it. She made a fist—and there was not even any of the small pops and cracks that age had given her. She could dye her wool and weave her cloth with all the speed of any young woman, and prove her worth beyond one who could only push out babies. "Thank you."

He looked down. "That will not last, sadly. I do not have much strength, here in the grass."

She opened her hand, closed it. "How—how much time do I have?"

"A few hours."

That wasn't long enough. "What could—is there anything I can do?"

He stared into the distance behind her, his strange eyes narrowing. "Just—if you could help me to come there, then I could heal you completely. It won't take much—I would use only a little of the power of your land."

"The land—here? There are no groves, only—only my tree." Her last link to her village. Could she give up her tree?

A nasty twinge ran from her shoulder to her wrist.

"Not the tree, which is from the mountains. From here, from this land." His voice was smooth, his smile comforting.

She had heard of fezrai who had laid waste to all they touched. Miscordia's village—had it been a wild beast, as Descendes claimed, or an angry fezrai? But this was a guardian—he was much too strong, too generous, to be anything else. Still, she asked, "Will you hurt the land?"

"Oh, no. The land will be as it was intended to be. As will all that grows upon it, and the animals that graze upon the plants. Everything will be healed."

He was offering to come and be a guardian for the village, and perhaps, yes, that was what this village needed. Perhaps then the other women would believe her about the fezrai. "What do you want me to do?"

"A small, very small thing. Put my token into the spring."

That seemed easy enough. "The one in my field, or the well

where the women draw their water each day?"

Concern flickered across his face, but was instantly soothed. He smiled. "The one within the rocks to the northwest. Don't you know it?"

"I've—never been that way." In all the years that she had lived in this village, she had never had an interest in those rocks. They lay on the other side of Descendes' fields, with an old, mean ram in the farthest one. The road to other villages swung far away from the rocks, and nothing grew near them that was worth foraging.

"You must go behind the rocks, then up through the narrow path. Within the stone you will see a spring and a pool of water. Drop in my token, that's all I ask."

"I…"

"And all the women here will marvel at your healing. They will pity you no longer."

Yes.

"It might be best if you do this quickly, before sunrise, while my powers are strong. And do not tell anyone about this—they would think you weak to use a guardian's power for healing, rather than your own strength."

How very true. "I will."

With that, the dream faded.

Pain woke Gynth, dull but brightening like the dawn. She had dreamed, but dreams were not real, and she was back in her agony. Now she had another misery, and needed to move to relieve herself. And so, cautiously, she used her good arm to push herself up—then saw on the floor, in the very early light of the new day, something which had not been there before.

She picked it up. A clay disc, half the size of a saucer, with strange symbols pressed into one side. The guardian's token. It was real, he was real. And she had been given the task of bringing him to the village.

Using a branch fallen from her tree to steady herself, Gynth hobbled along the footpath that ran between the gardens and the wild grass that grew as high as her shoulders. Stars still filled the sky that fit over the flat land like an overturned bowl, and only the faint violet line on the eastern edge hinted at the coming day. She could see forever across the flatness here, where the endless sweep of grass was broken occasionally by a stand of black rocks or the huts of distant villages. The only tree in sight was her own.

Beyond the gardens were the paddocks for the herds. A goat bleated here, a mare nickered there. Lambs cried after their ewes. As she passed the field where the ram wandered, the eastern half of the sky was light enough to wash out the stars. By the time she reached the rocks, gold limned the edge of the sky, then gathered to a single drop of molten light. She climbed to the cleft and looked down just as the first rays speared out, spreading light and soft shadows.

And found she had been deceived. For years.

There was indeed a spring here, splashing from a crack in the stone, and also a well-kept garden around a sculptured pool. Tiles lined the bottom of the pool, keeping the water clear. Red, gold and blue flowers bloomed in the garden, filling the air with their sweet and spicy perfume. Beyond the garden stood a ring of small rocks, each about the height of her knee, and then stone benches for sitting and enjoying it all.

A special place, kept from her. Now it would become home to the guardian that *she* would bring to protect the village, a guardian who would give *her* special privileges here.

She hobbled to the edge of the pool and carefully knelt. Pulling the token from her pocket, she held it above the water. A bit of the soft clay crumbled, attracting small golden fish.

You will be protected, she thought as she dropped the token in. They bit at it, then darted away, startled. Gynth looked behind herself, saw nothing. But she felt—stronger. Less pain. It was working.

"Remember your promise," she whispered to the water, then pulled herself to her feet. Yes, her shoulder hurt less. Things would be good.

"Mountain women heal quickly." Gynth worked with exaggerated slowness, pulling her wool through the carding combs as if her shoulder still pained her. No sense in letting the others know her secret. She had even kept her arm tied up for two weeks, doing her chores one-handed, rather than let them suspect she had a guardian's favor. Now as she sat in the bright sunlight, carding the long-neglected wool, she allowed herself the luxury of using both hands.

"Only bruised, not broken." Hentatia stared up at the cloudless sky, frowning, as she swung a half-filled butter bag in her hands. It came perilously close to the fire where Gynth was heating water to wash the next batch of wool. "Why hasn't it rained?"

"If it rains, I can't get this done." Gynth waved a hand at the pot and the fire. "Could you…"

"You should dye that before you card it." Hentatia raised her hand to Lulaine as the other woman walked by, a basket on her back. "Auntie! How are your plants?"

"Dry," Lulaine pulled off the basket and drew out a handful of limp greens. "And wilting in the heat."

"The well is going dry, did you see that? And so are the goats and mares." Hentatia held up the butter bag, thankfully moving it away from the fire. "This is all I've gotten today."

"We've gone without rain before," Gynth said, but neither of the women seemed to notice her.

Lulaine crossed her thin arms. "We'll lose our harvest if it doesn't rain. The plants were just flowering, and if they wilt now, they won't set seed."

"Hentatia!" It was Yemen, walking toward them, a wailing baby in her arms. "Do you have extra goats milk? I can't seem to satisfy my little one today."

The older woman frowned deeply. "The nannies *and* the women are going dry? This is bad. Very bad."

"Eeeeyaaaah!" Miscordia, behind the others, clutched at her stomach.

Dropping the butter bag, Hentatia turned and caught both of the girl's arms in her hands. "Is it the pains? Before the full moon? We should get you…"

"No! But if everything is drying up, how can I—what a

horrible time to have a baby!" She sobbed furiously, tears tracking down the dust on her face.

"You will be well, daughter." The older woman embraced the girl. "We will see that your baby and you are fed. We will see that it is born safely. You are protected."

Hentatia and Lulaine reached out to comfort the girl, and others from the village ran up. Yemen's child wailed on.

Gynth stood and caught her daughter's arm. "You can have my milk. I've yet to start the cheese today."

Her daughter nodded, but slowly. "What will you do?"

"My goats are not going dry. I have that spring in my field, remember? The grass is lush. I'll have enough to share with everyone." And yet, even as she said that, she wondered if the water bubbling up hadn't been lower than usual, and hadn't the bucket of milk been less full? But this was not the time, with the baby crying and Miscordia wailing, to voice such things.

"What's going on here?" Descendes stood to the side, her hands on her ample hips. "What's all this noise?"

"There's been no rain, and everything drying up." Lulaine glanced quickly at Yemen. "Everything."

Descendes brushed her hands on her wide sapan and looked at the chickens scratching listlessly at the dust. "I know. Even the roosters are ignoring the hens."

Lulaine paled. "It's the guardian, isn't it? She's left us!"

How did she know? Gynth thought, as chills ran down her spine. Then, *She?*

"Not willingly." Descendes spoke firmly, but it was same sort of firmness with which she said that the sons of the village would be fine when they left to find wives. "She would not abandon us."

"But she has!" Miscordia wailed.

"You—you have a guardian?" Gynth asked aloud. "A—she?"

All of the other women stopped and stared at her, even her own daughter. Then Descendes spoke, her voice harsh. "This has nothing to do with you. Go into your hut."

Gynth stood and stared into the other woman's eyes. "It

does."

Lulaine grabbed her arm, squeezed it hard. Her eyes narrowed. "You aren't of our village. You aren't one of us."

"True," Gynth spat out. She shook off Lulaine's grip and dusted off her skin. "I've lived among you for years, long enough for my daughters to have children, and I've never been accepted, but *you should have told me.*"

Descendes stepped back, her face paling to ash. "What did you do?"

"I was offered a bargain. I did not know you had a guardian already." Her hands clenched into tight fists.

Now the other women were drawing back, even her daughter.

"You made a bargain with—what?" Descendes raised her hands.

"Something that did not tell me he was taking the place of another." She clutched at her chest, touched emptiness where her missing amulet should have been. Where it should have protected her, protected all of them. "I put him in the spring."

"*He?*" Hentatia shrieked out. "You entered our circle, gave our power, woman's right, to a *he?*"

Lulaine whirled about and ran for the northwest, keening as she went. Hentatia dropped her butter bag and ran after, and then the others, even Miscordia, who waddled and panted as she moved. More women tumbled out of the huts and houses, joined the race. Behind them all, walking as if her legs were wood, Gynth followed them to the spring.

The spring still bubbled from the rock, but the water splashed into a brackish pool. Bloated fish floated on the surface; the plants were black with rot. Flies swarmed over the corpses of lizards, frogs and birds. And the circle of stones was thrown out of position.

The women walked about, dazed or crying, some beating on the stones, some ripping their sapans. Miscordia huddled on her swollen belly while Yemen held her screaming baby. Adril was there, her toddler sobbing against her mother's shoulder.

You did this, Gynth told herself.

Hentatia was first to notice Gynth. She drew her knife, thrust the blade forward. "You! You let it in! I'll kill you!"

"No!" Adril cried out, and moved in front of Gynth. But Yemen stayed where she was.

"Stand back!" Hentatia roared. She brandished the blade. "She did this—she'll pay with blood!"

Now Descendes stepped in front of her niece and pushed down the knife. "Not blood, not here. It would only make things worse."

Outside of this place, Gynth was certain, her life was forfeit. But here, if they listened to Descendes, she had a chance. They all had a chance. "Blood will seal the fezrai here."

Lulaine spat on the rock at Gynth's sandal. "What do you know?"

"I know what has to be done. What I have to do. My village fought fezrai all the time."

"Of course they did," Lulaine snarled. "With people like you inviting them in."

No, it was the trees that called the fezrai, or at least that was what the elder women claimed. And maybe her tree had called this thing. "But we also know how to fight them."

"How—how do you fight *this?*"

Gynth walked past the women to mouth of the spring, where the still fresh water bubbled out. The demon was in the pool below, where the token had dissolved. She picked up her tree branch, discarded on her last visit, and shoved the end into the spring.

Behind her, people gasped. Hentatia growled, low in her throat, "How could you…"

Gynth turned to face them. "Tear out all of these plants and remove the dead animals. Drain the pool, scrub it clean. When all trace of the pollution is gone, let the pool refill with clean water. Then you can call your guardian back."

Hentatia stood in front of her, stared into her face. "And you think that your pet demon will let us?"

"Fezrai." Gynth stared back. "You do your part, and quickly. My part is to deal with him."

Back at her tree, Gynth laid her hands against the rough bark and closed her eyes. Here and now, she breathed in the scents of cooking oil spiced with peppers, sour milk, dust and dry manure. She remembered the perfume of mountain flowers and sharp ash, the fire in her shoulder, the softness of dawn. Tears pricked her cheeks.

"You call for me?" That same voice, soft as a cat's purr. "Were you not paid well enough?"

In her dream, she turned to face him, to look into his eyes, into the brightness that poured from the slits. Golden light, bright as the sun above the Grassland, flowed around the shape of his head, his body. "You lied to me."

He smiled, the tips of pointed teeth showing between his lips. "I did all that I promised to do."

She waggled her finger in his face, anger where bravery failed. "You promised not to hurt the land or the animals! But look at this! There's no rain, and everything is drying up!"

"This is a dry land. The pathetic little god here was destroying it with her water."

"Destroying it? The crops, the herd, the people—all these depend on the water! You are the one destroying everything, by holding back the rain!"

The fezrai swept out his hand and caught her own "*Those* were destroying the land. Without them, the wilderness will return, and with it, the animals that *should* be here. This squalid circle of huts will be swept away, and all these pathetic women with them. I grant you the right to stay, and be rich beneath me, but all the others must go. Tell them this."

"I won't."

His grip crushed her fingers. "Do as you're told, or I'll scatter your bones."

Could she hold him off? The other women—were they working quickly enough? She had to keep fighting, but all she had was her will. "My daughters are among those you mean to drive away."

"So?" He laughed. His hand grew, covering her own. He squeezed, rubbing her bones together. "They have left you, become the others."

In her mind's eye she saw Yemen, not moving to protect her. But Adril had—and their children were her grandchildren. Miscordia was her co-wife, and her child—her child would be Gynth's step-child. "They connect me to the others. I am with them—and they are with me."

"Do you really think so?"

Was that a flicker in his strength? A dimming of his light? "Yes—they came to help when I was hurt."

He paused, as if noticing something.

She slapped his face, the face of a fezrai, with her free hand.

Red fire flared from eyes, and his hand burned her trapped one. He doubled in size, dangled her from his grip. "Bitch of the mountains! You dare!"

"Mountain women always have!" She kicked him, hard, though the blow landed only on his thigh, and slapped him again. "We have the strength of stone!"

"You're only a crack in the stone, the opening I needed among the women, the way into their protected spring." With that he flung her away.

She hit the ground with her shoulder, felt it snap. The pain wrenched through her as muscle and sinew tore. His giant foot rose above her, came down, and pounded the ground just as she rolled away. Gritting her teeth, she scrambled to her feet, faced his belly. Yes, he was smaller than before, but she couldn't let him notice. She drove her good shoulder into his stomach. "Do you really think you can command me?"

He staggered. "I am a god, and you are a—a woman."

"You, a god? A pathetic little trickster? A beggar, a thief?"

"Whore!"

This time the blow struck her hip, and she fell. But he hadn't killed her, not yet. She pushed to her knees, then to her feet, though the one leg didn't want to bear her weight. When she pushed herself up, she found herself looking at his neck, and there was barely any light around him. The last of his aura faded as he shrank to her own height. "I will kill you. I will crush you like an ant beneath my heel, and then this whole village."

She spat in his face, then dove to the side as his hand came down. She hit hard, on her injured shoulder and hip, but rolled quickly, out of the dream, into the dusty afternoon. Still in agony, she grabbed a burning stick from her fire and flung it into the straw and dung she had piled around her tree. Echoes of a scream swept around her as she fell into unconsciousness.

"Gynth!"

"Gynth!"

"Mom!"

The voices came closer, pulled her out of the darkness. Heat pressed on one side, a furnace. Cold water touched her face, dribbled on her chest. Hands patted her arms and legs, painful in their comfort.

She dragged open her eyes. "That—hurts."

"Can you rise?" Descendes crouched, her face almost touching Gynth's. "Can you walk?"

Just like on the walk back from the well, when she had broken her shoulder the first time. "Let me lie here."

"We'll carry you if we have to. We have to get back to the spring, and finish."

Gynth's eyes yanked fully open. All she had gone through—was for nothing? Unprotected, the fezrai would be back in that spring before, before… "You didn't call your guardian?"

"Yes, yes, we called her." Water splashed on Gynth's leg and she was aware, just aware, that the pain in her hip was easing. "But we must remake the circle of protection. We need you."

"Seal the crack," Hentatia stated. She was the one holding the water.

"And you want *me* to help you? When I nearly destroyed you?"

"You were the crack that let the evil in," Hentatia said.

Descendes waved curtly at her niece. "You were tricked. And you were right, we should have told you about our guardian. We should have brought you into the circle when you first came here, when you first became part of us."

"We should have tried to learn from you," added Lulaine as

she wrung out droplets from a cloth onto Gynth's forehead.

Gynth struggled to sit up, but everything still hurt, and she managed it only with help from the others. "I should have tried harder to belong."

"Then you would not have been Gynth." Descendes looked over at the heat, where a fire still burned around her tree. "I'm sorry you lost that."

"It's meant to take fire—that's how we keep the fezrai away. It's strong." She bit back the words, *Like mountain women.*

For their part, they pretended not to notice what she normally said.

Above their heads, there was a soft pop, and then another, and a third. The scent of spice tea filled the air, and then seeds from the newly opened pods spiraled down on little wings. Some went into the fire, but most caught the wind from the flames and blew out to the grasslands, there perhaps to sprout and grow.

Hentatia reached down with her strong arms and pulled Gynth to her feet. Yemen and Adril rushed over to support her, and the others, all the others, touched her back and arms. Even Miscordia was there, one hand under the swell of her belly, the other brushing Gynth's neck, and together they made their way across the fields to the Guardian's Spring.

A QUEEN OF ICE AND SNOW

by Kevin L. O'Brien

I once tried an activity monitor—for about a week before it irritated my skin so much that I got rid of it. The one thing I did learn from it was that I was more active asleep in bed than I was awake and reading a book. But I have nothing on Team Girl; they have actual adventures while their physical bodies are asleep.

Kevin L. O'Brien is a speculative fiction author who is a member of the Science Fiction and Fantasy Writers of America. He wrote "Shaman's Quest" which appeared in *Sword and Sorceress* 32, and he has been published in *Weirdbook* 32. He has also been granted an Honorary Mention by the Writers of the Future award. The further adventures of Team Girl can be found in *The Adventure of An Cupla* and *Team Dream Girl: The Adventures of Team Girl in the Dreamlands*, both available as eBooks.

"Nyarlathotep could be called the patron villain of the Dreamlands. Legend has it that he created the Dreamworld; he certainly maintains a proprietary interest in it. His stewardship is more like that of a mafia don than a satanic being, yet, he treats everyone within his domain as his property, to do with as he pleases, with no thought to their rights as sentient entities. If anything, his paternal oversight makes this realization even worse. Nonetheless, he seems to respect courage, audacity, and impertinence, and he demonstrates a sense of honour, fair play, and humour in that he will allow people to win and to reap the rewards of their victory without rancor—as long as he is shown some modicum of respect."

—*The Dreamlands for Dummies*, by Aislinn Síle

Eile awoke first, and she tried to burrow deeper into Sunny's back as they lay entangled in the bedroll they shared inside the lean-to. After a few moments, however, she pushed herself up on an elbow and looked past her partner towards the long-log fire. Aeul still knelt in front of it in deep meditation, just as they had left her before retiring, and Eile felt the gut-aching trepidation that once more she had failed to reconnect with her clan's spirits.

Eile extracted herself from the bedroll without waking Sunny and approached the Wendol shaman as quietly as possible so as not to disturb her. When she reached her she waited for some sign that she knew she was there, but finally she said in a quiet and gentle tone, "Any luck?"

Aeul made no move at first, but presently she stood up and turned around. She was naked, with the dusky skin and dark hair and eyes typical of her Neanderthal-like people, and she had lost all her tattoos and piercings during her transformation, but she looked like a pretty adolescent instead of the ancient ugly crone they had first met. Her expression said all that needed to be, but she confirmed Eile's suspicion: "No."

After Aeul had been purged in the Flame of Ice, Eile and Sunny decided to remain encamped near the Shrine to give her a chance to recover her strength, which she did after some sleep. However, when she tried to connect with her spirits upon awaking she could not contact them, or even feel them. After a day of near-constant meditation she tried fasting for three, then spent another day dosing herself with an hallucinogen before she once again meditated while they slept. Apparently to no avail. Meanwhile, she and Sunny along with Thundar their feline guide had spent the time exploring the area around the Shrine looking for anything that might help, but again to no avail.

"Is there anything else you can try?"

She shook her head. "I have tried everything I know to do. I am afraid the spirits may have abandoned me."

"But why?"

She shrugged. "Either I have offended them in some fashion, or my transformation has changed me in more than just a physical sense."

"Huh. Is there anyway you could placate them? Or get around yer handicap?"

"Possibly, but I can do nothing here. We might as well return to my village."

"Yeah. Okay, let me confer with Sunny." She went back under the lean-to, but first she got dressed. She and Sunny slept in their underwear because being together in the same bedroll was very comfortable, but outside was particularly chilly. At the very least they had to wear woolen shirts, trousers, and socks along with mukluks to keep from getting chilled, over which they wore parkas when traveling.

Once dressed, she nudged Sunny in the backside. Her partner tried to burrow deeper into the bedroll. "Just five more minutes, Dad," she murmured in her sleep; "there's no school today."

Eile kicked her harder. She came instantly awake, sat bolt-upright, and squealed in surprise and protest. "What?! Hey! Son of a—" Which was as strong as her language ever got. She threw Eile a nasty look. "Why'd you do that!?"

"Time to get up, ya butthead. Aeul wants to start back today."

"Why the urgency?" But she extricated herself from the blankets and stood up, stifling a yawn. Eile couldn't help staring at her plentiful bare bosom.

"She doesn't believe she can make contact with the spirits here, so she wants to get back home ASAP."

"Oh. Okay, that makes sense. Stoke the fire will you?"

Eile did as she asked as Sunny and Aeul got dressed. The shaman had made the arrival journey wearing nothing but a cloak made from devil-tiger hide and didn't seem to feel the cold. After her transformation, however, she had complained of being chilled, so the two of them gave her some of their extra clothes to wear under her cloak. Even so, she refused the socks and mukluks they offered and insisted on going barefoot, but considering that the soles of her feet were as thickly calloused as those of a Himalayan Sherpa, Eile reasoned that was the one place on her body that didn't need protection.

Thundar strolled into camp just as Sunny began to cook breakfast. As she had each morning of the past week, she offered him some, but he declined as usual and laid beside the fire to wash himself.

She grinned at him. “What was it this morning?”

“A fine fat partridge,” he said in his Munchkin-like voice.

“And you didn’t bring us back any?”

He paused long enough to give her a look of feline arrogance. “You do your own hunting.” And he went back to washing. She just crinkled her eyes and giggled.

“We’re taking off today, as soon as we break camp,” she told him, and she explained why.

“I’m sorry to hear that, but you might want to delay a day.”

“Oh?” Eile said. “Why?”

“Because I found something that might help.”

He couldn’t have surprised them more if he announced he had found a five-star hotel with a heated pool and a casino. They rushed through breakfast and after collecting their parkas, weapons, and Eile’s shield, they followed the huge beefy lynx-like cat deeper into the mountains. The Northlands stretched across the breadth of the Dreamlands and crossed over the northern Edge onto the Back Side. The Edge itself defined the Antipodal line that passed through the northern Antipode, what in the Waking World would be the North Pole. The northern Edge was the northernmost limit of the Dreamlands, where the horizon literally dropped off into nothing. They were nowhere near the Edge, so they had no fear of accidentally falling over the rim, but the mountain range that contained the Shrine followed the Edge from one side of the landmass to the other. Called the Spine of the World, it was anchored at its center by the Kadathian Range, which was centered on Mt. Kadath, where the Great Ones and Nyarlathotep resided in their onyx castle. The Shrine and their camp and Aeul’s village were located in the foothills on the Front Side, and Thundar had assured them the place he was taking them to was only a short distance from the plateau where the Shrine stood. But they could see the mountains further north through gaps between the hills, and each looked as if it could rival Everest in height.

A gibbous moon had risen while they ate, giving them enough light to see by. The Northlands lay beneath a perpetual overcast that normally blocked out the sky. If the underside of the clouds did not glow with a phosphorescent sheen, the region would have been as dark as a moonless night rather than twilight. However, the forces that maintained the integrity of the Dreamworld created storms over the mountains so violent that they pushed the clouds away, revealing an open sky of eternal night, illuminated only by stars and the moon. But although the women were handicapped in the darkness, Thundar could see his surroundings as if it were daytime.

The foothills were covered with a sparse coniferous forest that occasionally sported thicker groves, like the one they had encamped in. Thundar led them to another inside a tiny hollow. It was thick enough to shelter a few deciduous trees—birches, aspens, and dwarf oaks—but mostly it obscured the cliff-like back wall of the hollow. He took them through the grove to the cliff face and sat down in front of it.

"Doesn't that look like the Flame of Ice?"

When Eile got a good look at it, she came up short and her jaw dropped in awe. The whole wall was covered with carvings: low reliefs set inside sunken outlines, like Egyptian wall art. They stretched from left to right and rose up the wall as far as she could see; she actually had to step back a couple of paces to take it all in.

"Oh, my fabulous gravy!" Sunny said when she saw the wall. She focused on the central image. "You know, I think it does!" And Eile had to admit that it did indeed look like the frigid pillar of fire.

Sunny went behind Eile, opened her pack, and rummaged around inside, though Eile had a good idea what she was looking for. A moment later her assumption was confirmed when her partner reappeared beside her holding two batons made from ironwood on which Sunny had caste permanent light spells, turning them into torches. The light they shed was stronger than fire-based torches and they would last indefinitely.

She handed a baton to Eile as she stepped closer to examine the carvings more carefully. "What are those things floating around it?" Though abstract, they resembled winged stick figures.

"Angels, maybe?" Eile said.

"What are angels?" Thundar asked.

"Divine servants of God," Sunny said.

"Servitors then, like for the Great Ones."

"Yeah," Eile said, "I guess you could say—" She cut herself off with a sharp intake of breath and exchanged a shocked look with Sunny.

"Aeul!" Sunny squeaked. "Is it possible your spirits are connected with the Flame of Ice?"

"It is not only possible, but they are," she said.

"Theeen, maybe the reason you can't communicate with them is because the Flame has been extinguished!"

The shaman flashed a puzzle expression at first, but then her face broke out into a startled look when she realized what Sunny was saying.

"Are you suggesting that if we reignite the Flame, she'll be able to connect with her spirits again?" Thundar said.

"Yeah, I think so. At least, it can't hurt to try."

"Huh, maybe," Eile said, "but how do we do that?"

"I think the answer lies in these carvings. At the very least, we may find some clues. Like, I think this is Nyarly's snow queen avatar." She pointed with her staff at a large crowned and gowned anthropomorphic figure standing inside the Flame.

"Could be," Eile said.

"I guess that means that he's associated with the Shrine as well."

"No shit, Sherlock, but what's this then?" She indicated a smaller stick figure standing in front of the snow queen at its feet.

"I think that represents all the shamans who came to the Shrine to be purged." She lapsed into silence for a moment. "You know, I think we goofed."

"Whaddya mean?"

Sunny gazed at her partner. "I think that maybe we screwed something up when we saved Aeul."

Eile glanced at the shaman and noted that she wore a

distressed look. "Are you sayin' we shouldn't've defended her?"

Sunny didn't hesitate. "No." She turned her attention back to the wall. "We may have accidentally done the wrong thing, but it was for the right reason." Eile saw that Aeul relaxed at that comment.

"The thing is, it's now our responsibility to set it right."

"Okay, but how?"

"I don't..." Sunny hesitated, sounding unsure of herself, which normally wasn't like her. "I'm...not sure. I just don't see anything in these carvings that shows how to reignite the Flame."

Aeul stepped up between them. "What might this be?" She pointed at what appeared to be a tiny flame at the base of the fire pillar below the two figures.

"Hmmm," Sunny said. "If this were a design schematic, I would say that almost looks like a pilot light."

"What is that?"

"Well, in the Waking World, devices that run on burning gas, like stoves or water heaters, need an ignition source to set the primary burners alight. That source is usually a tiny flame placed next to the burner's gas-jet; that's called a pilot light."

"But we didn't see anything like that when we examined the base of the Flame the day after," Eile said.

Sunny made a spitting noise. "Pilot lights don't hafta be flames. Anymore, they're usually devices that create electrical sparks or use heated surfaces."

"But the Flame was cold, not hot. How could a pilot light of any kind work on that?"

Sunny flashed a 'well, duh' look. "Obviously, it has to be some kinda cold pilot light."

"Huh. Well, ya know, that almost looks more like a gem or crystal than a flame."

Sunny stiffened as her face sported a pop-eyed expression coupled with a goofy grin. Eile recognized it: she had just gotten one of her screwball ideas. All that was missing was an audible 'boing' and a lightbulb appearing above her head.

"Of course!" she squealed. "A cold crystal!"

Eile had to admit, that made sense. Cold crystals were among the rarest of the rare; they had never seen one themselves, though they had heard rumors of samples that might exist. They were said to be able to lower the temperature of a confined space down to well below zero.

So if anything could reignite the Flame of Ice, Eile figured a cold crystal would be the likely candidate.

Still: “Okay, but where do we find one, ya spaz?”

That seemed to stump her. She made ready to say something, but even as she opened her mouth she fell silent with a downcast expression.

Thundar had wandered off, probably to do some hunting Eile surmised, but he came trotting back with some alacrity. “There’s a snow devil out there.”

Despite the ominous name, Eile knew that it was just a mild whirlwind that kicked up snowflakes and ice crystals into a vertical column, like an arctic version of a desert dust devil. They were common in the Northlands, and were rarely dangerous. Still, considering that Nyarlathotep was involved, she didn’t think they should take anything for granted.

“I’m gonna check it out,” she said.

“Let’s all go,” Sunny said, and she and Aeul followed Eile as she and Thundar made for the edge of the grove. They found a white column a dozen yards high that danced over the ground, first one way, then another, as it gyrated and undulated like a belly dancer. Streamers that resembled sinuous arms waved around in the air as the column spun around its center. As Eile watched it, however, she began to imagine that its resemblance to a dancer wasn’t figurative. In fact, she got the idea that it was trying to lure them out to it.

“I think we oughta follow it,” she said.

“Why?” Sunny squeaked.

“Because it acts like it wants us to. Besides, here we are stymied for a cold crystal, and then this thing shows up.”

Sunny smiled and nodded. “Yeah, that’s definitely too much of a coinkydink. Let’s go.”

They advanced towards the snowy whirlwind, and it retreated before them, vindicating Eile’s suspicion. It stayed a dozen yards in front of them no matter how fast they traveled, but neither did it try to evade them. It led them further into the foothills, almost to the foot of the mountains, but then detoured into a ravine that narrowed the deeper they went in. Finally, it stopped in front of a high-relief carved into the rocky back end that looked like a human skull, except it had a three-lobed eye and a wide grinning gash of a mouth.

The snow devil took up a position in front of the open mouth, but did not dissipate, so they tried to approach it, but it intensified in strength and pushed them back with tornado-force winds and stinging clouds of snow and ice.

"Huh," Eile said after they recovered, "I didn't expect that."

"I did," Sunny said. "Nyarly wants to play, so we hafta expect obstacles."

"Okay, so, how do we get past this one?"

Sunny glanced at Aeul. "Do you know any magic?"

She returned a startled look. "Just devotional rituals for the Great Mother; nothing as practical as what you can do. About the only one I know that might help us creates a form of the Wall of Naach-Tith."

Sunny nodded. "I don't know that one; that could come in handy."

Aeul removed a bone pipe from under her cloak. "Let me know when you need it."

Sunny smiled and crinkled her eyes, then turned her attention back to Eile. "I have an idea. You guys get ready to move when I tell you."

"What've you got in mind?" Eile asked in an anxious tone.

Sunny winked at her with a mischievous smile and approached the snow-devil. She got as close as she could without being blown away, steadied herself with her staff, and pointed at it.

"Zaparoonie!"

The whirlwind became englobed in a sphere of voltage. At first, Eile thought her partner was trying to dissipate it. Like her usual zap spell, it consisted of a magical electrical attack, but on a more powerful scale. It wouldn't just stun a target, but also sear it to a cinder. Instead, however, the snow devil rose into the air, contorting wildly as it resisted.

"Go; *go!*" Sunny said.

Eile ran for the mouth; Thundar overtook her as Aeul kept pace beside her. When Eile charged inside, she let Aeul continue on as she turned to find Sunny. She in turn leapt through the opening just as the whirlwind settled back to earth. As if enraged, it pulsed, sending a blast of wind into the relief sculpture, catching Sunny in the back and pushing her into Eile's arms.

Eile caught her, but they collided with enough force to knock Eile off her feet. She landed on her back and Sunny fell on top of her. They lay together stunned for a few moments, then Eile focused on Sunny's face. She in turn crinkled her eyes and smiled.

"Under different circumstances, this might be fun," she said.

Eile rolled her eyes. "Put a sock in it, ya bimbo."

Sunny just giggled.

They stood up and turned towards the back of the relief sculpture. An opening led outside, and Eile realized the skull penetrated the rock wall of the ravine, providing passage through the earth.

"How'd you subdue that snow devil?" Eile asked.

Sunny shrugged. "In the Waking World, dust devils can generate a lot of electricity, which can interfere with the earth's magnetic field and cause them to levitate into the air. I took a chance that a snow devil does the same and I supercharged it to give it some extra umph! Piece of cake." She made a spitting noise.

The four of them emerged into what looked like an amphitheater; open to the sky, but with no seats in tiers. The upper rim was also defined by a series of icy pinnacles of varying heights, like upside-down icicles. Eile scanned the interior, but it appeared empty. At one end stood a throne on a dais inside an alcove in the ice wall behind curtains composed of a lacey frost, but it too was empty.

They wandered into the center of the arena, and Sunny let

loose with an ear-piercing whistle that made Eile jump. "Alright," she called out with the full force of her prodigious lung power, "we're here. Show yourself and let's get this over with!"

Before Eile could ask who she thought she was speaking to, a storm broke over the tops of the pinnacles. The wind came howling in, carrying clouds of snow and ice particles as they swirled and frothed, and formed a cyclone that dipped into the alcove, obscuring the throne. The clouds were sucked into the space, where they compacted and coalesced into a gowned human form of snow and ice wearing a crown. Once the figure fully formed, the storm abated and the curtains drew apart, revealing the snow queen seated on the throne.

"I thought you had destroyed her," Aeul asked.

"None of Nyarly's avatars can be completely destroyed," Eile said, "and he can recreate them whenever he wants."

Sunny approached, but stopped a fathom away from the alcove and bowed. "Greetings, Snow Queen. We thank you for your invitation."

It bowed its head in return, its porcelain-mask face inscrutable.

"We have come for a cold crystal, to reignite the Flame of Ice and reconsecrate the Shrine. Please show us where it is."

The Snow Queen turned its head to the left and gestured with its arm and hand. A veneer of ice crumbled from the face of a niche in the left wall and revealed a faceted oblong crystal that looked as if it was made of ice covered with a dusting of hoar frost, floating in its center.

Sunny glanced towards it, then looked back at the Snow Queen and bowed again. "Thank you, Mighty One." Eile couldn't believe it would be that easy; she expected another shoe to drop at any moment.

Even as Sunny made to turn, however, the surface of the wall beneath the niche shattered and out stepped a humanoid figure. Eile recognized it as some kind of golem, in this case consisting of a man's body encased in a shell of ice. The man looked to be a Viking warrior, complete with horned helmet and Danish axe, and she wondered if he might have been an adventurer like them.

The ice golem stepped forward, brandishing the axe, and Eile understood he was the guardian of the crystal, issuing a challenge.

"That's not fair!" Sunny chided the Snow Queen. It simply shrugged with arms and shoulders as it settled into the throne to watch the match.

"I'll handle this," Sunny said. And she made ready to throw a spell.

Eile stepped up behind her and placed a hand on her shoulder. "No, let me; it's my turn. Besides, warrior's code and all that. You and Aeul step back outta the way." She drew her thick, short-bladed broadsword.

"I'm not gonna let you face this alone!"

She leaned in close to whisper in her partner's ear. "Nyarly wants a fight. That'll let me keep him distracted while you figure out a way ta nab the crystal and get us outta here."

Sunny flashed a surprised look, but then smiled and crinkled her eyes. "Sounds like a plan, partner." She retreated to join Aeul.

Eile turned to confront the golem and slapped her sword against her ironwood shield. "Okay, you asshole, you wanna piece of me? Then come and get it."

The golem lifted the axe in its right hand and charged straight at her. Though slow and ponderous, it came on like a bull elephant, sufficient to trample her underfoot. She waited until it came close enough to strike, then she dodged to her left as the axe blade bit into the ice-covered ground. She chopped with her sword and splintered the handle, then swung the shield and hammered the golem's head with enough force to turn it and drive it back. Screeching a battle cry, she slammed her shield backed by her body into its torso. She did that twice more and steadily drove the golem towards the center of the amphitheater. Recovering, it swung at her with the section of axe handle it still clutched; she deflected it with her shield, but the golem brought it back around on the return swing and got it past her defenses. She tried to parry with her sword, but the handle smacked her across her shoulders and forced her to one side.

When she turned to face the golem again, she found herself looking towards the niche with the cold crystal, and she spotted Thundar deftly crawling up the ice wall towards it. She deliberately retreated a dozen paces, as if trying to put distance between her and the golem, to goad it into advancing further into the center of the arena. She didn't want to take her eyes off it to see if the Snow Queen was focused on them; she just had to hope it was.

The golem wielded the axe handle like a singlestick and Eile fenced with it as she continued to retreat towards the Snow Queen's right to keep its attention away from Sunny and Aeul. At the same time she studied the golem to spot any weaknesses she could exploit when the time was right. The main possibility seemed to be that its ice shell was not unbroken, but consisted of segments, with gaps between them where the body core needed to be flexible, such as the joints, thereby exposing that part of the body. At the same time, she thought Thundar was taking an inordinate amount of time retrieving the crystal, and she was beginning to feel fatigue creep into her muscles.

"Eile! We've got it! Break off!" Eile looked to her right and saw Thundar lay the crystal at Sunny's feet. Aeul was already retreating back towards the entrance as Sunny picked up the crystal and slipped it into a pouch on her belt.

Eile dropped and rolled between the golem's legs. Getting up into a squat, she stabbed it in the back of one knee between the leg segments of the ice shell. The golem staggered forward a couple of steps and fell onto its face.

"Fire in the hole!" Sunny shouted. Eile looked behind herself and saw Sunny point at the golem.

"Inferno!" A great gout of flame, like the discharge from a flamethrower, streamed towards her. Eile rolled to her left to avoid it, and it splashed on the golem. A column of steam rose into the air, obscuring the tableau, but it was quickly replace by a thicker column of grayish-black smoke rising from the burning body.

"Eile! Look out!"

She looked past the smoke at the Snow Queen. It had risen from its throne and stepped outside the alcove, and it grew as she watched to three times its original height. At the same time it transmogrified into a black three-legged monstrosity with a blood-red tentacle for a face. Once it achieved its full height it strode towards her as if intending to grind her under its heel. She didn't miss the irony.

"RUN!" Sunny screamed, but Eile had already scrambled to her feet and was rushing for the back of the skull sculpture. Aeul was already there, standing just inside the entrance playing her flute, and Thundar sped past her. Sunny waited for Eile to catch up with her and together they raced ahead of the avatar lumbering behind them like Godzilla slowly approaching Tokyo. The two of them reached the entrance just ahead of the god's feet, but as Eile passed the threshold it felt like the air in front of it had thickened, as if it had become gaseous tapioca.

Aeul completed her tune shortly after that, but she didn't retreat with them, and they stopped just behind the skull's mouth and looked back at her. Nyarlathotep reached the opening, but came to an abrupt halt, as if encountering a barrier. Which, Eile realized, it did, though magical and invisible. Nyarlathotep made no sound, but it hammered and kicked at the air in a furious manner as it tried to break through, but to no avail.

"Come on, ya butthead!" Eile said, and Aeul finally turned and jogged towards them.

"No worries; not even Nyarlathotep can break through the Wall of Naach-Tith. We will be safe for some time." She caught up with them. "By the way, remind me sometime to teach you some of our insults." And she grinned.

Eile return it with a chuckle. "Heh, yer on."

They hurried down the slope of the foothills back to the Shrine, but saw no evidence that Nyarlathotep followed. When they reached it they stood in a circle around the base where the Flame of Ice once burned, and for the first time Eile saw a hole in the center of the larger pedestal. Sunny removed the crystal from her pouch and held it up with a questioning look on her face.

"It's why we went through all this," Thundar said.

"Yeah; go for it," Eile said, and Aeul nodded.

"Hold on to your butts," Sunny said, and she bent over and placed the crystal in the hole. After a moment it dropped down and disappeared inside. A glow appeared and streamers of sparks like from a sparkler shot out. They retreated from the base just as a small blue, aquamarine, and silver flame erupted. It quickly grew in height and width until it covered the base and rose dozens of yards into the air. Eile grinned and flashed a thumbs-up at Sunny and Aeul.

Thundar perked, swiveled his ears, and looked up. "Does anyone else hear that?"

Sunny tilted her head. "I think I do; it sounds like fla—" She suddenly stiffened as her jaw dropped and her eyes popped out. "Huge wings flapping!"

When Eile heard it, she had to agree, and her gut turned to ice as the hairs on the back of her neck stood on end and her flesh goosepimpled. The flapping descended behind them, and they all whirled around to face the source. At first all they saw was a shadowy mass with great wings, the only visible details being a burning three-lobed eye and grinning gash of a mouth.

Sunny didn't hesitate. " Zaparoonie!" The entity became engulfed in the electrical globe, but it shook it off as it stood up on its hind legs. Then it transformed into the Snow Queen. At first it just stared at them, and Eile got the sour feeling that they were all dead, but after some moments it bowed deeply with garish gestures of its arms. As it straightened up, it grew once more, but this time it changed into a large snow devil, which continued to grow and expand. Streamers blew off from it, which were absorbed by the pedestals of the statues. Soon after that the frosty whirlwind dissipated, but the statues began to glow; even the empty pedestals showed misty patches of shining silver. Even as Eile wondered what was going on, the glows leapt into the air above the shrine and flew around the Flame like moths.

"I— I can feel the spirits again!" Aeul cried. As if confirming that, the glows soared into the perpetually night sky and disappeared amongst the stars.

"What were those?" Sunny asked.

"The souls of my predecessors. They have gone to join the spirits, to become spirits themselves."

"Huh," Eile said. "I never would've guessed Nyarly could be such a good sport."

Sunny smiled and crinkled her eyes. "Well, you know what they say: he's just full of surprises!"

Eile grinned. "Heh, yeah."

The three women and the cat stared up into the eternal night sky and watched as the stars danced in celebration.

THE CAPTIVE IN THE TOWER

by Pauline J. Alama

Not everyone trapped in a tower should be rescued, and being a hero does not make one omniscient.

Pauline J. Alama is a former medieval scholar and author of the quest fantasy *The Eye of Night* (Bantam Spectra 2002). Her first professional story sale was to *Marion Zimmer Bradley's Fantasy Magazine*, and if she hasn't miscounted, this is her thirteenth story in *Sword & Sorceress*—an ominous number, perhaps, as the anthology is regrettably coming to an end. She hopes that her duo of damsels-errant, Ursula the swordswoman and Isabeau the sorceress, will be able to continue their adventures in another publication. Pauline writes grant proposals during the work day and fantasy on the bus to work; when possible, she strives to keep the two genres separate.

It's curious that rain—a necessary element for life—has an almost endless capacity to unsettle everyone's temper. Galen would say that this cold and moist element engenders a phlegmatic humor of calmness. Evidently Galen never spent a wet week following a knight-errant through the Forest of Adventure. The horses were muddy and dispirited, and the Maiden of Révie, or Knight of the Unicorn—my friend Ursula—was muttering darkly about rust on her armor and mud in unmentionable places, while Laetitia, my fledgling dragon, mewed discontentedly.

"Oh, stop whining, dragon!" Ursula burst out. "It's your own fault we were kicked out of Lord Philip's hall after our last rescue."

"That was unfair!" I protested. "That tapestry was only slightly scorched—and it was such shoddy work that anyone with taste ought to have thrown it in the fire."

"Maybe so, Isabeau. But Lord Philip didn't share your

opinion, and his tasteless mead-hall must be nice and dry right now."

"Well, you're the one who thought something called the Forest of Adventure sounded like a delightful place to go from there," I retorted. "Now we're lost. I guess the map-maker thought 'Forest of Adventure' looked better than 'I have no idea what's over here, really.'"

"We're not lost," Ursula said, "We're exploring uncharted territory."

"And the difference is what, exactly?"

Instead of answering, Ursula cocked her head at Laetitia. "What's she excited about, all of a sudden?"

Indeed, Laetitia's mood seemed transformed. The wings that had drooped under rain now beat impatiently, catching a fresh breeze. Laetitia lifted her gleaming snout, sniffed deeply, chirruped, and took off with a running start. She hovered a while, tossed by erratic gusts, her immature wings not yet strong enough to make much headway.

"She scents something," I said. "Let's find out what it is."

"What kind of scent could she catch that the rain doesn't wash away?" Ursula said. But she joined me in following the dragonlet's sequence of flights, hops, and crawls toward whatever attracted her. Either the rain lessened or we paid it less heed now that we had a direction.

"It's curious how the underbrush has changed. These plants might have healing virtues," I was observing when Ursula shushed me.

She put a hand to her ear. "Was that a song?"

I shrugged; I'd heard nothing.

She pointed in the same direction Laetitia was headed. Interesting. I left off my study of flora and followed them.

As we pushed through rain-soaked vines, I began to perceive what had caught Ursula's ear: a distant voice singing, a smooth clear tenor—God help us, another beguiling troubadour. Would Ursula ever tire of them? Still, it was the first sign of human habitation we'd encountered since we'd entered the wood. And what good would it do me to complain? Both my companions, human and beast, were united in their direction, and I had no alternative to offer.

A massive willow cast a curtain of trailing greenery across our path. Laetitia went wild for it, grasping the leaves with her forked tongue and savoring them with growls of appreciation. Ursula reined in Fury and paused to watch, chuckling. "Look at our fierce guard dragon: a terror to leaf-kind!"

"Don't laugh: you'll be glad to have a dragon on our side one day," I said. "Besides, willow is special. It's a powerfully magical tree—probably very nourishing for her. Maybe she'll grow big at last." I dismounted for a closer look and laid my hand on the willow. Sure enough, I could feel magic coursing through its veins, strong as springtime, though it was near the drowsy end of summer. No wonder Laetitia savored it so eagerly. I stroked the bark appreciatively, then drew out my best knife, the one I'd purified in dragon fire. "Your pardon, Lady Willow, for my impertinence, but would you kindly let me take a lock of your splendid hair?" Such courtesies might not be necessary, but the lively power I sensed in the tree made me cautious. I cut a long spray just beyond the node, where the pruning would stimulate new growth, and bound it to my belt. Then I parted the trailing branches and passed through.

As I might have guessed, the willow dwelt on the bank of a stream that lay across our path. But the stream looked quite shallow, despite the rain, and the breeze from the other side brought a tantalizing scent of herbs. Eager to find what I could gather, I shed my shoes, tucked them under my arm, hiked up my skirts in my other hand, and waded in, trusting Ursula to get the horses across and Laetitia to follow me when she was done gorging on willow leaves.

Once I reached the other bank, I scarcely knew where to set my feet. Every pace of earth that was not blocked by trees teemed with a profusion of healing herbs, some of them rare and curious. Behind me, I could hear Ursula fussing at the horses, who seemed to have spooked at something. Laetitia came fluttering, skipping over the water like a side-slung stone, and settled down to browse this new bounty of fragrant greenery.

"No, Laetitia," I told her firmly. Though the road ahead was still veiled by trees, I knew we were no longer in the wilderness. "This is someone's garden."

"Is it?" Ursula came up beside me, leading both horses. "It looks fairly wild."

I pointed to a lacy plant with familiar pods. "Cumin doesn't grow wild around here, and it must take care and skill to grow it in such wet terrain. We may be on the outer edge of an estate, or possibly an abbey."

"Whoever they are, I hope they'll let us stable the horses," Ursula said. "This damp isn't good for them."

"Whoever they are, I hope they see us as guests, not trespassers. Tread lightly among these herbs." I called, "Up, Laetitia!" and the dragon settled herself on my back, her prehensile forefeet on my shoulders, her hind legs wrapped round my waist, her head resting on mine. Soon she'd grow too big for this. That would be a good thing—she should be much larger—but I'd miss the closeness.

The rain seemed to abate as we walked. The singing began again, and this time we were close enough to hear the words: "Alas, my lady, you do me wrong/To guard me thus so jealously/For never was there a cage so strong/As to hold love where it would not be."

"There he is!" Ursula positively glowed as she surged toward the voice. "The hall can't be far."

I followed with less enthusiasm. It would be nice to get indoors, but tiresome to watch Ursula fall in and out of love with another troubadour. As we passed into a clearing, the tower came into view. The singer—a golden-haired man with a smooth-shaved face—leaned out of a high window, caterwauling about the folly of jealous love.

"Hallo up there!" caroled Ursula. "Sweetly sung, troubadour! Can two lost travelers come indoors and applaud you in comfort?"

"Come no nearer, fair maidens," he said. "This is no civilized hall but a prison. A jealous enchantress holds me captive—for love, she says, but it's a poor kind of love that holds the beloved in prison. Perhaps she has deeper designs on the secrets I've learned in my travels from court to court—for I am Marcelin the Golden, famed for my songs far and wide. If you seek shelter here, the enchantress may kill you to keep the secret of my captivity."

"High walls and guarded towers cannot compel love," Ursula said solemnly; whether she'd heard it sung or extemporized the words, I did not want to know. "Fear not: help is at hand. We are no hapless travelers but a knight-errant and an enchantress. You may have heard of the Maiden of Révie, as the heralds style me?"

"They say she took the St. Gall's Day Tournament by storm. Are you indeed that prodigious maiden?"

"I am, and I will rescue you if I can. How many guard this tower?"

"Only two, but most mighty and most merciless: a giant Black Knight and a cruel magician."

"Never fear: Isabeau and I will outmatch them."

I dearly wish she would not overpromise. "Wait. What sort of magician? An alchemist? A numeromancer? An herbalist, perhaps—here in this garden rich with potent herbs? Or, God forbid, a demonologist?"

"Alas, wise damsel, how should I know?"

"If we make haste," Ursula said, "we need not stay to find out. I have a good rope. If we could just get the end of it up to your window, you could use it to climb down."

"I don't know..."

"It's very strong rope." Ursula unhooked it from her pack. "Here, Laetitia! Be a good dragon and take this up to the window," she cooed, holding out the rope. Laetitia approached her slowly, nibbled meditatively on the end of a rope, then turned away.

"Oh, for heaven's sake, Ursula, don't *tell* her what to do. You'd never make that mistake with a horse. Give me that." I looped the end of the rope into a halter, then reached to stroke the dragon's neck. "Here, Laetitia. Easy, now."

Laetitia shied away.

"Come on," I coaxed. A bribe of dried sage leaves from my herb pouch got her to hold still while I slipped the loop of rope over her head. "Good dragon. Good Laetitia." I rubbed her ruby-red neck-scales, hoping the rope would not chafe them too much. "Now, songbird," I called to the man in the tower, "call to her. Her name's Laetitia."

"Call the *dragon*?" This one seemed thick even for one of Ursula's fancies.

"Who else?" I snapped. "Does Ursula have wings? Of course, the dragon. If you can get her to the window, take the rope from her at once."

"Laetitia," he called tepidly, as if unsure he wanted her to come.

"Solomon's beard," I swore, "you called Ursula temptingly enough. Surely you can do better than that! If you have any aromatic herbs—even something nasty like camphor—hold it in the window as bait."

So he called a little more heartily, holding a finger-bowl of potpourri, and Laetitia fluttered upward. But every time she got near the window he'd flinch or cough or make some sudden movement, frightening her away. And so there we were—Laetitia on the ground resting from her last flight, me glowering up at the tower, and Ursula looking for hand-holds to climb up—when our adversaries came round the side of the castle.

The Black Knight was huge indeed. At first glance I thought he was riding an ox; at second glance, I decided his horse must have been squashed down shorter and thicker by the bulk of his armored body. "*Urs*!" I shouted.

"I know, Isabeau!" she panted, sprinting for Fury. She clanged her visor into place, leapt into the saddle, and rode at the knight. His mighty sword-stroke, aiming for the gap between plates in her brigantine, went awry when Ursula turned Fury aside. Like his rider, Fury was lighter and nimbler than his opponent.

As for me, I did not bother mounting. The slight man who followed the knight wore no armor and rode no steed, but I could feel the forces gathering about him from earth and air, from below and above. An experienced enchanter, he would know well how to wield those forces. I used to wield forces like that myself as my grandmother's apprentice on her Isle of Sorcery; but once I left her domain, I discovered how much harder it was to draw power from ordinary terrain that has not been tuned to magic.

Then in a flash I realized that I was not on ordinary ground. The herbs should have tipped me off. This was a sorcerer's domain, more like my native island than any place I'd seen since I left home. Could I turn it against the older and more practiced magician?

I began with my easiest trick, summoning bees to harry our adversaries. The sorcerer chuckled tolerantly and traced a pattern in the air with his wand. All the bees swarmed around his hand—never touching, but orbiting it endlessly on a complex path. I calmly pondered my next move. If he slung the bees back at me, I knew they would not sting me; I might even make them guard me. But instead, he cast the whole swarm into a crabapple tree, where they circled a branch, endlessly following the same path. A neat trick: I wished I had time to work out his method. Again he gathered forces toward himself, and I recognized the shape of his spell: he meant to freeze us, stealing heat from our bodies.

So it was heat he wanted, was it? "Laetitia!" I called—but my dragon was engaged in a battle of her own with a prodigious hound, alabaster white with red ears and one green hind paw, swifter than fire. Brave Laetitia! She could have flown out of its reach at any moment, but then the hound would have attacked me or Ursula. I saw a way to get the hound off our trail—a truly elegant solution. There was a fly buzzing around it; I cast a glamor to make the fly appear like the perfect prey, a white hare as magical as the hound with scarlet ears and a green forepaw, cunning and full of trickery, attainable only to the perfect hunter. The fly landed on the dog's hindquarters, and the dog went into a frenzy chasing his own behind.

Meanwhile, Ursula clashed swords with the Black Knight; his blows were harder and heavier, but she held her own with faster moves and better horsemanship. Heated by exercise, she did not seem to feel the chill as the magician drew warmth from our bodies. But if he went on like this, in time it would slow her. "Laetitia, to me!" I cried. She perched on my shoulders. "Give me fire!" I took the heat of her flames, spiced it with the heat of my own anger, and fed it to the magician.

"Solomon's fat bottom!" he swore, along with a number of oaths I consider improper to commit to writing. As the rain steamed off his body, he threw down his wand, which glowed like a brand in the fire.

Unbothered by the heat, Laetitia flew to fetch it.

"Oh, no you don't!" The magician scrambled to retrieve his wand just in time to see Laetitia seize it. Bereft of one tool, he seized another: the rope that still trailed from Laetitia's neck. "Ill-mannered beast! It's time someone house-trained you." He yanked on the rope, pulling the dragon toward him: either a bold move or a desperately foolhardy one. A mature dragon would have met him with white-hot fire. Laetitia—young, frightened, and sodden—steamed like a kettle without managing a proper flame. Yowling, she fluttered ineffectually as the magician reeled her toward him. Then she dropped the wand, perched on top of the magician, and relieved herself on his head.

Everything that comes out of Laetitia's body is powerfully intoxicating. Ever since we found her, I had been pondering how I might store some of her fewmets to use against an enemy, always frustrated by the impossibility of handling them without becoming too befuddled to go on. As her urine soaked into the magician's black hair, his ridiculous pointed beard, and his robes, the effect was immediate. Soon, instead of pulling the heat out of me and Ursula, he was swashing his arms wildly at imaginary enemies, shouting broken fragments of spells.

Laetitia took advantage of his distraction to flee back to me. The wand still lay on the wet grass, which steamed like overcooked spinach around it. I slipped on the heavy glove I use to gather nettles, cast a small cooling spell, and picked up the wand. I could still feel the heat through the glove, but it didn't burn through. Until I could touch it, I couldn't hope to wield the wand, but at least I could keep my adversary from using it when he recovered. I freed Laetitia of the rope, then looked to see how Ursula was doing.

The Maiden of Révie used a clever feint to put the Black Knight off balance so her next blow knocked him to earth. The crash of his armored body falling was like the time Grandmother's tirade at the cook made every pot in the kitchen hurl itself at the wall.

Ursula leapt from the saddle to seize her fallen opponent. She pulled off his helmet to reveal the leathery face of a man in his thirties with a huge curving mustache. "Villain, tell me—"

But the fallen knight spoke at the same time. "Take the curse off my poor dog, I beg you. Whatever grudge you and your witch have against the captive in the tower—or me—you can have none against my Belami."

Ursula choked on her intended threat. "What?"

"Why you need keep a maiden prisoner, I cannot fathom," the knight said. "What you do with me is no consequence; every knight-errant expects to fall some day. But please spare my hound."

Ursula cast her eyes up at the tower window. There was the troubadour, cheering her on to kill. She spoke in a low voice: "Play dead."

"What?"

"*Play dead*!"

The Black Knight went limp.

She swashed her sword theatrically and made it ring against the black armor, then dragged the knight into the bushes, heedless of the priceless herbs she trampled on the way. I hastily bound the magician in the willow spray I'd cut for myself and dragged him along, hoping the horses would follow us across the stream, out of this sorcerous land.

On the way, a branch snagged my arm, and to my astonishment, a blackthorn tree spoke to me: not in words, of course, yet I had the clear intimation that it was angry with the way somebody had used it, and wanted to be free.

Gathering both ends of the willow spray carefully in one hand lest I lose my grip on the magician, I touched the blackthorn branch in what I hoped was a calming gesture. "I know exactly how you feel."

The branch came away in my hand—a wand voluntarily given, the most powerful kind. If only it were not so prickly to hold! Reverently—and carefully—I tucked it into my belt, and followed Ursula to the stream.

She had dragged her captive into the water, but could not make headway: the stream that had seemed so tame and shallow on the way in now reared up into a wall we could not break through. "A water boundary, of course," I said. "We're not getting out easily. Let's find a hidden spot for a council." The Black Knight was starting to struggle, so I hissed to him, "Stay dead till we're hidden."

Huddled in the shelter of a thicket, I set the willow-spray between us and the castle, hoping it would mark us as outside the boundary, outside the surveillance of whoever watched from the castle.

"What's going on?" the Black Knight sputtered. "Why didn't you kill me?"

"Please! I'm not a barbarian," Ursula said. "I would have spared you when you released the prisoner. Besides, a man who showed such care for his hound couldn't be the monster we were led to believe."

"*Me*, a monster? *You* were supposed to be the ruthless knight who held the lady prisoner. And what has your witch done with poor Ambrosio?" He pointed at the magician, who sat listlessly in the mud, the worst of his madness past.

"Nothing really," I said. "He's addled by fewmets. The rain will wash off the last of it. If you catch rain in your helmet to wash him with, you can speed it up."

"Here, I'll catch some. My helmet's as wet as it could get, anyway." Ursula took off her visored helm, astonishing the knight again.

"A girl! Mother of God, I can't believe how close I came to killing a girl."

"Not very close." Ursula tossed her head. "What lady was I supposed to be holding captive?"

"The one around the other side of the tower, of course."

"*You* were supposed to be holding a troubadour prisoner," Ursula said, "on our side of the tower. He wanted to see me kill you—I could see that at the end. It made me suspicious. A real troubadour would honor chivalry and mercy."

I rolled my eyes, but said nothing.

At that point, Ambrosio the magician shook himself like a wet dog and demanded to know what was going on. "Are we prisoners, Rodrigo?"

"Only if you insist on fighting us," Ursula said. "And I'd rather not make more sport for the liars in the tower who set us upon each other."

"While the damsel told us to protect her from a knight and a witch," Rodrigo told him, "a man on the other side of the tower told these maidens that *we* were holding *him* captive."

I gazed thoughtfully at my new blackthorn wand. "The whole scene was obviously a trap for heroes. They lured us with the things we each wanted: music for Ursula, even some sort of scent that tempted the dragon's nose. And then the water boundary that the horses hesitated to cross should have made me suspicious—but I was too eager to reach the herb garden. Even the name on the map: the Forest of Adventure, indeed! I of all people should have recognized it as a trap."

"Why?" said the magician.

"Because I was once the bait in such a trap," I said, "as the *Damsel in the Garden of Delights*: another name carefully chosen to attract adventurers."

"Not only bait, Isabeau," Ursula said. "You were the jaws of that trap, too."

"The Garden of Delights! Wasn't that a creation of the enchantress Ettarre?" Ambrosio said.

"Yes. Lady Ettarre is my grandmother; I was her apprentice and slave until Ursula—that is, the Maiden of Révie—helped me break free of her."

"You've learned her arts well," said Ambrosio. "That was a powerful glamor you put on Rodrigo's hound. I do hope you'll take it off; it would be a lengthy process for me to unravel it."

"I'll disenchant the hound when we're ready to deal with our true enemies," I said. "I don't want to alert them prematurely that we've united against them."

"Are you really the Maiden of Révie?" the Black Knight was gushing at Ursula. "I've heard of you. Maybe you've heard of me, too? Some call me Rodrigue-le-Noir in these parts." He groomed his excessive mustache with cultivated nonchalance.

"Ah, yes! Lord Philip spoke highly of you," Ursula said.

"Let's not waste time in compliments," I said. "We have too much at stake. Why did those rogues in the tower go to such trouble to set us against each other? What enemies do you have who might set such a plot in motion?"

"What knight-errant can avoid making enemies?" Rodrigo said. "A highwayman here, a tyrant prince there—"

"To say nothing of jealous husbands and unpaid creditors," muttered Ambrosio, "but I doubt any of them capable of such refined enchantments. What about you maidens? Unless you have an enviable rejuvenation charm, you seem over-young to have earned such enemies."

Ursula considered. "I did kill Long Luc, and I've troubled some other highwaymen, but if they had sorcerers in their retinues, I think I'd have heard from them sooner. Now, that brother and sister we met at the St. Gall's Day Tournament—she was a sorceress, all right—but perhaps not as powerful as—"

"My family," I said.

Ambrosio raised an eyebrow; Rodrigo looked sympathetic. "Ah! The deepest wounds come from the closest hands."

"If it *is* my family," I said, "they're trying to bring me to heel, not kill me. Probably. But was the trap set only for me, or for all of us? Or for knights and sorcerers generally? If we can find out their motive, we may find in it their weakness."

"I take it you don't mean to attack them straight on," Rodrigo said.

"Of course not," Ambrosio answered for me.

"What's our one advantage now?" I said. "We know they're false, but they may not know we know it. We have to pretend they've gotten their way. You'll have to play dead until we've scouted out their weakness."

"You ladies expect us to sit passively by while you put yourselves in the enemies' hands?" Rodrigo was aghast.

"Don't worry," I said. "We'll be well armed."

I had little time to take the sense of my two new wands—willow from outside the garden, blackthorn from within—but they spoke eloquently about the bindings that had been put on the land and the violence done to it to create this trap. The willow lamented the misuse of the waters, and the blackthorn raged at being made an agent of harm. I could sympathize: I had been like the blackthorn, constrained by my grandmother, Ettarre, to use my magic to imprison and oppress; Ursula, perhaps, was like the willow, flexible and nimble, a creature of water and freedom. I let the blackthorn pierce my skin, and bound it with blood and forgiveness. Then I twined the willow around it, covering and blunting its sharp edges till it was safe to hold.

While I communed with the woods, Ambrosio helped create the illusion of gore on Ursula's armaments, and Rodrigo dug the semblance of a grave in the woods in case we needed to display one. "Impressive bloodstains," I said. "Who had to bleed?"

"I gave a bit of blood," said Rodrigo. "Ambrosio magnified it. Will you free Belami now?"

"Yes, but keep him out of sight," I said. "I'll need to pretend he's dead, too." I took the glamor off the fly. The hound sniffed about confusedly, then settled down to sleep by his knight. "Now, Ambrosio, will you free the bees?" I handed him back his wand.

He took it gingerly and looked at it from the corners of his eyes. "Hm. Plenty of fire inside. You and your dragon may have reshaped it permanently." He waved it at the trees in a complex geometrical pattern, and the bees dispersed. "Not altogether a bad thing, either."

As the men and beasts hid in the brush near the boundary, Ursula and I approached the tower. "Well, Marcelin, we've dealt with the Black Knight and his magician," Ursula called up to the troubadour. "I told you we were a match for them."

"What do you mean, dealt with them?"

"What do you think?" I said. "We killed them. As you urged us to do."

"I never!" he gasped in feigned consternation. "Rash, foolish women! You've entangled yourself in a thicket, all right. When word gets out what you've done, all will despise you. But come within; we'll find a way to erase the taint of your blunder."

"What!" cried Ursula. "But what about the sorceress who guards you so jealously?"

"I may have spoken harshly of my mistress, who is understandably jealous when I speak to other women. But she will know what to do about your predicament. No one is guarding the castle now. Walk around widdershins and you'll find a door. Come in, have some mulled wine, and we'll discuss what may be done."

We circled the tower until we found the door, which opened at a touch. Up a staircase we found a sitting-room with cushioned chairs, a broad embroidery frame, and a hearth cheerfully ablaze. A platter of aromatic meat and wine sat on a small table. Marcelin rose to greet us with a fox-like smile. His companion did not move from her seat by the fire, but her cornflower-blue eyes sought me avidly, and the forces gathering around her were thick as storm clouds.

She wore a gown of green embroidered with leaves, flowers, thorns. Her hair, dark as my own, was caught up in a golden net. She appeared a maiden in her twenties, scarcely older than I was; but if Ambrosio wanted to observe a masterful rejuvenation spell, he should examine her more closely. "Great-Aunt Alcine! Little did I think to find you here."

"Grandniece Isabeau," she said, "why so surprised? Did my charming sister Ettarre insinuate that my powers were slight? Welcome to the stronger branch of the family. And don't bother to pretend you're too moral to sully yourself with our methods. I heard how shamelessly you seduced knights on Ettarre's behalf. And now you and your Maiden of Révie between you have murdered the courtly wizard Ambrosio de Salamanca and Sir Rodrigue-le-Noir, heroes for whom many tears will be shed.

When it comes to the moment of truth, you're as much a killer as the rest of us, darling."

Ursula glowered at Marcelin. "What have you made me do?"

"Nothing that wasn't in your blood, lioness. Didn't your heart exult with the thrill of the hunt, the triumph of having him at bay, the bright spurt of blood? You're a magnificent predator."

"They have a point," I said to Ursula. "Think of all the petty people who've tried to take advantage of us. Your brothers. My grandmother. The merchants who tried to cheat us of fees for guarding their caravans. Why should we tolerate them? We're strong enough to take what we want."

I held my breath, waiting to see if Ursula could play her part in the pageant; her feelings show too easily. She kept her response brief: "Why indeed? Maybe it's time to cast our lot with the winners. But what do they want from us? And what do they offer in return?"

"What do we offer?" Alcine purred. "Freedom from the petty scruples that have restrained you. And a share of the spoil, of course."

"What share?" Ursula demanded.

The minstrel gave his most predatory leer. "Enough to sate the appetites of a lioness."

"Your share will be negotiable as you prove your worth and loyalty," Alcine added.

Ah, yes: loyalty. Why do dealings with my family always come back to that word? Aloud, I only asked, "Prove how?"

"I may send you to chastise certain enemies and secure certain property that should be ours," Alcine speculated. "Or I may begin by asking you to fortify the boundary of my domain."

"I'm glad you mentioned that," I said. "I did notice a potential weakness at the border—but perhaps I was mistaken—"

"Show me," Alcine commanded.

Heart pounding, one hand resting lightly on my wand, I led her and her consort to the water boundary. I gestured Ursula toward the stream. "See here: as my friend approaches the water, it forms a wall." I remarked, keeping my voice carefully neutral.

"As well it should," Alcine said.

"Sufficient to keep a mere warrior inside. As for myself—suppose I do this." I immersed both hands in the water and called on the purity of the Unicorn, as I had done to clear brackish well water. Then, salt had left the water and coated my hands; what would this enchanted stream leave on my skin? I could feel it, almost smell it: an insatiable magic that would not be content until it had swallowed all other powers into itself.

"What are you doing?" Alcine said. "I don't believe I've ever seen that spell before."

Of course she hadn't: it wasn't a spell, really, but a gift of the Unicorn. I hoped the gift would not desert me when I used it for purposes less innocent than purifying water. "I suppose you haven't, Great-Aunt Alcine. Nor this." I wrapped the power I had drawn from the water around my thorn-and-willow wand, using the anger of the trees to anchor it. Then I jerked the wand forward like a whip, sending the lash of hungry power—her own power—at Alcine, to slake its hunger upon her, eating magic out of her.

Taken by surprise, she had no defense to counter her own magic turned against her. "You lied to me, you double-dealing little witch!"

"I'm not a witch. I'm as much an enchantress as you are!" I said irrelevantly. Alcine struggled, weakening, aging. The minstrel had some notion what was happening—he was an enchanter too, though of lesser power—but he was busy battling Ursula. His swordplay paled beside hers, but with his left hand, he cast a spell to shake her bones within her, so she struggled to hold her ground against the double assault of steel and magic.

"Attack a woman, will you?" Rodrigo charged out of hiding to defend Ursula—and doubled over with his share of the bone-shaking spell.

All the while I drew on the power of willow and blackthorn to immobilize Alcine. The blackthorn tree was in a vengeful mood, so I gave its thorns free reign to grow and pierce her, as she had made it pierce others. The roots of the trees snaked over to her and sucked up her power, and I drank it from the wand, taking her strength and her knowledge into myself. I knew now what she'd been doing, how she egged on knights and sorcerers to commit one crime, then used the first rift in their souls to drive them to greater violence, doing her dirty work throughout the land. Working through me, my grandmother had once tried to raise an army enchanted into submission; Alcine, more subtly, aimed for a band of assassins enslaved by their own guilt. She would spread all this poison through the land: souls persuaded of their own worthlessness, plunging ever deeper into evil.

I tightened my fist, and thorns bit Alcine from all sides like the teeth of predators. As she bled in the mud, I sucked up her power until I felt as ravenous as she was. I would devour her—and then that slippery minstrel of hers would be a last choice morsel—and then—

Suddenly I saw myself defeating Alcine only to become her. "No!" I unclenched my fist, letting loose the stream of power.

For an exultant moment, Alcine took control again, and began reeling power toward her. That would not do either. I seized my wand so hard that my hand bled, and with all my will sent her power back into the living and growing things, the bitter blackthorn and the cool willow.

The blackthorn beside me grew higher than the oak, wider than the oldest beech tree, more abundant than grass. It sent runners through the enchantress's castle. Branches burst through the stone, toppling walls.

Alcine fell to the ground, tearing her gray hair in frustration. "Traitorous pet of Ettarre, what have you done?"

"I've given your powers back to the wood."

Free of her assault at last, I looked around to see how my companions fared. Ambrosio finished off the minstrel with a choking spell, freeing Ursula and Rodrigo of their pains. He pointed his wand at Alcine. "You haven't killed her."

"No," I said. "I've stripped her of power."

"Yes, I can feel that," he said. "But it won't last."

"I know. But it will take her years to gain back anything like the strength she had. And this wood will never be hers again; even the crabapple trees will refuse their fruit to her."

"Stop talking about me as if I'm not here!" Alcine rasped.

"You think yourself better than I am, do you? You pathetic ill-begotten harlot!"

Ambrosio still held his wand poised to strike her. "I've never killed a woman before. Or a disarmed foe."

"*Then don't*!" I said sharply. "Don't you see it's what she wants?"

"To die?"

"No, to see others take a step toward moral degradation. Especially people like—" I gestured at myself, Ambrosio, Rodrigo. The word I'd had in mind stuck in my throat till I rested my eyes on Ursula. "Heroes. People trying to do some good. Alcine drew power from the corruption of what might have been good." I turned to my fallen enemy. "Alcine, I don't know if I'm better than you. I've done things that shame me. But I've never yet killed a human creature and I'm not starting for *you*. Live with *that!*" It took all my will to turn my back on her.

I went to the stream, stood knee-deep in the abused water, and called again for the Unicorn's power to make all clean. The twisted magic that had infested the water coated my hands as a sickly green scum. I gathered it into a ball, then called Laetitia. I had not seen her during the fight; I assumed the little dragon had gone to ground to hide.

The mighty beating of wings surprised me. Willow fronds trailing from her mouth, the dragon perched on the blackthorn tree, which thickened its branch to bear her weight. She was growing even as I watched, fed on the power of the wood.

"Laetitia!" I tossed the ball of magic.

She understood; a puff of flame reduced the ball to a mere ember that guttered and cooled on the wet grass.

Ursula stared up at her. "She's grown too huge for any hall. Isabeau, where will we take her?"

"This wood is her home now," I said, then turned to Alcine. "Not yours."

Laetitia swallowed a bite of blackthorn, then swooped down, caught the fallen enchantress in her claws, and swept her away.

Rodrigo watched the dragon's flight with creased brow. "I hope we'll be able to leave more comfortably than that."

"As soon as the water subsides," I said. Freed from enchantment, the stream now behaved naturally for a brook swollen by rain. "I've removed the ban from the water—and it's not you the trees are angry at. But before you leave, consider: if it's adventure you're seeking, this wood may be richer than ever. The pent-up magic I've let loose could take any form."

"Intriguing," said Ambrosio. "And yet—no one here seems to need rescuing."

"Small chance of glory," agreed Rodrigo, "and none of pay. And if Alcine managed to corrupt other knights before us, they're out there doing harm. There's glory to be won in fighting them."

"You ladies could travel with us a while," Ambrosio said. "We might learn some useful things from each other."

"I need to stay in the wood until Laetitia's well settled," I said. "She's still young, for all the growing she's just done. But Ursula, I'll understand if you feel like Rodrigo does: small chance of glory, and no bards to sing your praises in this wilderness." I would hate it, of course, but I wasn't going to act like my family and try to keep her bound.

She shrugged. "There's more than one kind of glory. Why leave, when the forest has just become so interesting? It's all magical now, isn't it? Uncharted territory. Maybe it's really a Forest of Adventures now."

I met her eyes. "Maybe the lie has become truth."

"There's just one thing," she said. "The castle's a wreck. Where can we get out of the rain?"

As if in answer, Laetitia flew back, perched on the branch above us, and spread her wings over us.

I smiled up at the scaly rose-colored wings. "I told you someday you'd be glad to have a dragon for a companion."

GNAT

by Patricia B. Cirone

Nobody underestimates you like your family.

Patricia B. Cirone has published numerous short stories in various anthologies and magazines. Until recently she had to intersperse her writing with a job that paid for writing supplies that took most of her time. Now that she is no longer working at a "real" job, she is moving forward on writing the various novels she has started and stopped along the way. She lives with her husband and two cats and hopefully nothing she hasn't noticed—like that bat in the attic that surprised her.

"Hey, Buzzfly!" her brother Logan shouted.

"Naah, she's too small to be a buzzfly," said her older brother Daneel.

"She's just a gnat!" Logan snickered.

"Yeah, a gnat! Hey, Gnat," he called again. "Get me some more porridge."

"Why don't you get up and get it yourself!" Amiah replied. "Now, Amiah, don't be rude," their Mam said. "The boys work hard and need lots of energy. Get your brothers another bowl of porridge." Amiah swallowed her anger and waited on her brothers. Yes, they worked hard, but so did she. At least they got to work outside instead of in the stifling confines of the house on days like these. It was barely past dawn and already she could feel sweat gathering on the back of her neck where the collar of her tunic met her hair. At least the boys got to breathe fresh air and catch any breeze that might lift the heat a little bit. Every day for the past two weeks everyone in the village had gone out and searched the skies for any sign of rain. But the sun just glared down and baked everything drier. The ground cracked wherever it was bare, and folks eyed the wells nervously, for fear they would run dry. But no one voiced their fears. That might make it come true. Instead they made the blessing sign for water and went out and worked the fields, hauling water from the shrinking streams to save what they could in the fields and to water the livestock.

Logan and Daneel left to go out into the fields and Mam turned to Amiah. "We've put it off as long as we can—we'll have to wash some clothes and sheets today. The least we can get by with, I'm afraid." Amiah greeted the news with relief. Ordinarily she hated doing laundry, but today the water, even if it only barely filled the bottom of the tub, would be cooling. She wiped her hand across her forehead and gathered tunics and trews from the bedrooms. She and Mam sorted through them and picked out the most dirty to wash. Later, when she was hanging the laundry out to dry, she regretted wishing she could work outside. The glare of the sun

felt like a weight pressing down on her back. Her sleeves and the front of her tunic, wet from the washing, had dried within seconds of coming outside. She glanced upwards into the sky. It would be cooler up there. It always was cooler up higher, when she flew. Sometimes there would be a breeze, even if there were none on the ground.

She wished she could dare shed her tunic and day shift and let the wings that were her magic come out. She'd fly high and just drift, maybe glide south and land in the woods, where there would be some shade. Maybe she could even spot some clouds in the distance that might be rain. She wished she could "call" them—that would be a more useful magic than flying. Anything would be a more useful gift than flying, according to her mother. Flying didn't get the work done; flying didn't put food on the table. Flying made her a laughing stock, and worse. In order to fly, she had to shed both her tunic and day shift and wear only her upper underwrap, which was downright indecent. Flying wouldn't get her a marriage proposal from any good family in the village.

She'd heard it all, and more, ever since her gift had made itself known a year or so ago, as most gifts did, during puberty. She sighed and went back to putting the laundry up on the line.

At least it would dry fast and they wouldn't have to put it up, dripping, inside the cottage as they did when it rained. Oh, for some rain! When she finished hanging all the laundry they'd dared to do with the scant water Mam would allow to be used for it, she stretched her back and looked up into the sky again. The edge by the trees on the horizon looked greenish and threatening. It didn't look like rainclouds, but it didn't look good, either. Amiah hauled the empty basket inside and spoke to her mother about it. Mam went outside and looked for herself, frowning.

"Eh, that's not good. Maybe it will pass."

"What is it?" asked Amiah.

"Just more heat, if we're lucky," her mother replied, and wouldn't say more. Amiah knew better than to pester her. "Least said, best luck," her mother would just reply tersely. To say something out loud was to risk bringing it. And by the look on Mam's face, she didn't want to bring whatever it was if they weren't lucky.

The boys came home, sweaty and hungry after a day in the fields. Logan carried a fish.

"Stopped by the stream," he said. "They're gettin' harder and harder to call." He handed over the medium sized fish to Mam. Calling fish was Logan's magic, and one that had helped to put food on the table many a time. She could understand Mam being miffed at her odd talent. Fish calling was respectable and would bring him good offers of marriage when the time came. Daneel could calm bees, another good talent. He could go right up to a hive and take the honey without a single sting. He'd even moved a few hives close to their garden plot where they pollinated the plants and the one apple tree they had. Both were good talents: common enough that they were known but not so common that every household could boast of having one. They weren't freakish, like hers. No one had ever heard of anyone who could sprout wings out of her back and fly.

After supper, Amiah went out to feed and settle the chickens for the night. Even with the sun going down, it didn't feel any cooler. But at least the sun's remaining glare wasn't strong enough to feel like someone beating on her back and head. Even the chickens seemed lethargic and settled quickly. Soon it was time to crawl up to her small bed high in the loft. She opened the shutters on the tiny window, but not a breeze stirred. She lay on her back, wishing she dared take her sleeping shift off, but Mam would kill her if she found out. She lay there wondering if she would ever get to sleep but must have drifted off because she woke with a start, the aftermath of a lightening bolt streaking across her eyes. Another one crackled across the sky outside the loft's window, ending with the sound of wood cracking and a boom that shook the house.

Amiah bolted up, barely missing hitting her head on a beam. She leaned over the edge to call down to Mam and the boys, but before she could open her mouth, the clang of the fire bell in the village's center sounded. She hastily donned working trousers and jammed a rough tunic over her night shift. She slid down the ladder to find Mam and the boys similarly attired, with Mam shouting at the boys to stop and grab axes and buckets before bolting out the door.

Mam handed her a hoe and a bucket before they followed the boys out the door. Amiah expected rain to be pelting down but the air was as dry as it had been for weeks. Another bolt of lightning split the sky and she ducked instinctively even though it was high overhead. Mam muttered something beside her as they ran to the center of the village. They could see the eerie light of fire and hear the shouts of voices.

"It's the Donnings' house," Mam said. Amiah nodded, too out of breath to reply. The biggest problem was getting water. The buckets had to go so far down the well to reach water, it took twice as long to fill them and pass them along the line that quickly formed. Those that came up the line from the creek were only half full since the water was too low to sink the buckets right in. Everyone was sooty and sweaty by the time they managed to put the fire out. But they had stopped it from spreading to any of the nearby houses. The worst of the eerie lightning had spread to the south, where it lit the air over the woods with its hellish glare.

Amiah stood and watched it, wondering if it would come

back and fire more of the village houses. As she gazed at the woods, the sound of horses' hooves thundered into the village from the direction of the keep. The man beside her spat onto the ground and muttered, "Always late and always short," under his breath. But the King's men weren't here for the fire in the village.

"Men and boys! Round up! Stirth woods is on fire. Grab axes if you have them, hoes if you don't. Each of us will take one up behind him. Anyone without a ride follow behind as fast as you can!"

Faces looked at each other uneasily in the gloom of the torches and lingering embers of the Donning's house. The Stirth woods was massive, with tongues of it coming right down to the village on three of its sides. As well as supplying most of their lumber, it was vital to the game that kept them supplied with meat throughout most of the year.

"What about the women?" a voice called out.

"Do what you can to start building a fire break at the edge of the village," he said dismissively, as if the village women were weak and pampered as those of the nobility usually were. "It's headed this way. See if you can cut down those trees—they're not too big," the leader yelled, pointing at the east end of the village.

"But that's our orchard!" someone protested.

"It won't bear fruit if it's burnt to the ground, and you won't be here to harvest anything if your houses go with it!" came the answer. "And do what you can to pack up to be ready to leave if we can't stop the fire from spreading," he added grimly. By the look on his face, he seemed to think that likely.

With a thunder of hooves and a clanking of tools, the men and boys of the village clambered up on the backs of the horses and the cavalcade moved off, some of the villagers running behind. Amiah noticed a few of the older girls and women following after the men.

"Mam," she said, pointing after them. "Can I go?"

"Tish," her mother replied dismissively. "Those are women with useful skills. Damia can lighten a load, so that the men hauling trees and brush away from the fire line can move more, and faster. And Remidah can run like a deer, carrying messages. What could you do? Wave air at the fire with your wings?"

Amiah winced, her shoulders slumping. "You go and pack our belongings. Just the minimum of what we might need in a few packs. We may need to hurry, and your brothers might not be back in time to help. Just clothes and cooking utensils, mind you," her mother told her.

"What about... the brick?" Amiah asked softly.

"No, leave that for now. We can grab that in a hurry if we have to," her mother said, referring to what small savings they had hidden behind a loose brick in the fireplace. "And don't come back; you'll just get in the way."

Amiah nodded and turned back towards their home, jogging as she went. She soon had small packs of work clothes and their good clothes packed and ready to go, as well as some small essential cooking pans and a few pouches of herbs. No point in packing eggs, since they would never last in a pack while travelling fast. But she pulled down a few sausages and wrapped them well. Soon there was nothing to do.

She stood in the doorway and looked towards the edge of the village, but houses blocked her view. The sky was dark, with just muffled flashes of lightning and thunder off to the south. But east, where the Kings men had said the main fire was she could see a haze of yellowish orange. It looked evil. Unnatural.

She looked around the house for something, anything to do. Nothing. She couldn't just stand here and do nothing, but Mam would be mad if she went back to the edge of the village after she had told her not to. But she hadn't said she had to stay at the house...

Amiah eyed what she thought she could see of the fire glow off to the east. If she were up in the air, she could see better—maybe even tell if the fire was actually headed toward the village. She looked around. No one was near. She knew Mam would be mad—with all the village out, anyone could see her. But she couldn't just stand here and do nothing! Amiah tore off her tunic and night shift, tightened the binding of the undercovering that wrapped around her upper chest and over her shoulders and let the magic that was her gift free. Delicate wings formed and unfurled from her back and a moment later she was soaring upward, high over the village.

She could see the villagers working hard along the eastern edge of the village, but thankfully none looked up. She looked toward the glowing haze but couldn't see actual fire. The hills had too many gullies. She flew higher and angled closer to the ominous haze. Maybe if she flew over to the high road that came down from the Keep she would be able to see.

Quickly she worked her way over to the higher ridge. The air up here wasn't still like that down in the valley. Winds swept up the slopes, carrying the smell of smoke with it. She hovered over the road and tried to see which gully the smoke was coming from—not easy in the darkness of the night.

"Hey, you!" a voice called out from just below her. Amiah started and looked down in dread. A figure sitting on a horse was looking up and waving at her. One of the Kings men, seeing her half undressed like this. Mam would kill her. She thought about just swiftly flying away but dismissed it right away. Enough people in the village knew of her weird gift that just a few questions would be enough to identify her. And then she would be in trouble for defying a Kings man.

Slowly, and ashamedly, she drifted down and landed beside the mounted soldier. Only... it wasn't a soldier. It was the Princess. Princess Zhurah, the one that often dressed like a man and liked swordplay more than embroidery. Folks didn't know quite what to make of her, but then royalty always had their quirks that lesser folk didn't understand and knew better than to question.

Amiah stared upward. "How high can you fly and how far?" the Princess demanded.

"Uhh... high enough to have trouble breathing?" Amiah stuttered. "Umm... I don't know how far. Pretty far..."

Princess Zhurah stared down the road, thinking. "Any other gifts?" she asked after a moment.

"N...no, at least not that I know of," Amiah replied.

The Princess seemed to mutter to herself. "If that... then that... might do...."

Amiah looked up, waiting. Princess Zhurah's horse shifted, snorting slightly. It didn't like the smell of smoke. Smoke which seemed to be growing stronger. The Princess nodded her head decisively and looked back down at Amiah.

"Do you know what a *sight vassal* is?"

Amiah's eyes widened. "Ummm... the King uses the royal gift to link to another person to use their eyes? Like, like a spy?"

"Well, yes, it can be used for a spy. Though usually its just for having eyes and ears in many places the King can't be at the same time. It's not just the King. Any member of the Royal family with the Royal gift can do it. I can do it. Will you let me do it to you?"

Amiah gaped at her. "Isn't it... permanent? I'm just a village girl. Why...?"

"You can fly. I can't. If I can see with your eyes, and you can see the fire, then I can see the fire."

"So, you just want to know where the fire is? I can fly closer and come back and tell you."

"Not just know where it is. I have to be able to see it. I have another gift, a regular personal gift. I can throw things, even huge heavy things as far as I want to, as long as I can see where they are going to land."

Amiah looked at her, puzzled.

"I can throw water," the Princess half whispered to her. "The fire is out of control. It has spread down several gullies. It is threatening the Keep, the town of Ockton and several villages. It's cutting off many of those who are trying to fight it. Some have died—died horribly. And more will, if we can't stop it. But if I can throw water on it—huge heaps of water—then I can slow it down enough for the men on the ground to get ahead of it and stop it."

Zhurah looked down at Amiah. "I know it is a lot to ask. You have no training. You'll have no time to adjust to having me in your mind, in your eyes, in your ears. It may even drive you mad. But..."

"Do it!" Amiah said. She thought of her brothers, out there fighting the licking flames, possibly watch it come at them and surround them. She thought of her Mam, helping the other villagers, all the people she knew in the world, try to save their houses, their homes, their livelihood. "Do it," she repeated.

The Princess nodded. "Get up behind me. There's a deep lake up ahead that's fed from the mountain streams higher up. We'll go there."

Amiah scrambled up onto the back of the horse, mentally apologizing to it for the awkward way she did so. She had never ridden a "real" horse, only some of the village plow horses when she had been much younger, and someone had lifted her up into place.

"Grab on," Zhurah said and they took off before Amiah had barely managed to grasp the back of the Princess's tunic. The horse charged up the path, winding higher into the forested hills. It seemed like only moments before they stopped along a ridge looking down onto the deep lake the Princess had mentioned, barely discernible in the dark.

Amiah slithered off and the Princess dismounted beside her. "Last chance," Zhurah said. "I don't know what will happen to you, and I don't know if I can undo it if..."

"Do it," Amiah said again. Princess Zhurah nodded and stared deep into Amirah's eyes. In her hand, Zhurah grasped an amulet that had been hanging around her neck. The air around her hand seemed to glow, making her eyes gleam in the darkness. She spoke low, in a language Amiah didn't understand, and the glow from the amulet grew, brightened. And then she was hearing Zhurah's voice twice, in her ears... and in her head. The Princess shuddered and dropped the amulet. It fell, glowing, onto her chest. She staggered, and Amiah reached out grabbing her arm to steady her.

"No time," the Princess muttered and passed a hand over her eyes. "I didn't expect..."

"Are you all right?" Amiah asked anxiously.

"Yes," Zhurah replied and lowered her hand. "I have to be! Go fly, little girl, and save us all!"

"Amiah. My name is Amiah."

The Princess smiled. "Go fly, Amiah, and be my eyes for me this night."

Amiah unfurled her wings and flew upwards. She felt odd, a bit heavy, a bit dizzy. But she flew higher, looking for the licking flames that were putting all of them in danger. Winds buffeted her and she coughed from the smoke.

Careful, little one. Don't get swept away by the winds or breathe too much smoke, Amiah heard in her head. It was a soft sound, like someone whispering to her. Amiah nodded, flying faster and higher, searching, searching.

And she saw the flames, licking up the side of a gully. And another ridge, bathed in the light of torches the size of trees. They were trees. The trees of the forest. Small figures ran and scurried around the edges of the flames. And ahead, more flames, more fire.

A billow of smoke caught Amiah unawares, and she coughed, eyes tearing. *Steady* the voice in her head told her. *Steady now, while I...*

A gust of wind blew from behind her and a huge ball of water rushed past and plummeted down onto the flames along the ridge. A huge hissing sound and billows of smoke and steam rushed up. Amiah bobbled, nearly rolling over and desperately pumped her wings to move higher and away from heaving cloud.

Right, said the voice in her head. *We need to work on this a bit...* Amiah almost giggled. Everything was so strange, so unreal. She wondered if she was dreaming. She shook her head and her vision blurred. *Careful!* Shouted the voice in her head. *I know this is hard but concentrate! Don't fall on me, Amiah. Stay focused!*

Amiah swallowed and almost nodded her head, but the dizziness stopped her. She had to do this. She couldn't lose herself in the strange sensations, or lives would be lost. Her village would be lost.

Steady, now, the voice said. *I'm going to send another batch of water.*

Amiah was glad the Princess had warned her. She tightened

her shoulder muscles and held steadier as again a gust of wind and water droplets sped by her to land on the flames below. This time the Princess had aimed better, getting the leading edge of the fire. Faint shouts sounded from below, as the men frantically try to beat back the flames saw the water rain down on them, dowsing both the flames and the workers. Princess Zhurah warned her again, and yet another batch of water sped by them, getting more of the flames and pushing the fire back up the gully to where it had already burnt out most of the wood and fuel.

Time began to blur for Amiah. The Princess had her fly on to the next tongue of flame and the next gully filled with fire and death. She got used to bobbing out of the way of the huge balls of water and the hissing gouts of steam. Her throat was raw with coughing. Her eyes leaked tears from the smoke. She saw the edge of one village engulfed in flame, and saw the water land on it, drenching the houses and the small figures trying to throw tiny buckets of water at them. It wasn't her village. But it was her people, her Kingdom. *Her* Kingdom? Amiah's thoughts blurred again. She was so tired. It was getting hard to tell her own thoughts from the voice in her head. Were those her eyes that were looking down at the forest? Or someone else's? She couldn't see any flames. Something must be wrong if she couldn't see flames.

Come here, Amiah, her voice said. Some voice said. *We're done. Come down, back to the lake, back to me...*

Amiah felt herself drawn down to the small figure far below. She drifted closer, down, her shoulders aching with tiredness. And then she was down, staggering as her feet landed on the path.

A strange figure rode up to her. No, it wasn't strange, it was the Princess. And her horse. There still weren't any flames. Amiah blinked and coughed hoarsely.

"Come," Princess Zhurah said. In two voices again. Her ears and her head. The Princess reached her hand down and helped haul Amiah up and onto the back of the horse. "We did it!" Her voice sounded as tired as Amiah felt. "Let's get you home."

That sounded good, Amiah thought, as she slumped against

Zhurah's back falling asleep before she even felt the horse move.

Dawn was breaking when Amiah woke to the feel of the Princess's hands lifting her down off a horse. She was in front of her family's house. How... ?

"There's some bleeding of thoughts," the Princess said. "We should be able to stop that with time. And some training. For both of us..."

Amiah blinked up at her. So, she hadn't dreamt all of this, then. And she wasn't crazy. At least she didn't think she was. And her village was still standing. And inside the house she could hear her brother Logan exclaiming:

"You should have seen it! Huge balls of water the size of a bear! The size of a dragon! Just huge balls falling out of the sky, from, from nowhere! It must have been the Gods! It must have been!"

"Knight Tomas said it was the Goddess Kariel!" Daneel chimed in.

Amiah walked in. Silence fell and then her mother exclaimed: "Where have you been! And in such a state! You get some clothes on you right now! I swear, you don't have the brains of a flea!"

"A gnat!" Logan cried out. "The brain of a gnat! And she's been off flitting around while the rest of us were working, weren't you, Gnat!"

"Gnat!" agreed her brother Daneel, disgustedly.

And then Princess Zhurah walked in behind her and the silence fell again. This time it lasted much longer.

"Your sister," said the Princess, "worked as hard as any of you. Harder. And it was *she* who saved all of you. Your lives, your village, the Keep."

Her Mam and two brothers just stared at her. Amiah swayed a bit, still feeling as though she'd lifted and thrown those huge gouts of water herself. And flown for days, for months.

"What?" asked her mother. "How... ?"

"She is my eyes and my ears. She is my sight vassal. She flew for all of us this night and guided the water to the flames," the Princess declared.

Her mother stared at her. Her brothers' mouths hung open.

"She's not a gnat, but a Knight," the Princess added.

"I'm not a Knight!" Amiah exclaimed. "I'm just, I'm just a villager."

"Well, you're my sight vassal now, and you'll need to live up at the Palace to get training. After what you did tonight you are sure to be honored with some sort of title."

This time it was Amiah's mouth that hung open.

Her mother seemed to come out of her trance and took in the fact that a Royal Princess was standing in her doorway. "Your, your Majesty..." she stuttered, and looked frantically around the plain, humble living area.

"Just your Highness," replied Princess Zhurah. "Majesty is for my father. And speaking of which, I had better get back to the Keep before word is sent to him that I am missing.

"Amiah, get some rest. I'll come back tomorrow—or rather later today—no make that tomorrow, and pick you up. The sooner we get you to the Palace in Toberin for training, the better."

She turned to Amiah's mother. "I'm sorry, ma'am, but it seems I must take your daughter from you. Her gift is invaluable, and since she agreed to become my sight vassal, she will need training in that and in other duties. You should be honored to have such a daughter."

"Of, of course," Amiah's mother answered faintly. The Princess turned and walked out the door. Mam, Logan and Daneel gawked at her. Amiah was too tired to think, or to answer the questions she saw bubbling behind their eyes.

"Ummm..." she said. "I better go get some clothes on..."

She turned and walked to the ladder to the loft and climbed it, up to her bed. Instead of donning clothes, though, she fell onto the bed and wondered, as she quickly fell asleep, what tomorrow would be like. Different, she thought. Definitely different.

THE QUICKENING OF THE BARRENS

by Dave Smeds

Healing magic may have more uses than the obvious one.

Dave Smeds sold his first story in early 1979 to the anthology *Dragons of Light*, edited by Orson Scott Card. He describes himself as a non-prolific writer, but has nevertheless sold hundred of stories since then. In addition, he has written novels, screenplays, comic book scripts, reviews, and articles. His work ranges across a variety of sub-genres, but he particularly enjoys crafting imaginary-world fiction. He has done so for the Sword and Sorceress series nineteen times. His novels *The Sorcery Within* and *The Schemes of Dragons* will soon be re-released along with a concluding third volume, *The Wizard's Nemesis*.

Vahema's oath-nieces wept when they saw the barrens. Vahema mourned with them, though fury kept her tears stillborn. When she had last seen this land, farms had sprawled one after the other over the broad alluvial plain, crops verdant, barns full. Now all was blighted. No structures remained—only a few charred fence posts jutting skyward, memorials to slain livestock. Despite recent rains, the only growth pushing up through the ash were clumps of thistle or blood nettle or coils of stink briar.

General Mazhul had always been a foul man, his hordes infamous for their killing, their raping, their pillaging. But it was in retreat that the emperor's field marshal had shown his worst side. "Burn the haystacks. Foul the wells. Salt the earth." He had given the command. His lackeys had obeyed. The land was now beyond ravaged. It was cursed. Rain and sun, tilling and husbandry, would not cure it. Only sorcery could.

The women chose a spot for their camp. At Vahema's insistence, all three of her nieces rested while she unhitched the team and laid out feed and a trough of water for the poor, patient creatures. Fetching broken bricks and fieldstone, she created a simple hearth, hung a kettle, and set beans to soak, then she went in search of deadwood for the evening's fire—the land still could provide that, if not much else.

Thessa drank five dippers of water from the barrel and still seemed thirsty. Ardis could not stop pacing from the stiffness in her back. Worst off was Kalahi, who stripped to her small clothes to expose more of herself to the breeze. She leaned back against a wagon wheel, a damp cloth on her forehead, and regarded her two sister-initiates with envy. They suffered less from overheated flesh than she, even though their pregnancies were closer to term.

They nevertheless allowed themselves only two hours of recuperation. The afternoon was well advanced, and they had agreed they would not forego even one session of spellcasting.

Thessa, Ardis, and Kalahi made a triangle, ten paces on a side, facing toward the center. Spreading their arms, they began to sing.

Vahema patrolled a circuit around her companions. From time to time she would check them for indications of strain, but most of her observation was outward, a wariness about what might be coming over the horizon or emerge from the gullies or the lifeless tangles of brush.

The enchantment blossomed as the harmony grew perfect. The volume was soft, the singers' full wombs denying them the lung capacity they usually possessed. Vahema wasn't worried. The magic did not require loudness, only heart. Thessa, Ardis, and Kalahi brimmed with that.

Vahema untied the plait from around her waist and let her long robes flutter. Her fingers kneaded their way along the knots, stroked the beadwork, and summoned up the essence embedded in the leather—the residue of two hundred years of spellcasting, her own and that of eleven previous adepts upon whom the plait had been bestowed.

The sentinels materialized. They were no longer translucent as when she had first tried to cast them a fortnight ago. They looked to be genuine, corporeal beings, strong likenesses of the very men that had started the journey with them. As usual she adorned them in warrior mode, with swords at their belts and helms on their heads, not that the real swords and the real helms had prevented the real men from being killed. She arrayed them so that they faced away from the triangle, seeming to share the burden of watchfulness with her, though in truth only she, with her natural set of eyes, was capable of discerning the approach of enemies.

Eventually the song's effect spread far enough to wrap Vahema within its embrace. She recognized its flavors as profoundly as if she were crafting them herself. The enchantment was at once a call to prosper, to grow, to be healthy. Even as Thessa, Ardis, and Kalahi were fecund, so was the energy they wove. The vitality pushed against the morbid taint of the air, the sickness of the soil, until the immediate area became a zone of unassailable wholeness.

Finally the younger women could sing no more. They closed their mouths and lowered their hands.

The three examined the ground at their feet. Grasses and wildflowers were already emerging, a few blades here, a sprig there, seeking the sun. The aroma rising from the matted remains of last year's verdure was no longer an assault to the nose. The signs of vitality extended outward about thirty paces in every direction.

Vahema fetched a small box from the wagon and upended it in the purified area, dumping out the moist soil it had held. A dozen fat earthworms, freed to go their own way, began the process of burrowing.

The women permitted themselves a few minutes to savor their accomplishment, then busied themselves with the preparation of the evening meal and the arranging of bedrolls and dew canopies. They wanted to retire early and sleep fully. They had so much more to do, and so few weeks in which to attempt it.

The next day, the group walked more than a mile to a place that they could tell had once been a farmwife's vegetable garden. They repeated the ritual. The day after that, they walked in the opposite direction and purified a duck wallow.

The curse magic had been expertly laid down. To quell it took all they had. They couldn't say how many breaches they would have to create before the whole shroud disintegrated. They only knew if they were to have any hope of success, it would come in the near term, before spring gave way to summer. Fail now, and they failed forever.

Vahema suddenly became aware that a pair of armed men were watching them.

Soldiers.

Vahema's heart thudded in her chest. They were no more than forty paces away. How could they have approached so closely without her noticing?

Immediately she caused her non-corporeal sentries to unsheathe their swords and turn to face the newcomers. Vahema hoped it seemed intimidating. Perhaps it was. The pair held back.

Or had they already been holding back?

Thessa, Ardis, and Kalahi huddled together. Vahema screened them.

The strangers were a combination of opposites. One was older, steel-eyed, his countenance criss-crossed by scars, his hair flecked with as much grey as her own. A hillman of Scantis, judging by his complexion. She sensed he had been handsome once, but that was long past. The other was a lowlander, wheat blond, round-faced, and...restless. He gazed about as if unable to pay attention long to any one thing.

At the crest of the slope behind them waited a small pack mule. It stood vigil beside a cutter loaded with a modest quantity of gear and supplies. The sled was rigged to be pulled by a man, not by a horse. If these were mercenaries, they were not the sort who commanded high wages.

The older man waved toward her conjured guardians. "As scarecrows go, those are well made, but you would be better off with only one. When you split your effort, their movement is unnatural."

Vahema reshaped the enchantment. One of the phantoms evaporated. The other now received her best effort. She sent it striding in their direction. One step. Two. Three. She put a glare in its eyes and made it tighten its grip on the sword hilt.

The younger man stepped back, eyes widening. Then he blushed, to have reacted to the threat despite knowing it to be an illusion.

"Better," the older man said.

Vahema let the spell dissolve. "What is your purpose here?" she demanded.

"We wish to be of service."

"How?"

"We make better scarecrows."

Vahema knew her life was in their hands, so she did not raise her voice, but she could not entirely omit the scorn from her tone. "We had protectors. Soldiers murdered them. Before that, other soldiers made widows of my companions. And it was soldiers who turned this land into what you see around us. Are you suggesting I let a pair of soldiers bed down at our campfire?"

The older man neither bristled nor laughed. He just studied her face without interruption while she did the same to him.

"I am Fhadric," he said at last. He pointed to the younger man. "He is Hon."

Vahema folded her arms.

Fhadric did not seem troubled that she had held back her name. He pointed at the abundance of healthy duckweed that had formed in the puddles of the wallow within just the past several minutes. "We mean to make sure your work is not interrupted. We will stay at a distance, though, since you prefer it."

With that, the men returned to their mule and cutter and waited.

Vahema continued to study the unwelcome guests. Thessa joined her. Together they watched Hon brush the mule while Fhadric checked the fastenings of the gear on the sled.

"Are they waiting for reinforcements?" Thessa wondered aloud.

"They don't need them. The hillman—the one who spoke—he could have cut me down like milkweed, if he'd wanted."

"Even with what you can do?"

"Yes. Even so."

"Then perhaps these are good men."

Vahema cleared her throat. "They are soldiers without allegiance. I have met too many of that sort. In all my years I only found one who I would say was good."

"Then what shall we do?"

"I suppose we must hope they are like that one."

Vahema and Thessa rejoined Ardis and Kalahi and made their way back as they would have done had the men not appeared. Except, of course, they couldn't help looking behind themselves as they walked. Every time they did, they saw the men following in their wake, a hundred or so paces back. They only ceased when the women reached their camp, and even then, it was only to turn away to the side to a convenient spot to make their own camp, and the separation they observed was unchanged.

As Vahema defined it, they were stationed like shepherds—in plain sight, close enough they could be summoned with a shout.

Vahema was neither a ewe nor a lamb, and did not want to be treated like livestock.

Fhadric was reassured to see the Iavan initiates knew enough to bank their fire once their meal was cooked, and not allow the glow to serve as a beacon of their presence during the night. The older one—the adept—went around at sunset laying down fetishes she had fashioned of sticks and twine. These Fhadric recognized as the perimeter of a ward spell. He assumed that when she started swinging that plait she wore, she was setting it. The measure was not sophisticated, but at least it would provide some warning of encroachment. He was sure it was the best she was capable of.

In most other respects, he was deeply concerned. The women had nothing near the degree of safety they needed, not with the bulk of two armies still killing one another elsewhere within the very same province. What he and Hon could provide was only a modest improvement of their circumstances.

Fhadric took the first watch, sitting on a log as the Garnet Moon drifted down toward the western horizon, a cradle of burgundy luster that cast shadows of an all too eerie nature. He doubted he could have slept yet anyway. The landscape was too quiet. There should have been cricket chirp, or the rustle of field mice. He heard no drone of mosquitoes, nor the flutter of bats on the hunt for them. The only noises came from Hon, who thrashed inside his bedroll and mumbled in his sleep, as if arguing with ghosts, begging them not to lean over him.

Perhaps ghosts *were* leaning over the poor lad. If so, the question was, were they the ghosts of this place, or the ones Hon had brought along?

Eventually it was time for the second watch. Fhadric felt as though he were doing Hon a favor by waking him.

"Easy," Fhadric murmured, and told the youth in simple words where they were, and how they had come to be there.

Hon nodded, put his boots back on, and threw his cloak over his shoulders. Fhadric waited for the signs that he might have to repeat his words, but for once, it was not necessary. Hon was actually awake.

"I don't like this place," Hon said.

"It plagues me, too," Fhadric replied. "As it would anyone with a heart. The sorceresses have their work cut out for them."

"They don't trust us. The sorceresses."

"No reason they should. But they need us. Should we leave?"

As usual, Hon needed time to roll the question around in his head, but the answer was what it needed to be, and what Fhadric knew it would be.

"We should stay," Hon said.

"There you have it." Fhadric took off his boots and pulled a blanket over himself, and began his nightly struggle to relax his sword hand.

The four women did not let the arrival of Fhadric and Hon hinder their schedule. In fact, for the next two days, Thessa, Ardis, and Kalahi conducted the ritual morning and afternoon, resulting in four more small tracts of enlivened terrain. Near their camp, where they had sung on the very first day, the unpoisoned area now extended to almost double its original extent. Bees had discovered it and were probing each spike of clover and each dangle of vetch.

They saw very little of their uninvited guardians. The first day, by chance, Vahema noticed Fhadric emerging from the thicket of stunted duskwood where he had been concealed. The second day, she spotted Hon along the edge of the river, a strung bow in his grip and a quiver of arrows on his back. Vahema had to admit she was reassured that he was patrolling there. The waterway and its riparian fringe of brush and reeds were untouched by the poisoning, leaving too many places for a lurker to hide.

At the end of their labors, on their way back to their camp, the woman came across a strand of four fat catfish hanging from a stick near the path.

Vahema began to stride past. The next meat day was a fortnight away, and even if it had been the height of the Harvest Feast, she was not about to accept the gift of any swordsman. But Thessa swept forward and hefted up the entire strand.

"If you don't want yours, I'll eat *two!"* she told Vahema.

Vahema felt blood rise to her cheeks. She hadn't considered what her nieces might need. Even the strictest matrons of their order acknowledged that pregnant women could eat fish or fowl without regard to the usual regimen, and even red meat if they craved it. That was even more the case with women called upon to exert themselves as Thessa, Ardis, and Kalahi had done. Two ceremonies of renewal per day was an extraordinary pace.

"If they get close enough to speak to again, let's ask for a brace of pheasants," Kalahi suggested.

The next day they set out intending to conduct only one ceremony, so as to conserve their strength. However, fortified by the previous evening's fish dinner, they decided they would continue. The compromise was that the second spot they chose was not far from the first. That was not necessarily a disadvantage. Nature often appreciated random patterns.

It was perhaps a tactic they wondered if they should have employed earlier, because the session went well. Seedlings burst up as vigorously as any so far.

On their way back, they came around a bend and discovered two corpses lying on the ground, blood still seeping from the mortal wounds they had suffered—one to the throat, the other to the midsection.

They were not Fhadric and Hon. Vahema was surprised that this concern was the first that sprang to her mind.

Sounds of anguish drew them farther on, where they found the hillman and the lowlander kneeling down over a third man who breathed his last just as they approached.

Neither Fhadric nor Hon appeared marked by the incident except for a tear in Fhadric's left sleeve.

Hon was shaking. Fhadric reached out and placed a hand on his companion's shoulder.

"It's done. It's done," he said softly.

Hon stumbled to his feet and staggered away, hands covering his face. Vahema would have said he was sobbing except that the noises were so choked off she wondered if he might be having a seizure. Thessa started after him.

"Leave him be," the hillman said. "His injury is not of the flesh."

"Even so, can we not comfort him?" Thessa inquired.

Fhadric sighed. "You would have to unwind time."

Ardis and Kalahi could not bear to stay where the dead men were. Thessa escorted them on.

"Who were they?" Vahema asked Fhadric. "Do you know?"

"Bounty hunters. Searching to see if anyone of your sect was out here doing precisely what you're doing. Mazhul is offering a ten-stack of copper and a set of silver stirrups for every head brought to him."

Vahema frowned. In these times, it was all too easy to find men willing to sell their mothers for a five-stack of copper and a meal.

"You were right to stay," she said.

She appreciated that he did not seem smug. "I will see to the bodies now," was all he said.

"The graves should be in one of the areas we've purified. No one deserves to be laid to rest in tainted ground."

"I agree."

"Do you want to borrow our wagon?"

He shook his head. "The oxen won't like the smell of blood. Nor will Hon's mule, for that matter. I have the cutter. It will serve."

She left the grim task to him.

In the morning, the women moved their camp, not only to broaden their effort into fresh territory, but so as to get themselves away from the spot where the bounty hunters had fallen.

For the next fortnight, they saw no further sign of hostiles. On one occasion Fhadric cautioned them not to light their evening fire. They did as he recommended. All remained well—or if it were otherwise, the matter was dealt with out of their view.

Hon at first was completely silent, not answering when they greeted him and seeming to prefer only the company of the mule, if that. But over time he resumed his patrols. Eventually he began to help in other, small ways, though they did not ask it of him. He raked plots of purified soil, sowing seeds in places where the natural allotment was meager. He tidied up the debris of burned-out farmhouses.

One afternoon Vahema found herself watching the young man laboring in an orchard plot her nieces had blessed with their song several days earlier. A number of trees were starting to regenerate. Inevitably, some of that resurgence was in the form of suckers emerging from the roots, competing with the established trunks. Hon was proceeding along pinching off the unwanted growth, like a farmer tending to his own parcel.

"He seems better," Vahema commented to Fhadric as the hillman approached.

"It's the sort of work he knew before he picked up the sword.

It brings him some measure of peace. Not as much as he needs, though. He should never have been a soldier. Should never have seen what he has seen."

Over the next three weeks, the women sang as much as their stamina would allow. Throughout it all, Fhadric and Hon watched over them as they had promised. They did not attempt to shift their camp closer. They continued to find small ways to make the burden easier, such as escorting the oxen to the river to drink or fetching extra firewood. They even supplied the brace of pheasants Kalahi grew bold enough to ask for, though given the barren landscape they were unable to fulfill the request until they managed to find a cock and a hen hiding in the river brush.

By the end of that time, Vahema realized she had come to trust them.

On a warm day—the warmest so far, heralding the summer—a man came into sight poling his way up the river, his raft bearing a variety of trade goods, his loose shirt festooned with a myriad of beads and ribbons.

Ardis grinned. "It's a Six Bridges peddler."

It was a welcome sight. One always expected a certain sequence of visitors to a battlefield after the armies had left. First the looters, then the crows. But wait long enough and finally the peddlers would turn up, seeking out survivors in the midst of reestablishing their lives, folk who might be in need of a spare kettle or a shovel or a wagon hitch. They only appeared after conditions had become peaceful.

"I will speak with him," Fhadric offered.

Vahema knew him well enough by now to know he meant to trek to the riverbank alone while she and her nieces remained out of sight, with Hon as sentry, until the newcomer's character was certain.

"I'm coming, too," she said.

Fhadric nodded as if he had been certain she would say precisely that. They went down the bluff together.

At the water's edge stood a small pier. The reavers had set fire to it but its heavy timbers had resisted the heat. Fhadric tested it and found solid purchase on the platform. Vahema joined him.

The peddler's dog noticed them and began barking. The peddler shaded his eyes, took in their measure, and began poling toward them.

Vahema knew dogs. This one was dancing about and wagging its tail in a way that said it was delighted to be encountering new people. That told her what she needed to know about the man the hound shared the raft with.

The peddler reached them, looped a mooring rope around the last piling, and immediately the dog was with them, noting their scents and getting a pat on the head from Fhadric, then he bounded off onto shore to get in a good run.

Fhadric chuckled.

"Fine day," the peddler said.

"It is," Vahema replied.

"I thought I might be the very first to pass through here," the man said.

"We've been here several weeks," she said.

"Even before the war ended, then?"

"Has the war ended?"

The peddler nodded. "Indeed it has. The emperor has given up all claim to this province."

"And what of the field marshal?" Vahema asked.

"Mazhul? The emperor had him blinded and castrated and left to beg along the byway. Claimed he was entirely to blame for the atrocities."

Vahema knew "entirely to blame" was far from the truth, but "to blame" was unquestioned. At least some justice had been levied, even if only to the scapegoat.

The peddler was pleased to chat for several more minutes, but once he understood them to have no money and nothing to trade, and no particular need of what he had to offer, he was eager to be on his way, so as to make it past the blighted terrain before sunset.

The dog was disappointed to have to climb back onto the raft so soon, but obeyed once he had been petted a final time by both

Vahema and Fhadric. Within moments he was occupied trying to catch a dragonfly without tumbling into the water.

As Vahema and Fhadric wended their way back up the bluff, he told her, "I believe you will no longer be hunted. Perhaps it's time that Hon and I moved on."

Vahema was taken aback. "Do you have somewhere you need to be?"

The hillman shook his head. "All Hon and I have ahead is the road, but we are used to it."

"Then I suggest a different plan. I have already talked the matter over with my nieces. In just one week's time, my nieces and I will be returning to our chapterhouse. We would like to hire you and Hon as our bodyguards for that journey."

"A week? Will the work here be done by then?"

"Thessa and Ardis are both well into their eighth month. Within a week, or maybe less, they have to stop spellcasting or risk the health of their babies. The curse cannot be broken by fewer than three singers. It may harden into place, except for the few places we've saved already. If so, that is that. There will be nothing more we can do."

Fhadric weighed it. "We will keep the vigil, as before, and escort you to your home."

"Good."

"The curse will yield," he added. "You will succeed."

"Are you a seer?"

"No. But every time I have encountered a Six Bridges peddler, it has been a good omen."

Fhadric had spoken only as a form of encouragement, adopting the philosophy that a confident frame of mind might help the spellcasting. In truth, he doubted the women could fulfill their mission. Of late, Ardis, Kalahi, and Thessa had been struggling just to stay upright as they sang.

But on the third day after the peddler had passed through, the trio abruptly stopped in the middle of their ceremony. Smiles broke out on their faces. Vahema's, too.

Fhadric had never been able to sense magic in any direct

way. No colorful auras to dazzle his vision. No tingles up his spine. But he understood at once how completely the pall upon the land had shattered. The clamminess of the air gave way to blossom-kissed breezes. A flock of birds changed course, no longer ranging outside the edge of what had been contaminated terrain, but turning and landing within it. Green growth appeared *everywhere*.

He clambered down the rock outcropping where he had been standing sentry. He nearly stumbled as he reached the four women. It had been so long since he had been part of a victory, he had forgotten how drunk it made him feel.

"This is beyond what we expected," Vahema said. "The land was in torment, and now it is at peace."

"Like a baby that gets what it needs and stops crying."

She seemed startled that he would come up with that particular analogy.

"Yes," she said after she had thought about it. "Like that."

Thessa came forward. "We should mark the occasion. Perhaps you and Hon will share our evening meal with us?"

Thessa looked at Vahema. And Fhadric looked at Vahema.

"Yes," Vahema said. "Please eat with us this evening."

"Gladly," Fhadric replied.

Fhadric realized Hon had not joined them. He had been stationed on a hillock to the west.

And there he still was, gazing out at the landscape as if still seeing some sort of threat in it. Or worse. Fhadric was sure he was weeping.

"Do you think he is unaware of what happened?" Vahema asked.

Fhadric sighed. "If I am not mistaken, he is thinking of comrades he would like to have beside him, to share the moment."

"Would those comrades not be glad that at least he is alive and able to be part of it?"

"They would, I'm sure," the hillman said. "And they would tell him so, if they had the chance. Perhaps he would listen to them. He does not hear me when I make the argument."

~o0o~

After the women had left, Fhadric waited where he was until he saw that Hon was no longer crying, then he trudged up the hillock.

"You worried them," Fhadric scolded.

"I'm sorry," Hon mumbled.

"They've invited us to supper. Perhaps we could catch some fish, or hunt down some rabbits. Otherwise I fear it may be just porridge and vegetables. What do you say?"

"Rabbits."

"Rabbits it is." Fhadric had suspected that would be the answer, and was glad it was so. To find rabbits or any game of similar sort, he and Hon would have to journey an hour or more to the nearest edge of what had been the barrens. Wildlife would be turning up there, repopulating former territory now that it had been purified. A long walk, a lengthy hunt—that would distract the young lowlander. He was at his best when he had a task to focus upon.

They headed out. Fhadric did not attempt to lure his companion into conversation. They simply shared the chance to amble along through terrain that no longer smelled of fungus or putrefaction.

Was that a butterfly? First he had seen in all these weeks. Fhadric pointed it out.

Hon nodded. No smile, but at least he was not completely barricaded within himself.

When they came to a suitable zone, they split up in order to double the chance of encountering prey. Hon turned toward the north, strung bow in one hand, arrow in the other. Fhadric took out his bolas and headed off toward the south.

He encountered no rabbits, but within the hour he spotted a nice fat partridge, one that apparently had no awareness of what it meant when Fhadric started to twirl the weighted cord over his head. Down it went.

His shoulder objected to the vigor with which he had flung the weapon. Why he could not remember he was no longer young enough to apply full force, he didn't know. Once again he had paid the price. He decided he was done hunting for the time being.

The afternoon was still barely underway when he reached the camp. He held up the partridge and was pleased by the reactions. But after he had hung the bird from the side of the wagon, he turned to find that all four women were gathering around him.

"What is it?" he asked.

"It's about Hon," Vahema said. "We believe we can help him."

"Go on," Fhadric said.

"I don't know if you've quite understood the nature of the sorcery we have been wielding these past few weeks."

"A spell of healing, I thought."

"Yes and no. At its core, it is a lullaby of forgetfulness. We made the land forget its wretchedness and remember how it was before Mazhul's wizards afflicted it. You said what Hon needs is to unwind time. We could do that. The energy has not yet dissipated. We could tap it. We could sing to Hon. Sing *for* him. And he would forget his pain."

"Take his memories?" Fhadric's shoulder throbbed. He rubbed it, buying time to think. "Can it be undone?"

"No. Whatever he forgets will be forgotten forever," Vahema said. "The good and the bad."

"But our control is reliable," Thessa interjected. "We sing for a certain length of time, and the most recent year's worth of memories would be gone from his mind. Sing that much longer, and he would forget another year. We would go back only as far as he says he wants to go."

"You said he was happy once," Vahema said. "When was that?"

"I'm not certain," Fhadric said. "Tell me, why are you bringing this up now, to me? Why not mention it to him first?"

"We are concerned about the soundness of his mind. If he says yes, we need to know he is not grasping at a remedy that will not actually serve him. We know you well enough to know you will tell us what is right for him."

"It has to be his choice," Fhadric said immediately. "But I

can tell you that if his answer is yes, he will be the better for it."

"Then we will ask him," Vahema said.

Hon agreed so immediately—and so calmly—it removed any doubt Vahema might have had that she and her nieces were leading him into something he would regret.

Four years, he told them. He wanted to erase four years, taking him back to age sixteen, before his father had insisted he go off and distinguish himself in battle. Vahema was astonished to learn the lowlander was only twenty. She had guessed he was at least five years old than that.

The partridge and two handsome rabbits were arrayed on skewers over the fire and soup was simmering in the cauldron as Thessa, Ardis, and Kalahi gathered in a triangle around Hon. He lay down on the grass, closed his eyes, and they sang.

This time, there was no curse magic to resist the trio. They had only to reach out with their power and focus a small fraction of the ambient vitality that pervaded the air around them. The entire ritual took barely a minute.

Fhadric knelt down beside his comrade. Hon opened his eyes.

"Where am I?" Hon asked, with an attitude of curiosity rather than alarm. "How did I get here?"

Fhadric replied with the basic details Hon himself had said he would want to hear first. As he began the longer account of what the past four years had included, and why Hon had chosen to burn that part of his book of days, Vahema and her nieces retreated to a discreet distance.

Just as the food was ready, Fhadric and Hon joined them. The change in the younger man was profound. He instantly smiled at them—even though he had to be introduced to them anew. He was eager to talk. He moved with a puppyish sort of abruptness not unlike the peddler's dog.

When Kalahi leaned near him to hand him his plate, he blushed. What a change that was. In the weeks past, he had hardly shown any sign that he was aware how beautiful Kalahi was, a loveliness that her pregnancy had done nothing to diminish.

Vahema studied the expression on Fhadric's face as Fhadric watched Hon.

Fhadric became aware of the scrutiny. "I did not know him when he was this way. He was already half-broken when I met him. It is a fine thing you've done."

"You know, tomorrow, there may still be enough of the energy left to repeat the process. We could do for you what we did for Hon."

Fhadric shook his head.

"Unless I am greatly mistaken, you are burdened even more than he was," Vahema added.

"You are not wrong in thinking that." His voice dropped a register. "But my situation is not the same. I was not the best I could have been when I was younger. I do not wish to be the person I was then. You would not wish it, either."

"I see."

"If they offered to sing for *you*, would you do it?" he asked. "Give up the progress you've made?"

Vahema considered trials and nightmares she had endured, and the being forged from them.

"My choice would be the same as yours," she responded. "I am as I am."

As twilight deepened and the sky became a vault of stars and moons large and small, the younger women announced they were not tired in the least, and they should have a celebration. With Hon's help, they made a bonfire nearly as tall as themselves, knowing they no longer had to conserve their stack of firewood. The trio began to sing.

They were not spellcasting. They were making music, for the joy of making music. They warmed up their voices with the chant of the Thousand Lakes, a favorite piece ideal for their particular blend of voices. Soon they proceeded into the Ballad of the Milkmaid and the Farrier. They giggled as they tried to recall the third stanza, and clapped their hands as Hon supplied it—he proved to have a fine tenor voice.

"We can stand here and watch," Vahema said to Fhadric, "but it is bad form not to participate in some way."

"I can't sing," he replied.

"Nor can I. But I do know how to dance. I have the strange feeling you do as well."

She moved to a patch of ground free of trip hazards, and beckoned him.

When he had accepted that she meant it, he unbuckled his sword belt and laid his weapon aside. She untied her plait, tossed it to the edge of the circle of firelight, and unbound her hair.

He set his hand gently in hers, fingers only. Contact without lure. She held the hand as would a sister tutoring her brother, and led them step by step, twirl by tilt.

In mere minutes, muscles began to ache—the rust of years of a skill unexploited. She kept on anyway. So did he.

MISS ARGENT'S SCHOOL FOR MISLAID MAIDENS

by Melissa Mead

We used to joke: "another day, another damsel, another dragon in distress." In the stories we've bought over the years, the dragon is more likely to be in distress than the damsel, although sometimes it's both.

Melissa Mead lives in Upstate NY. She currently has a novel on submission, her stories have appeared in *Daily Science Fiction*, *IGMS*, and several volumes of *Sword & Sorceress* (among other places), and her web page is at https://carpelibris.wordpress.com.

"I need your help to rescue a dragon," said the girl on my doorstep.

"Rescue who from a dragon?" I said. My hearing isn't what it used to be after all those blows to the helmet. Plus, it was the small hours of the morning. This girl had roused me from a warm bed. I wasn't at my sharpest. Or most patient. "Cranky Old Lady" doesn't even begin to cover my mood at that hour, and my knightly training was barely holding my temper in check.

"No, rescue a dragon! Miss Argent. She's our teacher. I'm from Miss Argent's School for Mislaid Maidens."

"Whaa? Get in here, kid. It's chilly out there."

She scampered in. I poked up the fire, put on a kettle and rummaged for my packet of Hotshot tea, the kind that can keep the Sandman himself awake for a week straight. Clearly, I wasn't going to be getting any more sleep tonight.

"So, how d'you mislay a maiden? And what's your name?"

"June." The girl scowled. "And we're not really mislaid. Miss Argent thought the name was funny. Dragons are weird. But at least she didn't leave us chained to rocks, or trees, or just dump us out in the middle of nowhere and hope a giant lizard would eat us up like the stupid king did."

Now I really needed that cup of Hotshot. My head was spinning. I was so out of it, I gave a mug of the stuff to the kid. Big mistake. The Hotshot sent her mouth into triple-time, bypassing her common sense entirely.

"There's twelve of us. Miss Argent calls us January, February, and so on. 'Cause dragons are weird, y'know. Jan, that's what we call January, Jan says that this sacrificing maidens thing is the King's fault. Jan's the oldest, and she's got red hair, which really makes no sense for somebody named January and Augie's— that's short for August, which I guess is really a boy's name but Augie's a girl and she *should* have red hair 'cause August is hot but it's just sort of a washed-out blond but at least her hair's curly while mine just frizzes even when..."

"Focus, child! What was that about something being the King's fault?"

"Oh, right. The King's an idiot, Jan says. 'Cause he thinks chaining girls to rocks will keep dragons away. He hates dragons, Jan says. But he's not stupid enough to kidnap one, I don't think. Miss Argent's been missing for two weeks."

Privately, I agreed with her opinion of the King. The latest of the dynasty didn't approve of "old ladies playing Knight," so he'd torn up my contract. Freelancing is tough enough when you're a young, strong fellow. Almost nobody wants to hire a grey-haired grandam with more wrinkles than an antique treasure map, even if she can bench-press more than any skinny young man. And now I knew for sure that my hearing was going, because there was no way I'd heard the kid right.

"Wait...your teacher's a dragon?"

"I *said* that. Miss Argent. "Cause she's silver. She says that any common wyrm can collect gold, 'cause it doesn't tarnish, but silver takes *care*, and besides whoever heard of gold teapots anyway and a lady appreciates good tea and is punctual and Miss Argent's always punctual and now she's been missing for *two weeks*!"

"Maybe she's just out hunting?"

"Miss Argent says eating raw meat is vulgar and causes

unladylike disturbances. She gets our food from markets across the river. 'Cause she says a town that's stupid enough to offer up its daughters to a dragon's probably ignorant about basic sanitary food-handling procedures and..."

"Breathe, child! All right, I'll help you find your mislaid dragon. In the morning."

"Technically it is morning, because I left the cave at midnight and it took me ages to get here because of the rocks, which look like they're sedimentary but..."

"When there's daylight. And we've both had some sleep. Here. Drink this."

I suppose giving her a mug of Blackout on top of the Hotshot was a bit like spurring your mount into a gallop and then hauling on the reins, but we both got some much-needed sleep, and if June was a bit groggy the next morning, well, at least I could hear myself think.

June refused to take me to the dragon's lair, or school, or whatever it was.

"Once knights start tramping up here in their ridiculous tin-can suits, we'll have no peace whatsoever."

"Quoting your teacher again?"

"Er, yeah."

"So when and where did you see her last?"

"Two weeks ago, just outside the lair...er, school. She said something about working on a surprise for us. But she hasn't come back, and May heard a rumor about the king sending a dozen of his best knights into the hills to...to slay the dragon and take its treasure, and we're so afraid somebody's made Miss Argent into a wall hanging. She'd hate being a wall hanging. She says such things are gauche." June sniffled.

"Well, it would really help if you'd take me back there, so I'd have a place to start my search and maybe get an idea of what her tracks look like..."

"Oh, I can show you her tracks! Her favorite sunbathing spot's not secret. C'mon."

June led me on a roundabout hike so obviously intended to keep me away from the dragon's lair that I could've triangulated the location of her "school" from the places we avoided. My knees were starting to protest by the time we came to a sandy, sun-dappled clearing flanked by a natural stone wall.

"Miss Argent says that the stones absorb heat from the sun and radiate it back later, so this spot stays extra warm."

"Hm."

The stones also looked familiar. Like I'd seen them before. Only from further below, and from the other side. Judging from my aching joints, we were pretty high up.

"What's on the other side?"

"A long drop, some boring building, and a big empty dirt patch."

Now I was sure I'd see the wall before. My better judgment and every muscle in my body screamed at me to stop, but I clawed my way up to the top and had five seconds of triumph that I'd made it before I realized that June was already there and looked like she'd been waiting awhile.

Kids. They don't know how easy they have it.

"See? It's just a boring..."

"Barracks."

"And an empty..."

"Training field. You said something about the King sending a dozen of his best knights up here?"

"Um, yeah."

"How long ago?"

"A few weeks, maybe?"

"And what happened to them?"

"Um, I dunno. I think some of them went missing, but we've all been too worried about Miss Argent to keep up with the news."

I did a quick mental calculation of the weight of your average armored knight, the prevailing winds, and the likely location of the nearest clearing.

"I have a feeling that when we find out what happened to the knights, we'll find your Miss Argent."

"You don't think they made her into a wall hanging, do you?"

"Oh, I'm not worried about her."

The kid looked so hopeful I didn't have the heart to tell her that I suspected that her teacher'd gotten so concerned about food safety that she'd gone looking for some meat that came pre-packed in nice shiny in tin cans.

I was right, sort of. After half a day's hike in the direction I'd calculated, we came upon a pile of discarded tin cans...I mean suits of armor. And claw prints.

"They all attacked her at once?" June wailed.

"Kid, I'd be more worried about the knights!" I snapped, but June went on sobbing at a volume that ruled out any hope of surprise.

"She never hurt anybody! And she taught us reading and deportment and how to set a table for sixteen, and... How *could* they!"

She was too worked up to hear the crunch of approaching footsteps. Big footsteps. Enormous footsteps. I wasn't, but abandoning a kid to a dragon is about as unknightly as it gets. Besides, if a dragon really wants to eat you, running just makes you pre-salted in your own sweat.

"Oh, do stop bawling, child! You know I detest maudlin displays of emotion."

The voice sounded like my grandmother, if my grandmother had been a forty-foot lizard.

"Miss Argent!" June ran to embrace a leg like an armored tree trunk. "We thought the king's men had made you into decorative tapestry and dog food."

"Nonsense! Consider your lessons in observational logic. There's no sign of a struggle. No blood. No one was harmed here."

"No one?" I said. "Including the knights who used to be inside this armor?"

The dragon eyed me up and down. "I don't believe we've been introduced."

"Morgan Redland, late of the King's Guard. And you must be June's mislaid headmistress."

"I am never mislaid, and I cannot truthfully say I am pleased to make the acquaintance of another of the King's Guard. But I thank you for accompanying June."

"But where have you *been*?" June demanded.

"*Another* of the King's Guard?" I echoed.

"Oh dear. This is getting dreadfully complicated."

"Look, I'm not exactly pleased with His Temperamental Majesty myself," I said. "I did say *late* of the King's Guard. But if you've made twelve young men into barbecue, we've got a problem."

"Barbecue? How dare you make such an uncouth suggestion, Lady Knight?" Miss Argent heaved a sigh that flattened a nearby sapling. "Very well. June, dear, I'm afraid I'm going to have to spoil the surprise I promised in order to reassure your companion. It really is a pity you couldn't have waited, but I can't fault your loyalty and affection. And they *are* being frustratingly recalcitrant."

The dragon lead us to a campsite. A clearing in the middle held a sturdy pen. Inside were all twelve of the missing knights, stripped to their gambesons and mad as hornets, but otherwise unhurt.

"Oh, do settle down, boys! See: I've brought company. Including one of my young ladies that I've told you about. If you behave nicely you can come out, and we'll all go home and have tea and cake together."

"Just what's going on here?" I demanded.

"Well, my young ladies are growing up so fast, they'll be wanting husbands before long," said Miss Argent, with a fond look at June, whose jaw dropped. "And these fellows are all strong and healthy, and I'm told that human knights are trained to a code of honor where human females are concerned. Really, it seemed ideal. I don't understand why everyone's being so stubborn."

"The girl's what, ten?" shouted one of the captive knights. "And this ain't how it works!"

"'Isn't,' my dear boy. We've discussed your regrettable grammar before, you know."

"I'm twelve!" June shouted back. "But really, Miss Argent, he's right. This isn't how humans get married. Jan's the only one who's old enough, anyhow."

"Oh dear." A steaming dragon tear splashed and sizzled on the forest floor. "I'd planned everything so carefully, with a lovely dowry of silver for each of you, and some of your birthstone gems. Yours has both pearls and moonstones, June dear."

Now the knights perked up, and I didn't like the looks on some of their faces.

"Miss Argent," I said, "you're obviously, um, a lady of refinement..."

"Thank you," she murmured.

"...whereas these men are used to a rougher sort of environment. Fortunately, I've trained as a knight myself. Would you allow me to talk to them?"

"Oh, please do!"

"And I'll explain why we girls can't get married yet," June whispered in my ear. "I toldja dragons are weird."

It took some discussion, some of it involving a demonstration that yes, the "old lady" did know how to handle a sword, but eventually I got the point across that if any of the knights harmed the dragon or her girls, their future was likely to be short and unpleasant, and that trying to make off with any of Miss Argent's treasure would be a singularly stupid idea.

Turns out, they weren't a bad lot. For one, they'd all volunteered for this dragon-hunting mission to get away from the new king. Smart bunch. Some of them thought that tea and cake (and meeting red-haired January and her impressive dowry) sounded like a sweet opportunity. So we struck a deal.

So yeah, you can call me Captain Morgan. Official trainer of the Argent Guards, Defenders of Mislaid Maidens. Robin Hood's got nothing on us. Pay's great. July makes a currant cake you wouldn't believe. Anybody comes around causing trouble, we subdue 'em, make 'em drink two double-strength mugs of Hotshot tea, and send 'em babbling back to the king. In their gambesons. Which Augie and April generally paint rude pictures on first. Everyone thinks it's hilarious, except Miss Argent. She calls it "unseemly." But like June says, dragons are weird.

ABOUT THE EDITOR

Elisabeth Waters sold her first short story in 1980 to Marion Zimmer Bradley for THE KEEPER'S PRICE, the first of the Darkover anthologies. She then went on to sell dozens of short stories to a variety of anthologies. Her first novel, a fantasy called CHANGING FATE, was awarded the 1989 Gryphon Award. MENDING FATE is the sequel to it. Elisabeth also writes short stories, in addition to editing the SWORD AND SORCERESS anthologies.

She has also worked as a supernumerary with the San Francisco Opera, where she appeared in La Gioconda, Manon Lescaut, Madama Butterfly, Khovanschina, Das Rheingold, Werther, and Idomeneo.

Made in the USA
Monee, IL
15 July 2020

36618845R00173